"Children of mine, the world without is dying. Have you the courage to be part of the healing?"

The Grey Lady spoke, her voice a sad ache of a whisper. "I came to these caverns, this home of the First People, through lands savaged by war, stripped of the beauty, raped of bounty. I went past rivers running crimson with blood, silver with tears. That was many hundreds of years ago, when there was no Mannish, no Elvish, only the Second People. Many hundreds of years ago—when the Sorcerer fought his first war against us.

"I need a body, I need hands and heart to guide the magic. I need a child of both Man and Elf."

Joze looked at Kicva; the Elven turned to look at him. And so their eyes were met, locked tight as though theirs were not glances but hands clasped, when ghostly Aeylin told them that they must bring her the child of Nikia who is the Princess of both Mannish and Elvish, the child of the Hunter-Defender who defeated the terrible Sorcerer and then tore down his Souless fortress with fire and wild magic.

"And you must use whatever means there are to bring that babe back here to me."

Ace Books by Nancy Varian Berberick

SHADOW OF THE SEVENTH MOON
A CHILD OF ELVISH

A CHILD OF ELVISH

NANCY VARIAN BERBERICK

ACE BOOKS, NEW YORK

This book is an Ace original edition,
and has never been previously published.

A CHILD OF ELVISH

An Ace Book / published by arrangement with
the author

PRINTING HISTORY
Ace edition / April 1992

ISBN: 0-441-85429-X

Ace Books are published by The Berkley Publishing Group,
200 Madison Avenue, New York, New York 10016.
The name "ACE" and the "A" logo
are trademarks belonging to Charter Communications, Inc.

PRINTED IN THE UNITED STATES OF AMERICA

10 9 8 7 6 5 4 3 2 1

Again, for Bruce:
You are the answer to my question.

Prologue

ON MIDWINTER NIGHT, WHEN THE FULL MOON HUNG LOW ON THE western horizon, when a hot wind stolen from summer soughed from the north where no such wind had ever before come, the Elf-King's daughter woke from a dream of fire, a dream of magic gone wild. Head aching, heart pounding, she left her bed. She moved carefully, silently; she didn't want to wake her husband. Yet, despite her care, Garth stirred restlessly when the motion of the bed told him that his wife was gone from his side. But he didn't wake, and for that Nikia was grateful.

Once she'd got safely into the unlighted corridors, Nikia made no hand-fire. She could have—a whispered prayer to the Deity of Fire, a plea to the Deity of Magic, would have filled her hands with soft blue light. But she prayed no prayer. This night her dreams had all been of a time when she'd nearly lost control of magic. Now even friendly blue hand-light would have made her shudder.

She went silently into the winter moonlight of the Queen's Garden. The night should have been sharp with frost, but was instead hot as a summer noon. Her blue cotton bedshift clung to sweat-sheened breast and thigh, to the hard new swell of her belly. Barefoot in the bone-white glare of the moon, she followed the familiar circular path around the Queen's Garden as cicadas droned their dull winding song. The dry wind sent dust chasing after, rattled the thin brown leaves of the basil bushes, chattered among the rosemary's dead, sapless stems. They were not winter-withered, for winter had not come to the Mannish kingdom this year. The plants were drought-killed.

In the autumn past, when these plants were yet alive, she'd taken clippings and cuttings and rootings to preserve against the hard seasons to come. As the garden, those plants, too, were dead.

Pausing to brush a clinging strand of silvery hair from her neck, Nikia looked up at the sharp-edged moon. No rain, she thought, and none to be expected when the moon's thin edge is so keen. She could not truly remember the last time the sky had granted rain. But it didn't matter when she'd last felt the rain; what mattered was when rain would be granted again. And no one, not even her father's most skilled mages, could predict that.

Canny spell-crafters, wise in the ways of magic, they filled the ears of the Seven Deities with their prayers as they tried to work their long-practiced weather spells and enchantments. But though the Seven would grant small prayers, small magics, they would not grant these most desperate pleas. Some of the Elf-King's mages had died giving the last of their strength to this arcane struggle against the Sorcerer's land-killing spells, the effect of which they managed to keep away from the Elvish forests but which grew ever stronger in Mannish even all these months after the Sorcerer's death.

Nikia shuddered, for the memory of the evil one's death, for the killing she herself had done with the Ruby's fiery magic. The Twin Kingdoms had won the last battle against the Sorcerer. Yet it seemed that they had lost the war.

The Sorcerer was dead. Souless, his mighty stone fortress, was naught but sand and broken rock in Carnach's Straits. But his last terrible spells survived. For though the southeast skies above the Elvish forests shone brightly by night with shivering curtains of many-colored light—manifestations of the labors of the Elf-King's mages in behalf of the afflicted Mannish kingdom—no rain ever came to soothe the dying farmlands. The wasted River A'Damran, once a strong tumble of water from northern Raeth, limped only wearily past the city walls.

Here in Damris, in the Mannish city where she had chosen to live, Nikia often came out into the night to watch the mage-lights dancing. Elf-light, the folk of the Citadel had taken to calling those shimmering colors, and some said it with hope in their voices, though most with the bitter kind of scorn that is the withered fruit of starved faith. But tonight Nikia hadn't come to watch the Elf-Light, nor to join her prayers for rain to the pleas of her father's mages.

Tonight she had come fleeing a question which had for an answer only fear.

Walking slowly, directed by habit, Nikia crossed the garden, stopped when she came to the stone bench in the far west corner opposite the solar doors. Moonlight made the shadows of a rosebush's naked branches seem like dark webs on the smooth stone, like something she wanted to brush away before she sat.

Soft on the night air came a harp's voice, rising and dropping, lilting then thrumming beneath a master's fingers. The King's Bard worked late tonight and his music came like a bird gliding from a window high above. Nikia heard none of the song's words—she could not have from this distance; still she knew them.

She settled against the bench's low back, smiled a little, and maybe truly for the first time that day. At least she knew what the words had been that morning when Dail had come into the hall to begin teaching this song to his bards, to her their Lady. But this was a new song and the words could yet change, though subtly, until Dail had found precisely the right ones to frame the vision his heart saw.

And he sees his vision so clearly, Nikia thought, *as though the Lady of the Blue-Silver Eyes stands beside him each time he takes up his harp to make a song for her.*

Nikia envied her friend, for once she, too, had seen Aeylin that clearly. A time was when she dreamed often of the ghost of the ages-dead queen.

Heal the damage, the voice in her dreams had said. *Daughter*, said the Lady of the Blue-Silver Eyes, *find the strength to mend what the Sorcerer has broken*.

And each time she'd dreamed, Nikia woke with renewed strength to go again before Alain, her husband's father, and convince that heartbroken king one more time that he must hold to hope, and trust that magic would cure what sorcery had wrought.

Nikia folded her hands across the swell of the new life within her. She'd not been before the King in many weeks, had not spoken to his restless Council in as long. Her dreams of Aeylin had vanished, had never returned after the day she first knew she was carrying a child again. And with the dreams had gone her will to look into the King's old eyes and see his fear. With the dreams had gone her strength to face resentful Council members, the lords of the five provinces of Mannish who feared this drought-stricken winter, this unnaturally hot season, and dreaded what summer must bring. These things she left for Garth to do now.

A cicada's drone rose in the darkness, and below that harsh rattling a cricket piped, summer songs eerie on a Midwinter Night. Nikia closed her eyes, breathed softly, as one who is afraid that things she'd been hiding from would find her. And, of course, they did. Fear loves the night.

Rising in memory, she heard the curious and solicitous voices of folk who today had noticed for the first time that she carried a child. Or, for the first time, had spoken to her of noticing. All who saw her pressed congratulations upon her. Many said that it was a sign of hope that their prince's wife was a-bearing in so terrible a season. But whispered in corners, discussed in shadows, was a thing everyone remembered: Nikia, the Elf-King's daughter, the

Mannish prince's wife, had conceived a child once before and miscarried it.

"Oh, aye, she lost the babe, poor thing," a chambermaid whispered. "It would've been a boy—though, mind you, I don't know of my own seeing. I wasn't there. Serving in the kitchens, I was then. . . . But it's what I've heard."

And: "Oh, but surely you know," a lady's maid murmured to a companion newly arrived at court. "Surely you've heard that she lost the baby?"

Lost the baby . . .

Nikia hated those words, for in them she heard a kind of accusation, as though somehow she had misplaced her little, never-born son, been careless of him; as a child is careless of her puppy, lets him follow her to the crowded market-fair, and losing him, stands weeping among the gaily colored stalls, a small island of misery amid the shouts of fruit-sellers and tinkers and fishwives, not knowing whether she has abandoned or been abandoned.

And yet, painful as the whispers were to hear, painful as the memories which they called up, these Nikia could have borne, and more like them, if she could escape the memory of the unspoken question in her husband's eyes—in her own, each time she looked in the polished silver mirror. She and her husband, and only two others, knew that the child Nikia carried now might not be Garth's.

Husband and wife, and the kings who were their fathers . . . only these four knew the story of the rape which had occurred at the Keep of Seuro, a rape at the hands of a mage who had once been Alain's trusted advisor. On that night, from that crucible of humiliation and fear—and finally, hatred—had come the fiery Hunter-Defender, a creature of magic and godhood who'd possessed Nikia's own body to channel the terrible strength of the Ruby of Guyaire, to direct the Jewel's power to kill the Sorcerer and end his unholy war.

Nikia still dreamed about the fire and the power. Often she dreamed about the crucible. And after each dream she wondered:

Had this child within her womb been made on that same night?

Yet none, not Garth, not the two kings, not Nikia herself, had put words to the wondering. None asked: Is the child Garth's? Or is it Reynarth's? None of them seemed to have the strength to think about what must be done with a child who showed evidence of a fathering that was not Garth's.

Now the wind dropped, the night became still. Nikia raised her hand, again to brush her hair from her cheek. At that same moment, from deep within, her child stirred. Only a little, and it was no more of a motion than a windflower rising to spring's breath. But it was the first motion, the first stirring she'd felt from within, and it was startling; delightful and frightening all at the same time.

The babe was real, a life forming as part of her. Not thinking of anything but that, Nikia whispered, "Who are you, little one? Are you a child of my husband's love, or . . . little one, are you the child of rape?"

The fluttering within stilled.

Terrified, suddenly colder than she'd ever been, Nikia sought desperately for the timid motion of the babe within her, searched past the singing of her own blood, the thundering of her own heart, for the stirring of life.

From the Citadel, from the high chamber where Dail sat with his visions and his harp, one clear note rose into the night, and when it had gone, no more followed.

In the silence Nikia felt her child move again, a motion like a moth's fluttering.

And then all perceptions changed, all needs and wants and hopes fled but one—and this one Nikia felt deep in her, deeper than the place where her child grew, deep as the place where her soul was. Swiftly she covered her belly with both arms, as though she could hug her child even closer.

It doesn't matter who fathered you! My child, it doesn't matter! You are mine! And I will keep you safe. I won't lose you. I promise you, child. I won't lose you. . . .

Chapter One

ON APRIL'S FIRST MORNING, JOZE WOKE SWEATING FROM ANOTHER dream of the flame-shrouded fortress. Often when he'd wake from these dreams, he had trouble knowing where he was. Often he thought he was still huddled on the brittle shore of the Straits of Carnach, wounded and sick, his will strangely drained away so that he could not move but to breathe. Joze had seen the destruction of mighty stone Souless. He remembered it nightly.

Yet this waking was not the same as all the others. This time Joze woke knowing that he was still being watched, and the knowl-edge that the watcher was yet near crept along Joze's skin, cooled his sweat like thin fingers of north wind. Before that knowledge his nightmare shredded to vaguely remembered tatters.

Joze got quickly to his feet, scattered dirt over his camping fire. He looked for his horse, saw the roan gelding safely hobbled. He reached for his short-sword, then let his hand drop.

What use to unsheathe the sword, he thought bitterly, *when all I'll see is nothing? All I ever see is nothing.*

As though it understood Joze's thoughts, the gelding shook its head, snorted once. Joze dragged his fingers through his short dark beard, ran his hand up the side of his face, feeling as though he'd not slept at all. Tired, he bridled the horse and freed it from the hobbles. Taking up the saddle, he led the roan out of the shadows of the few trees that crouched in the lee of the hill where he'd made his night camp.

Two weeks old the spring—and this morning already burned hotter than a summer's noon!

Dead dust sighed up from the ground where he stepped. Dry grass, last year's seared leavings, brushed against the sides of his boots, rustled underfoot. The cracks of the boulders he passed, the new crevices in the sun-split earth, were filled with the grey powdery dust that had only a year ago been rich dark soil.

"Ashes," he whispered. "The earth is the color of ashes. . . ."

How could this have happened to Raeth Province! Once the richest farmland in the Mannish kingdom, now it was a wasteland, lifeless and blowing away before hot winds.

Yesterday, at sunset, Joze had come out of the eastern forest to this place. Its barrenness had wrung hot tears from him. All through the winter he'd heard rumors of the land-sickness, the blight on his homeland. Nothing had prepared him for the reality.

Who would want to follow him into this ruined place?

Tall mountains, the steep-sided northern shoulders of the Kevarths, rose in the east behind him, thick with sharp-scented pines. Their tops blushed faintly in the dawn's rosy light. Those eastern mountains, the green forest lands vibrant with health, were Elvish lands. No blight touched them. Rain fell there as often and sweetly as rain always does in the spring.

Not so in Mannish lands.

And yet, though his throat grew thick with dread at the thought of the long ride south and west through these aching and empty farmlands to his home in southern Celed, Joze thought it best to leave the flourishing Elvish woodlands behind.

Because Alain, his king, had wished it, he'd fought beside Elves in the great war, found them good fighters and sometimes

trusty friends. And, while many of his countrymen didn't like
having old enemies for companions, Joze hadn't minded the Elves
too much.

"They're uncanny, I'll grant you," he'd told his grumbling
friends. "But for me, I find it hard to curse a man who can call
fire to soaked kindling in a downpour."

Still, for all his practical advice to his friends, Joze did not forget
that his father and his grandfather had fought in wars against the
Elvish in former days when the dreaded Sorcerer had been no
more than a legend, in the time when no treaty bound the Twin
Kingdoms against the legend come to terrible life. Now, a year
and more after the alliance between the two kingdoms had been
struck, a season after the Sorcerer was well and truly defeated,
Joze wondered if the two races would or could easily forget their
ages-long enmity.

Hot wind sent dust whirling high, and Joze squinted against
the grit.

At the war's end he'd found himself among a band of Elvish
hunter-scouts. They'd tolerated his company through the winter
because he was, like them, a soldier of the alliance caught far
from home. He'd heard them boast often through the snowy
months that their king's mages would heal the land. He thought
now that the Elf-King's mages were doing a fine job keeping
their own lands safe. They weren't doing a very good job with
Mannish lands, though. Stepping from the Elfland forest to Raeth's
withered farmlands was like stepping from a cool hall into a sun-
seared courtyard. No border existed between the two places, and
a long-legged man could stand with one foot in health, another
in affliction. It made a man sick to see.

Joze looked away from seared Raeth and back to the green and
healthy forest. He didn't want to ride home through sick lands, but
his Elvish winter-companions had warned him—as friends, they'd
assured him—that his safest route home would be the most direct
route out of Elflands. He'd taken that warning very seriously, and
he didn't think there was much of friendship in it. He'd spent close
to seven days riding out of the Kevarth Mountains. Each of those
days had seemed like an age. He'd been watched all the way, sure
that the watcher was one of the Elvish hunter-scouts sent to make
certain that this unwelcome Mannish soldier found his way back
to Alain's kingdom.

And so he'd believed until last night, the first he'd spent in
homelands since leaving the Elves. Last night, crouched by his
small campfire, he'd known that the watcher had followed him

here to the foothills. And last night, though the moon had been dark, starlight had given him his first look at the one who followed him.

He'd seen no more than a dim, shadowy form, darker than darkness, drifting between the trees. The shadow-figure had been small and bulky—like a man bent low to avoid striking a silhouette. Whoever it was had not offered to harm him, but had watched him all night.

"And that's not a good feeling," he said to the roan gelding. He watched the horse search for better food than scorched grass. "Ah, horse, I've a feeling there'll be lean meals for us both from now on." He glanced uneasily over his shoulder. "Still, we'd best be going."

They went south and west with the dawnlight at their backs, their shadows long and dark before them, south and west toward the ruined farmlands of Raeth and the dusty brown line that could only be the dried bed of the River A'Damran.

Soft behind the young man and the horse, stepping silently, came the watcher, keeping carefully to the edge of the lush green woodlands and the shadows of the trees, finally stopping at the edge of the woods. Sunlight, harsh and bright and hot, proved to be a stronger barrier than the watcher could pass.

Kicva stopped at the forest's edge. Shading her eyes against the sun's glare, the Elven looked out into the wide farmlands, foreign Mannish lands, and felt familiar queasiness rise again. She hadn't meant to come this close to the woods' edge; she didn't like to see those bleak, disease-savaged lands. Leaning her back against a high, scaly-barked pine, she took long slow breaths, filled her lungs with the tangy scent of the woodland. Sometimes, when she was too close to the sick places, close enough to smell the lifeless dust of dying earth, she'd found that she could only barely control the urge to vomit. Sometimes she couldn't control the wrench at all.

She was grateful now, bitterly thankful, that she managed to control her belly. An Elvish hunter-scout should have more strength, more control—you Seven Deities, more grace!—than to be spewing her food each time she saw something distasteful. Knees weak, quick shame racing in a deep flush up her neck to her cheeks, Kicva edged around the trunk of the pine until she'd put her back to the seared lands and the sun's glare.

She'd separated from the hunting band she'd wintered with only four days ago. Though she missed their company, she'd been eager for her home in the southern forest, eager to return to her family and to Mage Aidan.

Aidan . . . .

Kicva flushed again, her cheeks flaming scarlet. She knew what that proud young mage would think of her if he saw her cowering against this tree, afraid to look out into the sick lands. She sighed. He'd think that he'd do well to find himself a better woman, one with more courage than she. Mage Aidan despised weakness of any sort. He'd welcome none in his betrothed.

The Elven pushed away from the tree. She knew she had at least four more weeks of walking before she left the upland forest and came again to southern woodlands and Verdant Hall. In one week, maybe a day more or less, she would arrive at the eastern shore of the Landbound Sea. Another week walking along that stony shore would bring her to the River Altha.

Maybe, she thought, *if I'm lucky, I'll find a fleet out fishing and be able work my passage down-river and home.* That would be easy work, and welcome. Her father was a fisherman, her mother a maker of fine strong nets. Kicva had been raised on the river, and any fine dream she had saw the sun-spangled water, heard the Altha murmuring.

How proud they'd been, that simple fisher-family, when their daughter had gone to be a soldier in the war. And how frightened. She'd left her home in the darkest time, in the summer before, when the Sorcerer's armies had swarmed south. The farewells spoken then, as the starlight gleamed on Altha's shining water, had been tearful. Maybe final. Kicva had no idea whether her family had survived the war; none about Mage Aidan, her betrothed. This terrible uncertainty had made the winter a long one.

High in the pine's thick boughs a black-capped chickadee piped its light-hearted morning song; another answered, voicing its own joy in the dawn. The Elven looked up, searching the shadows for the small birds. She didn't see them, but she knew where they were—seed shells from the cones they pried open in search of breakfast drifted down through the branches and caught in her hair. Kicva smiled as she combed the shells from her short curls. Some things, and certainly the carelessness of birds, never changed.

Then, mid-stroke, she stopped, pressed her back to the tree once more.

She saw the shadow again.

That shadowy figure had been tracking something last night. She'd seen it from a distance, a dark shape in the moonless twilight, tracking and watching and tracking again. Kicva had given it a wide berth, let it go on its way unmolested. Some small woods-creature, or so she'd thought, and so she hadn't bothered it, holding that the forest-inhabitants had as much right to hunt as she did. Yet here it was again. She'd never known an animal to hunt this determinedly, never known one to keep so close, so purposefully on the trail of its prey.

Her curiosity roused, the Elven watched now and waited silently as the creature passed between two boulders not a man's length from her. Because she was west of the tracker, she saw its shadow before she saw the creature itself. When the shadow vanished into a pool of darkness beneath one of the boulders, when the tracker stepped into her line of sight, Kicva used every bit of her will to keep her hands away from her bow and quiver.

No woods-creature this! And it was not Elvish, nor was it Mannish. A shiver crept along the back of Kicva's neck. Could one of the Sorcerer's loathsome, brutish aberrations have survived his fall? She'd heard that none had, that when the fires consumed the Sorcerer's northern fortress all the life went from the hideous monsters he'd made to fill his armies. The Sorcerer's magic defeated, his misborn soldiers had fallen like string-cut puppets, lifeless where they lay.

But, if that were so, what was this thing?

It caused only the smallest rustling when it passed over leaf and mould; it was a careful walker. Short, thick around the neck and shoulders, the tracker stopped near the edge of the woods upwind from her.

Head low, thick shoulders high, as one tensing against fear, the creature stepped out of the woods and into the sunlight. Low and deep, the thing moaned. Then, faster than a trout darting, it fled back to the forest's shadow again.

Kicva drew a careful breath, waited for the strange creature to fade back into the forest darkness. Because she knew what to listen for now, the soft whisper of old fallen leaves, the barely heard hiss of brown pine needles slithering on stone in the wake of almost-silent passage, she knew when the tracker had gone far enough into the forest to be no threat to her.

Her curiosity stronger than her fear of sickness, Kicva forced herself to step out of the shadows, out into the ravaged lands. At once she saw what the creature had been trailing: A horse and rider headed west into the wastes of what had only a year ago been the rich, fertile farms of the Mannish kingdom.

The Elven knew, by the rider's bearing and the short-sword at his belt, that here was another soldier returning home. Mannish, too, by the look of his stocky frame. Quick pity rose in her heart, pity for a soldier who had to return from battles to a land sick and dying. As she watched, the horse stopped, the rider dismounted. He was not so far away that Kicva couldn't see the sag of his shoulders or the way he bowed his head as though in bitter defeat.

She was a soldier, she knew what grief looked like; when the stocky young man mounted again, turned his horse back to the forest, Kicva made a decision.

She'd not often been comfortable working and fighting beside these Mannish, for they were not used to the idea of women as soldiers. If they were not gallantly trying to defend their female companions-in-arms in battles where they'd have better served themselves and everyone else by looking to their own safety, they were ungallantly trying to get their female companions into their arms . . . and their blankets.

But she'd learned to tolerate them, after they'd learned to respect her boundaries, and so for the sake of old comradeship, the Elven waited in the woods for the Man's return. She thought he should know that he'd been followed.

It was always Joze's opinion that he wept too easily. When he was a child he'd often been teased by his friends for this sign of weakness. As a youth on his father's farm, he couldn't drown kittens without true regret, and he couldn't ease an old hound out of pain without shedding tears.

As he turned away from wasted Raeth, fled back to the cool shadows of the forest and Elvish lands, tears made thin trails on his dusty cheeks, caught in his dark beard, and he didn't know how to stop them. He wept for the dying land as he'd have wept for the deaths of kin and friends.

What use, he thought, *trying to find my way home through these wastelands? Me and the horse, we'd starve before two nights passed*.

Better to take whatever risks he'd have to take riding south along the Elvish borders. At least there he'd find forage for the horse, be able to hunt for his own supper.

Joze kicked up the roan, set him into a quick trot, eager for the cool pine woods. Not so eager though, that he didn't keep his wits about him, didn't listen, sharp-eared, for all the things a man must listen for in a land where he is unwelcome; in a land where he'd been followed to the border and beyond. And so he heard the dry rustle of bushes and old leaves off to his right, saw the shadow separate from the darkness of the forest.

The watcher!

Instincts born of a long year of war flared. Joze turned the gelding sharply, wheeled him in a tight half-circle, kneed the roan till, squealing, his mount reared high, struck out at the shadow with sharp hoofs.

But this was no shadow at all!

Only a girl, crop-haired, tall and thin. She flung up an arm to protect her face, tried to dodge the gelding's deadly hoofs, but her foot twisted on a rock and she staggered. Joze shifted his weight in the saddle, tried to undo the battle maneuver which he'd instinctively launched, but he couldn't stop the horse in mid-strike. The girl went down under iron-shod hoofs, fell hard with blood streaming from a ragged tear in her cheek, and her right leg twisted under her in a way no leg should twist.

And then Joze saw the real watcher. Short and squat, head low between hunched shoulders, it stood in the shadows at the edge of the woods. This creature was no Man or Elf bent low to avoid being seen. A chill spidered along Joze's arms, crept down his neck. He didn't know what this thing was.

Slowly, very carefully, Joze laid his hand on the hilt of his short-sword.

Chapter Two

THE WATCHER MOVED RESTLESSLY IN THE FOREST'S SHADOWS. IT didn't come forward, didn't move backward. Like a small bear scenting the air for danger, it planted its feet and weaved from side to side, short neck extended, shoulders hunched. A bird chirruped in the pine above the watcher and the creature gasped, hunched its shoulders higher as though frightened. Drawing another breath— maybe to calm itself—it crooned low in its throat, a soft and troubled sound.

Hearing no threat in the noise, Joze relaxed his grip on the sword's hilt, looked quickly at the girl. He hadn't noticed it before, but he saw it now: She was Elvish. The slim, delicate taper of her ears, only partly hidden beneath soft curls of roughly cut golden hair, told him that. Too, her face was shaped like an Elven's, broad at the forehead, narrow at the chin. Tall, as most Elvish are, she wore the rusty tight-sleeved blouse, high sturdy boots and softly tanned hunting leathers he'd come to know in this year past as common among their hunter-scouts.

Joze shot another look at the watcher, saw that the thing held its position. Too, he saw that it carried no weapon. He slid from the roan's back, dropped the reins and stepped on them, ground-tying the gelding.

The watcher raised its head.

Joze had the impression that the thing looked at him, but he could not see its eyes, hidden as the creature was in the shadows. Slowly, he dropped to one knee beside the Elven. She had the expected quiver of arrows at her hip, long-shafted, fletched with white but for the cock-feather which was bright green; she had a longbow slung across her shoulder. Joze had never seen a hunter-scout, man or woman, without beloved bow and quiver. He moved these out of her reach and continued his careful search. He relieved her of a sheathed dagger and reached for her blouse, sure that he would find the sharp little knife most women hunter-scouts carried hidden in their smallclothes.

As he untied the laces of the blouse, just as his fingers brushed the soft skin at the base of her throat, the watcher in the shadows made a low, growling sound.

"All right," Joze muttered. "Don't worry, I don't mean her any harm." He removed the little knife quickly, then looked up, flushing suddenly. He tucked the knife into his boot, then sat back on his heels.

The watcher took a short step forward, then stood still. Joze was beginning to get the idea that, though the thing had trailed him through the mountains, watching always, perhaps it didn't mean him harm.

Yet certainly it had not liked the idea of a man groping beneath the Elven's blouse. Perhaps the two were companions? He pointed to the watcher, then pointed to the hunter-scout. "Your friend?"

The little creature cocked its head as though considering the idea, but said nothing.

"Is it all right with you if I look to see how badly she's hurt?"

Bracing bulky shoulders, the watcher advanced another step, then stopped suddenly when sunlight touched it. In the moment before it scuttled back to the shadows Joze saw its skin, rough and glistening, and grey. He shuddered. Some of the things he'd seen in the Sorcerer's army had skin like that.

And yet Joze didn't fear this watcher. For, though a feeling of strangeness emanated from it, he didn't feel the *wrongness*, a sensation of aching, sliding nausea, he'd experienced when he'd encountered the Sorcerer's monstrous creatures.

Joze held up his hands. "I only want to see how badly she's hurt." He smiled, more at himself than at the watcher. "I'll behave myself. I promise."

He wasn't sure whether the creature understood his words, but it seemed to understand his intent now. Safe in the dark and cool shadows, it nodded once.

Hands gentle, Joze brushed the Elven's golden hair from her forehead. The girl bled from a cut near her scalp, from scraped cheek and jaw. The most damage, however, was done by the fall beneath the roan's sharp hoofs. Her left leg was broken.

The horse had hurt her badly.

Ah, no, Joze thought. *Not the horse: me. I hurt her.*

He glanced at the little watcher, said defensively, "But she was coming at me from nowhere, wasn't she?"

The watcher made a sound like water gurgling in a stream, a sound like an old man clearing his throat.

"And I thought, watcher, that she was you. We'll portion the blame half and half, aye?"

Maybe the creature didn't understand even his meaning this time; it made no noise and didn't gesture or move.

Joze sighed heavily. "But I don't know what I'm going to do with her. Doesn't look like I should move her, does it?"

The watcher kept silent.

Joze looked at the forest, then over his shoulder to where the dry and brittle farmlands lay stretched painfully beneath the hot blue sky. "Maybe what I should do first is try to bind up that leg . . ."

The watcher moved now, drifted silently along the border of sunlight and darkness, moved closer to Joze and the Elven. The thing stopped when it ran out of shade. Though Joze sat on his heels, the two were only just eye to eye. Drawing a deep breath, the watcher spoke.

"Tall, I have a home."

Its voice sounded old, like small stones rattling down scree, and as though it hadn't been used for many long years. The language it used was Mannish, but carefully spoken as though this were not the creature's native tongue.

Joze answered slowly, speaking clearly. "Is your home nearby?"

"Not close, Tall. Not far."

Carefully, Joze asked: "What are you?"

The watcher rattled in its throat, and the sound needed no thinking about—it was laughter.

"Not an ill-wisher."

Joze rested his hand lightly on the Elven's shoulder. "She needs help."

"I have some," the watcher said.

The Elven moaned softly. Joze leaned closer, heard her shallow breathing hitch in a short gasp as pain found its way to the dark place of unconsciousness where she was. That pain would be ghostly now, but she would return to consciousness soon and then she'd feel its full force. Joze made his decision quickly and he didn't make it based upon sound logic or good sense: He made his decision based on sorrow for the Elven's pain and regret that he'd caused it.

"What do you swear by, watcher?"

Crooning softly in its throat again, making that sad and troubled sound, the creature spoke no word.

"Tell me," Joze insisted.

"For what?"

Joze narrowed his eyes, studied the creature closely, trying to determine whether, despite its earlier declaration, this reluctance meant that the thing planned mischief. "I want to assure our safety. I want to swear you to it."

The watcher considered this, then rattled laughter. "Tall, what is your sacred thing?"

"Why?"

"Too, I want you to swear my safety."

Fair enough, Joze thought. Aloud he said: "I swear by my honor."

"Is it good honor? Tall, is it bright?"

Joze bristled. "I haven't heard any complaints about it."

"Then maybe I will not complain," the watcher said. Waving a hand, it signaled Joze to join it in the shadows. Reluctantly, Joze left the Elven. Carefully, as though it was uncertain of the creature that stood before it, the watcher touched the palm of Joze's hand with the palm of its own. "I swear by the Lady."

Joze refused to shudder while the creature's palm, moist and cool, lay against his. He held himself still, asked evenly, "Is she a good Lady?"

Joze heard pride in the watcher's reply. "I know she is."

"Then maybe I'll swear by her, too. I'll not harm you, watcher."

"Nor we you." The watcher gestured to the Elven with one hand, toward the horse with the other. "Tall, put that friend on that beast. Follow."

Joze gathered the weapons he'd taken from her, fastened the bow and the quiver to the gelding's saddle, put the Elven's dagger in his own belt. Then he lifted the Elven as carefully as he could. When he had his arms full of her, she moaned again.

"Hush," he whispered. "It'll hurt for a while—but it'll be better soon."

The girl in his arms was thin. He saw the marks of war on her, a purple scar in the sinewy place between her neck and shoulder, another trailing down from her collarbone to the hollow between her breasts. At once moved to tenderness, Joze brushed his lips against her torn cheek, kissed her gently.

For apology, he told himself.

In the shadows the watcher's laughter rattled again, this time softly.

Joze glared at the creature. He lifted the girl onto the roan, then vaulted up behind her. Holding her steady, he took up the gelding's reins and followed the watcher into the deep shadows of the Elfland forest. He wasn't sure this was a very good idea, but he had no better one.

They went far into the forest, travelled eastward for a long time. As he rode, guiding the roan carefully to lessen the chances of jostling the Elvish hunter-scout in his arms, Joze observed his guide. He had no idea what kind of creature this was, but clearly it was not Mannish, nor was it Elvish.

One thing Joze did know: He didn't like to look at the creature's eyes. Long, as Elvish eyes are, they were set farther apart in its face and seemed to absorb all light into their deep sockets, sending it back as a pulsing glow the color of pale daytime fire. The sight of that glow and those huge eyes made Joze shiver. For warmth against his shivering—though he told himself that he wanted to keep her safe from painful jolting—he held the Elven close.

The watcher walked easily on two legs, rolling from foot to foot like a sailor who'd spent more time on a ship's deck than on firm ground. For all that, it moved quickly and with little sound over stone and leaf-strewn forest floor. It was fascinated by Joze's mount and often it came close to the beast, touched velvet muzzle or rough mane. It didn't stand as tall as the gelding's broad chest, and once when it reached up to lay gnarled fingers on the Elven's wrist, it had to stand on the tips of its broad splayed toes and stretch its arm as high as it would go.

"Is the friend worse, Tall?" the watcher asked.

"I don't know," Joze said, "but she's no better."

"Soon we will be in my home."

He was glad to know that. The girl had stirred once or twice since they'd entered the forest, then fallen still again. Her breathing seemed shallower now, her skin cold. He held her closer and followed the watcher again.

From what Joze could see, the creature was hairless, had no beard, and its arms and hands were rough and glistening as wet stone. The broad dome of its head, white-skinned and shot with thin blue veins, was naked as rock. For clothing it wore a pair of breeches, raggedly cut at the knees, bound round its thick waist by a leather plait. It wore no shirt, only a thin leather vest. It didn't seem to need shoes or boots; sometimes it stepped on rocks and didn't appear to notice sharp edges that would have made someone else wince or curse.

The watcher didn't like sunlight very much. It kept always to the shadows, hissing when even the small dapples of light drifting down through the closely growing trees touched it. Though it didn't mind the rocks and stones that would cut or bruise naked feet, it avoided stepping into those small bright spots of sunlight the way one would avoid treading barefoot on burning coals. And it didn't seem to be very fond of the forest's inhabitants. Hares leaping in the bushes startled it so that Joze could see the pulse leaping in the watcher's neck; birds darting from tree to tree actually frightened it.

What are you? Joze thought. *You don't seem too afraid of me, yet small birds and harmless hares scare the wits from you!*

The sun was an hour gone, the new moon early up, a slender shaving of light in the purpling sky, when the watcher stopped suddenly, raised its head to sniff the air. Pine and last year's fallen leaves, newly unfurled wood poppies and shady thyme, rich mould and the salt hint of the sea which lay beyond the mountain's shoulder—among these twinings the watcher seemed to find a smell he knew.

One he likes, too, Joze realized. The watcher was rattling again, laughing.

Moving about quickly now, it plunged its hands into a small thicket, hummed happily to itself as it cleared away brush and leaves. A few moments' work exposed a pile of tumbled rocks. Though some of those rocks were as large around as the watcher itself, the creature tossed them aside with little effort. When its work was done Joze saw a long narrow opening in the earth.

"Home-come," the little watcher said. It gestured to the dark crack in the ground. "I am home-come, Tall."

Doubtless the narrow opening formed an entrance to a cave, and that didn't really surprise Joze. The watcher looked like something that lived in caves, grey-skinned and loving darkness. Joze eyed the narrow space skeptically. It seemed only barely wide enough to accept the roan's width.

"I don't think the horse will want to go in there."

And the horse, Joze thought, wouldn't be the only reluctant one. The watcher lifted its shoulders in a shrug. "Horse stays here."

"No."

"Horse can't fit through."

"I can see that. But I can't leave him here. Maybe there's wolves."

"No wolves, Tall. Not this far down the mountain." The watcher pointed to the high crests of the Kevarths, seen only briefly through the thick trees. "Wolves hunt up there. More game is there now than before." The watcher swept its arms wide, embraced the forest. "Deers and hares and bears and squirrels have run to here from the hurt lands. And so squirrels and bears and hares and deers who once lived here"—it pointed to the mountains again— "have run *there*. This old home is too crowded now. Wolves are happy where they are."

Aye, Joze thought, *probably that's true*.

Close on that thought came another. It was very likely that the people at home were hungry if all the game had fled to the mountains. And with no crops planted now, when wheat and barley, oats and corn, should just be starting to turn the fields to waving green seas beneath fresh spring breezes, Celed folk would be hungry come the winter.

No food . . .

"No wolves," the watcher said again.

"I can't leave the horse," Joze said. He was no longer thinking of wolves. He was thinking of hungry people to whom the roan might look like a month of good meals.

"Leave him. The friend needs a place to get well. Horse won't fit through."

The Elven stirred in his arms, sighed shakily. The blood from her scalp wound had dried, the cut was scabbing over. Joze knew that the cuts should be cleaned, the broken bone set. He knew, too, that if the Elven came to consciousness, the pain of setting her leg would be terrible and immediate. If he managed to set the bone while she was still unconscious, maybe the pain would seem like only a bad dream.

Again Joze made an impulsive decision. He gathered the girl tightly to his chest, slid from the gelding's back. When his feet hit the ground she cried out; her long eyes fluttered open. For an instant Joze saw startled fear. Then her eyes clouded and her head fell forward onto his chest again.

He settled the Elven on the ground and quickly dragged the saddle from the roan's back, slipped the bit from its mouth and the bridle over its head. The gelding snorted, pushed at Joze's chest and nearly rocked him off his feet. Absurdly, Joze felt his throat tighten. He did nothing to send the horse on its way, only turned and picked up the girl again.

Surprised, he saw that the little watcher had slung bridle and saddle over one shoulder. The Elven's bow and quiver dragged on the ground. The creature was strong!

"What are you doing with the gear?"

"Horse won't stay where he can't smell you. Better for him. Better for you."

Joze had expected a bear cave, a small musty hole in the earth draped with the roots of the trees above, close and smelling of earth and old, old leaves. He saw nothing like that as he followed the watcher.

He saw nothing at all. Holding the Elvish hunter-scout tight in his arms, he walked into darkness more complete than dreamless sleep—and forgot how to breathe.

"Watcher!" He heard the brittle edge of panic in his voice, gasped deeply for air. He told himself firmly that this sudden feeling that he couldn't breathe was only an illusion, conjured by the fact that he couldn't see; told himself that his ability to do each, to see and to breathe, were not connected. None of the telling did any good.

Soft scuttling, naked feet padding on stone, Joze heard the watcher come back to him.

"I did not remember," the watcher said. "No lights here." It touched Joze's elbow lightly, then laid a broad palm on the young man's chest.

At the watcher's touch, the security of knowing that he was not alone, Joze found himself able to breathe again.

The watcher whispered something, a word or two as though speaking to itself. Then it said, "Tall, I know a place where light can be. Follow?"

"I can't follow. I can't see."

Long fingers closed around Joze's wrist. In the forest above he'd shuddered to feel the cool moist touch of the watcher's hand on his skin. Now he relaxed, accepted the touch as he'd have accepted a friend's hand. He heard the sound of a weight falling to the stone floor, the jingle of iron that could only have been stirrups and saddle cinches, the rattle of the Elven's bow and quiver. Joze felt soft leather lines pressed into his hand and knew that the watcher had given him bridle and reins. A small tug, the kind he might have used to coax the roan forward, told him that the watcher had hold of the other end of the reins.

"I will guide and lead," it said gently. "You can follow now, Tall, yes?"

Darkness pressed against him from all sides. Joze tried not to think about it, tried to think only of the Elven stirring again in his arms. She groaned deeply; her head moved weakly against his shoulder.

"I can follow," he said. "Yes."

The watcher led him carefully, assuring him from time to time that no obstacle lay in his path, rattling its strange laughter when Joze began to trust its guidance and step more confidently.

He heard no echo as he walked, and so he knew that the walls were close, the ceiling low. Air, light and cool, brushed against Joze's skin, came to greet him from far places. Joze was no city man but a farmer used to air's wonderful freshness. Still, he'd never breathed air so sweetly clean as this. When he said as much to the watcher, the creature said:

"Air comes in, it goes out, changes always, but slowly. Stone keeps it sweet, and water helps. Another reason to leave Horse outside—bad smells stay for a long, long time here."

Soon Joze was able to tell when they'd left the corridor to turn down others. When he saw the first faint traces of illumination ahead, caught a sudden scent of smoke, he breathed a deep sigh of relief. He thought he'd never seen a light more lovely, not even the gleam of sun shining on gold. Smoke reminded him of cooking fires, and that reminded him of hunger, though he tried to forget about the yearnings of his belly. He didn't know what this watcher ate.

Maybe things so strange, he thought, *that I wouldn't want to eat them, or wouldn't be able to.* It was probably best to endure hunger for a while.

"Home-come," the watcher said.

Joze felt the reins slacken, then heard the soft whisper of leather falling to stone as the watcher dropped the lines. For the first time since entering this strange dark place, he saw the watcher, but only as a dim shadow hurrying on ahead.

"Wait! Watcher, wait!"

"Follow!"

And the watcher was gone, slipping through a high, arched doorway and into the light. Arms and shoulders aching from having carried the Elven this far, Joze let the bridle fall and followed, using the welcome illumination as his guide now.

Later—much later, when he had time again to think—Joze decided that the watcher had been sensible in not wasting its breath trying to prepare him for the sight that greeted him when he finally found the light.

Chapter Three

JOZE STOOD AT THE EDGE OF A GREAT STONE FOREST.

Trees rose from the cavern's floor. For trunks those trees had stalagmites, thick around as the greatest of the great mountain pines. The stone columns, smooth or scaled or gnarled as wood is, stretched high to meet vast colonies of hanging stalactites, some so thinly made that they resembled the long switches of willows, others so thick that they suggested the spreading branches of oaks. And yet, as similar as these formations were to trees, nothing stirred them; the cool breeze wandering through the chamber couldn't move them.

There was light in this place, splashes of soft glow from small braziers at the bases of the largest trees. Joze drew a deep breath and held it, took illumination into himself as though it were air. Stone walls, stone trunks, stone branches caught and held the dancing light, gave it back in playful shimmering.

Snow lay in this rock-forest, stone snow. Clusters of delicately spiked crystals gathered thickly at the gnarled bases of the trunk formations, like winter drifts. And they were not all white. Some

gleamed faintly pink, called to mind dawn's light on newly fallen
snow; others shone blue, and Joze thought of noon shadows
caressing drifts. The most lovely were the purple clusters. These
captured the exact shade of a snow-covered field under twilight's
fading glow. All the hours of a winter day gathered here in this
wonderful place beneath the ground where no snow had ever
fallen.

There were blow-downs in this stone forest. Huge columns, top-
pled in some long-ago age, stretched across chasms like bridges,
grown with time to merge with other columns, with the walls
themselves. Though he craned his neck as far as he could without
overbalancing, Joze saw no roof above, only darkness. He heard
water below and to his left, gurgling musically in a deep, winding
channel, lapping at shores of stone, working patiently to coax rock
into a new pattern in the splendid design.

Joze held the Elven closer. "A forest of stone," he whispered.
"Hunter-scout, I wish you could see this now."

A long-fingered hand touched his wrist. Startled, Joze clutched
the girl, looked down to see the watcher.

"The friend cannot answer yet," it said. "Come with me. I will
show you the help I have."

They went along winding paths lighted by the ground braziers.
The paths were not always smooth, and sometimes they climbed
short hills, then dropped into dips and swales. Though his arms
ached from carrying her, still Joze held the Elven close, tried
not to jostle her. She never stirred, but Joze knew that she still
breathed shallowly; he felt her warm breath on his neck.

In truth, her breath felt good; the warmth of it eased the rising chill. As he and the watcher walked on, the air became
cooler.

"Watcher," he whispered once. "Who made this place?"

The watcher looked back over its shoulder, then shrugged.
"Gods did, and their goddesses."

Through the wonderful forest, past stone trees, over fallen columns bridging deep chasms, Joze followed the watcher. After a
time he realized that the forest was thinning, the distance between
the stony trees widening. Now he saw walls rising to his left
and right, had again a sense of being within a vast chamber.
The walls circled and nearly met but for a small dark crack.
Joze didn't think that crack would be tall enough for him to fit
through.

The watcher pointed to the narrow split in the wall. "Tall, do
you smell the smoke?"

He did, just as the question was asked. This was not the coal smoke that drifted up from the braziers, but wood smoke, wispy and grey. "A hearth?" he asked.

The watcher nodded. "And the Lady. Be ready to bow low, Tall."

Suddenly uneasy, Joze looked down at the watcher. "To your Lady?"

The watcher rattled laughter. "No, no, Tall—to the top of the doorway. It would hurt to hit your head."

Arms and shoulders aching, Joze followed the watcher again, bent low when he was warned, and stepped out of the stony forest into a wide chamber. The chamber glowed with light from a free-standing hearth in the center of the floor. The hearth was a thing to make the wonders of the stone forest seem pale indeed.

Someone had captured rainbows, snatched them right out of the sky and brought them here to this far place below the ground. This rainbow-hunter had set the gleaming lights, shimmering bands of purest white, of red and blue and gold and green, in spans of crystal and built this circular hearth with them. There could be no other explanation. The fire in the marvelous hearth leaped and danced, as fire does everywhere, but that dancing made the exquisite bands of color seem to move, swirling and spinning within the crystal hearth. Beyond the light lay darkness so thick that Joze could make out no shapes. He didn't try to; like a moth drawn to a candle's flame, he wanted only the light. He didn't realize that he'd gone close to the hearth until he felt the heat of the fire, heard the watcher say:

"Put the friend down." It gestured to a long smooth depression in the cavern's floor at the base of the hearth. "Rest her here, close to the fire. She is not awake, but maybe she is cold, yes?"

Joze sank to his knees, eased the Elven gently into the shallow place. His arms, free of the burden of her weight, felt suddenly light and buoyant. Then, just as suddenly, they began to ache fiercely again. He reached high, flexing stiff muscles, then sat back against the crystal hearth, checked the Elven carefully. The hearth's colors moved gently across her face, like dream-light. She was very pale. Pain had etched thin lines around her wide mouth and her long Elvish eyes. She breathed now as one would who didn't care very much about breathing.

Joze looked around the chamber, peered closely into the darkness. He saw nothing beyond the hearth's light, knew nothing more about the place than that it was a chamber within the earth, smelling of stone and the hearth-smoke drifting slowly toward some unseen vent in the ceiling. He heard nothing but the watcher's rough breathing, the hiss of the fire in the marvelous rainbow hearth and, faintly, far away, the tap of water on stone. He wondered where the Lady was, but he didn't ask. He needed to care for the Elven now, and questions about the watcher's mysterious Lady might delay that.

"Watcher," he said, "is there water and cloth for bandaging? And maybe something to make splints with?"

The watcher shook his head. "No bandages. No splints. Water, yes. Are you thirsty?"

Joze eyed the watcher narrowly. "You said you could help her."

"She can be whole again. Yes. But—"

One hand on the Elven's shoulder, the other close to his short-sword, Joze said, "But?"

The watcher didn't look at the sword. Slowly, purposefully, it reached for the hunter-scout's shoulder, covered Joze's hand with its own. "Then you must help my Lady."

Joze held his hand still beneath the watcher's. Remembering his pledge of peace in the forest above, he took his right hand away from his weapon. "And how would I do that?"

"She will tell you."

Joze glanced quickly around the empty chamber. He saw nothing, no darker shadow hiding in the blackness beyond the hearth. He heard no sound of breathing, no soft, secretive slide of foot against stone.

"Watcher," he said coldly, "I don't see anyone here but you and me and the girl."

"The Lady is here. She can make the friend whole. She will if you promise to help."

"I don't make promises without knowing that I can keep them."

"Wise," the watcher said. "And honorable." It reached for the Elven, touched her face tenderly. "Then we will trust you to help when you know that you can. See."

Joze saw, and felt his heart tighten, caught between elation and dread.

Light, green and shimmering as sunlight glancing across a waving meadow, veiled the cuts on the Elven's face. As Joze watched, the skin healed, grew back clean and smooth. The deep gash at her hairline closed as though the wound had never been.

"The Lady can mend the bone, as well."

Stomach loose with quick sickness, suddenly dizzy, Joze whispered, "How—how do you do that?"

"Not me, Tall. The Lady."

Joze closed his eyes, groping for balance. This was not natural. Almost he thought, *This is not right!* But he caught the thought back. It didn't look natural, but it didn't feel wrong. Yet, despite his acknowledgment, he didn't find the balance he'd been groping for, found only fear and confusion.

What had he come into? What had he brought the hunter-scout into?

"Damn it!" he shouted. The echoes of his cry skittered round the chamber, sound lapping at the shores of silence. He drew a long breath, let it out slowly. When he spoke, he spoke quietly, though not yet calmly.

"*What* Lady? There's no one here but you and me and—"

But that was not true, though it had seemed to be when he'd started to speak. The smoke from the hearth, once arrowing straight for a vent somewhere in the ceiling, drifted sideways now, stretched outward like grey arms, encircled the girl in a ghostly embrace.

The Elven stirred once, cried out. It wasn't a cry of shock or pain, but one of joy and recognition. When she settled again, the lines of pain around her mouth and eyes had smoothed. The smoky veil, the ghostly arms, withdrew. The Elven's breast rose and fell in the soft rhythm of a sleeper's breathing.

"That Lady," the watcher said proudly, its wide-set, glowing eyes on the retreating smoke. "My Lady. She has redeemed my promise to you, Tall. Now she wants to know if you will consider her request."

Eyes still on the smoke, mouth suddenly dry, Joze said cautiously, "What does she want?"

"She will tell you. She can explain it best."

The watcher rose, stepped away from the hearth, but Joze closed a hard hand around its wrist.

"You're leaving?"

"You sound like you are thirsty, Tall. I have help for that." Gently, the watcher disengaged Joze's grip. "I will be back."

Beyond the light of the rainbowed hearth the darkness was like blindness. Joze watched the creature step into that darkness and vanish as though it had never been.

A chill, sharp as dread, crept along the back of his neck when he knew that he was alone in the chamber, alone with the sleeping hunter-scout and the watcher's ghostly grey Lady. His hand on the Elven's, his heart beating thickly with fear, he waited for the Lady to become more than smoke.

Chapter Four

SOMETHING CHANGED IN THE CHAMBER OF THE CRYSTAL HEARTH; something else did not. The hunter-scout roused; the smoke continued to hover over the hearth, disdaining the draft from an unseen roof vent. Eyes on the smoke, Joze didn't realize that the Elven had waked until she snatched her hand from his, caught it to her as though recovering something stealthily taken.

Joze looked away from the hearth and the hovering smoke, a reassuring smile ready. The smile fell away when he saw that the hunter-scout's hand lay upon her breast where—if one had been there—she could easily slip a hidden weapon from within her blouse.

"I have the knife," he said, trying hard to keep his tone casual. It was not an easy thing to do, for as the color mounted from the Elven's throat to her thin cheeks, Joze found that his fingers seemed to remember all on their own the softness of the skin beneath her blouse. To give his suddenly restless hands something to do, he took the small knife from his boot and handed it to the Elven.

"Don't worry," he said gruffly, "I didn't—"

A softening expression of relief flickered across her thin face, then vanished, hidden away behind a hard, scathing smile. "Lucky for you."

Wisely, Joze said nothing about whether or not he considered himself lucky.

The hunter-scout watched him coldly from beyond the gleaming blade. Then, eyes darkening as though remembering dreams of pain, she slipped her hand along her leg. "You're the one with the horse."

He nodded. "I'm sorry about what happened. I—"

"Who are you?"

"My name is Joze. You?"

The hearth's colored light danced in the Elven's short curls, played across her cheeks, glimmered along her neck and throat as she weighed the ideas of telling and not telling him. At last she said:

"Kicva. What happened to my leg?"

Joze answered carefully, thinking it was best to lead her slowly into that strange territory. "It was broken. Now it's not."

He waited patiently while she considered this, tried to marshal answers to the questions she would surely ask. She had a question, but it was not one he'd expected.

"Where are we?"

Joze wished she would stop glaring at him from beyond that glittering knife blade as though he harbored villainous intentions. They were touchy, these women hunter-scouts. They seemed to have the idea that every man who came near them wanted nothing more than to yank them out of their hunting leathers and into the forest for a quick—

"Well?" she demanded.

Joze shook his head, summoned patience. "I don't know for certain. Beneath the ground—"

"I can see that," Kicva said coldly. "How did we get here?"

Joze didn't think it would be a good idea to smile now, yet a smile tugged insistently at his lips. He ran a hand slowly along the length of his jaw, combed his blunt fingers through his dark beard. "I walked in. You got carried in."

The Elven slipped the little knife into the sheath beneath her blouse, put a hand on the many-colored hearth, and pushed herself to her feet. She gave Joze one uncertain glance, then walked around the hearth, putting high stone and low fire between them. Her first steps were limping ones, as though she'd expected to stagger. But soon she found that her leg was as sound as it seemed. None would know from watching her that a little while ago her leg had been broken; her stride was long and smooth, a cat's gliding. And, like a cat, curious and cautious, she circled the hearth, eyes on the rainbow of crystal and the fire.

Joze started out watching the Elven, for her slender grace was something worth watching. But soon he found all his attention taken by the soft grey smoke hovering above the hearth. Deep in him, in some far place where he was not used to looking for observations, he realized that something waited within that smoke. And he understood suddenly that what waited did so with less patience than it had only a moment ago.

Above the hearth the smoke shifted, stretched now, but not toward the vent. It stretched outward, like two arms reaching.

"Kicva—" Joze said, eyes on the smoke, sudden fear making his voice rough and low.

She looked up sharply, but didn't move.

"Kicva, come over here."

"Why should—?"

"*Now!*"

It was Kicva the soldier who responded to his warning shout, and responded like an arrow shot from a taut bow. She hit the floor and scrambled away from the many-colored hearth, scurried to Joze, along the way scraping arms and elbows, bruising knees. Joze gathered her close as fire roared and leaped high in the hearth. Flames flew toward the dark roof like bright-winged birds hungry to feed on the darkness. Kicva, long light eyes on the fire, sat quiet in his arms.

Quiet, Joze thought, but for her heart leaping like a startled hare! Nor was his own heart any steadier.

As quickly as they'd raced to life, that quickly did the flames subside. And the watcher's Lady took shape in the heat-shimmering air above the hearth.

Though the figure in the smoke didn't become much more solid than a dream, Joze was surprised by the form it took. He'd expected to see some short, squat female version of the watcher. He saw, instead, a tall lithe woman, long-eyed as Elvish are, hair the color of a sun-struck raven's wing. Her eyes were the same soft blue as is seen in the depths of highly polished silver. She wore about her an air of regality, the look of one used to commanding and to having commands obeyed.

Kicva drew a soft, wondering breath. Joze saw the hard suspicion fall away from her face, saw something lighten her eyes, soften her expression, as though she'd rediscovered a pleasant, long-forgotten memory.

"Ah, you," she said. "Lady . . ."

Joze thought of queens and bowed his head.

"My children," the Grey Lady said, and Joze shivered deeply. "Joze, my faraway son, Kicva, my distant daughter: I am Islief's Lady."

Faraway son, Joze thought. *Distant daughter?*

And in almost the same moment, he thought: *Islief. So that's its name.*

Kicva shot a suspicious look at Joze. "Who's Islief?"

Joze said nothing, for his thoughts had raced to wondering how this ghostly lady knew their names.

"Joze, I know your names," the Grey Lady said, "because I heard you speak them; and you'd have known Islief's if you'd asked. Son of mine, it would be kinder—and truer—to think of Islief as 'him' and not 'it.' "

Curiosity helped Joze to find his voice. "Does it—does *he* think of me as 'it'?"

The smoky image wavered, then settled again, giving Joze the impression of gentle laughter. "No. Islief knows what you are. So do I, faraway son."

Again the strange naming! Joze leaned forward. "Why do you call me that?"

"Because it's what you are." A finger of smoke drifted toward Kicva, who leaned a little forward in Joze's arms as though to meet it. She sighed, a sound filled with yearning.

"Lady. Lady, I dreamed . . ." Her words fell away, clearly silenced by wonder. Kicva accepted the Lady's touch as calmly as she would have accepted a mother's caress.

"Daughter," the Grey Lady said, "it was no dream."

"It was you who made me well."

The ghosty hand withdrew, left only an impression of tenderness and a wisp of grey smoke behind. "Children, come close to the hearth-pit."

Kicva gave Joze a quick, startled look, as though she'd suddenly realized that she'd been sitting close in his arms. She scrambled to her feet, took a bold and quick step toward the hearth. Joze followed, watching the light from the hearth shimmer like a jeweled necklace on the Elven's throat as fire stirred again in the hearth-pit. The flames didn't reach for the darkness and the ceiling this time, only breathed gently, then fell still, leaving a vast bed of coals in the hearth-pit, coals dancing with heat and light.

"Once," the Grey Lady said, "and not so long ago, the Sorcerer used a pit like this."

Kicva drew a tight breath. "In his Souless. Lady, I'd heard that he could see the whole world in his fire pit, and that he watched the battles and stoked the war as though fighting was fire and he was always cold."

Despite the heat emanating from the embers, Joze shivered. He'd heard much the same about the magic fire pit deep in the sea caves below evil Souless.

The Grey Lady seemed to rise taller. "You saw that place destroyed, son of mine?"

"I saw it," Joze said. His voice sounded hollow in his own ears, empty as he remembered the dream that haunted his sleep always, recalled the helplessness when his will to do more than breathe was stolen away from him, his muscles aching and trembling with exhaustion and fear as fiery enchantment scattered the stones of Souless as though they were grains of sand before the wind. He shuddered, as he did each time he woke from the nightmare of burning Souless.

Softly, barely felt, a hand touched Joze's shoulder, trailed warmth down the length of his arm. Kicva, her eyes on the ghosty smoke, tucked her hand into his own. The expression in her eyes told Joze that she didn't know that her hand lay in his.

The smoke drifted around the Lady, as a thin silk gown drifts in soft breezes. "Children, the Sorcerer's fire could only show him what is, not what *was*. And so it didn't remind him of his first defeat, his first failure at my hands, long ago in ancient times. Maybe if he had been obliged to see his history, he would not have let one of the Jewels fall into the hands of another hunter-defender."

Within Joze's grasp Kicva's hand trembled; then her fingers tightened to a fist. Her long light eyes blazed with fierce pride, the kind Joze had often seen when his Elvish winter-companions spoke of their Princess Nikia. Man or woman, not one but would have gladly laid down his life for their king's daughter, for Nikia gone to live in Mannish, gone to foreign lands to be a treaty-warrant and the wife of a stranger-prince. Not a man or woman of them but spoke with glowing pride of Nikia who had unlocked the secret of the Ruby of Guyaire and become the Hunter-Defender, silver-eyed Nikia who had defeated the Sorcerer.

The Grey Lady spoke softly, spoke to Joze's own thoughts. "Nikia, too, is a distant daughter."

"Lady," Kicva said, "is your fire like the Sorcerer's? Can it show us the world about?"

The smoke thickened, darkened; the Lady faded. But only a little, as though she had turned away to think. And then the smoke thinned and the lithe, dark-haired woman appeared again.

"This hearth-pit is like, and unlike. From the Sorcerer's pit," she said, "the seeing globes were created. The last of those is gone, shattered. There will be no more, for that pit is destroyed, the fire and the sorcery quenched forever. My fire cannot make a seeing globe. But maybe it can make hope." The smoky form moved again; the Lady held out her hands. "Children, in the world without, the land is dying. Have you the courage to be part of the healing?"

"Lady, how?" Joze whispered.

"Come see what was, and you will learn what can be."

Again Kicva took a step forward. She laid her hands on the crystal hearth, leaned eagerly to see what might be seen. Joze followed, but reluctantly. Something in the way the smoke moved above the hearth made him think that what he would see would not be an easy thing. He was not so sure of his courage as Kicva seemed to be.

In the hearth-pit, heat shifted, rose up to embrace them. Embers danced, trembling with light. The Grey Lady spoke, her voice a sad ache of a whisper:

"I came to these caverns, this home of the First People, through lands savaged by war, stripped of the beauty, raped of bounty. I went past rivers running crimson with blood, silver with tears. That was many hundreds of years ago, when there was no Mannish, no Elvish, only the Second People. Our people. Many hundreds of years ago—when the Sorcerer fought his first war against us."

Joze caught his breath, let it out slowly. The shifting embers before him fell into patterns and shapes, made a glowing picture which, in spite of his unease, drew him to watch.

Chapter Five

A YOUNG WOMAN WENT HURT AND LIMPING ALONG THE RUINED BANK of a river, a bank scarred as though by the brutal dragging of a wide-bladed plough. Trees and bushes lay twisted, agonized, with secret roots exposed to light they should never have felt. The soft moist soil beneath stone and rock dried and crumbled beneath the sun's hot glare. The woman stumbled, fell to her knees. She bled from many wounds, as though she were an icon of the land.

Joze looked away and he didn't look back again until he heard Kicva murmur, "Lady, she is you."

"She is Aeylin," the Grey Lady said. "Yes, she is me."

And Joze looked again, saw the young woman fall against a wall of stone, saw a wide door in that stone, dark and yawning beyond the woman's shoulder.

Wretched, nearly dead of sorrow and pain, Aeylin entered the dark cool caverns. She was ravaged and naked as the forests and the fields, torn as the river banks were torn, bleeding as the earth bled, weeping as the river wept.

Hot on his own cheeks, hotter maybe than the fire in the wonderful crystal hearth, Joze felt tears running, tears for the woman Aeylin, tears for the damaged land that was, for the plague-struck land that lay above these caverns now.

Aeylin laid herself upon the stone floor as though she believed she laid herself upon her bier. She closed her eyes as though she believed it a final and irrevocable sleep to which she fled. But after a time, she knew that she was not alone.

The warmth Aeylin felt then, the low and gentle voice she heard, were to her as the graces of the Deity Lif-Hori, whose name means Life and Hope. It may have been that none so badly needed the favors of the Deity of Life. But it was not the god Lif who touched her, nor the goddess Hori who held the torch which streamed like a brave banner in the breeze from the ruined river.

It was only Islief, silent and watching. Islief, old then, old many hundreds of years ago.

Joze stepped closer to the hearth, saw the watcher—his watcher—fall to his knees. Careless of the heat, responding only to the terrible sorrow he sensed in the images, Joze reached his hand to the embers, to the little tongues of fire and light, to Islief and the young woman.

With a sudden cry, Kicva pulled his hand away from the licking flames, held tight to his wrist. "Have you lost your mind?" she hissed.

The Lady spoke kindly. "Islief is a lot like you, Joze. My friend could never look upon the hurt or dying without wanting to help. He wept at the sight of me. Islief is one to whom beauty despoiled is a thing more grievous than death itself. I was no beauty then, torn and broken. But Islief believes that what can be broken can also be mended. I pray that he is right."

Joze freed his hand from Kicva's, wiped his palm across his wet cheeks as he watched the fire's play and the image of Islief weeping.

Islief dragged his hand across his eyes, wiped away his tears. He rose and slipped back into shadows. But he was not long gone, and when he returned he had others, two small men, with him. With great care they lifted Aeylin and carried her into the caverns. They carried the woman down a dark corridor, through the wonderful stone forest where other small folk, thickly built people who looked much like Islief and his companions, hurried along brightly lighted corridors.

As people in Damris hurried along the streets, Joze thought.

As Islief and his friends passed them, the folk stopped, exclaimed over this stranger-woman, and many followed him.

"For I was a wonder to them, children," the Grey Lady said. "A woman of the Second People. They knew about us, knew that we'd come to this land from across the Eastern Sea. And they knew that we brought our old enemy, the Sorcerer, with us. He came following with war, and the First People left the land and went to live here, below the ground. They were not interested in our wars and strivings. They hid themselves and hoped that we would not do what we did; hoped that the Sorcerer and the Second People would not tear at the world when we meant to tear at each other.

"Still, they welcomed me. They were a kindly people. They did their best to make me well, and so Islief's foundling, the woman of the Second People, lived. But, when Islief begged me to stay with the cavern-folk, I said that I could not."

In the fire-image, Joze saw tears sheen Islief's wide, glowing eyes. When he looked up to the smoke-image, he thought he saw the shadow of those ancient tears in the ghost's eyes.

"I was a hunter-scout," she said. "Kicva, like you are. Daughter, you know what that means. I was bound to the service of my king by an oath which cannot be broken, pledged to the protection of my kin."

Kicva nodded solemnly. Though she said nothing, Joze knew that an understanding had been forged between the Elven and the Grey Lady. Perhaps one he couldn't share.

"The Sorcerer raged without check," the Lady said. "He savaged the lands and my people. Islief warned against my leaving, told me I'd find nothing but death up above. And I told him that to stay would be death of a kind, too, the death of honor. I could not hide in safety while my kin died under the Sorcerer's fell hand."

In the fire-picture, Islief's eyes grew sad, achingly tired. Joze heard an echo of that weariness in Kicva's sigh. She was a young woman, not much more than a girl, but hers was the sigh of an old soldier who understood that a sundering was coming.

An echo of an echo, Joze heard sadness in the ghost's voice. "Islief sorrowed for me," the Grey Lady said, "and for the ravaged lands up above. None loved the beauty of the world, the deep caverns, the great forests and the star-filled skies, as well as Islief did. I think—in his heart—Islief confused me with the land. And so, maybe, his people should not have been surprised by what he did."

Joze caught his breath, looked away from the fire pit and the images. Though his heart trembled to think what the answer might be, he asked a question.

"What did Islief do, Lady?"

"He sinned. He sinned terribly. Because I asked him to. Look at the fire, children."

The scenes shifted rapidly now, accelerating in quick jerking fashion as though Joze were seeing them through the eyes of one who was running down deep corridors, racing through narrow hallways. When the fire-vision settled again, he saw a low-ceilinged chamber, circular, and much smaller than the one he was in now. The chamber was unfurnished, empty but for a slender pedestal, a stone column of what seemed to be black diamond. Upon the pedestal, placed high as though it were a sacred thing, rested a crown.

All jewels and gold and lustrous silver, the crown leaped alive in the fire's vision. A simple band of silver-chased gold. At each of the four cardinal points was set a gem: emerald, sapphire, diamond and topaz. In the center of the crown, warded by the others as though this one jewel above all must not flee, was set a ruby.

Kicva caught her breath, let it out in a slow sigh. Joze shared her wonder. He'd never seen the Ruby of Guyaire, but all through the winter he'd heard tales of it. All through winter he'd dreamed of the terrible destruction its magic had done.

"Lady," he said, "the ruby is . . ." He could not finish.

But it was Kicva who answered him, her voice thrilling. "The Ruby of Guyaire," she breathed. "The Jewel the Elf-King's daughter brought to your prince. The other treaty-warrant."

Smoke rose high above the hearth; an arm of flame leaped within, tinting the smoke scarlet. Joze backed away, heart pounding, throat tightening with nightmare-fear and instinctive dread of the Ruby's terrible crimson beauty.

"War's Mistress," the Grey Lady said. "Within its magic Nikia became the Hunter-Defender; with its power she pulled down terrible Souless. But the Ruby is only part of the Crown, that gift of the Deities to these people. Whole, the Crown is the embodiment of the earth's spirit and potency, holy beyond holy. As long as there is the Crown, then so will the powers of the earth move in balance."

The cool breeze dropped, and the effect of its stilling was as though a warmer one had risen. Or maybe it was the effect of the sudden warming of the ghostly woman's voice.

"There is a chant these people used to sing in the presence of this gift:

> Hail to you!
> Emerald: Proud Ruler of Nature!
> Sapphire: Gentle King of Air!
> Diamond: Wild Prince of Water!

Topaz: Golden Thane of Fire!
Ruby: Fearsome Mistress of War!
Hail to you!

"It was no prayer, my children, only a simple greeting to the five Powers, humble acknowledgment of their strength and place in the world of both Peoples."

The Lady fell silent. Joze heard no breathing but his own and Kicva's. This Lady sighed sometimes, but she didn't breathe. This Lady was a ghost, a spirit. A haunter.

But Joze didn't fear her as he would have feared a ghost, for in the hearth-smoke, in the heat-shimmering air, he tasted her sorrow and . . . He held his breath, not sure that what he suddenly felt was indeed what this proud ghost-woman felt. Shame?

The ghost stirred; the smoke-image wavered.

"A magnificent Crown, yes?" Her voice trembled a little, and Joze knew in the deep places of him that the trembling echoed an old eagerness. "Four of its Jewels embody all the powers of nature. In the fifth, in the Ruby, lies the power to destroy all that the four rule. It was a source of great pride to Islief's people that they were entrusted by the Deities to hold and keep this Crown, to stand watch over the spirit of the earth.

"And I knew the moment I saw the Crown that I would persuade Islief to blasphemy. I knew that if the Second People stood any chance against the Sorcerer, it lay with this Crown.

"Children, see what I made my friend do."

With dread fascination, the kind a bird feels as it watches a snake's hypnotic weaving, Joze looked again at the fire-image, at the shifting embers in the hearth-pit. And watching, he saw the enactment of a deed which had haunted the last age of the world.

Islief and Aeylin entered the chamber. As soon as his eyes rested upon the Crown, Islief knelt as one who worships. Wide eyes glowing, huge with sorrow, he lifted his hand, touched a finger to each of the Jewels in turn.

Joze's heart ached with pity. He understood it, as surely as if he'd been there: Islief knew right then that he would sin.

"When Islief called me to him," the Lady said, "I went. I knew nothing of the ways of the First People, but I knew this: I stood in the presence of something holy. I knelt, I could do nothing else. And that gesture was Islief's undoing. I think he could have turned back from his sin at any moment before I did homage to the Crown. He could have dug a shallow defense, though deep enough to save himself, had I stood boldly in the presence of the thing he and his kin held most sacred. But I knelt, and he was lost. When I asked him for the Crown, he gave it to me."

Islief lifted the gleaming Crown from its column of black diamond. His long-fingered hands were steady as he held the treasure. He told Aeylin that no one of the Jewels must be used alone, warned that this would be imbalance. But, used in balance, he said, they would restore to the world what the Sorcerer had torn from it: the symmetry of magic moving in tandem with the earth.

The smoke wavered, trembled. The Grey Lady raised her hands, as though she again reached for the mighty treasure which Islief had offered her.

" 'Save your people,' Islief whispered to me. 'Save the earth,' he meant. My children, the Deities and his own people called him sinner for giving me what he did. Even now, even today, I do not think he cares what people call him. None so loved the earth, none took greater pain in her sorcerous agonies, in the tearing of her soul, the despoiling of her bounty, than Islief."

Memory, like a hard and cruel hand, came to squeeze Joze's heart, memories of impotent dust and hot, hot winds blowing down the sky over barren Raeth.

"Yes, Joze, Islief is a lot like you. It was in his hands to restore balance to a world run mad with sorcery. He knew the Seven had decreed that the Crown should never leave this safe place, he knew the Deities would exact payment for his sin. And so they did."

His throat thick with tears, Joze could not speak. But Kicva did, defiantly, boldly.

"It was *his* choice as much as yours."

The Lady lifted her hands, empty ghost-hands. "Daughter, it was never Islief's choice that I break the Crown. But that is what I did, for I was a warrior, and thinking only of war, I made the Crown a tool of war. I made it a thing it was never meant to be. When Islief placed that treasure in my hands I felt its power, and though I took the Crown whole from here to the upper world, the first thing I did upon reaching a place of safety was to have the Jewels struck from the band. The first thing I did was break the balance."

"You did what you had to do," Kicva said stubbornly. "Lady, you had no choice: You were a soldier; you'd sworn an oath to your king!"

"I'd sworn an oath," the Grey Lady said, and in her voice Joze heard the weary recriminations of many hundreds of years. "But what I did in those days made me little different than the Sorcerer."

"You used the Ruby?" Joze whispered.

"No." The Lady laughed, a bitter sound. "I was foolish, but not mad. I knew what that terrible Jewel could do, and I knew that it would take a greater strength than mine to wield its power. I used two others, the Diamond and the Topaz. With the Wild Prince I raised the seas against the Sorcerer, with the Golden Thane I commanded fire. They were enough to cause him to flee these lands. I thought they were enough to teach him that the Second People were a folk to be reckoned with.

"And you know, my children, for you have only just finished fighting him, that I taught him no lesson. All I did was break a greater balance than any of his sorceries could have broken. In that breach was a place for him to re-enter the world, strong again for having rested. And the Jewels became lost down the ages— the only one kept was the terrible War-stone. The Ruby."

Joze turned away from the hearth. He'd been caught by the Lady's tale, followed her words and the images in the fire. Now, looking into the darkness, he understood something fully, a thing he'd only vaguely considered before. The images the Lady had showed him, the story she'd told him, were of a time long, long ago. An age lost in legend.

"Lady," he asked, his mouth suddenly dry with fear of the answer. "What price did Islief pay for your sin?"

Aeylin was a long time answering, and when she spoke at last, her voice was so thin and low that Joze heard her words more clearly with his heart than he did with his ears.

"He has lived through centuries, my faraway son. His own people are long dead, gone to the place the Seven have made for all people when our time in this world is done. Islief alone remains, condemned to wait here until this new age could be born from the old, when the balance could be restored.

"You call him Watcher. It's a good name for him. Here, in the embers of this hearth he saw me drive the Sorcerer back. He saw the Second People grow strong, watched while we fought our own wars for power and dominance. He knew it when we forgot that we are one race.

"Islief saw the Sorcerer return, saw him corrupt all he touched. When the evil one cast the spell which caused the land to sicken, Islief saw that. And he felt the Ruby's power like a wild wind in his ancient soul when Nikia lifted it against the Sorcerer. He rejoiced when that evil creature finally died, for he knew that a new age was being born. He understood that the end of his long punishment was near."

Suddenly weary, immeasurably tired, Joze walked away from the many-colored hearth. Kicva came to stand stiffly beside him. She didn't touch him, didn't offer even the warmth of her hand. Long blue eyes on the smoke, she said:

"The Sorcerer is dead, Lady. This new age you speak of has come. Why is Islief still here?"

The Grey Lady answered sorrowfully. "All is not balanced yet. Kicva, you've seen what damage has been done to the earth. It is the Sorcerer's doing, for he was stronger this last time than he was the first. He found his greatest powers in the skewing of the world's balance, in the wild void I created.

"His damage—*our* damage—needs undoing now. Islief felt my spirit abroad in the land when I came to coax the Hunter-Defender, the Elvish princess, back from the temptations of godhood. We are old friends, Islief and I, and so he welcomed me again when I did not return to the Seven, but came to seek him out. He welcomed me again even though I came begging another boon from him."

Joze's shuddering breath hurt raggedly through his whole chest. "Lady, what more could you ask of him?"

"That he stay here a while longer, stay to make the Crown again."

"Why?"

"Because I need to help in the restoration of the damaged balance. For reasons of their own, the Deities condemned me not at all, unless with a conscience. Still, I know that mine was the greater sin. Islief gave me the Crown whole. I broke it, took its enchanted Jewels. They should never have been separated."

Softly, Kicva said: "Have you the Jewels, Lady? Even the Ruby?"

"Yes, child, all of them. Even the Ruby."

"And so Islief will remake the Crown?"

"For a fee."

Sudden anger flared in the Elven's eyes. "A fee! Lady, I'd think he'd be glad to remake his precious heirloom! What *fee* could he ask?"

"A simple one, daughter. That the land be healed, made well again. With the Emerald's help, I can do that. I can undo the damage that has been done by the Sorcerer's land-killing enchantments. With the Emerald, I can heal the land. With it . . . I can heal my own sin."

"And so, Joze," she said softly, "we have come to the part about promises. The one Islief kept, the one you made in return."

Joze drew a long breath, let it out slowly. He'd been dazzled by fire-pictures; he'd been in conversation with a ghost. But he hadn't forgotten his promise. "The fee for healing the hurt I'd done Kicva."

The Elven shot him a quick glance, wary and mistrusting. She slipped a hand along her thigh to the place where her leg had been broken. Long eyes narrowed with suspicion, she said, "You've promised something for my sake? That's as much as making a promise in my name. What have we promised?"

"A favor for a favor. The favor Islief asked was that I grant his Lady's wish. If I could."

Then, shuddering, thinking of Islief the Watcher who had once and long ago granted this ghost-woman's wish and paid a price for the granting that Joze could yet only a little comprehend, he said:

"Lady, Islief kept his promise to me. If it's within my power, I'll keep mine to him. What is your wish?"

"I need a body, I need hands and heart to guide the magic. I need a child of both Man and Elf."

Joze stopped breathing.

Kicva didn't. And her face flamed with color, eyes widened with sudden fear.

But the Grey Lady laughed gently. "Child, be easy. Your sons are yours to keep until they go out to meet their own fates. The babe I need is already growing strong in her mother's womb."

Joze looked at Kicva; the Elven turned to look at him. And so their eyes were met, locked tight as though theirs were not glances but hands clasped, when ghostly Aeylin told them that they must bring her the child of Nikia who is Princess of both Mannish and Elvish, the child of the Hunter-Defender who defeated the terrible Sorcerer and then tore down his Souless fortress with fire and wild magic.

"And you must use whatever means there are to bring that babe here to me, Joze."

Chapter Six

"NO, LADY," JOZE SAID FLATLY. A CHILL BREEZE WANDERED through the chamber, made the smoke above the hearth waver, grow thinner. Still he said on. "I'm no kidnapper, Lady."

Beside him Kicva drew a short sharp breath. "Joze, what do you mean? You've promised—"

"I promised to listen, Kicva. I didn't promise to become a kidnapper." Though it seemed that the disappointment he'd sensed in the Lady was now reflected in the hunter-scout's long eyes, Joze held firm. "And this is a matter between the Lady and me."

"Oh, no it isn't. You made that promise for my sake. That makes this my business."

"Think what you like," he said coldly. "But know this: I'll have nothing to do with child-theft." He looked away from her, squared his stance, and eyed the smoke above crystal hearth as though gauging an opponent's strength. Heart pounding thickly, afraid even as he spoke, he said:

"I mean it, Lady."

"Joze, I cannot heal the land-sickness without hands and heart and soul to call the magic."

He gestured toward Kicva. "You healed the hunter-scout simply enough."

The smoke rose high, the ghostly image sharpened for just a moment. Cold the Grey Lady's voice now, and far colder than Joze's had been.

"You are a fool, Joze," Aeylin said, "to challenge when you don't know what you are talking about. Your people tossed aside their heritage of magic uncounted years ago, forgot the ways of enchantment, and from your superstitious fathers you have inherited only ignorance. As well compare a raindrop to the sea as to compare that simple healing-spell to the magic that must be done to unknit the Sorcerer's land-killing spells.

"Without this child, the healing power of the Emerald will stay forever locked within the Jewel. Without Nikia's daughter—this child of Elf and Man—I can do nothing. Nikia's child *must* be brought to me."

Joze knew nothing about magic, nor did he understand the ways of spell-crafting. But he knew how he felt about child-theft. Any man who'd ever seen a mother smile over her newly come child knew that this was a crime which left behind sorrow forever unhealed.

"Why this child? Lady, there are mages aplenty in the Elflands. Why not send for one of them to act as your hands and heart?"

It was Kicva who answered, her voice low, low and soft as though she had herself only just understood the reason for Aeylin's need.

"Because no mage of Dekar's was born to this, Joze. No mage—not even his most powerful—was born of a woman who has the strength to wield one of the Jewels. And that strength is not physical."

From behind, from somewhere in the blind darkness, drifted a deep and weary sigh. "The friend is right, Tall."

Kicva tensed, then turned slowly. "Islief," she whispered, and her voice sounded ragged, as though she—who had these moments past been in easy converse with a ghost—now saw something to give her pause.

Islief's wide-set eyes glowed warmly. He nodded once to Kicva, a silent greeting, but continued to speak to Joze.

"The friend is right, Tall. No mage of her king's is child of Man and Elf. And yet did they all have such parents—no one of them was made for this magic-working. Only *this* child. No good—and much harm—would be done if another tried to call the Emerald's magic. This the Deities have said. The Lady and I, we know it.

"But still, Tall, your choice is not easy."

A child made for magic . . .

Joze closed his eyes, tried to think. But what else to think about except the very thing he didn't want to consider? He was being asked to fetch—by fair means or foul—a helpless child, one not even born yet.

"Choice?" he laughed harshly. "The way you tell it, Islief, there *is* no choice."

"There is choice. There is always choice. This one that you have is between one hard thing and another hard thing. But, Tall, you can help my Lady restore health to the sick lands."

Kicva relaxed a little. "He's right, Joze, we can help. We *must.*"

Joze rounded on her, said in a tight, strained voice, "Kicva, we're talking about stealing the child of the Hunter-Defender."

"We're talking about the land! Your homeland—and if this land-sickness isn't stopped, mine, too. And we don't have to *steal* the child."

Islief nodded. "The friend is right, Tall. You could ask for her."

"Ah, certainly," Joze said caustically. "Why didn't I think of that? Surely the Princess would gladly hand over her newly born babe to us. Or maybe she'd even be happy to come here for the child's birth." He looked around the stone chamber, the cold rock floor, the rough, shadowed walls. "What a nice change it would be from giving birth in a warm bed among physicians and ladies' maids."

Flames leaped in the hearth; the rainbowed crystal threw brilliant color shadows across the stone floor, sent them bounding up the rock walls. Aeylin laughed, but gently.

"Son of mine, do you think I intend to harm the daughter of the Hunter-Defender? Do you think I mean to do anything but preserve the only hope left in the land?"

"I don't know what you intend," Joze said. "I don't know what you mean to do."

"And you do not trust me."

Joze let silence be his answer, and when it became clear what his silence meant, Kicva stepped forward, chin high, proud and eager as a soldier before her captain.

"*I* trust you, Lady. Joze made a promise for my sake. If he doesn't want to honor it, I will do my best to." She glanced disdainfully at Joze, then smiled, a cool, crooked lifting of the corners of her mouth. "That should content everyone, Joze. Yes?"

Stung by her derision, Joze turned away, looked to Islief. But Islief was busy wiping wet hands on his old breeches, carefully leaving Joze alone to answer both Aeylin and Kicva. Feeling trapped, suddenly wanting nothing more than a quiet place to think, Joze quit the chamber, stalked out into the deep and cool darkness of the great underground, leaving the ghost's question unanswered and Kicva's challenge unmet.

Joze wandered in the eerie forest of stone, the silent place where brazier-light flickered and slight breezes drifted. The slender rock-willows, the tall, broad stone-oaks, the spiky rock-made reeds at the edge of the channel where the underground river ran, didn't breathe and live as their counterparts did in the upper world. But for the river running, he heard no sound until, behind him, not too close, not too far, came the small rattle of a displaced stone. Someone followed.

Joze stopped to listen, hoping that it wasn't Kicva. He was in no mood to sort out his confused feelings about a young woman who could cling so warmly and trustingly to him in one moment and sneer so coldly at him in the next.

And I don't have time, he thought, *to think about this moody hunter-scout when I need to be thinking about kidnapping.*

Kidnapping . . .

Ask for the child, Islief had said.

No, Joze decided firmly. That was impossible. No mother would hand over her child to a man who said he wanted to bring her to a ghost so that the dying lands could be healed. Rather, she'd hand *him* over to the nearest man with a big sharp sword. No matter what Kicva said, no matter what Islief hoped, they'd not bring this child to Aeylin unless they kidnapped her.

Behind him, stones rattled again. He cocked his head, listened to the soft footfalls behind him. The scuffing of bare feet on the cavern's rock floor was no more than a whisper. Islief. It could be none other. Joze went on. Though he was glad that he didn't roam this strange underground world alone, he didn't stop to wait for Islief to catch up. He wanted to be alone, or as alone as he could safely be without becoming hopelessly lost in this strange land beneath the world.

As he walked through the silent cavern forest, he came to think that the place was like a memory caught in time, a place captured, as insects were preserved undecayed and unchanged in chunks of amber found at the edge of the sea. A long ache of fear caused his belly to go weak.

Reath too was becoming like a memory. And in southern Celed, were the meadows filled with birdsong? Were the fields flowered, the farmlands bountiful? Or were they stricken as Raeth was? Joze shuddered to think that the farms and meadows of his home province might well have been seared by heat, made infertile by land-sickness. For if that were so, soon their sweet green life, their boundless fruitfulness, would be nothing but memories caught in someone's heart and held there, motionless, unchanging, unliving.

And that only until the last of us dies, for we will not live long in such a place.

Could it all be saved by magic? Could it be restored by enchantments and spells woven by placing a lump of green glittering stone in the hands of an infant?

Cold acknowledgment drifted through him, unwavering acceptance. The lands had all been ravaged by a spell. It must hold that they could be healed by enchantment. Joze's heart sank, for

he knew that he'd come to the point of seriously considering
child-theft.

Just ahead, Joze heard the dark water of the underground river
gurgling in its stone channel, lapping at rocky shores. No part of
the forest was alive but the river, murmuring as though over secrets
long held. Secrets of an ancient sin, of the long, long penance Islief
paid for granting Aeylin help in a distant time when legends were
being born.

*Islief helped her to steal a crown; now I must decide whether
to help her steal a child.*

Joze listened for Islief and didn't hear the Watcher's scuffing
footfalls. Nor his rattling old man's breathing. Alone with only
the gurgling river and the lurking darkness beyond the brazier's
light, he whispered, "Islief?"

As though his whispered word called the Watcher back, Joze
heard the scuffling footfalls. But not from behind; this time they
came from a small distance ahead, and as Joze peered into the
stony forest he saw Islief's glowing eyes. He had to squint to
make out the outline of his small squat body in the dim light.
Saying nothing, Islief waved an arm in a come-ahead gesture
and walked into the darkness. Joze didn't stop to consider, he
followed.

They didn't go far before they left the stone forest for a narrow
corridor, a high-ceilinged hallway in which light sprang up just as
Joze needed it to see. This was not firelight—it didn't come from
any brazier squatting on the ground. It was even and white as
sheets of lightning spread across a dark summer sky, illuminating
the corridor with a strange twilight glow. He peered at the smooth
stone floor, the rough rock walls of the corridor. Never did he find
any sign of the light's source.

"Islief," Joze whispered, "where's the light coming from?"

Islief glanced back over his shoulder. "From the same place
the brazier light comes from."

Joze looked back over his shoulder to see the light fall away
in the wake of his passage, the darkness stalking him. He hurried
to catch up with Islief and kept close behind him the rest of
the way.

Again they didn't walk long, but they walked in silence. Islief
seemed to sense that this was not a time for talk. After a short time
Joze began to feel a strange sense of familiarity to the corridor.
Though he knew that he had never been here before, still the
feeling of having seen these walls, this floor, these winding ways,
persisted like a dream remembered.

And in that dream, he thought, *I was running . . .*

Understanding settled upon him like a well-fitting cloak. He had not dreamed this place; he had seen it in the glowing embers, in the vision-giving pit of Aeylin's crystal hearth. *He* had not run breathless down this hall, heart pounding like thunder; Islief had, and many hundreds of years ago.

When they stepped out of the corridor, left the twilit hallway, Joze didn't have to wait for the uncanny white light to leap to life ahead of him. He knew without having to be told that Islief had brought him to Crown Hold.

The black diamond pedestal, the slender dark column, stood empty, hungry, naked in the unwavering white light.

This is what a lonesome cry of yearning looks like, Joze thought.

Islief reached up, touched Joze's hand with his gnarled fingers. "Tall," he said, "soon there will be a Crown here again."

Joze looked away from the pedestal, looked down at Islief the Watcher. He remembered a time—surely only hours ago—in the upper forest, when he'd not liked to look at Islief's strange eyes; remembered a time when he had to steel himself against the moist cool touch of the Watcher's hand. Here in Crown Hold, here far beneath that upper-world woods, that time seemed long ago.

"You've remade the Crown?" he asked gently.

"The work is not finished; the Crown is not whole yet." Islief's eyes glittered.

And glittered feverishly, Joze thought, as though he were exhausted. Why not? You can get very tired after hundreds and hundreds of years of waiting.

"Tall, I will not set the Emerald yet. He has work to do, and this work he must do alone, without his brothers to help, without his terrible sister to hinder." Islief sighed, a low crooning sound for the Crown's completion delayed. He tugged at Joze's hand. "Come."

His hand still in Islief's, Joze followed the Watcher to the far wall, the one opposite the lonely pedestal. There he saw a doorway and leaping golden light beyond.

"Bow low, Tall, because—"

Joze smiled, stooped as they went through the low doorway. "Because it would hurt to hit my head. I know."

Islief turned, rattling laughter. "Yes." He sobered abruptly. "And because you have come into the presence of the Crown."

He had indeed.

Two cresseted torches lighted the small anteroom, one on each wall to either side of a low stone table. Upon that table lay the

Crown. Though the silver was young, the gold was brightly new, Islief had exactly reproduced the elegant band Joze had seen in the fire's vision, the one Aeylin had broken so many long years ago. Safely held at three of the Crown's four points, home again after centuries of wandering abroad in the world, the blue King of Air, the golden Thane of Fire, the white wild Prince of Water kept watch around their fearsome sister, the Ruby of Guyaire, the Mistress of War. The light of the torches breathed in the Ruby's crimson depths, like hot whispered memories of nightmare.

Joze looked quickly away, searching for something better to see. He found that better thing at once. Cool and green, glowing in the torchlight with the same color as newly opened leaves under the first sunlight of spring, the Emerald, the proud Ruler of Nature, lay beside the Crown, waiting.

Emerald and Sapphire, Diamond and Topaz and Ruby. Joze sighed, as a man sighs who understands a thing he didn't know he'd been wondering about. The colors of the crystal hearth echoed the colors of the five Jewels of the Crown.

"Deities made these," Islief said, wide eyes still on the Jewels. "Irthe and his Aerd made the Emerald. Waian and his Vinge crafted the Sapphire. Vuyer and his Fyr worked the Topaz, and Wazer and his Vetr fashioned the Diamond. Diwan and Deyja created the Ruby. Lif and his Hori quickened them. Chant and Ylf set them in balance, wove magic around them all."

Islief bowed his head in homage. "Hail to you," he whispered.

Joze echoed the greeting. As Islief did now, he bowed his head. As Aeylin had so long before, he went to his knees. He could not have done less, and as his knees touched stone he felt the power of the Crown ringing like a deep-toned bell in every part of him, echoing in mind, thrumming in muscles, pealing in his heart.

These Jewels were vessels for the spirits of the world, this near-made Crown a symbol of Deities who had been little more than legend to Joze all his life. He did not much pray to gods, nor did he often call upon their goddesses. His mother used to talk about them sometimes, but his father seldom did. And so they had been little more than almost-real creatures from childhood's legends, these Deities, and Joze had quickly forgotten them when he put aside the things of childhood.

Yet he knew that should he come home again, home to the farmlands and friends and kin—should his mother look at him and say, "Where have you been, boy of mine?"—he'd have to tell them all that he'd been in the land of legends. He'd have to tell his mother that he'd been in the presence of Deities.

Joze felt Islief's hand, his cool and age-gnarled fingers, on his shoulder.

"Tall, now we must talk."

Joze nodded, agreed that they must. He waited for Islief to speak. But Islief, speaking, didn't say what Joze had expected him to say, made no appeal for him to honor his promise.

"Tall, ask me your question."

Though he'd not known before that he had a question to ask, Joze understood now that he did. "Islief," he said, "why did you follow me?"

The Watcher smiled, a ripple of amusement passing over his craggy face. "I thought you might become lost."

"No," Joze said. "I don't mean just now. I mean, why did you follow me when we were in the upper world? Why did you follow me out of the Kevarths and right to the edge of the forest?"

Islief watched the torchlight gleaming in the Crown's band, followed the play of golden light in the Jewels. Some time passed before he answered.

"Tall, I followed because in the winter I watched you in the Lady's fire."

"Why? And—I thought that fire could only show what *was*."

"Only that. You did a thing one moment, some moments later the fire showed me."

Joze held himself still, waited for the chill of knowing that he'd been observed through all the winter past to creep along his neck and arms. No chill came, no fear.

"Why me?"

The Watcher's wide eyes seemed to hold in them all the many-colored reflections of the magnificent Crown. He laughed, that slipping-scree rattling in his throat. "Tall, who has made the fire knows why and why not."

"Aeylin."

Islief shook his head. "The Lady does not make it. She only asks for it. The Deity of Fire makes it. Vuyer does, and his Fyr helps. This I know: I was to follow and to wait for you to see what you would see beyond the forest. Tall, I knew I needed to be near when you saw your homeland."

Joze didn't have to ask why. He'd already learned the answer to that question. "And Kicva?"

"Ah. The friend."

Joze grimaced. "Not too much of a friend, if you ask me," he muttered.

Islief didn't comment, only said, "I was not following the friend. She only happened."

Joze snorted. Yes, she'd "happened." She'd happened like a soft spring day turned suddenly wintry and dangerous.

"I wonder what these Deities think about that," he said.

"I wonder, too."

One of the torches snapped, sent golden light and dark shadows flowing along the stone table and the Crown. Though four of the jewels reflected the light, the Emerald took it into itself, shining.

"Tall, have you made a choice? Will you try to bring back the child?"

Joze drew a deep breath, let it out in a long sigh as he looked away from the Emerald. "Try? I thought I *had* to do it."

"It would be good if you did do it. But now, Tall, you can only choose to try."

In the world above, where none even dreamed that a place such as Crown Hold existed, out to the west and beyond the lush Elvish forest, farmlands withered beneath a brutal sun, vanished, erased by hot winds. The woodland creatures, the creatures of field and meadow, had fled into Elvish lands, had left hungry people behind.

And my own farm, Joze wondered. *What has happened to my own farm? Is it failing and dying like the Raeth lands? My parents, my grandfather—ah, neighbors, the farmers and the villagers, the miller and the merchants—are they starving too?*

Was there really a choice to make?

"I'll try," Joze said, his voice shaking. "But, Islief, I don't know how—I don't know how . . ."

Islief left Joze's side, went to stand before the glittering Crown. Slowly, he reached out; gently, he touched the Emerald. When he turned again, Joze saw compassion in his wide, wide eyes.

"Tall, you are thinking that you have just promised to be the one to bring great sorrow to the Elf-King's daughter. You are thinking about child-theft, yes? You do not think the Hunter-Defender will give you her little child."

Joze shook his head. "Do you?"

"No. I don't think so."

Torchlight flared, the Crown flashed and sparkled. The Emerald pulsed with light. Joze whispered, "Then why am I doing this, Islief? Why am I promising to attempt something you think I'm going to fail at?"

Wry amusement tempered Islief's laughter. "Tall, I can't know why you are promising. That is yours to know. Maybe you won't fail if you have help."

"Kicva?" Joze shook his head. "I don't know how much help Kicva and I will be to each other."

"No," Islief said slowly. "You don't know. How could you know? You and the friend have not done all the deeds you need to do yet. But I am not thinking of the friend when I think about help. I am thinking of me."

Small the Watcher before him—old, old son of a race no one remembered. What could he do, who startled at a hare's leap, shivered before birdsong? What kind of help would he be when he could not even bear to let sunlight touch him, had not seen sunlight before these few days past in many hundreds of years? How would Islief survive the sick lands?

Joze tried to keep the disbelief from his voice, but didn't wholly succeed. "You?"

Islief stood as tall as he could, lifted his bald head, stiffened his beardless jaw. "Me, Tall. I am Islief of the First People."

In that simple statement Joze heard an echo of what kind of pride the Watcher might have had in his far distant youth, and, hearing, was touched by it.

"The Hunter-Defender knows me, Tall. In a dream she listened to me. Maybe she will listen to me again."

"She knows you? The Princess Nikia knows *you*?"

"Tall, you weren't present when Nikia became the Hunter-Defender."

"And you're saying that you were?"

Islief the Watcher nodded solemnly. "I dreamed of her; she dreamed of me. With my words on her lips and my knowledge in her heart, the Elf-King's daughter freed the Ruby's power. Maybe she will heed my words again. And if she will not . . . there is a harp-master in Damris. He knows who the Lady is. He knows her well. *He* will know that we mean the Elf-King's daughter no harm, nor her babe. I'm thinking the harp-master will aid us."

Joze shook his head. For help he'd have a bard who was on familiar terms with a ghost, and a creature who was older than old. "You're saying you want to come with me"—he stopped, remembering Kicva and her vow to the Lady—"with us?"

Islief smiled now, again gently amused. "Why are you never certain what it is I am saying? Yes. I will come with you. I do not feel easy in the upper world, I am not comfortable there anymore. But once I was, and I am feeling that it has been too long since

I have heard the wind in the trees, and the birds and the hares in the brush. I have not heard the thunder in many hundreds of years. I have not felt the rain on me in that long. Yet these are things I once loved, all things . . ."

Islief didn't finish his thought, but Joze knew what the unspoken words were: . . . *all things I risked the Deities' anger to preserve.*

"Tall, I will go with you to speak to the Hunter-Defender. Maybe it will help."

Maybe it will, Joze thought. *Or maybe this bard, this harpmaster, will be able to help.* And so maybe it would not be a matter of kidnapping after all.

Before he could change his mind, Joze held out his hand. "I must swear, Islief."

The Watcher blinked. "Pledge what, Tall?" But, though he questioned, Islief readily pressed his cool palm to Joze's.

"I swear by my honor that I will try with my every strength to bring back the child of the Hunter-Defender. It's all I can do."

Islief dropped his glance, suddenly shy. "You swear by your bright honor, Tall, and you have not asked an oath from me. Here is one: By the Lady, I swear that should you come to a time when you have no more strength to use, you will have mine."

A chill crept along Joze's neck, raised the hair on his arms. He didn't like the sound of the Watcher's promise, didn't like it for his own sake, didn't like it for Islief's. He glanced toward the Crown, the only witness to the oaths given here, and saw the five jewels pulsing with light. And he remembered a thing Islief had said to him in the forest above. *Not an ill-wisher . . .*

Joze clasped Islief's gnarled, ancient hand. No, not an ill-wisher, he thought, and surely an unlooked-for friend.

The torches guttered, one failed. Soon it would be too dark for Joze to see. "Come on, Islief. Let's go find that prickly hunter-scout and tell her that she can come with us if she promises not to be so nasty."

Islief smiled, but forbore to comment.

Joze didn't think that he would actually extract a promise of gentler behavior from Kicva. He didn't think that such a request would be met with other than haughty scowls anyway. That one, it seemed, was only sweet and fair when she was asleep. As he followed Islief back to the chamber of the crystal hearth, Joze

decided that he would simply tell her that he'd made up his mind
to go seeking the unborn daughter of the Hunter-Defender, and
prepare himself to endure whatever behavior he must.

But there was no chance to tell Kicva anything. When Joze
and Islief returned to the rainbowed hearth, they learned that the
hunter-scout had left some time before, directed by the Grey Lady
to her weapons and the small cave which was the way back to the
upper world.

Chapter Seven

AT THE END OF APRIL'S SECOND DAY—A HOT DAY THAT BORE
no likeness to spring—Darun Lord Calmis went looking for a
friend. He ran up the winding stone steps to the Citadel's highest
tower, not caring that the stairwell was dark and full of shadows.
He well knew the way to where he was going. And though
the darkness was hot, stifling in this close stone fastness as it
was everywhere else, he didn't pause for breath on the first
landing, but took the next flight two steps at a time. As he
started up the third flight, he wished heartily that the King's
Bard would move back to his old quarters off the Citadel's main
gallery.

Where normal people live, Calmis thought. *But no, he's decided
that he needs a tower room where you have to* really *want to see
him if you want to see him.*

At the top of the stairway pale light sheened the walls, gleamed
from the flagged stone floors and relieved the darkness only a
little. Calmis stopped, winded. Filling his lungs with the hot
musty air, he looked along the tight, high-walled corridor to
the far end, where the wan light had its source in a narrow
window. From far down the corridor *Dashlaftholeh*, the harp
whose name meant Song-Bringer in the Elvish tongue, spoke
of quiet hunger, of her master's melancholy, and a lady lost to
time and all who love her. Calmis knew the song, he'd heard it
from Lizbet.

> Of moonlight her robe is spun.
> No gem has she but starlight's strands
> Braided fair in her hair.

> Of dawnlight her cheek is made.
> No gold has she but sunlight's mantle
> Soft to wrap her in.

"And he'll tell me that's another of Aeylin's songs," Calmis muttered to the wall.

All of the court thought it was so, and maybe the bard believed it, too. In Calmis' opinion the verses made up the best description of Nikia he'd ever heard. Although the part about the gems and the gold wasn't accurate. The Elf-King's daughter did not lack for jewels; Garth's wife did not want for gold.

Well, maybe that was bard's talk for the color of her hair and skin. As for the moonlight robe . . .

Suddenly uncomfortable with his imaginings of his friend's imaginings, Calmis pushed away from the wall. As he followed the sound of the harp, he wondered what made Dail think he had a chance at successfully pretending that he'd turned his love for Nikia into simple friendship.

Calmis snorted. One doesn't hide from *that*, and he knew it well, who loved his own wife, his own Lizbet, dearly. There wasn't enough magic in all the Elflands—let alone here in Damris—to make a man forget love. And it was another of Calmis' opinions that his friend was a poor fool if he thought he could hide from his love in his visions of a long-dead queen, or even in this far chamber in the Citadel's highest tower. He had no opinion, however, on the subject of what Dail might do about this love of his.

The thick wooden door to Dail's chamber stood slightly ajar. Calmis raised a hand to knock, then decided not to risk the chance of being bidden to go away. He didn't have much time for arguing. He opened the door upon the usual mess that was Dail's quarters.

The place was a litter of broken harp strings, half-made songs scrawled on parchment, broad-pointed reed pens, slender-tipped quill pens, and dried-up inkpots. Dust motes danced thickly in a hot shaft of aging sunlight, and the bed, a shambles of unmade linen, was barely to be seen beneath a heap of discarded clothing. The place looked like a bear's den. Calmis wrinkled his nose. It smelled like one, too. The servants didn't get up here very often, and in his new love of solitude, the King's Bard didn't object to their neglect.

And like a bear brooding at the mouth of its cave, Dail sat in the window embrasure, hunched over his harp. As Calmis stepped into the room, the bard rubbed his hand along his jaw, ran his fingers through his beard ungently. He didn't like that beard, Calmis knew, and he'd only lately and grudgingly stopped complaining about the thick dark growth. Like Calmis, Dail had always been cleanshaven until the drought forced a close and careful husbanding of water, a conservation which didn't admit of granting water for shaving, and too rarely allowed enough for bathing.

Soft again, Dail caressed *Dashlaftholeh*'s strings, called up his moonlight and starlight song. But the harp sang only a note or two before the bard became aware of another's presence and laid a hand across the strings to still the music. In the silence, faintly from far below, came the incessant drone of cicadas.

Dail showed no surprise at seeing a visitor, only smiled, a sleepy kind of smile as though he'd not been disturbed from a song, but from a dream.

"Ah, my lord of Soran." Dail's tone made the formal address something else altogether, an acknowledgment of longstanding friendship of the kind that didn't admit of titles. "What can this humble bard do for you today?"

Humble bard . . . Calmis snorted to show his opinion of that contradiction in terms and the ill-fitting whimsy which had prompted it. "Have you forgotten? The Council meeting is about to start."

Dail yawned. "I haven't forgotten, Darun. I'm not coming."

A diplomat trained, and skilled at it, Calmis knew that no sign of his disappointment showed. Still, beneath the training, behind the skill, he felt it. "Dail, Garth needs you there."

"Me? I don't think so. I'm no Council member." The harp strings sighed beneath his touch. "Just a—"

"—humble bard. So you've said. Now, there's a load of—"

Dail's laughter, sharp and humorless, overrode the barnyard expression. "I've a rival word-smith! I'd better watch myself, eh? Still, you're probably right. I suppose I'm not all that humble. But I am just a bard, Darun, even if the King's Bard. No, Garth doesn't need me there. He needs his father."

"The King won't be at Council today," Calmis said flatly. Hot wind sighed at the window, for a moment muting the cicadas' droning. "He sent his usual message."

"Ah. 'The King will not attend. You may feel confident that the Prince will act in all things as I myself would.' That one?"

"That one. Dail—"

The King's Bard shook his head. In the sunlight Calmis saw patches of silver glistening in his friend's dark beard. "No, Darun.

Garth doesn't need me there. He has you. And you're more made for what goes on around that table these days than I am. Come back later and tell me what happens."

He picked up his *Dashlaftholeh* again, ran a hand along the curve of her breast as gently as though the harp were a woman. He loved his Song-Bringer, and this love he didn't have to hide. He cradled the harp against his shoulder. His left hand high on the strings, his right low, he closed his eyes, sighed the sigh of which he himself was never aware. This he always did when he prepared to sing, when he was about the business of banishing everyone but his sweet-voiced *Dashlaftholeh*.

Calmis held tight to his patience with both fists. He would not be made invisible by the music. All through winter Dail had kept to his high aerie. Aloof and distant, he made his Aeylin-songs, his ballads for the long-dead queen which were in truth laments for the Elf-King's daughter. And around him the kingdom fell to quarreling factions as the land died beneath their very feet. Hard to remember that it was Dail who'd once done the brilliant work of heartening the people against the Sorcerer!

"Ah, bard," Calmis said, "it's always that way with visions, isn't it?"

Dail looked up, blue eyes narrowed, his mild and sleepy expression gone. "What way is that?" he asked coolly.

"You start out thinking that the vision belongs to you—but soon you find that you belong to it. And then one day it's no vision at all, but blindness."

Dail put his harp carefully aside. "Darun, I don't tell you how to go about your statecraft. I'd appreciate your not telling me how to go about a bard's work."

"This isn't about bard's work." Frustrated, angry now, Calmis gestured around the room, the carelessly kept den. "This is about something else. You know it." Hedged round by need, by the things he must soon do and didn't want to, Calmis cried:

"Dail, come out of here, come down to where the hard things are! I don't want to tell you what happened at Council. I want—I *need* you to witness it today."

In the silence between them the thin hot wind passed across *Dashlaftholeh*'s strings like a phantom's hand. The music that vagrant wind called from her was softer than any a man's hand could make. Dail reached to quiet the harp, then changed his mind, let her sing her own song.

"What's going to happen today, Darun? What do you know that I don't?"

A lot, Calmis thought wearily, *and just a little bit more than I want to*.

But he said only, "Come and find out."

Dail drew a deep breath, let it out in a long, exaggerated sigh. "All right, then. Just give me a few minutes to clean up here. I'll be along."

Calmis kept his feeling of relief private. Smiling wryly, he looked around the room. "I'm talking about *today's* Council, not next year's."

"Today's . . ." Dail scratched his beard absently. "Right. Let's go, then. We don't want to be late."

Shaking his head, Calmis followed his friend from the room, stopping only to close the door behind him. But when he reached back for the door, he saw a thing he'd not noticed before among the clutter.

Propped against a heat-twisted candle on the small table near Dail's bed lay a scroll case. A shaft of late afternoon sunlight fell upon the wax-spotted leather. Calmis recognized the tooled design, a long, twining pattern of leaves and vines. And so he knew that Dail had received yet another message from Dekar, Nikia's father.

There had been many like it in the winter past, accompanying Dekar's letters to Nikia or his messages to Alain. Calmis knew of four times when scroll cases such as this one had come alone, the sole purpose of a messenger's long hot ride from the Elvish forests to Alain's drought-ridden kingdom. In them were old Elvish songs and tales, chosen by Dekar because they had to do with Aeylin. Often the tales and songs were so old that only a scrap of an ancient Elvish poet's fancy remained in allusions to the ages-dead queen. From these, from his own vision, from his need of solitude and hiding, Dail's best songs were made. If some of them were thinly veiled love songs, many were not. Between them, Dekar and the bard had contributed much to Aeylin's lore. All the Elf-King asked in payment for his generosity was that the Aeylin-songs make their way back to him.

And they did, for sometimes Dail left his high chamber, brought his *Dashlaftholeh* down into the hall to teach the new songs to his bards and to Nikia, who was their Lady. Then the harp's music, and her master's voice, would be heard in the hall again. The servants would come from their tasks, the ladies from their bowers, to linger near the hall, as hungry for the songs of the King's Bard as bees are for nectar.

And then, unburdened of his songs and trusting that his bards would send them abroad, that Nikia herself would send the words and music of them to her father, Dail would quit the hall and the company of his bards, the company of the woman for whom he truly wrote his songs.

Lizbet once said that the King's Bard, taking his leave of the hall, looked shining somehow, like a clear vessel emptied and ready to be filled again. Calmis considered this notion of his wife's fair and foolish women's talk. That was a lean and hungry man who fled the hall for his high tower, and the exhaustion that paled him had nothing to do with weary satisfaction in a task well done.

And he's not shining at all, Calmis thought now as he shut the door of Dail's chamber. *A dead queen, a love that he cannot nourish . . . nothing shining in that.*

What Nikia thought of this, what the Lady of the Bards felt about Dail's erratic patterns of feverish work, no man or woman knew. The Elf-King's daughter, serene and lovely, shared her thoughts with no one, and so Calmis didn't know whether Garth's wife understood for whom the songs were truly written.

Dail returned the greetings of the men gathered in the Council Chamber with quiet words or a silent nod. The lords of the Council, even Garth himself, seemed surprised to see him come down from his tower.

His greetings given, Dail didn't take his usual seat at the wide oval table, the golden board of polished oak which dominated the Council Chamber. Instead, he went to sit in the deep window embrasure in the north-facing wall. The fierce sun, which had glared with high summer's worst heat all through the winter months and blazed ruthlessly now in early spring, had baked all the lingering chill out of the Citadel's massive stone walls. But at least here the air stirred a little. And here, in the comfortable corner, Dail had the illusion of remove and solitude.

As Calmis had said he would be, Alain was conspicuously absent from the Council meeting again. The lords of the provinces were not happy about that. And yet, Dail thought, the Council couldn't be less happy than Garth, who was left by his father to pretend once again that Alain was not what rumor named him, a heartbroken old man made powerless by grief and fear. Dail glanced at Garth, and a familiar, aching confusion of feelings crowded his heart.

Prince, he thought, *cousin, friend . . . husband of the woman I love, the husband she loves well.*

Dail clamped down hard on the thought, tried to forget about the ache. He leaned his head against the stone, closed his eyes wearily, shut himself away from the unmarked sky, the restless men in the Council Chamber. In the sun, with the baked stone at his back, he could have slept.

Despite what most people thought, the King's Bard didn't spend all his time with his visions, or the secret he had given up trying to hide from himself—the one he gave voice to between the harp's notes. To his high chamber, often in the latest part of night, came a call to bring him ungrudgingly out of his solitude: the King's.

But Alain didn't only call to hear Dail's songs. He called to have his company, to share silences, sometimes to share his brokenhearted confidences with this nephew of his who, of all those around him, wanted nothing from him, and most especially not the strength he no longer had. For Alain had lost a lot in the recent war: the health of his kingdom, his own health, and—the King felt this as the most dire of all blows—he'd lost his beloved older son, hard-drinking, arrogant Fenyan, a prince who left behind him only an orphaned yearling child for an heir.

This child, young Ybro, should have represented the kingdom's hope, yet in him Alain found only despair. An infant king, he said often, is no use to anyone but the men who would make a pawn of him. And yet, for all that he acknowledged the imminence and the danger of little Ybro's fate, Alain did nothing to prevent it. He abandoned his grandson while he sat brooding and ailing in his chambers.

Just as he'd abandoned Garth, Dail thought.

It seemed that neither Garth nor Ybro were Alain's idea of what a king should be. Fenyan, or what he'd pretended to be, had embodied that idea. Alain didn't sleep much these nights, and so neither did his bard.

The weary breeze fell still. In the Council Chamber voices droned, deep and troubled, dry from thirsty throats, mimicking the rasp of cicadas heard endlessly night and day. The lords of the kingdom's five provinces brooded over their troubles, enumerated them as old beggars who tell over their sorrows.

And it's what we all look like, Dail thought, *old beggars, dusty and dry, hungry paupers waiting for the almsgiver to come and ease our afflictions.*

But there were no alms to be had. None for stormy Karo, whose Raeth was near blown away; none for rat-eyed Fargut, who saw the land-sickness encroaching on his Hivard province. For lean Liam of Celed and for old Celedon of Rigg, whose lands had only felt the drought, there was nothing to offer, not even the hope that the land-sickness would stop at their borders.

Hard and sudden as a crack of thunder, a hand slapped the oaken board. Karo of Raeth lifted his leonine head, glared around the table. Dail found it hard to believe that this fierce man was the father of gentle Gweneth, the sweet, grey-eyed woman who had died giving birth to Fenyan's son. But in his bearing, his arrogance, his gradual assumption of leadership among the Council members, Karo didn't let anyone forget that he was grandfather to infant Ybro, the heir to Alain's kingdom.

"Prince," the Lord of Raeth said, "my people are *hungry*." His voice landed heavily on the last word as though the emphasis would somehow change the way Garth understood it.

Dail sat forward attentively. Karo of Raeth spread his hands, as though to show them wide and empty of all but helplessness. And yet the look in the man's narrowed eyes let all who saw know that Raeth's lord was anything but helpless.

"My people are starving, Prince, each man and woman and child of them."

Fargut of Hivard province nodded agreement, his beady eyes flicking from Karo to Garth and back to Karo again. For an instant he looked as though he were going to speak, but the impulse died swiftly. Most often, Fargut didn't speak unless Karo suggested that it might be a good idea to do so.

"Karo," Garth said calmly, "if you think that the King is not aware that Raeth-folk are starving, if you think that Alain doesn't know that those of Hivard and Rigg and Soran and Celed are thirsty and only a little less hungry, you are wrong. If you think he has some salve for the land's wounds, some potion for the sickness"—the Prince shook his head—"you are wrong."

"And so," Karo said, brow lowering, voice tight, "and so because the King cannot see the solution, we starve."

"What solution do you see, Karo, that the King does not?"

Karo didn't answer Garth's question directly, and only sullenly. "They don't starve in Elvish lands, Prince. In Dekar's kingdom they are not thirsty."

Celedon lifted his head, an old hound scenting trouble. Liam, seated next to Fargut, sat back in his chair, seemed to draw himself in and become even leaner.

"And well they don't starve," Garth said coolly. "Else my father-in-law would have a hard time being as generous with hunting rights as he is. What is your point?"

Something dangerous ghosted across Karo's face, something cunning and deadly; the look of a man surveying his enemy's stronghold, searching for the undefended place.

"We can't feed ourselves from the poisoned earth," Karo said. "The rivers and streams are dying. In Raeth there are no fish to eat but those which the sea-fishers catch, and the catches are lean these days. You're lucky here in Soran, the seas are yet generous. Fargut and I are not so fortunate. The waters off *our* shores are quickly being deserted. And there's yet some game to be found here in Soran, but none in Raeth. It has fled the land-sickness.

"It has fled into the Elflands. And so I don't understand, Prince, why you speak of your father-in-law's generosity. He only gives us back what is ours."

Fargut muttered agreement, his full attention on Karo now as he nervously stroked his wispy blond mustache. Karo's dark eyes narrowed as he leaned across the oaken board.

"Aye, Prince," the Lord of Raeth said softly, "in your wife's land they feast well and often—on *our* game as well as theirs. It's very convenient for them that the cures their mages have sought through magic for the land's ills have not worked in our kingdom, but seem to work so well in theirs."

Calmis sat straighter, leveled a stare every bit as dangerous as Karo's own at Raeth's lord and drew a breath to speak. Garth gestured sharply, signaled Calmis to silence. He said coldly:

"An accusation, Lord Karo?"

"If you've ears to hear it."

Garth flared, his brown eyes keen as a blade's edge. "Against whom?"

Karo smiled, a sneer only poorly hidden. He'd tested the stronghold with only one brief sortie and found the undefended place.

"Oh, not against the Princess, surely. After all, she's still here and not fled to safety. Or not yet."

Dail shivered, an icy-fingered chill trailing along his spine, like a ghost from a winter past, a cold grey phantom from a time when whispers of suspicion haunted the Elf-King's daughter and all those who cared about her.

"Not ever, Karo," the King's Bard said, and didn't realize that he'd spoken until he heard the words hanging in the hot, unmoving air of the chamber, until he saw Calmis look around at him, a flicker of alarm in his brown eyes, until he saw Garth's expression soften with sudden gratitude.

Garth drew a long breath, let it out slowly. Inclining his head to each of the Council members in turn, he said:

"My lords, again I apologize for my father's absence. I know that the King wouldn't have wanted you to waste your time idling here when you must have other things to attend to. I'm sure he will want to recall this Council when he has been freed from whatever matter has delayed him. May I tell him that you will await his call?"

Karo's smile was little more than a smirk as he nodded. "Oh, aye, Prince, you may tell him that. We've matters to discuss with him that will not vanish simply because he doesn't want to hear them."

So saying, the Lord of Raeth stalked from the Council Chamber. Fargut of Hivard scurried after. Liam and Celed were slower in taking their leave, remaining behind to assure the Prince that they would be nearby when Alain again called a Council.

"Thank you," Garth said tightly. He tried to smile, but though his lips moved, the smile failed utterly. His eyes were too cold for it.

Dail abandoned his seat in the window, ready to take his own leave, wanting to be well away from here if Garth or Calmis brought up the matter of Karo's thinly veiled insinuations against the Elf-King. Such a discussion would inevitably bring Garth's thanks for Dail having spoken on Nikia's behalf. Accepting gratitude innocently offered in the belief that it was innocently earned would be no different than stealing.

Dail started for the door, but Calmis gestured for him to wait. Uncertain if this was also Garth's wish, Dail looked an inquiry at his cousin, hoping that Garth would let him leave.

"Stay," Garth said, low. "I need you to witness this, King's Bard."

Eased suddenly by Garth's formal use of his title, Dail understood that what was about to happen here now would have nothing to do with him personally. Curious now, remembering Calmis' insistence that he join the Council meeting, Dail resumed his seat in the window embrasure.

Neither Garth or Calmis marked his presence. They stood, each watching the other while the relentless drone of insects framed their silence. Garth was the first to look away, and Dail knew, as surely as if he'd heard the words, that between Soran's lord and the King's son a question had passed and been answered.

"It's time," Calmis said gently.

Garth said nothing, only drew a long breath, let it out shuddering.

"Prince," Calmis said, "if we don't do it soon, we may not be able to do it at all. You see how Karo is."

"I know. I know, Darun. But . . ."

He bowed his head, and when he looked up again, the misery Dail saw in his cousin's eyes moved him to deep-felt pity.

"Ah, Darun!" Garth cried, "it would be like saying that my father is dead—no! Worse! It would be like saying he's . . . incapable. Incompetent." Garth's voice dropped low, shaking. "Impotent."

To Dail, unbidden, came the memory of the King in his chambers, the old man who was not old a year ago, lost now among his losses.

"It doesn't have to be that way, Garth," Calmis said, still gentle. "Ybro needs a regent. He'd need one even if Alain were well. The appointment should have been made in winter. Whoever speaks for Ybro speaks for the kingdom. And someone must, Garth. The kingdom cannot be ruled by five hungry and frightened men."

Genuine anger leaped in Garth's eyes. "A regent rules *only* if my father is dead. Only then."

Heart racing suddenly, Dail looked from one to the other, listened to the silence between them. So much gets said in silence, and he had an idea what was being said between the two men now:

Garth was not Alain's idea of a king, and so Garth was not his idea of the man who should train Fenyan's son to kingship.

And in honesty, Dail thought, ashamed for thinking it, *Garth isn't my idea of a king, either. But who else is there with as much right to be Ybro's guardian?*

Karo.

"Karo," Calmis said, as though he'd plucked the name from the bard's mind. "Garth, if you don't get yourself appointed regent, Karo will. He's the boy's grandfather. That already gives him as close a tie of kinship as you have. Some might say closer." Calmis leaned forward, eager now to press his point. "Garth, Karo is a very dangerous man. He had no love for the Elvish alliance when we first made it. Now he can't—or won't—see that Dekar's good will is all that's keeping Raeth-folk from dying of hunger. Karo speaks of the game that's fled Raeth as though it were his. Maybe it was once, if any man can lay claim to deer and pheasants and rabbits. But that game's gone now, run to the forests for food and water. The right to hunt in Elvish forests is Dekar's to give or withhold. We're damned lucky your father-in-law has better feelings about the treaty than Karo has."

Dail had seen stags look like Garth did now, just before the hunter looses his bolt. Trapped and desperate. He glanced at Calmis, and suddenly he understood that the Lord of Soran had manipulated Garth, hunted him to this place. Dail dropped from the embrasure, a half-formed idea of stopping what was about to happen. His boots on the stone floor made a flat thud. Garth looked up, but Calmis ignored him as though he'd never moved.

"Garth," Calmis said, "for Ybro's sake, we *must* talk about an effective regency, and one that will uphold the alliance with Dekar. *You* must become regent; and unless Alain abdicates, your regency will be useless to Ybro and to the kingdom. Your father can be convinced that you're the one who should guard the boy's rights."

Garth swallowed once, then nodded. "Do it," he said, bitterly. "If you think you can convince him, do it."

As he watched Garth leave the Council Chamber, a thought came to Dail all unlooked for: He, who had envied his cousin many things, didn't envy him now, for if Calmis had been the skillful hunter, Garth's own sense of duty had been the hound to drive him straight into the trap Calmis had laid for him. And, like it or not, Garth would soon be Ybro's regent if Calmis had his way.

Dail looked away from the door, back to the Lord of Soran standing beside the Council table. He remembered the time, not long ago, when in jest he'd told Calmis that he was more deadly in a Council chamber than most soldiers are on a battlefield. Then he'd meant it as a compliment.

Now Dail wasn't so sure that he'd mean it that way again.

Chapter Eight

CALMIS STARED, UNSEEING, AT THE SMOOTH STONE WALLS OF THE Council Chamber. He didn't hear Garth's retreating steps on the stone stairs outside the chamber, nor did he see the narrow-eyed way Dail watched him. He was thinking of an evening, almost two years since, when he'd stood with the Elf-King and shared an old wine to celebrate a new covenant.

That evening the spring breezes had whispered across the Altha, ruffled the water's surface, carried the clean scents of forest and river all through Dekar's Verdant Hall. The wine that Nikia's father had offered tasted sweet as the last hint of honeysuckle on the cool air. Quietly proud of himself for having negotiated the lengthy and complicated treaty between Alain and Dekar which would culminate in the marriage of Garth and the Elf-King's daughter, Calmis had pledged Dekar and pledged the success of the treaty.

"You have convinced us all, my lord Calmis," Dekar had said, "and so, your king and I, my daughter and Alain's son—we have put ourselves in your hands."

The Elf-King had smiled, and Calmis was not so far gone in Elvish wine or his own pride to know that Dekar might send his daughter off to be wed to the son of an old enemy, but as for himself, he rested comfortably in no one's hands. Neither did Alain in those days before the war. No man could have made either king come to the board of peace if he didn't think it was a good idea. Calmis had worked tirelessly for nearly two years to convince the kings that the treaty, the marriage, would be the best thing for both kingdoms.

He still believed so, now even more strongly than he'd believed it then. There would have been no hope for the Twin Kingdoms to survive the Sorcerer otherwise.

We'd none of us have survived the Sorcerer, he thought, *if Nikia hadn't seen the Ylin tapestry and drawn her own conclusions about the Ruby of Guyaire. And having survived, we in Mannish would soon be dead of these terrible seasons without Dekar's good will.*

And his hunting rights.

"Your goblet is empty, my lord Calmis," the Elf-King had said on that distant spring night. Tree frogs had piped at the river's edge, crickets sang in the forest. In the swaying willow outside the starlit window a nightingale trilled. "Let me fill it again, and drink to my lord Calmis who is the author of our fates. You are a skillful fellow, indeed."

From that day till this, Dekar's words had haunted Calmis. In darker moments he felt that he was responsible for the fates which had lately befallen. In better moments, he simply felt that he must use all his skills to assure that nothing threaten the treaty between the Elf-King and Alain.

Nothing, he thought. *And no one, my lord Karo.*

The thought of Raeth's lord brought Calmis forcibly back from his memories. Again he heard the dry, buzzing whine of the cicadas. The stone walls of Alain's Council Chamber replaced memory's vision of the carved oak columns, the gleaming, tapestry-hung cherry wood walls of the Elf-King's hall. No sooner had memory faded than did a voice, flat and disgusted, speak in unknowing parody of Dekar's long-ago politeness.

"You are a skillful bastard, Darun," Dail said. "I'll give you that."

Calmis closed his eyes, drew a long breath for patience. "Thank you. I think."

For the first time since entering the Council Chamber, Dail took a seat at the board. It was Karo's, though the bard didn't seem to notice, or care if he did. He leaned forward, faced his friend across the wide oaken expanse. His voice, losing none of its antagonism, sounded more accusatory than questioning.

"Darun, what kind of a regent do you think Garth will make?"

Calmis resumed his own seat, leaned against the carved wood back, suddenly as weary as though he'd covered the leagues between Verdant Hall and this chamber not in memory but upon the hard back of a need-driven horse.

"I don't know," he said honestly. "But I'll tell you this: Alain's right in thinking that Garth isn't the man to make a good king. He could acquire the skill for it, though he doesn't like to admit that. But he hasn't got the taste for it; Garth doesn't want to be king. I don't think he ever did. Me, I think that's a fine quality for a regent to have."

"And you don't think Karo has this particular quality?"

Again Calmis answered honestly. "If you mean, do I think Karo has a yen for kingship, the answer's yes. I've a feeling—and others agree—that if Karo were made regent, Ybro would have a hard time getting his kingdom back from my lord of Raeth when he comes of age.

"Dail, Alain underestimates his son. Garth will do what he sets out to do. He'll hold the Council together."

"And yet how is a man who has no desire for kingship going to teach Ybro to be king?" Dail met his friend's eyes and held them. "That's the other part of a regent's duties, Darun."

Calmis smiled, but only tiredly. "Garth will have someone to help him teach Ybro the business of kingship."

The silence between them was only as long as a heartbeat. "And who would that be, Darun? You?"

Calmis laughed, genuinely and with sudden relief, and seeing Dail's eyes narrow yet again as he tried to gauge whether he was being mocked, only made him laugh the harder. Only now did Calmis understand that he'd been dreading this question since first he'd known that there must be a witness to what he'd encouraged Garth to do. To have the question asked at last, to have the challenge set down and to be able to answer, was like having a fear laid to rest.

"No, Dail, not me. I don't know anything about being a king. I only know how to deal with them."

Not amused, Dail said, "Tell me who you have in mind to teach the boy kingship."

"Someone who was raised to rule, someone who's been trained to it as Garth never let himself be. Nikia is stronger than any of us, Dail," he said gently. "Ybro will need the strongest for his teacher."

Sunlight poured hot across the oaken board, turned the polished wood to gold. Cicadas rasped as Dail silently traced an aimless pattern in the windblown, ever-present dust. When he spoke at last his voice was low and reminded Calmis of the sad, yearning notes he'd heard sighing from *Dashlaftholeh* earlier.

"Darun, have you spoken to her about this?"

"Garth has."

"Ah." It was a lifeless sound, a whisper, no more. Calmis, who understood a good deal about his friend, didn't understand why Dail's voice should sound so pale now, why he should look as though all the blood had been squeezed from his heart. "And from there?"

"From there," Calmis said, suddenly moved to speak kindly, though he didn't yet know why kindness was needed, "from there it's up to Garth and Nikia. But at least we'll have a regent to lead the Council. It's not the same as a king, but it's better than what we've had. Karo has a head full of very dangerous ideas, my friend, and the things he says against the Elf-King, the sly insinuations he makes in Council, are only a little of what he says in private."

Dail looked up, light kindling again in his eyes. "And how would you know what he says in private?"

Calmis shrugged. "Sometimes he speaks to the wrong people."

"Spies, Darun?"

Calmis didn't like the word. Less did he like the way Dail looked at him when he said it.

"No," he said, more sharply than he'd meant to. "Not unless you want to think of Liam of Celed as a spy. We of the Council don't speak to each other only in this room, Dail."

Dail left the table, went to stand at the window. He stood there for a long time, staring out at the drought-ravaged Queen's Garden, the brown, heat-seared meadows, the feeble, sluggish stream that used to be the wide A'Damran.

"Darun, my friend," he said at last. "You're a better man than I am if you've got the heart for the work that's ahead. Me, I have no heart for this."

Calmis said nothing as he watched his friend leave the Council Chamber. He sat for a long time in the empty room, then went to the window and stood for a while longer. He watched the sky turn a hot, bruised purple with twilight, then watched the moon rise. Steely blue, new and shaped like a farmer's scythe, it hung above the eastern forest where the Elf-light shimmered. Tonight, as every night, Dekar's mages exerted their strength to find in enchantment the cure for the sickness which sapped the goodness from Raeth's farmlands, which marched ever deeper into Alain's drought-ridden kingdom.

His eyes on the light, the rainbowed gleaming, Calmis remembered the last message Nikia had from Dekar. In it, she said, her father had informed her that five mages were dead of their exertions.

That message had come in March, weeks ago, when the moon was full. Calmis wondered now whether others had died as the moon waned and darkened, and he wondered how many mages were left to take the places of the fallen.

When the first stars pricked the darkened sky above the weary river, the Lord of Soran went to seek an audience with his king. But when he was bidden by Alain to enter the chamber, he found that someone else had been there earlier, for before he could speak, Alain suggested that he would do better to take whatever matter concerned him to the Regent.

"The Regent?" Calmis hoped that only normal, expected surprise showed on his face, hoped that the terrible fear he felt was hidden well.

Not Karo! Please, he begged silently. *Please don't tell me that Karo has been here while I've been staring out of windows!*

"The Regent," Alain said dryly. "My dear son."

Swift joy, barely controlled, set Calmis' heart racing. Were he anywhere but in Alain's presence, he'd have laughed aloud, for he remembered the words he'd only lately spoken to Dail, the assurance that Alain underestimated his son.

And Alain's not the only one who underestimates our new Regent! Garth will do what he sets out to do. *And how much better for him—for us all—that he's taken the first step himself!*

But Calmis' joy was short-lived, dampened by the narrowing of the old king's eyes, by Alain's bitter smile.

"But you'd best be careful of him, Darun, if you've anything to ask him. My son is feeling like a thief tonight, and it's my experience that a man who is feeling robber-guilt will either give you more than you need in order to soothe his conscience, or he'll give you nothing for fear it's not his to give."

Calmis stood still in the hot night, listened to his own heart pounding hard and fast again in his chest, racing with fear now. In a voice tight and unlike his own, he said:

"Who names Garth thief, my king?"

Alain didn't answer. He turned away, straightened the linen bed sheets around himself. He reached behind to plump the pillows at his back, acted in all ways as though Calmis were addressing someone other than him.

"King, who's called Garth a thief?"

"The King is not here," Alain whispered. He glanced at the slim new moon to see the time. "Doubtless you'll find him sleeping in the nursery. As for my son . . . I was wrong about him, Darun, wasn't I? Garth has the strength to take what he wants. Let us see if he has the courage to hold it, aye?"

He had the courage to take the Regency, he'll find the courage to keep it, Calmis thought. But he said nothing of that to the old man sitting in the bed. Instead he asked Alain if there were anything he could bring to him, someone he could send for.

Pale against the bed linens, Alain said that he'd normally have asked for the King's Bard, but he believed now that Dail would better employ his time practicing the counting-rhymes and nursery songs that would please the King best.

And so Calmis left him, went along the corridor to his own rooms, and Lizbet, who was surely waiting. He'd set in motion another part of this tale he'd authored, and he was not certain whether he'd tangled the telling or made things clearer. Never was he more in need of the gentle comfort his wife was so capable of offering. Nikia had brought more than a waiting-woman with her from the Elf-King's forest hall when she'd brought Lizbet to Damris. She'd brought a woman who was, for the Lord of Soran, a greater treasure than any legend could name.

But when he came to the place where the stairs led upward, Calmis stopped, thought for a moment, then went to the high

tower to tell the King's Bard that the decisions he'd witnessed
this day had come to pass. He had to wake him to do it, and
that wasn't done easily. Dail was sleeping as deeply as a bear in
winter's cold.

When the bard received the news in silence, showed no joy,
Calmis was not surprised. There had been a time when Alain was
a good and strong king, and each man—Lord of Soran and King's
Bard—remembered that time well.

Chapter Nine

QUIET FILLED THE CAVERNS, THOUGH THE UNDERGROUND RIVER
still lapped at stony shores, though the pale, large-eyed fishes
broke the river's dark surface and a small wind ruffled the water
as it drifted along the channel to make whispering echoes.

The caverns beneath the Kevarths were quiet because Islief
was gone.

No ghost, Aeylin thought, could be said to possess life, for all
that she possessed will and want and even animation, and so the
caverns were quiet; for they were quiet of life.

How strange to feel them so! Such an empty feeling; as the
heart of a long-travelled journeyer when her comrade has turned
away, bound by fate or circumstance to take a different path at
the crossroads.

It came to Aeylin then—like a cool wind breathing—that she
missed Islief. Though he was not hours gone out into the world,
up into forest and farmland, she missed his courage and patience,
his wide-eyed humor and quiet strength.

"Old friend," the ghost whispered. "Dear old companion, I wish
I had told you at least once how much I have cherished you, my
only friend in exile."

A ghost shivering, smoke wavering, Aeylin wondered whether
she would be given time to tell him this when he returned to take
his last breath here in his cavern home, here with the stone beneath,
above, and around him. Would there be time to let Islief know—
time before the cavern became his deep grave, the mountains his
tall cairn—that he'd been so dear to her as to now be part of her
very heart?

Lonely, she determined that if she could not be with her old friend, still she could watch him, she could see him in the embers, her spirit following behind. Aeylin made a prayer to the Deity of Fire, another to the Deity of Magic. She wove spells to make the fire leap high, to burn brightly in the crystal hearth.

But a Deity's will caused the flames to drop, the embers to fall dark. Somewhere, at a great distance, a god whispered, a goddess murmured softly. These sounds made no echoes.

"Ah, Vuyer," Aeylin pleaded, "won't you let me watch? Fyr, mother of visions, won't you let me keep the flames so that I may follow along behind my friend; a spirit close to his spirit? Chant," she whispered. "God of Magic—Ylf, mother of spell-craft—please!"

The embers did not stir, though Aeylin heard a sound like fire breathing softly; a god sighing. She heard a sound like flames hissing; a goddess denying a prayer.

Now, Vuyer said, *you must learn patience, Aeylin.*

Patience, Fyr agreed. *For you have seldom before taken the path away when an opportunity to interfere lay at hand. This part of the healing is Islief's to do. This time, you must learn to trust, for trusting will not be the least of the skills you will need before the end.*

And the Deity of Magic—Chant, by his silence, Ylf by her wordlessness—approved of the judgment.

And so, compelled by Deities, in the silence, in the enfolding darkness, the long-dead queen steeled herself to stillness and patience. She made her form no more than a small thin wisp of smoke hovering above the crystal hearth.

And this state was enough like sleep to invite dreams. Dreams of restoration: Islief's to peace, her own to the Deities, and the world's to life.

The Elf-mage Aidan liked to do his scrying, his searching along the magical planes, in the reflection of moonlight on water; the only time he used a candle's flame—and then reluctantly—was at dark-moon. He was something of a traditionalist; a reactionary, if one listened to his few detractors. Aidan himself would have said he was a purist, for before there was fire, there was moonlight. Even those who liked the convenience of steady light which was not subject to waxing and waning with the demands of time did not fail to admit that old elements are strongest.

The Elf-King watched his young mage take a small bowl and fill it with clear cold water from a newly replenished ewer. No bigger, no deeper than Aidan's cupped hands, hollowed from a single crystal of black garnet, the bowl was worth a prince's ransom.

Dekar's thin lips twitched a smile. In fact, the garnet bowl had *been* a prince's ransom. Generations before, this bowl and three others like it had won back the life of Aidan's many-times great-grandfather when war-luck had been on the side of the Mannish. That royal prisoner's daughter—Fial of the Bow, Fial of whom bards yet sang—had taken the treasure back in later years when luck ran with the Elves again. Now the three other bowls were lost to time and later wars, as were the fortunes of Aidan's family.

For another man, this part of a lost treasure might have served as a bitter reminder of what time and change had taken from him, but Aidan had long ago decided that this heirloom would do better service as a tool. And so it had, for if Aidan, this last son of a once-powerful family, was not a prince in Elvish, his status was not to be despised. He was the Elf-King's Mage, a position envied him by many an older man and woman.

"Young Aidan," the Elf-King said, "you will not be searching for the stones or the ghost tonight. You're going out among the living."

No ripple of surprise marred Aidan's calm, though Dekar had expected his mage to be surprised. Had they not been searching for those five stones each night until Midwinter, searching for the ghost each night since?

A twice-made search for hope . . .

With his scrying, Aidan had found the five stones in winter. One beneath the deepest foundations of the great keep at Seuro; another in the rubble of the same city. The third had been part of some long-forgotten hoard of Eastland pirates, buried deep in caves beneath the sea itself. The fourth, and the most desperately sought fifth stone, had been found as parts of a necklace which decorated the brittle broken neck of a skeleton, of a person—whether male or female, Elvish or Mannish, Aidan could not say—who'd lain ages dead in a high pass in the Kevarth Mountains. All had been found after painstaking search.

And all had vanished, the five at once, on Midwinter Night, only a moment after Mage Aidan had seen the glittering image of the last two in the moonlit water of his scrying bowl. And though he'd searched each night until now, Aidan had found never a trace of the stones.

The lost Jewels of Elvish, found for a moment, were lost again.

Dekar believed that he knew, if not exactly where the stones were, who had gone to their far-flung hiding places and taken them. And Mage Aidan, privy to the Elf-King's belief in this matter, did not disagree. He'd spent each night since Midwinter searching for the one who had taken the stones and the hope.

Now, his canted eyes soft-focused, as though seeing dreams, Aidan found the exact center of the table, placed the black garnet bowl there. His hands cupped the bowl, long fingers perfectly still. He barely breathed, and the water, as though it sensed his quiet, stilled as well. When the new moon's silvery light filled the bowl, Aidan whispered the first words of a spell-chant.

Dekar, to give his mage privacy with the magic and prayers, went to stand near the window. The moon's light fell around him, but only faintly, for the sky was never truly dark now. Even at midnight, even in dark-moon, the sky was always filled with mage-light, like silvery twilight.

This light, this weary glow, was a reflection of the prayers and spell-strength of desperate mages, men and women who could get none of the Seven to answer, who could get no enchantment made to soothe the burning lands in the west.

And those mages were fewer now than they had been yesterday. Another had died of magic tonight. She'd given all she had to the barren prayers. She'd won nothing by her death but her own place in legend.

The Elf-King did not think, as once he would have, that they in Mannish had better be grateful for what his brave mages gave. He had no room for bitterness; fear filled him now. Though treaty-bound to help Alain, Dekar did not put his mages to such terrible work for the sake of a treaty.

And a weak treaty it is, he thought now. Though few know about that. For should Nikia's child be shown to have been fathered by Mage Reynarth, that treaty might well collapse under the weight of the child's bastardy and Dekar's own refusal to acknowledge a traitor's get as his heir.

No, Dekar's mages worked because, like a hungry beast, the land-sickness was moving ever south, and lately a little east toward the sweet green forests of Elflands.

Yet there might be a way to relieve the mages of this terrible task he'd committed them to; there might be a way to save his own forests, to heal Alain's lands. There might be, if the patterns he'd found in old legends and a bard's new songs were more than the patterns that wind traces in sand.

Oh, you Seven, Dekar prayed, *only a year ago we fought an enemy with a weapon from legend. The tale can't be ending now, the legends empty of hope. Let these song-patterns I've helped to forge become a road to healing!*

When Dekar stepped away from the window, Aidan adjusted the bowl's position to compensate for the moon's movement. The water again still, the light from the thin new moon again a motionless sheen on the water's surface, he said gently:

"Tell me what you need, King; tell me who you want to see."

Dekar did, and he said that he'd no desire to see this one only in a scrying bowl. He wanted to see him in Verdant Hall, the man himself standing before the Forest Throne.

For he may be able to resist my own invitations, Dekar thought, *claiming duties and the needs of his own king, but he'll not resist Mage Aidan.*

"I want to see him soon, Aidan. Make your suggestion a strong one. Make it one he won't resist."

"In your service," the mage said formally. "For your good." The cadenced words, spoken like a chant, were the beginning of his every invocation.

In your service; for your good . . .

The world around Aidan became silent and dangerous, wide and wild, filled with treacherous possibilities, deadly certainties. When he'd learned this practice of reaching for another's heart and mind through the scrying bowl, Aidan had been strongly warned of the dangers, told terrible tales of mages who'd become caught in the alluring web of emotions woven when one spirit reached out to touch another.

It was rare that a mage survived such an experience, and even so, he did not live long, died thin and white and looking as though he'd been taken by a wasting sickness. And so he had, for he'd left the most of himself, the most of his soul, trapped on the unseen plane where the nets of enchantment and illusion are woven. What came back to the body was never enough to preserve life.

Still, those were other mages, weaker ones. Aidan believed that he knew his own strengths, believed that he'd tested them enough to know their limits.

Now he closed his eyes, gathered his strength and centered it until he felt it all within, like fire leaping, water falling, wind blowing. Aidan did not need Dekar's indrawn hiss of breath to know that an image now shimmered, wavering and cloudy, on the moonlit surface of the water. He felt that image forming, taking shape slowly.

In the deepest parts of himself, the Elf felt all the things which moved the man in the image. His fears and his hopes, what he hated, whom he loved.

Aidan went deeper, to the place where there were no borders between him and his subject. He felt . . .

My strengths and weaknesses; all the things I need; all the things I can give.

The sensation now was like reaching for his own reflection in a mirror, and he saw, he heard, he dreamed . . .

The songs we know, the ones we'll make.

He became filled with songs known, songs unborn: exhilarating verses like spell-chants; tender ballads like solemn prayers; wild war songs wrapped in bright strands of glory like spun silver; dirges like dark-draped moonless nights.

Last, Mage Aidan heard and felt and tasted the thing which was part of every song, sometimes acknowledged, if only in a long slow minor chord, more often avoided: an aching sadness that spoke of time passing, of days gone, deeds not done. Aidan shuddered under the lorn, empty sorrow of love not taken. Mage and subject, they each groaned under the weight of that sorrow as though under the heavy weight of a dream unrealized.

A hard hand clamped on his shoulder, fingers gripping, hurting. Dekar hissed a warning, and Aidan, hardly aware of what he was doing, opened his eyes, exhaled sharply, broke the webs of allure as his breath broke the image in the scrying bowl into white wavering lines on black water. His hands shook, trembled like the water. Cold sweat stood on his brow.

Aidan whispered his own name, then spoke it aloud, once, strongly. And the image stilled again.

His own control securely recovered, Aidan picked gently among his subject's emotions and dreams, and quickly for all that he was careful. He did not want to come close or stay long. Shaken by what he'd felt, he did not want to be haunted by it. Nor did he want to remember that he'd nearly lost control under the burden of unrealized dreams.

When Aidan again knew the man as a separate being, a spirit safely walled within blood and skin and bone, he recalled a thing he knew about him. The strongest suggestion, the one this man was least likely to resist, was the one which looked most like his own good idea.

Aidan opened his eyes, filled them with the vision in the moonlit water. He spread his hands over the bowl and the water and the image, noted with distant satisfaction that his hands were steady again. Then he reached out across the distance. He spoke in his subject's own voice, spoke to the man as though the man were speaking to himself.

He gave him a good idea.

Chapter Ten

DAIL WOKE WHEN THE SLIM NEW MOON HUNG LOW ON THE western horizon and the many-colored Elf-light shone brightly in the east. He was roused by a thirst for music, a hunger for his harp's voice, and the sudden certainty that he'd not dreamed that Calmis had come to tell him that Alain had made his decision to abdicate the kingship. Considering it easier to slake the thirst and feed the hunger than to deal with the certainty that things were about to change here in the Citadel, in the kingdom, he searched for his *Dashlaftholeh*.

He found the instrument where he'd left it in the afternoon, on the window seat. Lifting the harp carefully, he held it to the faint starlight, turned it so that the stronger light, the Elf-light, shone on the wood, and saw that a crack, a small wound inflicted by dryness and the sun's merciless glare, marred *Dashlaftholeh*'s wood. The tiny separation had sprung up in the joining at the harp's slender pillar and her base.

"Ah, no," he whispered. Hands trembling, Dail stroked his harp as tenderly as he'd have caressed an injured child. "I'm sorry, my girl. I'm so sorry."

He looked around, spied the untidy table shoved up against the wall next to the bed. Sometimes he left the pot of linseed oil there; sometimes the soft polishing cloth was there, too. Or maybe the pot was on the mantel, the cloth in that pile of clothing in the corner?

Groping in the dark, he found a candle and taper on the bed table, knocked a leather scroll case to the floor and didn't care that it rolled under the bed. Then he stared blankly into the darkness,

realizing that he had no means of lighting the candle. He dropped
the candle, slid from the bed and went out into the corridor to find
a torch.

When he'd bracketed the torch in a cresset just inside his door,
Dail resumed his hunt, found the oil pot behind the chamber pot.
That accomplished, he abandoned his search for a soft cloth and
decided that an old pair of breeches would serve.

With oil and cloth, Dail fed the harp's hungry wood, polished
the dulled ashwood to a glowing sheen again and checked each
inch of the wood for further signs of cracking. There were none,
and the tiny separation at the base would be easily mended. Still,
he felt no better, for as clearly as though he'd spoken aloud, Dail
heard his own warning to aspiring harpers:

*Sometimes your harp will give you a mother's comfort. Often
she is as companionable as a sister. Times are when we caress
her like a lover. These are only guises we offer her, aspects she
likes to assume. She is none of those things.*

She is you. Treat her that way.

Now those remembered words sounded like an accusation as
the torch in the wall cresset snapped and orange light leaped high,
flung images of his debris-strewn quarters at him. Dail truly saw
the place for the first time in many months, and—seeing—he was
suddenly disgusted by the clutter and dirt, frightened by these evi-
dences of his inability to care about anything, least of all himself.

"My girl," he said to the harp, "one of us is in more trouble
than the other. And you will recover."

A breeze wandered in from the window, breathed like a sigh
across the harp's strings. And though the breeze did nothing to
ease the night's heat, in that wind-called music Dail heard the
memory of the cool and fragrant breezes of spring. His fingers
traced harmonies across the harp's spring-song, phrases like bittersweet memory of riches lost, treasure not found. Then, regretting
that he'd spoiled his Song-Bringer's music, he laid the harp gently aside.

"Ah, you're right, my girl. It's time we were gone from here."

The breeze dropped, the harp's voice stilled. As he began the
long hunt through winter's rubble for *Dashlaftholeh*'s old leather
case and a scrip to hold what little he would take with him, Dail
began to understand that he'd not just now minted this decision.
He was acknowledging one he'd begun to consider hours before
in the Council Chamber.

This afternoon, as he'd stared out the window to the seared
lands beyond the A'Damran, he'd found it difficult to sort through

Calmis' talk of politics and plans. He'd not been able to think of anything—of anyone—but Nikia.

Aye, Nikia: the Elf-King's daughter; the Lady of the Bards; the Hunter-Defender who had risen from the heart of fire and magic to defeat the Sorcerer; Garth's wife.

The Lady A-bearing, folk called her now. Many spoke of her in hushed, almost reverent voices. Lovely she was, all tall grace and glowing with health while the world around her withered beneath baleful magic. Once a symbol of peace between two kingdoms, Nikia had now become another kind of symbol. People treated her as though she carried not a child within her but the last hope anyone could expect before utter despair.

But Dail hadn't been thinking of her as any of those things this afternoon. He'd been thinking of a girl who was only newly turned nineteen. In that girl's eyes could be surprised a look which made Dail's heart ache; the wistful expression of one for whom care and trouble had worn away even the smallest memory of what it felt like to laugh or sing or feel the sweet kiss of spring's gentle sunlight on her face. Though young of face and form, Nikia did not seem young at all when that lost look was on her.

This was the Nikia he'd been remembering in the Council Chamber, and he'd wanted to go find her, take her up in his arms and carry her away, far away to a distant place where the world still remembered spring, where birds yet sang and green meadows were starred with flowers. And he'd been thinking how very much he loved her, and how badly he wanted to discover who she was when she was not all the things other people wanted her to be.

Yet all of that foolish, painful dreaming was nothing but that: Dreaming. For though Nikia was the woman he loved, she was not the woman he could have. She was a king's daughter; she would bear the child of a prince and help guide another to kingship.

Dail slipped the harp carefully into the case, tied the closure strings. "I'll tell you this, my girl: I do love her. Ah, but you know that, don't you? And you know something else, or you'd not have made your wind-song to speak so clearly of leaving, aye? It's time for us to go; time for me to get away from here before I grow careless as well as foolish. She has enough to manage these days. It was friendship I promised her all those months ago, and so I'm thinking the best part of friendship now is to leave her to find what peace she can and not trouble her with what she doesn't want."

He settled *Dashlaftholeh* in her case over his shoulder, took the guttering torch from the wall and left his high tower chamber.

In the corridor he found a bracket for the torch and, settling it, remembered that he'd knocked something—a scroll case—from the bedside table in his earlier search for light. That case had contained a message from Dekar, more bits and pieces of Elvish history . . . and another request that Dail come to Verdant Hall.

Three times before, Dail had put off the Elf-King's requests. And, aye, they were requests only barely disguising a summons. But each time Dail had refused the summons, claimed that he had duties in Damris, claimed that he could not leave. In truth, he *would* not leave, though duties—of which he had few—had nothing to do with his reasons for staying.

But now he had no reason to remain in Damris, and so Dail went quietly into the night and took a swift horse from the stables. By moonset he'd put the Citadel, Damris, and the muddy A'Damran behind him.

Nikia took Garth's hand and led him into the Queen's Garden. At the edge of the walk he stopped, looked up at the new moon hung low in the western sky. "Nikia, it's late. We should be sleeping."

His voice sounded weary and ragged. Nikia tucked his hand, a fist knuckled and hard, into the crook of her arm, stroked it gently until the fist unknotted. She didn't argue with him, for she heartily agreed that they should be sleeping. But they hadn't been. They'd been talking, going over and over matters until all sense and meaning had been lost from their words.

The decision Alain had made tonight was yet secret, but it would not stay that way for long. Before another night, all men would call Garth Regent. Many would mourn Alain's abdication, for he'd been a good king for a long time. But most would feel that it was well done of the old king to look to his grandson's future, better done to place a young man in power who would look to this troubled present. Even Karo, belligerent Lord of Raeth, whose contingent of followers had grown over the last months, would be obliged to at least present the appearance of contenting himself with Alain's decision. In this matter, the King's wish was final.

"And yet," Garth had said, often and often, looking out the window to the seared lands beyond the Citadel, "what good is it to secure the Regency, to keep the kingdom for Ybro, if the kingdom dies in my hands?"

Nikia had no answer for him, and so, hoping to offer him a short time of peace, she begged him to leave their chambers, to come out into the night and the garden for a while. She'd always found comfort in the night's stillness, in the starry darkness. And sometimes she even found peace here when, most often at moon-set, she heard the garden's secret music, the strains of harp-song as Dail worked late in his high tower room. Nikia hoped she'd hear the music tonight, for she wanted to share that peace with Garth.

Now the breeze quickened to a light wind, rattled the dry husks of last year's plantings. Nikia stood up on her toes, put her arms around her husband's neck. She didn't do this gracefully; her child had grown big within her these last months, heavy enough to make reaching awkward. Garth had to help her, hold the small of her back to lend her balance.

"There's a breeze moving," she whispered against his brown beard. "And the night is cooler—a little—out here. You could almost believe that it is April."

Garth smiled; she didn't see it, but she felt it in the way his lips moved.

"Wife," he said gently, "all your night roaming must have given you a better sense of that than I have. This feels like no April night to me."

He put an arm around her shoulder, she slipped her arm around his waist, and they walked in silence until they came to the stone bench at the far side of the garden. Garth handed her to a seat, then sat on the ground at her feet, rested his head on her knee.

They sat so for a long time, and for a long time Nikia listened to the night, hoping for harp-song. She heard nothing but insects droning, a tuneless noise; wind rattling dead plantings, an empty sound.

Garth pointed to the eastern sky, to the Elf-light veiling the stars there. Nikia looked, and saw a shifting in the light's pattern, a wavering in the fabric of illumination, then a sudden flare of all the colors.

"A magic is being done," she whispered.

Garth nodded. "They try, your father's mages." He drew a long breath, let it out slowly, and got to his feet.

"Won't you stay?" Nikia asked, still hoping for the secret music, still hoping to offer him peace.

"No. If there's no sleep for me tonight, there's work can be done." He gestured to the Elf-light. "He's a good ally, your father, and there must be times when that still surprises us both. I won't take him for granted, and it would be poorly done if I left him to learn of the changes here from rumor's mouth."

He bent and kissed her. After the briefest hesitation, he brushed his fingertips across the soft fabric of her thin cotton nightshift where the wombed child lay. As though roused by his touch, the child stirred, and when he felt that movement, Garth withdrew his hand.

"Don't stay long, Nikia. Of us both, you need rest more. That babe of ours taxes you, I think."

Nikia watched him walk back to the solar, watched as he took a torch from the hall and bracketed it near the door for her.

That babe of ours . . .

He was so careful, so very careful, to use just those words. And of late he hesitated only a little to touch her where the child nestled. Nikia wondered whether a time would come when he didn't hesitate at all, when he'd completely convinced himself that he believed this babe was his.

Trembling suddenly, Nikia smoothed the blue cotton shift, spoke to the child she could not yet touch, the child she fervently hoped was Garth's.

"But we won't know about that, not for certain until you are born. And then what will happen, little one, if you bear the stamp of Reynarth's fathering?"

She shuddered to speak that name, shuddered to think what folk would want done with a traitor's child. Any other man's child would be put out to fosterage, but Reynarth's child would be wanted nowhere in the two kingdoms his father had helped to damage so badly. And maybe few would blame Nikia for her ill-gotten child if the story were told, but none would suffer that child, none would care too much that his mother loved him as dearly as she would any child of her body. Maybe not even Garth would understand that.

Nikia forced herself to turn away from that thought, to put it firmly behind her. This was her child. Nothing else mattered. If he was Garth's all would be well. But if Garth could not claim him, she would find a way to keep him. She would have to, for she'd felt the terrible emptiness of child-death once before and she knew in the heart of her that no matter what else she'd lose, she could not survive the loss of another child.

Hungry now for the peace she'd so often found here in the night, Nikia listened for the first strains of the garden's secret music. But though she listened for a long time, she heard only the insects' incessant night noise, and once a shrill whinny from the stables. From beyond the garden wall came the distant bark of a dog, the weary sound of the A'Damran struggling past its drought-widened banks.

The night seemed darker than usual, hollow, empty.

In the morning the Citadel was abuzz with gossip, as word ran round the place that Alain would announce his abdication in favor of Garth's regency, and Nikia, fleeing for a rest from rumor and speculation, went to the Great Hall and her bards. There she learned from a young apprentice, who had it from a chambermaid whose cousin worked in the stables, that Dail had gone from the Citadel. The apprentice, mistaking Nikia's stricken expression for surprise, said, "Lady, surely you knew he'd be gone sooner or later. He doesn't stay long in the city, never has. Master only comes here for winter, then he's gone again, off along the spring paths like any wild young journeyman. He's been longer here this year than most. Maybe the strange weather confused him, maybe it took him a time to know the season by the way the moon and stars move." The apprentice shrugged. "But he's reckoned it out now. He's gone."

He didn't say that Dail would be back, for he took it as given that summer's end would send his master home again, took it for granted that the Lady of the Bards would know that.

Nikia was busy all that long hot spring day. She worked through the morning with her bards. The task gave her none of its usual joy, for the apprentices were full of nothing but their frustration that their master had gone roaming without them, and the bards who had the task of teaching were ears-cocked for the larger excitement brewing without the hall. She, their patroness, was oddly distracted.

And later she stood with Garth as Alain made formal announcement to the Council that the kingdom would now be ruled under his son's regency. Then Nikia watched carefully to see how each lord received the news. Some, by tone of voice, by expression, showed themselves to be happier than others. But Karo of Raeth sat like a man made of stone, betrayed no emotion when Alain, seeming as frail and withered as an old, old man, left his chair at the head of the wide oaken board and made way for his son.

Still later Nikia attended to the matters of ordering the Citadel, inspected the last kegs of bitter winter-brewed ale and had two taken up from the storage places beneath the kitchens. She dealt bargains with Saer, the sea-fisher's lad, who had come to

Damris from the coast. He'd wrapped his father's sea trout and flounder and ocean bass in seaweed and kelp, cached them in airy wicker baskets, and so, though he'd ridden all the distance of a day, many had not yet spoiled. Nikia was pleased to have them, for they would eke out the small roebuck and three braces of grouse the huntsmen had brought that morning. The evening meal would seem almost like the feast it would have been in better times.

Late in the night, while Garth sat talking in the hall with Calmis and Liam of Celed, when Lizbet had grown tired of waiting for her husband and gone to her own bed, Nikia, restless and weary but unable to sleep, went to sit by her bedroom window. As she sat looking down into the empty garden, she wondered where Dail could be this night.

Then, as she sat wondering and listening to the dry, hopeless droning of cicadas and crickets, to the hot night wind, she heard a rattle of hoofs from beyond the garden wall, saw two dozen men riding northward. In the hand of one, held high, was a banner. Hot wind rippled the silk, moonlight showed a device she knew: Shield and Sheaf, the banner of Raeth. Karo was quitting the Citadel.

As Dail had.

When she went at last to her lonely bed, Nikia did not sleep well. There came to her—stalking like terrible night-beasts— hard dreams of a time of fire and power, a time when she had stolen the will from every creature so that all who lived must stop and attend a god-woman's doings. In that dream Aeylin had not been able to call her back from power's excess, for in that dream Dail had not been near to speak for the Lady of the Blue-Silver Eyes.

Trembling from the dream, she awoke in the early morning, feeling the strong movements of life within her, the unborn child awakening. Ah, but uneasy the child, fretfully kicking. Nikia wrapped her arms around herself, hugging the babe within, trying to soothe the restlessness.

"There is only you, my child," she whispered. "And only me. Only us. We'll not be troubled by nightmares again, sweeting. No, nor will we be able to go walking in the poor garden by night hoping to catch foolish and fair dreams filled with someone else's songs. We'll sleep well in the night."

She knew this would be so, knew it certainly. For though she was far away from her father's Elflands, she was Dekar's daughter;

she knew a spell, secret words that would make sleep dreamless. Her eyes on the empty garden, Nikia whispered those words, and her right hand moved gracefully in the air before her, sketched a patterned web where dreams would be caught and held, powerless to haunt her when she was helpless in sleep.

This dream-killing was the first spell she'd cast since that night, many months ago, when she had nearly lost her soul to a Jewel's fire and terrible magic.

Chapter Eleven

THE KING'S BARD LONGED FOR THE GREAT DARK PILE OF THE Citadel, stone on stone, built high and wide, where the sun did not beat so brutally in its search to drink the last drop of moisture from a man's body. The Citadel, Damris itself with its buildings standing close together and leaning over narrow cobbled streets, provided a thing he could not find out here in the countryside where trees were mere bony hands scratching at the hot sky: Blessed shade.

Dail soon realized that, despite the sun's heat, it would be best to travel by day. He'd quickly learned that the night, while cooler and sometimes stirred by vagrant breezes, was full of danger. Hungry, thirsty, angry men prowled the darkness, hid in the shadows at the edges of villages and towns, took cover beneath rocky outcroppings and in skeletal oak shaws. They would kill him for the horse he rode and the sword he carried.

These men had been soldiers, had survived the war and come home to find drought and hunger. In better times many had been workers in the fields or in the villages. But there were no farms now, only withered lands, and in the villages the bakers did not bake for lack of flour—no man had grain enough to pay the miller's-portion for grinding, no miller had flour to sell to bakers. There was no work for the cooper, none for the iron-maker. The chandler had no tallow, and he, like his fellow tradesmen, had no need to hire help.

The men once housed and fed by their work in villages and on farms found themselves turned out onto the road, abandoned and changed into robbers by the pitiless sorcery of hunger and fear and rage. They ruled the night in packs, preying on lonely travellers. Even well-armed companies of hunters making their way homeward from the Elf-King's forest seldom reached their destination without having to fight off these marauders. No honest man dared travel after sunset.

And so, though day's heat was cruel, Dail chose it over the uncertainties of the brigand-haunted night. As he rode east to the Elf-King's forests, he thought about Dekar's messengers who had braved the pitiless sun by day, risked encounters with the ruthless bandits by night, to bring him scraps of Elvish poetry, an almost-forgotten song, a carefully copied parchment with— only possibly—a veiled reference to long-dead Aeylin.

And four times they'd come riding with summonses he'd never answered till now. Those wild young riders would gallop their horses through each of the seven hells for their king, and now— for he himself was surely baking in one of those legendary hells!— Dail wondered what the Elf-King wanted from him that was worth the risk he put his messengers to.

At night Dail found shelter in the homes of folk who knew him, and these were not a few. People had become used to looking for him in spring and summer, accustomed to watching for him in autumn as he went home again to Damris full of songs to ease the King's winter. Though these folk had little to offer as hospitality, many still welcomed him even in this season of want and hunger, and if not always for himself, at least for the sake of his harp and the profession it betokened. It was well known among the country-folk that he who turned a harper from the door courted ill luck.

In this bitter spring, none needed more bad luck; Dail slept before homely hearths if there was room, slept in haycrofts with hungry, thirsty cattle if the house was crowded. Wherever the bed they offered, Dail's hosts fed him as well as they could, gave him precious water—if sometimes only a scant dipperful—from their failing wells, and the payment they asked was one Dail had always been willing to make.

"I've not much food to give," said one farm-wife, come to the dooryard in answer to his called greeting at the end of his fourth day of travel. "But if you're wanting to pay for't, you can tender me a song, harper."

She looked past his shoulder, beyond fallen fences, past the crumbled well-walls all draped with the purple shadows of twilight, out to the dun stretches which should have been a rippling green dance of rye and wheat swaying in April's breezes. For an instant her eyes lifted to the rainbowed lights just starting to show above Dekar's forests. But only for an instant. She looked away from that wonder as from a promise never kept.

"Sing about rain, bard," she sighed. "Sing about the sound of it, the cool of it. Help me remember how it feels."

Dail ate as little of her food as he could, for he'd seen that she'd taken the smoked meat from a meager store. He took only a mouthful of the water she offered and gave the rest to his weary brown mare. He tried to pay the woman in the coin she'd asked for, but it was hard to do. His throat was parched, his voice unlovely.

Yet, had Dail's voice been as supple and willing as it used to be, he'd still have been hard put to pay the farm-wife her due. He remembered only a little better than she about rain and how it bewitched the senses. The best he could do was ride the deep ranges of the harp-strings, call a song of thunder to remind the old woman and her two daughters of what the promise of rain sounded like.

In the deep blue hour before dawn when the shimmering, many-colored Elf-light in the east still shone brighter than the pale warning of day's approach, the farm-wife's youngest daughter went to watch Dail saddle the brown mare. When he'd bid her farewell, was just about to haul himself up to the saddle, the girl stopped him, pressed a heel of dark bread into his hand.

"I wish I could give you more, harper. My da's out hunting, gone into Elflands. If you'd come after, when he's home again, then we'd have seen you on your way with better than bread ends. And I wish I could give you more water than this morning's mouthful. . . ."

Ah, but even if he makes it past the wayside robbers, Dail thought, *your da's not going to bring you back water*. Aloud, he said:

"I appreciate what you've given me."

The girl smiled and Dail saw that the light in this breathless hour was kind. As though some magic had escaped from the Elflands, her dry mouse-colored hair seemed to shine a little. And that light—if escaped it had—smoothed the wrinkles beneath her light brown eyes, hid the blisters that marred her lips. Dail remembered then, where he'd forgotten in the evening, that this girl was no older than eighteen.

And he remembered, the memory clutching at his heart, an April night three years gone when, at fifteen, this girl had not had mouse-brown hair, dried brittle by wind and sun, but thick chestnut curls which had fallen all around her smooth white shoulders and smelled of fresh breezes. That spring she'd been old enough to flirt with the King's handsome harper, old enough to make the jaunty switch of her hips, the toss of her head, the soft pout of her lips, something to dream about.

But three years ago she'd been too young for Dail to take seriously, even though the sweet-scented night had bid fair to confuse and enchant him, even when she'd sighed and said that there wasn't much she'd not give to be remembered in a harper's song. Wishing all the while that she were only a few years older, Dail had kept a firm grip on common sense that night and gently told her that she must hold him to account, that he'd come back and give her a song when a few years had passed.

Now this bitter drought, this hunger and thirst and brutal sun, had changed her, given her the look of a woman twice and half again eighteen. And Dail, moved almost beyond speech, said that he'd not forgotten that he owed her a song.

She thanked him for remembering, wished him well on his journey. Then she smiled, and in the brown wrinkled cheek a dimple came, dancing a little in a way that Dail remembered. But tears sparkled in her tawny brown eyes, as though she knew that the petal-soft girl she'd once been was forever gone, fled much too soon.

Dail turned the mare's head east into the sun, toward the dark line of the Elvish forests. As he rode, he made a song for the girl and the damaged spring. A song about things people hardly remembered these days, a hymn born of the memory of gentle evening breezes and the tender fragrance of dew-sheened wild roses clinging sweetly to wayside fence-posts with the same simple trust as soft-eyed young girls clinging to their lovers.

As the breezes of evening, alive with the dewy scents of night-blooming flowers, sighed in through his open window, Mage Aidan studied the image of the man on the brown mare—a man he'd watched often during the past six days. From the cool safety of his quarters in the Elf-King's hall, he'd observed the bard's journey, watched as sun hammered him, gritty wind stung him and the generosity of friends humbled him.

Aidan turned away from the scrying bowl and thought about the most interesting secret he'd learned the first time he'd watched this bard, the one he saw affirmed each time after: This bard made no song that did not have his hidden love for the Elf-King's daughter as its seminal impulse.

And the mage thought about Dekar, thought that his king was good at using the strengths of others to his own advantage, even better at finding ways to use their weaknesses. That his daughter, wed to a Mannish prince, was part of the soul of another man's song would be no surprise at all to Dekar. The Elf-King had known this since the summer before, when he'd first seen the bard in Nikia's company. And Aidan believed that this secret had been used to lay the foundation of Dekar's plans for the bard. Aidan was proud of his crafty king.

"And I am grateful," he thought, "that Dekar has chosen me to be the bard's companion, to see that the King's wishes are carried out."

It had not sat easy on him that he'd lost the five Jewels. Now he told himself that he'd dare anything for Dekar, risk what he must to bring back the Jewel that represented the world's hope.

Yet for all his determination, a chill spidered along Aidan's arms, the kind of chill a man feels when fate breathes near. He did not fear journeying into the sick lands; he was not afraid of encounters with brigands or the dangers of the forests and the mountain. He'd been well taught in weapons-craft, was adept at woods-craft. But the one skill he'd never learned, the one his mage-work never allowed him to cultivate, was the art of dropping his natural guard enough to admit even the most simple form of companionship. For he, gatherer of other men's secrets, feared most the risk that another might discover his.

And he had secrets—the best-guarded of them dreams that he himself did not want to admit, did not dare give life to. They had to do with love, those dreams, but not the love of a woman. They had to do with a love of power. Such dreams as these had long before seduced an Eastland mage to abandon the ways of natural magic—to wander far into the realms of ungodly enchantment, the lightless lonely places in a soul where no prayer or spell or chant was needed to work wonders. When he'd come out from those dark places of power and nightmare, that Eastland mage had been known only as the Sorcerer.

Shuddering, suddenly cold, Aidan left his chamber for the sweet spring night. His boot-heels rang hollowly on the old wooden bridge across the Altha. The air was misty with the mingling scents of water and reeds and the pine tar that the fishers used to pitch the seams of their light craft. And suddenly, though he'd not thought of her in many weeks, Aidan wondered whether Kicva, the fisher's daughter turned soldier, would come home soon from the war.

He'd had word from her parents—that news brought by another returning soldier—that she'd set out for Verdant Hall at winter's end. After that message, Aidan had heard nothing further. Neither had he searched for her image in his scrying bowl. Kicva was a sensible young woman and would find her way home with little difficulty or distraction. It was one of the several good reasons for marrying her. Capable, strong, pretty in an untamed way, Kicva would make as good a wife as any woman.

Aidan paused on the far side of the wooden bridge to watch the mist rising faintly blue in the twilight from the Altha's smooth surface. All in all, he thought, it was a good thing that his father had betrothed him to the daughter of his old friend Cowan the fisher, for Cowan—like Aidan's own family—came of far older blood than the present catch of Elvish nobility, a line which—like Aidan's—had once bred princes. Neither family had, or wanted, a chance at regaining the ancient glories of their houses. Still, both men had been pleased to join their lines again, as once, in the old days, they had been joined. All things considered, Cowan's girl would do very well for a wife.

And yet, as the mist thickened, swirling over the water, as golden fireflies winked in the twilit haunts of the forest where now full darkness never came, Aidan wondered what it would be like to love—to dream—as wildly, as terribly *willingly*, as the bard Dail loved and dreamed of the Elf-King's daughter.

Chapter Twelve

AEYLIN DREAMED IN THE QUIET BENEATH THE MOUNTAINS. IN dark caverns, she who was dead dreamed of a time when she had lived. And, dreaming, it was as though Aeylin had found a body again, for she was filled with an aching of memory.

Mayne! Dead so many hundreds of years that his own children did not remember him. Brawny Mayne, savage fighter, fierce prince, who had—for all his legendary strength—come closest to taming his wild Aeylin when she let him use tenderness. A thousand memories, some sweet, as many bitter, crowded round Aeylin in dream.

Theirs had not been a tranquil union, never that, for the marriage had been purchased, paid for with a treasure stolen from the

Deities, paid for with promises of peace. And yet, though their people kept a limping truce for a time, Aeylin and Mayne had little of precious peace in their own lives.

Too often compromises had looked like surrenders to Mayne. Too often Aeylin had seen agreement as weakness. They were both soldiers, the prince and the hunter-scout. They didn't know much about peace, and had no time to learn about it as the political alliance their marriage symbolized fell apart in bitterness and war.

Yet, sometimes they found a rare personal peace, peace as unexplainable as a miracle. And in those wonderful moments, Mayne and Aeylin were able to make love as though their bed were not a battlefield or a council table. Now, dreaming above her hearth, Aeylin understood that—whether by fate's design or simple coincidence—her children had been conceived in those peaceful interludes.

One, a son, had gone back to the folk in the Kevarths, by choice went to live with his mother's kin. His brothers had scorned him, and soon learned to call him enemy. Another child, a daughter, Mayne had given in marriage to a man from the mountain kingdom. Her sister had mourned her, and soon learned to call her lost. For the matters which divided the two peoples were not new, the wounds not easily healed. They'd been brought like baggage on the journey from the Eastlands. Mere compacts could not heal the pain or lighten the weight, for these were matters of pride and politics, matters of magic and worship. Mayne's kin had never been strong in magic; Aeylin's kin had called them false believers, charging that the man who could make no magic could offer no worship.

"Yours are godless people," Aeylin had once said, and said quietly in cold disdain.

But Mayne had not risen in anger to hear his folk thus accused, not that time. "This breach between our kin will widen," he'd said. "And our children will learn to hate each other. Aeylin, I swear to you, I think I will die of it."

And he'd spoken words of prophecy. He, as shy of magic as any of his folk, had spoken as accurately as the most potent seer because his prophecy was self-fulfilling.

Before his death, Mayne had fought in wars against his own son, against his daughter's children. Before his death he'd learned the new name his enemies went by: Ylf's children. Ylfish; the children of the Deity of Magic. Hearing this, he declared that his own people would then and forever be known as Mayne's children; Maynish.

Did he think—as his enemies accused—that he, himself, was a god?

Aeylin had never believed that he did. He only feared, as men will, that, nameless, his children would vanish and become forgotten. Instead it was he who had been forgotten, was today not even an echoed memory in the hearts of the people who bore his name.

"And yet, they are all our children, Mayne," Aeylin whispered to the darkness and the dreams, a ghost offering comfort to the spirit come to haunt her. "I broke a balance when I broke the Crown. *We* broke a balance when we sold ourselves for a treaty which celebrated the sundering of our kindred. And now it is time to let our children try to heal the ruin which resulted from broken balances. If it is meant to be done, they will do it."

Beneath the Kevarth Mountains, in the caverns where first she'd seen the Jewels, weapons and later a marriage fee, the ghost—who in life had possessed little patience—understood that she must learn in death that patience is to be prized. And so, dreaming, trying for patience, she waited for Islief to bring Nikia's daughter to touch the Emerald's magic, to reclaim the world's health, to redeem his own and a ghost's sins.

The Deity of Magic smiled, the god Chant and the goddess Ylf. They, eternally balanced, power against power, male moving in patterned rhythm with female to make a single and whole Deity, began to believe that a time would come when they would answer the world's dearest prayers again.

The Citadel was all but silent as Ina hurried down the winding stone stairs, trotted along the gallery, tugging her gown straight, patting her grey hair into place as she went. She smiled a little, grimly satisfied. There were few people up and about this hour. This morning she was determined to be first into the nursery, had risen at dawn for the very purpose of being there to wake and feed the new little King before anyone else could sweep in and carry the child off.

Aye, me *hurrying! In all this hopeless heat and dreadful dust, me hurrying and scurrying to get there before the Princess. But what else to do, when* she *will do as she wills be there no one near to advise against?*

As though dumping the poor mite down midst a chant of harpers all the morning long is a fit way to tend to a yearling child! Them with their lusty tavern ditties and lorn love-lilts; them with their terrible war songs and ballads for dead queens! Princess she may be, but that Elf-Lady will need to learn something about babes by the time that little 'un of hers comes awaiting.

Ina sniffed scornfully, grumbled not silently.

"A lot to learn, she has—and not e'en two months to learn it in if my eye tells me true. But does she come to Mother Ina? Not she! She'll have that babe of hers and likely set him on some harper's knee 'fore he's taken two breaths. . . ."

Everyone called the old woman Mother Ina, though she was no one's mother at all. Never had been. Still, hers were motherly tasks. She tended children of kings. She saw to their feeding, administered their baths. (Or had, when there was water for bathing!) Mother Ina soothed and mended their scraped knees, presided over the telling of nightly bedtime tales to start them dreaming.

She had done these things for the princes when they were but small; for Fenyan (and him dead of war this year past, poor prince!) and for Garth, him they called Regent now. She'd hoped to do the same for the dead prince's son, had *expected* to, until the Regent's wife decided that she herself—and none other—must have the care and tending of the little King.

"And, aye," Ina muttered, "that Lady Lizbet scolds and warns and says no good'll come of her o'ertaxin' herself. But does she listen? Not her. Taking up the work like she was no more than a servant herself. And her the daughter of a king and a regent's wife. Well, she'll have to leave the servants' work to me this day. She surely can't be up and about yet."

But Nikia was up and about, and Mother Ina caged a frustrated sigh behind clenched teeth as she opened the nursery door. Aye, there she was, sitting in a spill of early light, little Ybro upon her knee.

The sweet little King, and all that sunlight falling on his dear red curls like they were gold. Now, what's the matter with the Princess? Doesn't she know the sun's not good for skin as fair as Ybro's? She'll have him pink as a boiled crab . . .

"Good morning, Lady," Mother Ina said, pleased that she sounded as bright and cheerful as though she'd not hauled herself out of bed in the dark before dawn only to find that she'd done so for no good purpose at all. *She*, at least, knew her place and could behave as she was meant to. "Sun's quite hot today, don't y'think?"

Nikia looked up, smiled a greeting, and Mother Ina bobbed a curtsey.

*Well, you do give'er a courtesy; you do when she smiles like
that. A good deal she has yet to learn about child-rearing, but
she's nothing at all to learn about looking so sweet and good.
Like the soul of peace, this one.*

In the absence of anything else to do, Ina went to start the
morning's tidying, slipping sideways looks at Nikia and Ybro as
she worked.

She was beautiful, the Elf-King's daughter. None could dispute
that. Long hair like starlight, braided with green silk ribbons this
morning and wrapped like a crown around her head to show the
witchy cant of her Elf's ears. Slender, the Regent's wife, and tall
for a woman.

Yes, slender, Mother Ina thought as she pulled the sheets from
the infant King's bed, snapped them hard, and spread them near
the window to freshen. *Though she's round-bellied with child,
though her breasts swelled now to make ready for a babe's hungry
sucking. Her with her long back, her slim hands and arms; were
her back to you, you'd not know she carried.*

*Ah, but such a lost girl! One look in her eyes—only let you get
past how they make you think of the kind of silver never found but
in moonlight on still water—one look, and you see that she's lost
and trying her hardest to make the best of it.*

In that moment Mother Ina decided that the Elf-King, famous
Dekar, was no better than Ruf the Chandler who married his girl
Winset to the tallow-render's son for the hope of better rates for
his wax. He was a good man, that render's son, not too old and
not bad to look at; clean in his habits and hard-working. He neither
beat his wife nor abused her. Ina had even heard said of him that
he loved Winset, and so maybe he did. But Winset, poor child,
went about with the same lost look on her—hard to see if you
weren't looking close. Folk in Chandler's Way said she'd had her
heart set on another man.

Maybe the Regent's wife had loved a tall magical Elf in her
father's kingdom. Maybe she'd been swept away from a handsome
lover to come wed Prince Garth.

Or maybe, thought Mother Ina, the thought born of nothing
much more than the look in the Lady's eyes and the way light
shone like a song of starglow in her hair, maybe the sudden
vanishment of the King's Bard had something to do with that
look.

Master Dail had not been seen about the Citadel for nigh a week.
Friends those two, the Master of Bards and their Lady. Famous
friends from the recent war-days. And *him* it was brought her

back from that terrible northern Keep when the mad mage had kidnapped her right out from under her own father's hand. (*Some father, he! Sends her packing off to marry a stranger and can't keep track of her when she comes a-visiting!*) Rumors of dire magic—some done by the Princess's own hand—had gone abroad afterwards. But were those rumors true, the magic hadn't daunted the King's Bard, no. And for good measure, he'd rescued Prince Garth from dark dungeons, too, though everyone had thought him dead of war like his poor brother.

And so it could be that the Regent's wife missed her good friend . . .

But that's none of my business, the old woman decided firmly. *None of my business at all.*

"Lady," she said, her work (such as it was) done for the morning. "Will you let me take the babe for you? I'd be pleased to amuse him while y'go sit w'your bards."

Nikia smiled and shook her head. "No, Mother, thank you. I'm not sure we could do without this little one this morning. It seems to me that my bards play better for having him near." She tickled a smile from Ybro, stroked his red curls. "But thank you for offering."

Ah, well, Mother Ina thought on a sigh. And then, as she watched the Elf-King's daughter leave, she wondered if maybe all that wistful wanting was not about the vanished bard after all. Maybe it was nothing more than a longing for her own child to come.

Well, she thought, *two more months, Princess; if that. Then maybe you'll let me have my duties back! For surely two babes will be more than a fine Lady like you will want to handle.*

And maybe your bard'll be back before long . . .

Ina shook her head, as though to shake away that last thought.

"And *that's* what comes of hearing too many love-lilts," she muttered. "Y'start seeing things all starry-like, makin' lorn tales of a half-remembered tune and the sigh in a Lady's eyes. Ah, what fine and fair nonsense that little King's head'll be filled with!"

In the Great Hall, the tall and wide place that was so good for hearing harps and songs, Nikia sat in a fall of sunlight, Ybro on her knee. The child loved the music, and when a host of chords rose high, spiraling up to meet their own echoes, Ybro crowed laughter, reached his little arms high as though he were trying to catch the music.

"Like he's reaching for dreams," an apprentice said.

Nikia smiled, caught the little King in the moment before he overbalanced, and steadied him on her knee again.

"Yes, like that," she said.

And she was glad to hear the echo of her own voice, glad that she heard no clue there that her heart had gone suddenly heavy, as though with the burden of all the dreams she'd forbidden herself.

Chapter Thirteen

THE TALL-CEILINGED, AIRY CHAMBER BLAZED WITH THE LIGHT OF candles—slender white tapers in branched silver holders, and thick, short blocks placed all around the room. These single boxy candles gave off a subtle and poignant fragrance. Like old leaves in autumn, Dail thought.

Candlelight gleamed on cherry-wood walls and the intricately carved furniture, reflected from the glass panes of the wide double doors which opened to the outside. The glow of candles was welcome, for it was darker within doors than it had been outside. Out there by the river, it seemed that silvery twilight would last for hours. Restlessly, Dail crossed the flagged stone floor to the two wide doors and threw them open to the night air.

An exterior room, the guest chamber fronted the wide terrace that circled the sprawling hall itself. Surrounded on all sides by water, for Dekar's hall stood on an island, and the river flowed around that island as courteously as though nature itself must move aside for a king. Though these outer rooms were seldom used in winter, they were the finest in all other seasons.

"Is there anything I can get for you, bard?"

Dail turned away from the river and the unnaturally long twilight, back to the tall young man who'd greeted him near the west bridge and introduced himself as Aidan, the Elf-King's Mage. He'd shown no surprise at Dail's arrival, nor had he asked for his name or his business, though the latter was usually the first question an Elf asked—and from behind a drawn bow—when an unexpected visitor came this close to Verdant Hall. Stiffly courteous, the mage had offered Dekar's welcome and shown Dail to this room.

Strange, that casual welcome, but—weary from his journey—Dail had asked no questions of the Elf-King's Mage. He was certain that any he'd have would be answered soon enough.

Now Aidan stood patiently in the doorway. His long face was handsome, in the way that Elvish faces can be, deep-eyed, high-boned. The mage held himself so still that nothing, no gesture, no quickening or quieting of his breathing, no flicker of light in his eyes, gave even the smallest clue to the spirit housed within the tall, lithe body.

Dail, whose bard's eye always hungered for details, noted these things, and made of the sum a man who likely knew himself well, and liked to keep the knowing to himself.

"Yes," he said. "You can get me water. Not for drinking, though you could bring me some for that if your king has lately run out of wine. I want the water for bathing."

When the mage asked if he wanted the water heated, Dail—rank with the sweat of a five-day ride, several layers thick in dust, his hair and the damned beard fouled with both—stared at him.

"No," he said, carefully and clearly, "I do not. I want it as cold as you can find it, and you'd better warn whoever is bringing it that I want several changes of it. Mage, I haven't had a bath in longer than I can stand to think about, and I've felt nothing cool since before then."

Aidan, who kept himself at a distance several times more than arm's length—and perhaps not only for privacy's sake—allowed a sympathetic smile to break the surface of his calm. "Are you fond of those travelling clothes of yours, or shall I have new ones sent?"

"Burn 'em," Dail said, and then, as the mage turned to leave: "Wait, I've a question." He gestured to the twilight behind him. "The moon says that the night's well along. Why do my eyes say it's still gloaming?"

"You saw the light above the forest as you came here?"

Dail nodded.

"This is what it's like to live beneath that rainbow after the sun goes down." And saying no more, the Elf-King's Mage left him alone with the eerie twilight and the sweet breeze drifting into the room from the forest and the river.

They did not keep servants at Verdant Hall, but there were folk whose task it was to see to a guest's needs, and sooner than Dail would have thought possible, two men appeared with a wide and deep bathing tub, three others with buckets filled with cold, cold water.

"Call when you want more, bard," one of the men said. He was a northerner, perhaps originally from the foothills around the Landbound Sea as Darun's Lizbet was, a fact plainly spoken by his eyes, blue as shadows on snow, his dark hair, and the less pronounced cant of his ears. He cocked a crooked grin. "We've been told to empty the river for you, if that's what you want."

They brought food, as well, and though Dail could happily have fallen on a whole roasted pig and eaten it to the bones, he agreed that a meal of bread and cheese and thick broth was better for a belly that had gone nearly a week on rations which were short and sometimes questionable. Best, though, was the stone flask of wine, glistening with moisture as though it had been cooling for a long time in a shady brook filled with snow-melt.

Later, when he'd scrubbed off the road's grime, eaten all of the bread and broth, much of the cheese, and emptied the wine flask by at least half, Dail finally left the bathing tub—filled for the third time. On a thick stack of green-dyed flannel towels he saw something he hadn't noticed before: a fine-honed shaving knife and a highly polished silver mirror.

Blessing the Elf-King's Mage for seeing to even the smallest detail of Dekar's hospitality, Dail went about the business of ridding himself of his hated beard. Then, clean and finally shaven, he unpacked his harp, applied oil to the wood, saw that the crack at the base was healing, and went at once to sleep.

He did not remember to blow out the candles, but someone must have done that, for when he woke in the morning to a knock and a diffident Elven bearing Dekar's summons, Dail saw that the candles were gone, the room clean and tidy, and that someone had covered him in the night against the dampness and chill from the river.

Dail walked with the Elf-King on the terrace in the new morning. They spoke quietly of the changes which had come about in Damris. The sun had not yet cleared the top of the forest, nor melted the dawn fog, and so the sound of their footfalls on the wood-floored terrace was muted, like rumors spread to the distant rhythm of drumbeats.

"It's hard to see an old enemy succumb," Dekar said. At Dail's expression, he laughed. "You're surprised to hear me call Alain 'enemy'? Remember, bard: I knew him as such for a far longer time than I knew him as an ally. It was as my enemy that he

taught me to respect him. I don't know how they think of him
now in his Citadel, but the courage to let a stronger man fight
this present battle is what I'd have looked for in my old enemy.
Though summoning the strength to use courage like that can break
a man's heart."

It can, Dail thought. *And often bitterness fills the breach*. But
he kept his thought to himself.

Dekar respected the silence and said: "Tell me how my daughter
fares. How is Nikia?"

On the river's smooth surface a swan glided. She'd captured
all the frail light of the young day in the startling whiteness of her
wings, a luminous ghost. Under the guise of stopping to watch the
swan, Dail turned away from the Elf-King, hoped that his voice
would not betray him.

"Your daughter is well, King."

"Ah. Then her pregnancy doesn't trouble her?"

The swan trumpeted. The deep, rich, somehow lonely notes
stirred Dail's heart in the same way that the calls of the wild
geese fleeing winter always did.

"No, it doesn't," Dail said. "She blooms and thrives like a
windflower in spring, just as they say all happy women do when
they are childing. It isn't easy living in Damris these days, but
I've never seen the Princess in better health."

"Well, then I am happy. They say that no eye sees more clearly
than a friend's. What you say must be so."

Dail turned the conversation bluntly, and with little grace.

"King," he said, "I had the feeling when I arrived here last night
that I'd been expected. Is it so?"

Dekar smiled thinly. "My friend, I've sent you invitation upon
invitation to visit me here. One is wise to expect the guest one
invites. Even when he is late in arriving."

Along the riverside the fog thinned to rosy gold mist as the sun
lifted higher and forest-scented breezes stirred. Dail watched the
swan as it rounded a bend in the river and vanished; then he turned
back to Dekar. The look in the Elf-King's long, silvery eyes told
him as clearly as words that Dekar wanted something.

Feeling reckless, suddenly feeling as though he stood not on
the terrace outside Verdant Hall on an April morn, but at some
unmarked crossroads where time did not exist, where any step
taken would set him outside the lands he knew, Dail said:

"You want something, King. What is it?"

"The Emerald," Dekar said.

Dail stared blankly. "An . . . emerald?"

The Elf-King smiled again. That smile did not reach his eyes. "*The* Emerald, bard. One of the Ruby's brothers, one of the five."

"They're lost," Dail said flatly, as one who repeats automatically something everyone knows. He closed his eyes, and there in the darkness he saw again the fiery Ruby of Guyaire as Nikia flung it into night and darkness to fall into the rubble of a ruined city. "Even the Ruby is lost now, King."

In the forest, birds sang; the river lapped and sighed at the shores, kissed the island as it flowed past. These made strange harmonies for Dekar's next words:

> I found the Flame-stone and the Wind-stone.
> I held in my hand the War-stone.
> I took the Sea-stone and the Heal-stone.

"Those are Aeylin's words, friend bard. You know them well, don't you?"

Dail knew them. They were not Aeylin's words, they were his, a verse of a song made in winter and of the pieces of legends which Dekar had sent him. The song for Jewels that had been ages-lost, existing nearly invisible between the lines of half-forgotten legends for longer than any could remember.

"I want the Heal-stone," Dekar said, his voice low and urgent.

Dail wondered suddenly if the Elf-King's mind had become unbalanced. "But—they're lost, King."

"Not as lost as they have been. I haven't been idle these months past, bard. And, with my mage's enchantments, I'd located them all by Midwinter Night—even the Ruby which my daughter flung from a high window as though it were nothing more than cheap glass and paste."

"You found them . . . where?"

"Located them," Dekar said carefully. "Here and there." He handed out his next bit of information with a humorless smile. "I even learned that one, the Diamond, was in your Keep of Seuro, buried far beneath the foundations in a place so deep that dungeons would have seemed like airy towers."

A cold creeping, like wet winter wind or foul dungeon air, made Dail's skin prickle. He'd seen one of the Jewels used at Seuro, and he'd seen this Elf-King's daughter rise terrible and strong to the brutal song of magic that the Ruby had sung.

Uncomfortable with his thoughts, uneasy feeling what he felt in the presence of Nikia's father, Dail took a step beyond the crossroads and said:

"So you located the Jewels. But you don't have them."

"No. Someone has gathered them, bard, and hidden them in a place magic can't see into."

"Who?" Dail asked quickly.

"Only two people in my hall know about the Jewels. One is me, and the other is trustworthy. Who do *you* think has the Jewels?"

"King," Dail said carefully, "I'd have no way of knowing that."

"My question isn't an accusation, bard. Rest easy." Dekar looked at him for a long moment, judging. When he spoke at last, his voice was low, thrilled with an urgency which drew Dail farther into the lands of impossibility. "I believe that Aeylin has them."

Dekar laid a long hand on Dail's arm, and when he felt that hand trembling, Dail knew that the Elf-King was not as calm as he'd pretended to be.

"And she is someone you know well, friend bard. You speak with her. I hear her voice in your songs.

> I am the hunter bright, north-fled
> To dark places where no light shines.
> Dark's foe I am, hard-hunted
> To stone places where nothing grows.

When those songs are voiced, I see her."

Dail said nothing for a long time. He was listening to his own words, given back to him by the Elf-King. Those words hung in the air between them like the mist above the gently purling Altha.

And he was thinking about long winter nights, nights as hot as summer's noon, when he'd studied parchments filled with legends and bits and pieces of history, straining his eyes in the flickering candlelight and hoping that Alain would not call him too soon. It had always been hard to put aside those ragged whispers from the past, even to ease the old king's pain.

And sometimes, when his eyes were weary of pale light and wavering shadows, he'd take up his harp and go to sit in his window. Filled up with legends and history, the echoes of strange and ancient poems, he would labor over new songs, all the while caught between the vision of a ghost's blue-silver eyes and the sight of Nikia walking restless and sleepless in the Queen's Garden. He'd played with legends and made histories all winter.

Dail glanced at the Elf-King, saw Dekar's face in profile. Canted ears, long slightly slanted eyes, the structure of his face was just a little different from a Man's. The cheekbones were higher, the jaw a little longer. The same kind of face as a Man's, but not exactly.

So it was with Dail's Aeylin-songs; they used some of the same elements as the old histories and legends—but the two, song and history, were not exactly the same.

His songs were *not* histories, only new patterns made from the fragments of imperfect memory. And they were not made by a ghost.

> Dark's foe I am, hard-hunted
> To stone places where nothing grows.

Dail almost laughed, remembering how he'd labored over first the words of the songs Dekar had quoted, and then the music. No ghost had made these songs, though one had inspired them. Dail shook his head, moved to speak gently, for he was certain that he was about to break a fragile hope.

"King, Aeylin doesn't live in my songs. You gave me some bits and pieces to make them with, and I fitted them together as well as I could. But there were a lot of empty places that had to be filled with a poet's fancy."

Dekar would not be moved. "Poet's fancy or magic, it is an echo of words a ghost spoke to you. Bard, think: Heal-stone, Wind-stone, War-stone, Sea-stone, Flame-stone—I never sent you a song or history or legend with those words in it. I have one— a fragment of a text come recently to light—but I never sent it to you. Who told you these oldest known names of the Jewels?"

"Well, no one, but—"

"No one but Aeylin."

No! Dail wanted to shout. *Those expressions are nothing more than a bard playing among the words!*

But he had no time to protest, for Dekar went on hurriedly:

"Those are Aeylin's words. They are attributed to her in the text of the parchment we found. You must use your songs as though they were a map to her, bard. Go fetch back the Emerald."

"Fetch it back from where? And why?"

"Why? Because, as the Ruby has power over the things of war, so does the Emerald—the Heal-stone!—have dominion over the things of nature.

"From where? Aeylin was a warrior, she was a queen, but now she is a ghost. One whom you and my daughter know well, if the tale you both brought back from the war is to be believed. Where does one look for a ghost if not in the place she is bound to haunt?

What other place would Aeylin haunt than the place where she found the Jewels in the first place; where she brought them again? Be guided by your songs, bard, and I will be surprised beyond words if you don't find yourself very near the western edge of the Kevarths, in a place that would be exactly in line with Seuro were a line drawn between it and that city on a map."

"How do you know that, King?"

Dekar smiled wryly. "I don't know that. But think: There were people in this land before ever your kin and mine came here to live. Those folk were called the First People. They liked to call us the Second People. And it was from a parchment written by one of these folk that my daughter learned the spell to unlock the Ruby's powers. Nikia found that parchment in Seuro's Keep. The Kevarths, directly east of Seuro, are riddled with caves. In the oldest form of Elvish *kevarthi* doesn't mean 'cavern.' It means, 'hold.' The Kevarths would be a good place to start. Don't you agree?"

Shivering now, though the sun had risen high and warm, Dail remembered a song Nikia had taught him.

> . . . Hands of beauty, slim and fair,
> Fingers skipping, touching.
> Lady bold, how came you there
> In caverns dark and drear?
>
> What paths followed in your toil,
> Dim and full of danger,
> To kneel before the ancient spoil
> In caverns low and cold?

"King," Dail said, "are you asking me to find the Jewels and bring the Emerald back so that Nikia can use it?"

"Yes," Dekar said simply.

"Nikia almost lost her soul to that cursed Ruby!"

"But she didn't. She had you near to help her. She had Aeylin. I cannot speak for the dead queen, but I think you will not desert my daughter if she uses the Emerald to heal the damage that has been done to the world.

"And I tell you, bard, that if you don't find that Emerald and bring it back to her, Nikia will die as surely as each of us will. My mages have little strength left to fight the land-sickness. It creeps farther east and now it threatens the forests. There is not much time."

All the world fell silent as the wind dropped. The forest stilled, birds became quiet.

"Bard," the Elf-King said, "will you presume to make the choice for Nikia and condemn her to die? That is not love."

And so he was caught, and all the care he'd taken to keep his feelings well hidden amounted to nothing. Dail looked at Nikia's father, expecting to see the cold triumph of a king who had wed his daughter to his enemy's son for a treaty-warrant and used her to achieve his own ends still.

He saw nothing of the kind. Yet the sympathy he saw hurt almost as much as gloating.

"I'm sorry, bard. Truth is a cruel trap to catch a man in."

Wordless, Dail nodded.

"Will you do it?"

Voiceless, Dail formed a word with his lips. *Yes*.

Dekar thanked him, then told him that he would not journey alone. "I've chosen a companion for you, someone who knows the land well and can get you safely north. He is ready to leave with you now." Dekar smiled, this time genuinely. "I've had him pack your belongings this morning. He'll join you here shortly."

Dail watched the Elf-King walk away. It wasn't long before he heard the sound of boot-heels on wood and looked around to see Mage Aidan walking toward him with a harp case slung over his right shoulder, and two scrips—one Dail's, one his own—over his left.

Chapter Fourteen

ISLIEF USED THE MANNISH LANGUAGE CAREFULLY, WEIGHING words for their meanings; and he used expressions that Joze's grandfather's grandfather would have known.

Islief called anemones "breeze-blossoms." He called the red-breasted robin a "ruddock"; the sweetly singing thrush "a gladsome mavis." Joze listened to each naming and remembered how his grandfather Crey used to tell him that *his* own grandfather had spoken of the ruddock and the mavis.

"That was my mother's father," Grandfather Crey had said. "And he used to say 'feather-heeled' when he meant agile. A horse's fetlock was his 'foot-lock,' and we farmers did not engage in farming, young Joze, we engaged in 'earth-tilth.' "

Grandfather Crey would have gotten a great deal of pleasure conversing with Islief.

As well as being a repository for old-fashioned words and expressions, Islief was keen-eyed. The two were not an hour gone from the caverns, Islief still talking about how strange it was that Kicva had seemed so interested in whether Joze would decide to help the Lady and then gone suddenly off on her own— Joze trying not to think about anything but the best way to get to Damris—when Islief spotted what he claimed to be Kicva's trail. Joze was doubtful, cautioned that anyone could have passed this way; there was no certainty that these were Kicva's footprints on the soft ground.

Islief, head high, sniffed the air, then nodded, satisfied. "The friend passed this way." At Joze's startled look he laughed, pebbles slipping down shale. "I have been many years in the caverns, Tall, smelling only rock and water; only cave air. All other smells are strange to me now, and so I am careful to remember them. I know what the friend smells like: leather and smoke, the scent of her wooden arrows and the flint tips of them, the sharp smell of her knife."

Joze still doubted. "Anyone could have come past here carrying weapons like that, wearing leather and smelling of smoke."

"It is so, Tall. But no one else is wearing her skin and her hair. The friend was here not long ago." Islief cocked his head, looked up at him. "Do you think we should follow her? She will best know the way through the woods."

Joze wished he could assure Islief that they didn't need Kicva's aid. But he knew that wasn't true. He could find his way to Damris from these foothills of the Kevarth Mountains, but the way he knew led through Raeth, through seared, hungry places in thirsty lands.

He was only a little sure that he'd survive such a journey. He was afraid that Islief wouldn't. Islief still shied from sunlight. And though Joze hadn't asked, he believed that the light hurt Islief's eyes, maybe burned his skin. They must keep to the forest when they could, keep to the cool shady ways until they came nearly to the Elf-King's Verdant Hall. Then a westering journey across the Altha would put them in Mannish lands—in Joze's own home province of Celed. From there, if they were lucky, two weeks walking would bring them to Damris. By then it would be May, maybe early June. Perhaps two weeks in the burned lands wouldn't be too much for Islief . . .

Until then they must hope that they didn't come across any of the Elf-King's border-guards or hunting parties. Joze had not forgotten his winter-companions' suggestions that he leave the Elf-King's lands quickly. Trespassers were not welcome in Dekar's mountains and forests. And so, in the end Joze told Islief that they'd best try to find the hunter-scout.

"I suppose, we'd better follow," he said stiffly. "We'd be a lot safer in Dekar's forests if we had one of his people with us."

Islief squinted at the sun's dazzle on stone. "Well, Tall," he said thoughtfully, "some things have changed here in the forest since you have been away to war. I saw it in the Lady's fire. The Elf-King does not trouble hungry people who come into his land to hunt." He looked away from the bright splashes of sunlight. Wide-set eyes on the short-sword at Joze's side, he rattled laughter. "Tall, you do not look like a hunter, but maybe the Elf-King's folk will let us pass if they see us."

Joze considered this, and grudgingly said that they'd still need a guide. "Dekar was never so accommodating before. There are only a few Men who know the ways through the Elflands. I'm not one of them. You're right. We need to find Kicva."

Islief nodded. "And maybe the friend would be good company for you."

"I doubt it," Joze growled. Then, to soften his words, he smiled. "You're all the company I need, Islief."

Islief said nothing about that, only set out down the trail, keen eyes watching for the signs of Kicva's passage. What his eyes didn't find, his nose did. Islief kept them on course, and Joze was certain that they'd catch up with the hunter-scout by day's end.

They didn't.

The way down from the Kevarths' foothills was steep and rocky, a journey better endured on horseback than on foot. Still, if Joze missed his roan horse, he knew by the second day that he'd have missed more and better things if he'd gone horse-aback, for Islief's delight in the Open-tide—as he called the spring season—was contagious. Joze soon found that he looked forward to the quiet but intense rising of Islief's joy at the feel of the fragrant breeze on his face, his sigh of pleasure at the sight of a brilliant yellow brimstone butterfly dancing among the white breeze-blossoms.

They went always south down the steep flanks of the Kevarths. As they clambered over rocks, picked their way carefully along crumbling stony shelves, they followed Kicva's trail unseen, only scented by Islief. It was hard going, leaving Joze with little breath for talking, and a lot of time for thinking. He remembered his first encounter with Islief only a handful of days ago. Then Islief had been startled by every small sound of the forest. He no longer seemed so. At noon, when they stopped on the stony lip of an angular slope to rest from the morning's long walking, Joze asked how it was that Islief now felt more comfortable in the forests.

Islief didn't answer, only peered over the edge of the drop, tracked a seemingly invisible path down to the shady glade. He cocked his head, listened to the murmur of a small stream which cut the glade north to south. From this height, the stream looked like nothing more than a thin trickle, but even Joze could smell the water, and it smelled good.

"Tall," Islief said, "maybe we should fill up our water flasks."

Joze agreed, and followed Islief down the treacherous slope. Eyes on the path and the jutting rocks, he did not repeat his question, gave all his attention to the task of keeping his balance.

But Islief had not forgotten Joze's question, and when they'd filled the flasks and sat resting—Joze in the sunlight, Islief in the deep shade of the pines—he said:

"These forest sounds do not frighten me now, Tall, because I am waiting for them. I want to hear them. Before, I wanted only to find you and go back to home. Now . . . now I want to hear the noises. I want to see the Open-tide, and taste it. It is so beautiful, Tall. So gladsome and lovely."

It was a good enough answer, but Joze had the feeling that it wasn't the whole answer. Yet he asked no further, allowed himself to be diverted by Islief's delight in a chickadee's skipping flight over the water.

When the blackcap was gone, when the glade had fallen silent and Joze sat dozing in the sun, Islief, unwilling to venture into the light, pitched a pebble from out the shadows to get the young man's attention.

"Now come, Tall, it is time to go again. We must not let the friend get too far ahead or we will find no company for you."

Joze didn't growl this time, but not for lack of wanting to. He got to his feet and followed Islief along the stream, out of the glade and into the cool deep forest. Islief tracked steadily and Joze understood, though he'd seen no sign, that Kicva had recently been through the glade. He was grateful that she had chosen to continue her journey south to Damris along the easier paths of the forest.

But they didn't find her that day. Nor did they find her on the third day. On the night of the fourth day gone from Islief's cavern home—April a week old—thick clouds hid the moon and the stars, and Joze was a long time falling asleep for worrying that it would rain in the night and all sign and scent of Kicva be washed away.

Sunlight made jewels of the night's rain where it hung, small droplets, on the tips of pine needles. The campfire smoked fitfully. For the first time since he'd camped on the edge of ruined Raeth, Joze woke from the familiar nightmare of burning Souless. He lay still while his racing heart slowed, watched a green nuthatch creeping down the side of the pine's trunk. The bird stopped only a hand's length from Joze's shoulder and, head cocked, eyed him brightly before it went to tapping at the rough bark, knocking for breakfast.

Gentle, a hand touched his shoulder. "Tall?"

Joze started, heart leaping again; the nuthatch scolded—*yank! yank! yank!*—and fled the tree. Islief withdrew his hand.

"Are you well?"

"Bad dream," he said, trying to keep his voice steady.

Islief patted Joze's shoulder sympathetically. "Will you be eased to talk, Tall?"

Joze shook his head, unwilling to describe the nightmare which had haunted him this whole year past since the war's end. Then he laughed, but with only a little humor.

"Islief, the idea of going to Damris to find the woman who made the magic to blast a stone fortress to sand—*and* asking her to hand her child over to ghosts and strangers—will keep me well supplied in nightmares for the rest of my life."

"I will be sorry if that is true, Tall."

The dawn's breeze shifted course, and Joze caught the rich scent of hot food. Islief patted Joze's shoulder again and went to tend the fire. Joze watched Islief sniff the contents of the stone pot that sat on a flat rock at the fire's edge. This was the smallest of the three pots which Islief had taken with him from his cavern home, each carefully wrapped in thin sheets of softest leather, nested one inside the other and carried in a small sack. Last night they'd snared a rabbit, skinned it and roasted it, but Islief had not eaten. He'd eaten nothing in all the five days they'd been gone from his caverns. When questioned, he'd simply said that he'd forgotten about eating a long time ago.

"Because this alder-elde the Seven have given me—this long, long living—does not have to do with whether or not I eat or drink. I still go on. And then . . . I got out of the habit of going above, and nothing good to eat lives below. I don't like the taste of the pale fish in the underground river, and a flutter-mouse is all sharp teeth and leathery wings. What meat there is, is not loathly. But it is wearisome to catch enough of them to make a meal."

Joze had nodded sympathetically, but thought that no matter how much meat there was on a bat's bones, he'd have to be very hungry before he'd eat it.

Still there must have been a time when Islief liked his food, for the accumulation of years seemed to have had no ill effect on his cooking skills, which were as finely honed as such skills often are in one who enjoys a good meal. The rabbit he'd prepared for Joze's supper had been delicious, and what was left of that meal, simmering in the stone pot now, smelled even better, a mingling of odors—rabbit seethed with wild thyme and thin shavings of peppery lovage root—to make Joze's stomach growl eagerly.

And loudly, for Islief, hearing, said: "Maybe you want to go wash yourself, Tall. The food will be ready for you when you come back."

Joze got to his feet, stood looking at Islief. Small grey man nearly as old as the oldest tale anyone could tell, Islief yet shied from sunlight—even the dappling here in the thick forest—but he tolerated a cooking fire's light as long as he didn't look directly at it. As he did not eat, neither did Islief sleep. Instead he spent the dark nights peering through the spaces in the forest's roof, watching the stars winking, delighting in the progress of the moon across the vaulted blackness. Bright welkin-wanderer, Islief called that moon. At such times Joze would hear him draw a deep breath, let it out in a long and wondering sigh. Joze was glad that Islief at least needed to breathe, for that sigh of his was filled with more elation than even a child's, and it was good to hear.

Joze left the clearing, went to the black and silver brook running fat and swift with the night's rain. The promise of breakfast, the quickening of hunger, the sharp cold sting of the stream's water, drove away the last shred of nightmare. And when he shook the water from his hair, saw sunlight dazzling on the brown carpet of wet pine needles, he smiled. All tracks of Kicva's journeying must be washed away, but she'd make new ones. Surely today they'd find another trace of her, another line of footprints, a ring of ash from her campfire. Maybe, if they made good time today, they'd catch up with her by darkfall.

Kicva was tired. She was tired of walking, of climbing the rough rocky trails, tired of pushing her way through the forest. Mostly she was tired of trying not to think about Joze.

There was no reason to think about him, she decided on the day she left the caverns. None at all to remember how he looked, dark-eyed and broad-shouldered. No purpose to recall how it had felt to be held by him in the moment the smoke above the crystal hearth had become more than smoke.

And there was no reason to think that she'd ever see Joze again, she realized on the second day of travelling. Either he'd cravenly decided to renege on his promise to help the Lady, or he'd finally made up his mind to keep his word, in which instance he'd have struck out for his king's Citadel at Damris, hoping to see the Princess. Even if Joze had chosen the honorable course, Kicva wouldn't see him again, because she wasn't going to Damris.

She was going to Verdant Hall, to lay her case before Dekar. This was a matter for him to manage; the Princess was his daughter, the child Aeylin needed was the Elf-King's grand-daughter. This was no matter for foreigners to handle.

And so, determined to do the only sensible thing, she'd travelled for four days, threading rocky glens and finding the hidden pathways through the mountain forests. And each night, as she sat before her lonely campfire listening to owls and the wind in the trees, she told herself that she didn't care whether she ever saw Joze again.

Now, late in the afternoon of the fifth day since she'd left the caverns, with the foothills well behind her and the ground levelling at last, Kicva stopped to rest in a glade and found that it held a rock pool, water where she'd not thought to find it. It must be fed by underground springs, she thought. And then she thought that it looked like it had been made expressly for the purpose of bathing.

Surrounded on all sides by dense brush, with only a slender apron of grass where violets and white wood sorrel grew, it was oval in shape and the dark slaty color of the water told her that the pool was deep enough so that the water would come nearly to her elbows were she standing in the center, in the sunniest part by that broad flat rock rising. Yet, though the pool was deep, it was neither very wide nor very long. She'd only need to swim for a few moments to get to that rock.

Kicva sighed wistfully. A person could certainly enjoy the sun on that rock after the water had cleaned away the dust and grime of travel, washed away weariness. And even though the water would be icy, she'd bear the cold for a chance at getting clean.

During the last months of the war, for all the winter after, she'd been constantly on the move, often with barely enough time to

hunt, less to eat, even less to sleep. That hadn't left much time
for bathing, and sometimes Kicva felt as if it had been years since
she hadn't reeked of campfires and sweaty hunting leathers, ages
since she'd had the luxury of slipping into the Altha to bathe on
all but the frozen mornings.

"You are like the fishes we catch," her mother used to say.
"Even winter doesn't keep you from the water!" Then she'd hold
up one of her nets, pretend to cast it high, as though trying to catch
her daughter. When she was a little girl Kicva would scamper
away, shrieking with laughter.

To distract herself from a sudden wave of aching homesickness
and from wondering whether her parents were well, Kicva looked
up at the sky and reckoned the age of the day by the slant of the
sun. She decided that it was too late to go much farther and still
have any hope of finding a better place to spend the night than
this quiet glade. There'd be wood and kindling to gather for a
fire, dinner to catch, but at least she could pull off her boots and
roll up her breeches and bathe her tired feet.

She slipped her bow from her shoulder, the quiver from her
hip—then decided at once that she would do more than ease
walk-weary feet in the water. In moments she had her hunting
leathers and smallclothes piled neatly next to her weapons. She
stepped into the water, gasping at the cold, and struck out strongly,
swimming for the flat rock and the sun. She didn't see the two men
break the cover of the bushes and come to stand at the water's
edge until she'd reached the rock and turned, wiping water from
her face.

Heart lurching painfully in her breast, Kicva put the rock
between herself and the men, looked quickly around the glade.
She saw only these two. But they might as well have been a
troop, she realized helplessly: They stood between her and her
weapons. And her clothes.

These were not Elf-kind, but interlopers from Mannish lands.
One was tall. His clothes were filthy and ragged, his hair the
color of bleached straw. He looked like a scarecrow, rail-thin, as
though he'd been hungry for a long time. The other was short and
balding, his beard grey-streaked and as patchy as a mangy dog's
coat. He was thin, too, but his hunched shoulders and vaguely
puzzled, inward-turned expression made Kicva think of a man
who'd only just lately understood that some ache or illness is not
minor after all.

It was the tall man whom Kicva watched carefully, watched
with heart pounding, shaking harder than the cold water should

have accounted for. His eyes were flat and dangerous. As she would have before a wild dog, Kicva lifted her chin, eyed him levelly. Sometimes a cur backed down when it saw that its intended victim would stand and defend itself.

But Scarecrow only smiled, a malicious parody of geniality. He scooped up her clothes and, grinning wide enough to show bad teeth, he tore the rust-colored blouse from neck to hem and tossed the pieces away. The tanned breeches were harder to destroy; these he simply flung into the brush.

Kicva's heart hit hard against her ribs. This man didn't think she'd have further use for her clothing.

Laughing, he snatched up her weapons—the bow, the quiver full of white-fletched, green-cocked arrows, and the knife. He flung them after her clothes.

"Well, my girl," Scarecrow said, his voice dusty and dry, creaking. "You're going to freeze if you don't come out of that water soon."

The smaller man, the sick man, bent over and began to cough in deep racking gasps. When he stood straight again, Kicva saw a small bright splash of blood fouling his patchy beard.

His companion didn't even glance at him. He crossed the thin apron of grass at the pool's edge, trampling violets and wood sorrel underfoot. He held out his hand. "Come on, my girl, out of the water. Let's see if me'n Greil can warm you up, eh?"

Wet and shivering, eyes on Scarecrow, whom she judged to be the most dangerous of the two, Kicva tried to give the impression that she would offer no resistance. She waded slowly toward the outstretched hand. Trembling with cold, she lowered her eyes, knowing that this would make her seem to be ashamed and afraid.

She was both, and her shame was not for being forced to come out of the rock pool and stand naked before strangers. She was ashamed of having to expose her fear for the sake of keeping them off-guard in the hope that Scarecrow would think that this slender, naked girl who reached hesitantly for his hand was completely helpless.

She hoped desperately that she wasn't.

Chapter Fifteen

ISLIEF STOPPED IN THE CENTER OF THE SUNNY PATH. HIS BREATHing hitched—as though the light or warmth stung him—then he squared his bulky shoulders, braced himself to stay where he was. He stood as still as stone.

He *looks* like stone, Joze thought.

A brown rabbit loped onto the path, stopped upwind from them, raised up, nose twitching. It looked right at Islief and, taking him for nothing more dangerous than a tall rock in the path, hopped around him and went on about the business of foraging the tender grass at the side of the trail. Head low, wide-set eyes veiled, Islief did not turn to watch the rabbit as he normally would have. He didn't move.

If Islief breathed, Joze couldn't see even the smallest sign of it. The longer shadows of day's-end slid across his bald head, his pale, grey skin, in the same way they would slide along the sides of a rock. The hair rose, prickling, on the back of Joze's neck.

"Islief," he hissed, "what is it?"

The rabbit, startled, leaped into the brush, and Islief looked up. Wincing, he stepped into the shade at the side of the slender path. In the shadows his eyes gleamed.

"The friend is being followed, Tall. The men smell . . . bad."

A hard knot of fear twisted in Joze's belly. He was certain that Islief wasn't talking about road-dirt and old sweat. He slid his short-sword soundlessly from the sheath at his belt, and Islief pointed to the sun-dappled earth.

The path was narrow, perhaps originally an old deer trail which had been widened over the years by the passage of Elvish hunters following game. The dirt showed three sets of tracks. One was Kicva's, slender footprints with a distance between them which indicated her long, smooth stride. These were the oldest of the tracks, for the breeze had already swept old dry pine needles across them, started to smooth them over. The others were broader, deeper, the edges more sharply defined. They were more recent than Kicva's.

That at least one of them was made by a man, Joze didn't doubt. He didn't have Islief's refined sense of smell to tell him that, but he had eyes to see the dark damp place on the bole of a scaly-barked pine where one had relieved himself. Though the sun shone warmly on the tree, and would have been shining so for some hours, the bark was not yet dry.

Without thinking, Joze started quickly down the path, leaving Islief to scamper to catch up. He'd gone several yards before Islief grabbed his arm.

"Wait, Tall!" He tugged sharply at Joze's arm. "Better for us—and better for the friend—if we go carefully. Not better for the bad-smelling followers if we surprise them, yes?"

His eyes on the place where the path narrowed and seemed to vanish into a wall of brush and thickets, Joze agreed reluctantly that what Islief said made sense.

Islief went out in front, tracking as truly as he'd done before, and Joze followed, trying to see into the dappled gloom on each side of the path, straining his ears to hear every sound. When they'd gone farther still, Islief bent to pick up something from the ground. Joze's heart seemed to wither in his chest when he saw the white and green fletched arrow in Islief's broad hands. He groaned aloud when he saw others, two dozen at least, flung and scattered. The bow and quiver, the little knife Kicva kept hidden beneath her blouse, were not far from the arrows.

In the same moment, a high snarling scream—like a scalded cat's—split the forest's silence.

Kicva broke Scarecrow's wrist over her knee, and with almost the same motion drove that knee upward where it would do the most damage. When he was doubled over, howling with pain, she hit him hard with clasped hands just at the base of the neck. He dropped, motionless, at her feet. She turned swiftly, ready to press her advantage and bring the attack to the older man. But though he was obviously ill, Greil was not slow. He hit her hard, tackled her around the waist, and drove her to the ground. Kicva fell, twisting beneath the man's weight, skinning her knees on the rocks at the pool's edge. Greil's hands were hot and dry where they touched her, as though some fire burned within him.

Cold water lapped at Kicva's chin, mud and water filled her mouth as she struggled to throw off her attacker and gain the water again. Half-raised above her, Greil came down hard again, drove the heels of his hands into her back, blasting the breath from her lungs. The force of his blow ground her face against a rock, but Kicva, who could not breathe, could not feel the pain.

Scarecrow, his face twisted with agony, climbed to his knees, wavered there for a moment staring at his broken wrist, then staggered to his feet. His left wrist held protectively against his chest, he drew a dagger from within his ragged shirt, and though his clothing was shabby, the dagger was not. Intricately carved horn handle inset with semiprecious stones, the dagger's finely honed steel blade gleamed in the old ruddy light of the day.

His eyes flat and dead as a snake's, Scarecrow jerked his chin at his companion, and Greil—coughing now from his exertion, his breath wheezing in his chest with a terrible bubbling noise—staggered away with lurching, sideways steps.

Kicva held herself still, trying to catch back her breath, trying hard to block the terror she felt. She must not panic; she knew she must wait for Scarecrow to come close again. What her knee did before, her fist could do now.

"Nice work, Greil," Scarecrow panted.

An expression of distaste flickered briefly across Greil's face, then vanished. He turned, then suddenly spun back again, his rheumy eyes wide with panic. Before he could warn against what had frightened him, Kicva saw Scarecrow jerk upright, saw his hands—even the broken one—grab at his chest.

In the same moment, Greil fell to his knees, coughing with terrible wracking sounds. He crumpled to the ground and did not move. But Scarecrow made no noise at all when he collapsed again, one of Kicva's green and white fletched arrows in his back.

Fear ached like ice water in his veins when Joze surveyed the glade. The rangy thin man who had been crouched over Kicva was dead; his companion—though no bolt had struck him—had fallen into a heap of collapsed limbs.

Kicva lay between the two as though she, too, were dead . . . washed naked and killed on the mud-churned edge of the rock pool.

The quick breeze of twilight hissed in the brush, ruffled the pool's dark water with its cool breath, slid across Kicva's wet skin. It must have been cold, but she didn't move. Joze would have believed that she was dead were it not for her eyes, wide and glittering, and staring at him as though he were not a friend but another deadly threat.

Images from nightmare whispered around Joze like waves lapping at the sea-edge. He flung the bow aside, began to cross the glade, when Islief stopped him.

"No," Islief said. His voice sounded like sand drifting. "Wait, Tall."

Joze pulled away, and the light in Islief's eyes flared, almost to anger. Far back in his throat, Islief made a low, growling sound.

Joze had heard that sound once before, in the forest when he'd reached beneath Kicva's blouse to find and take the little knife she'd had hidden in her smallclothes.

"Islief—what—?"

Islief put himself squarely in Joze's path. "Give me your shirt."

Glancing over Islief's shoulder, Joze saw Kicva gather herself slowly to sit, arms wrapped around drawn-up knees, knees all skinned and bleeding. Her protective gesture made Joze realize suddenly that she was naked.

It wasn't that he hadn't noticed before now that she was without clothing—how could he *not* have noticed her long, tanned legs, the whiter curve of her hips, her slender waist? But he hadn't been thinking about that until now. He'd been thinking about saving her life, hoping desperately that, though he hadn't used a bow since the days before the war, he was still a good shot.

But now, now he was watching the old red sunlight gild the scar that pointed down from Kicva's collarbone to her breasts.

Islief punched his arm, ungently, and Joze hastily lowered his eyes. He pulled off his shirt and handed it over, then cast around the glade, saw Kicva's blouse torn in two, the rest of her clothing carelessly scattered. Feeling suddenly awkward, he went to gather up what was not damaged.

Kicva's boots in one hand, her smallclothes in the other, and the tanned breeches over his arm, Joze saw that Kicva had pulled on his shirt and stood now at the edge of the rock pool. The shirt hung loosely on her, came to mid-thigh. Her back was to him, and Joze saw other scars, the shallow trail of an arrow along the back of her left thigh, the shorter mark of a knife or dagger halfway down her right calf. And he saw the soft skin along the sides of her knees, scraped raw only a little while ago and still bleeding.

Joze was confused, caught between the respect he'd have felt for any soldier with honorable badges of courage like Kicva's, and the startling, sweet-aching desire to gather her into his arms and soothe her hurts, the old and the new. He wished suddenly, fiercely, that Elvish women would stay at home—where all sensible women belonged!—and not go running off into the wild forest to be hunter-scouts and soldiers.

As though she felt him watching, Kicva turned, her long eyes narrowed. "You have a bad habit of staring," she said icily.

Joze cleared his throat awkwardly, muttered an apology, and made to approach her. Again Islief stopped him.

"Tall," he said, "we did not take all of the friend's arrows from the woods. Go make them neat in the quiver and fetch them back."

And I suppose I should take my time about it, Joze thought. But aloud he only said, "All right," left Kicva's clothes on the ground and went to do as he was bidden.

He did take his time, and returned to the glade just as the first pale stars studded the purple sky. Kicva and Islief were sitting at the water's edge, working hard at something. When Joze went to look, the Elven glared at him, but Islief held up a piece of white linen, a thin undershirt, and said that they were washing the friend's clothes.

Joze, who didn't even dimly understand why they were doing that, made himself busy again. He removed the bodies of the two dead men, dragged them far into the woods and upwind so that carrion eaters wouldn't need follow the scent of meat through or around the glade. He didn't look at the tall thin man; he was not one who liked to look at the faces of the men he killed. But he did examine the older man, the one who was dead though no arrow had killed him. That one's face had a strange blue tint, and blood fouled his patchy greying beard. Even now, lifeless, the man's body emanated the fierce heat of sickness. Shuddering, Joze wiped his hands down the sides of his breeches, then wiped them again.

"We might as well camp here," Joze said. He glanced up at the waxing moon hanging sweetly in the darkened sky, framed by the trees ringing the glade. "Doesn't make sense to travel farther tonight."

Islief agreed, but Kicva—glowering at Joze—said that she'd sooner make camp in a wolf's den than here.

Joze wished she'd said something about that before he'd done all the work of dragging the corpses out of the glade, but he kept silent, leaving the matter to Islief, who seemed to have found a rapport with the Elven.

At least, Joze thought resentfully, *she doesn't snap Islief's head off every time he draws breath to speak to her.*

Even so, it was a time before Islief could get Kicva to agree that Tall was right, they needed to make camp now. He suggested that everyone's purposes would be served if they simply removed to the other side of the rock pool.

"Fine with me," Joze said, shrugging. "Does that suit you, hunter-scout?"

The Elven gave Joze a hard look, then shouldered past him. Joze thought she was going to walk ahead, but she didn't. She stepped to the edge of the rock pool and dove into the water, struck out for the other side.

Joze watched her swimming, watched the reach and stretch of her arms and the way his shirt, soaked and heavy, clung to her hips and slender thighs.

"What's the matter with her, Islief? She carries on like *I* was the one who'd attacked her—instead of being the one who rescued her."

"Can you not understand, Tall?" Islief asked as he gathered up Kicva's clothes.

"Well—" Joze gestured over his shoulder, vaguely in the direction where the Elven's attackers lay. "She's had a scare, but . . . she's all right now."

Islief looked at him as though he'd expected a different answer. "Come along, Tall. We still need to find a place to stay on the other side. And we need to find supper and firewood."

Kicva was not interested in supper. She did not leave the water when Joze called to her that Islief had gotten a fire started, did not even look their way when the cool night breeze carried the aroma of roasting woodcock out over the water. She stayed in the water for a long time, past the point when Joze was certain she'd freeze to death. Time and again, she dove deep, rose up to twist in the water, graceful and sleek as an otter, and dove again.

"What's she doing, Islief?"

"She is getting clean, Tall."

"Clean? You'd think she'd be bleached by now." He reached out to turn over the Elven's clothes, spread near the fire for drying. The tanned breeches were only warming, but her smallclothes were yet damp.

They were very pretty, those undergarments: a thin white undershirt of fine linen which was—unexpectedly—laced in front with pale green ribbons. Joze looked at the second piece of clothing. Breeches seemed too rough a word to apply to these, though breeches they certainly were. These, too, were trimmed with green ribbons, ribbons at the waist and stitched down the length of each leg. These last seemed to have no function beyond decoration. Joze imagined that these pretty breeches would reach to only mid-thigh.

"Are the friend's clothes dry, Tall?" Islief asked, looking at him sideways.

"No," Joze answered evenly. "They're not."

"Ah," Islief said, then said no more.

The night breeze was cool; April in these northern woodlands did not make warm nights. Joze edged closer to the fire, for he missed his shirt. Wide-set eyes glowing with amusement, Islief suggested that Joze get some sleep.

"We all must talk together in the morning, Tall. It will be better to do that when you have slept." He gestured to Kicva, rising again from the water. Moonlight dazzled on her wet hair and skin, Joze's shirt hugged her tightly. "And when the friend is feeling cleaner."

Joze said that he supposed this was so, and saying no more, he stretched himself out before the fire. He was, on one hand, certain that he wouldn't sleep for the sounds of Kicva's splashing in the icy rock pool; on the other hand, certain that if he did sleep, he'd be visiting the land of nightmare again.

Neither was the case. He slept at once and dreamed of green things; of sun sparkling on new leaves; of delicate green ribbons; of the Emerald as he'd seen it in Crown Hold, pulsing with the light of torches as though it were a heart beating.

Kicva left the water when she was certain that Joze was asleep, moments after Islief had come to the edge of the pool and said that he believed it would be best now to come back. She hadn't answered him, for the first reply that had leaped to her lips was a surly one. She hadn't wanted to speak to him that way, for she'd been glad to see him with Joze. And when he'd seen her earlier today, frightened and shivering, Islief had been friendly and kind, neither asking questions nor standing around staring.

Islief it was who'd suggested that she'd feel better for having washed her clothes, and she'd worked at the washing for lack of anything better to do while waiting for her hands to stop trembling, her heart to stop quaking. And in the end, Islief had been proven right: She'd at least calmed enough so that she could speak without wanting to sob. But just now she could find no agreeable words in her, so she kept silent, only nodded, and then watched Islief go into the woods.

She hurried to the fire, and after she'd made certain that Joze, stretched out on his belly, face turned from the fire's light, slept soundly, Kicva peeled off his wet shirt and stood as near the fire as she dared. Rubbing her arms and legs, sloughing water from her, she tried to get warm and as dry as possible before she dressed again.

When she'd pulled on smallclothes and breeches and boots, she saw that there was yet a whole roasted woodcock warming on a flat rock near the flames. By the time she'd finished her meal, Islief was back, slipping silently from the deep dark beneath the forest's eaves. He walked wide around Joze, careful not to disturb him, and went to sit opposite Kicva at the fire.

"Are you better now, Friend?"

She nodded.

"All clean and dry?"

Kicva smiled, eased by the fire's warmth, and the memory of the simple kindness Islief had shown her in these last few hours. "All clean and dry, Islief."

"But still very angry, yes?"

"No—of course not."

"Not angry?" Islief cocked his head. "But, Friend, those men did not mean you well. They—"

Kicva laughed hollowly. "They surely didn't. But there's no need to go on about it. Forget it. I'm fine. I'm just fine."

Islief looked as though he wanted to say something more, but he let the matter go. "Where is Tall's shirt?"

At the mention of Joze, a thread of irritation ran through Kicva's new feeling of well-being. She reached behind her for the shirt, held the sodden muddy thing at arm's length, then tossed it in the general direction of the sleeping man.

"Ah, Friend," Islief said, "someone is going to want that shirt dry." Islief retrieved the shirt, spread it out to dry near the flames. "Maybe *you* will want it to be dry in the morning."

Joze stirred in his sleep, turned onto his back. Firelight gleamed red in his dark beard, orange on his sun-browned face. He raised his arm to cover his eyes, never waking, and Kicva saw shadows sliding along his wide shoulders, showing muscles in relief beneath tanned skin.

He looks like a farmer or a smith, she thought. *Only farmers and smiths have shoulders that wide, arms that strong. Wielding hammers or wrestling with stubborn plough horses . . .*

"It is a hard thing when feelings get jossed and janglesome, isn't it, Friend?"

Kicva shrugged, admitted nothing. But unbidden came the memory of how good Joze's rough cotton shirt had felt when she'd slipped it on. It had fit her like a tunic, still warm from his own body, with the smell of him—smoke and sweat and the deep mysterious scent that was peculiarly a man's—lingering in the fabric. That warmth, that scent, had almost dispelled the cold creeping along her skin, the loathsome feel of Greil's fevered touch.

No shirt of Aidan's would have smelled like Joze's. Mage Aidan's clothes smelled clean, windblown, with only the faintest traces of the enigmatic odors of mage-work clinging: incense and arcane combinings of herbs and earths. Any shirt of slender Aidan's would have hardly covered her decently, would have left her shivering and cold.

And so, for a brief moment, Kicva had felt that she could hide in Joze's big loose shirt, and no one would know that she'd been so wretchedly, helplessly terrified of hideous Scarecrow. And then she'd looked around, found Joze staring as though he'd seen right through her to her very heart still cravenly shaking with fear.

"I don't want Joze's shirt," Kicva snapped.

Islief resumed his seat, pointedly not looking at her attire, breeches and boots and thin linen undershirt. "Well, well, Friend. Maybe you will want it tomorrow. Or maybe Tall will. So best we dry it, yes?"

"As you will," Kicva said.

Then she excused herself and went to the edge of the rock pool to find a place to sleep where she could hear the water lapping, for she knew that the gentle sound would lull her to sleep. She was very tired, weary and aching. She hoped to dream of Aidan, who waited for her to return to Verdant Hall. She hoped that her dreams would flow with memory's echo of the River Altha running past Verdant Hall.

But, though the water in the rock pool whispered soothingly, Kicva was a long time falling to sleep. Earlier in the evening, she'd heard Islief tell Joze that they all must talk in the morning. No doubt about the search for the Hunter-Defender's daughter, Kicva thought now. And no doubt Joze will want to go straight to Damris to lay the matter before his own king.

Strong in her rose the conviction that this was not a matter for the Mannish king to decide. This was about one of the lost Jewels of Elvish, and so it did not concern foreign kings at all. But she would not try to convince Joze of that. And he and Islief could talk all they wanted to, it wouldn't matter: She would simply let them go their own way, and she would go hers.

So determined, she fell asleep at last. And she did dream, but not of her betrothed or of her home. Her dreams were hazy, ill-defined. They carried no real impression but that of the comfortable scent of Joze's shirt.

Chapter Sixteen

DAIL KNELT AT THE EDGE OF THE POND, LISTENED TO THE TWO horses snorting and stamping in the grove. The pied gelding was restless, the brown mare impatient to begin the day's journey. High in the forest's leafy eaves redstarts and chickadees, warblers and woodlarks racketed. Not an arm's reach away from where Dail knelt, a tiny grey water shrew left the tall grasses at the edge of the misty pool and rose up on its hind legs, blinking rapidly in the new light of the day.

From behind him, Dail heard the campfire snap as flame found pockets of sap in the wood, heard Aidan suck his breath between his teeth, hissing. He didn't have to look to know that Aidan had burned his fingers again. The Elf-King's Mage was much better at summoning magic to make fire than crafting it with flint and steel striker. He burned fingers or wrist every time, and last night he'd come perilously near to setting his shirt on fire. Clearly the Elf had seldom had to bother with building or tending fires before now, and Dail considered his insistence on learning to make fire the hard way a waste of time. But Aidan only said that he didn't like to turn away any knowledge.

Dail looked out over the rosy dawn mist rising from the still pool, then, wincing, peered through the mist to find his reflection on the water's surface. He scratched his jaw and wished fervently that he hadn't shaved his beard. The new growth itched, and the dark stubble was chased with more silver than he'd expected to see. He had no means of shaving again unless he wanted to scrape the keen edge of a dagger over un-soaped skin. He didn't want to do that. Itch and disconcerting grey, he'd have to get used to these again.

In the pool, a barely seen shadow beneath mist and water, a brown trout wandered lazily out from beneath the overhanging bank. With a sudden hard thrust, the fish rose in a surprising leap, its sides flashing silver as it broke the water's surface. A long slim hand arrowed past Dail's shoulder, snatched the trout at the arc of its leap.

Dail jerked around, startled, and glared at the mage. The fish wriggled desperately in Aidan's hands, its mouth gaping. But it would not regain the water, for Aidan knew how to hold it lightly in the cage of his fingers. To grasp or squeeze would have sent the slippery trout shooting back into the pool.

"Mage," Dail said from between clenched teeth, "you really want to stop sneaking up on me like that."

Aidan shrugged an apology, then nodded to the gasping fish in his hands. "I didn't want it to get away."

Smoke from the newly roused campfire drifted on the dawn breeze, slid across the pool to mingle with the mist. A spotted woodpecker hammered insistently on the trunk of a nearby oak.

"Shall I call another fish?" Aidan asked. "Or do you think one is enough for breakfast?"

"One's enough," Dail said evenly. "I'm not hungry."

Aidan shrugged again and went to wrap the trout in broad leaves and prepare it for baking on the flat rock which had been heated in the embers of the fire all night. Dail watched him for a moment, then got to his feet and went to saddle and bridle the horses. As he spoke quietly to the beasts, he found that he was yet thinking about Aidan.

He was a strange fellow, the Elf-King's Mage. His strangeness hadn't to do with the magic he used so casually. The calling of trout to breakfast, the shadowless blue hand-fire he made to light their way through the dark parts of the forest, even the way he listened to birds singing or squirrels gossiping for news of the woodlands were small magics compared with the raging sorceries Dail had seen worked at the end of the Ruby War. Mage Aidan's strangeness had to do with a disharmony between his distant politeness and an undeniable sense that for all his cool demeanor he, through some agency the bard did not understand, knew more about Dail than Dail himself had told him.

And yes, Dail thought as he slipped the plaited leather bridle over the head of Aidan's gelding, *I've a reputation—even in Elflands, they sing my songs. And so there's much Aidan could know about me, and a lot more that Dekar could have told him.* Still, that couldn't account for the sure knowledge Dail sometimes saw in the Elf's long, canted eyes. In Mage Aidan's company Dail felt as though he'd shared large secrets and small, but had somehow forgotten the occasion of the sharing.

That was one strange thing about the Elf-King's Mage. The other was that he spoke about the Deities—so long forgotten among Dail's countrymen as to be little more than lifeless names in oaths or curses—as though they were familiars. Hearing him speak thus, Dail came to understand that Aidan and his Elvish kin had managed to keep hold of a sense of wonder and perception of the spiritual that Dail hadn't even known his own people had lost.

So thinking, the bard finished saddling the horses and went to sit near the fire while Aidan had his breakfast. He listened stonily to Aidan's words of thanks to the Deity he sometimes called Irthe and other times called Aerd, before he freed the trout from its leaf wrapping and ate. Dail wondered if he'd ever learn the reason why these gods of Aidan's seemed to have two names.

Then he put aside his wondering, reached past *Dashlaftholeh* snug in her case for the leather pouch which contained the maps Aidan had brought with them. At the same moment, Aidan—with the expression of one who does a thing while thinking about something else—picked up the case, rifled through the maps it contained, and handed him a folded parchment.

"This one," he said absently. "It shows the best way to Lindens Lee."

It was the very map Dail had been thinking of, the one which showed the lands along the northern length of the Altha where the river shouldered to the west and widened, running fast and hard as though to find extra strength in order to feed the Landbound Sea.

"Lindens Lee?" the bard asked, trying not to let his annoyance show. Had the mage read his mind? "What's Lindens Lee?"

"A village, a small one. But they know about the mountains there. Sometimes they are called the Stone-Elves, because of all Dekar's folk only these build with stone and not wood. When you want to know about the mountains, it's probably best to go talk to the folk who live there. If we are lucky, we'll be there in three days."

Dail grunted, a noncommittal sound that was barely acknowledgment.

Aidan sat lonely as he ate his breakfast. He watched Dail studying the map and tried to wrap himself in silence and the kind of solitude which had once been so easy to maintain but was no longer so. The maxim had it that there was magic even in the least skilled of bards; magic of the kind even the most masterful of mages did not possess. That old saying was likely heavy-freighted with bard's hyperbole—surely no proud mage would have coined it!—but Aidan thought he could attest to its having some truth.

Be it enchantment or music's allure, spells or poetry's beguiling, a bard carried about him the same kind of deceptively simple magic a polished silver mirror did: the magic of reflection. In his songs a bard shows the world what he has seen; displays visions of himself, visions of those around him. This was a Deity's grace, the gift of the god who was called Chant, the goddess named Ylf. This was a bard's best skill.

And a mage's best skill, Aidan reminded himself, was invisibility; the protecting silence; the neutral and uninviting expression; the quiet movements which would bring no unwanted attention.

But it was hard to be invisible in front of a mirror, Aidan thought as he chewed a breakfast gone suddenly tasteless. Hard to avoid peering into it to see what could be seen. Harder still to avoid looking into *this* mirror, this one which he'd so often and so secretly looked into before now.

What scrying had shown Aidan of this bard's soul uncovered the kind of hunger Aidan felt in his own spirit. They each yearned for that which could not be had—worse, for that which should not even be dreamed of.

Ah, that bard, Aidan thought, *who like could have any woman he turned his smile upon, dreams hungrily of a woman he must not love. And I, who have worked magics Dekar's mages have not the strength for, dealt in powers they have not the skill for—I long secretly for a chance at the kind of power I dare not name.*

Suddenly frightened at having come so close to acknowledging his dangerous dreams of power, his powerful dreams of danger, Aidan tried to fill his mind, his heart, with prayers to the Deity of Magic.

Chant! Oh, Ylf—please! It is not mine to do! Please help me see that it is not mine to do!

Yet, even as he prayed, there was a part of him—treacherously weak—that wished Dail would stop poring over the map, wished that the bard would give voice to a chant, a ballad, perhaps one of the Aeylin-songs he'd heard Dekar play throughout the winter.

And so, as he watched Dail, Aidan both wished that the bard would lay aside the map for the harp, and was deeply grateful that Dail did not.

For it is true, Mage Aidan thought—that thought still a prayer to the god Chant and the goddess Ylf—*it is true that did he sing the smallest line, pluck the softest minor chord of melancholy, did he make me feel even once more how he loved Dekar's daughter, this mad idea of mine, this hidden harbored secret, would find a reason to spring to life in me. And I don't know how I would find the strength to do anything but enact it were that to happen.*

• • •

Joze woke alone, to a breakfast of cold woodcock and the sound of Islief and Kicva in disagreement. While he ate, he listened to them as they talked together in the shadows. Islief's voice was always calm, a soft sound like sand gently sighing. Kicva's rose in anger, lowered mutinously, then finally grated as though she forced her words from between clenched teeth.

That must be agreement of some sort, Joze thought sourly. He massaged his temples, tried to smooth away a headache. *Likely teeth-clenched is as close to agreeable as that one gets.*

Islief came to the edge of the shadows, gestured for Joze to join them. Joze went reluctantly, feeling mutinous himself. He stood stiffly, not looking at the hunter-scout longer than it took to notice that she was still wearing his shirt. He made himself listen silently as Islief told him that Kicva had agreed to guide them as far south as Verdant Hall.

"Then, Tall, we must decide."

Joze eyed Islief warily. "Decide what?"

"Whether we wish to accompany the friend to her king, or go onward to the city where the Hunter-Defender lives."

"Go to Dekar? What does this have to do with the Elf-King?"

Islief drew breath to answer, but Kicva overrode him. "It has everything to do with Dekar," she said. "Nikia is his daughter—"

"And the wife of the Prince of Mannish."

Kicva imperiously ignored him. "And the Emerald is one of the lost Jewels of Elvish. As the Ruby was ours, so is the Emerald. Dekar will decide how this is to be managed." She smiled with false sweetness. "And so you see, Joze, you won't have to worry about becoming a child-thief after all. Dekar will manage both his daughter and his Emerald."

Joze glanced at Islief, and when Islief made no move to refute this absurd claim of ownership, he said, "Hunter-scout, I think Islief's Lady would disagree with you. That Emerald belongs to her."

"Oh, yes," Kicva said, still using that patently false sweetness. "And Islief's Lady is Aeylin. And Aeylin was—is—Elvish. So, for that matter, is your prince's wife."

"Pity my poor prince," he muttered.

Kicva ignored that, too. "So even *you* must see that this is wholly an Elvish matter. Dekar will decide how best to handle it." She brushed past him, then after a few strides turned and said impatiently: "If we want to make Lindens Lee by nightfall, we won't do it standing around here."

Joze opened his mouth to argue again, but Islief laid a hand on his arm.

"Peace, now, Tall. We have our guide."

"Yes, but we don't want to go to Verdant Hall. We need to get to Damris. Islief, no matter what Kicva says about the Elf-King, we can't waste time."

"I know it, Tall." Islief shrugged his bulky shoulders. "But for now, we are going to Lindens Lee."

"What's Lindens Lee?"

"The friend says it is a village."

"What do we need to go there for?"

Islief smiled for the first time that day, his wide-set eyes glowing. "Horses, so we can get to where we need to go faster."

"Well, that would be good luck," Joze muttered. "And it would cut the time I have to spend with that woman by half." He watched Kicva pacing restlessly in the path. "She's not very good company, Islief."

And as he followed Islief around the edge of the clearing, he wondered how matters had come to this end, wondered how it was that every word he spoke to the Elven was delivered like a challenge.

What had happened to the sweet-aching sense he'd felt in the forest that first day, that feeling that he'd come upon a fair pretty flower?

Joze sighed. Kicva had turned out to be no fair flower. She'd proven herself a briar, all twisty and hard to follow, full of stinging thorns. He cocked an eye at the sun just topping the tall trees in the east. It was going to be a long day. He wiped sweat from his forehead, massaged his aching temples again. And likely a hot one.

Chapter Seventeen

DAIL HAD LOST HIS SENSE OF TIME PASSING. EACH DAY IN THE Elfland forest was much like another—rosy dawns, misty midmornings, sunny afternoons, cool purple twilights which lasted till dawn. And sometimes, like a blessing, rain fell; the soft cool rain that Dail had longed for all through Damris' unnaturally hot winter and brutal spring. But none of this sameness made a way to count time passing, and so his journey had taken on the seeming of unreality, an endless passage through greening woodlands—a timeless voyage through the landscapes of his own winter-dreams as he and the Elf-King's Mage followed the Altha north.

Came a morning when the dream ended, a morning when, disoriented by the feeling that he'd lost track of time, Dail asked bluntly how many days had passed since they'd left the Elf-King's hall. As though this were the most reasonable of questions, Aidan said that they were now only a day's ride from Lindens Lee: three weeks gone from Verdant Hall.

That would put this day in May's first week, Dail thought, wondering again how he could so completely lose track of time.

"Likely," Aidan said, "we'll not see the lights over the forest tonight. Likely we'll have true dark tonight and not the endless twilight. For that light of magic doesn't extend over all the realm."

When Dail asked why this was so, the mage shrugged.

"Bard, that light over Verdant Hall is like a sheen of sweat on a man using his every effort. Dekar's mages try to hold back the land-sickness from the forests and seek for a cure, both. But sooner or later, their strength will run out. The rainbow light—the Elf-light, as you say—is no healing-light. I need the Emerald for that, yes?"

"You need it?"

Aidan smiled mildly. "So that I can bring it to Dekar for his daughter to use."

"And do you think," Dail said carefully, "that Nikia will be able to use the Emerald as she once used the Ruby?"

Aidan rode silently for a while, then said stiffly: "Bard, I think it would be a hard thing to have to ask the Princess to risk again what she risked then."

"You know what kind of power those Jewels offer?"

"I am a mage," Aidan said. He smiled coolly. "None knows better. Yes, I think the Princess could use the Jewel, but I think it's too bad that she'll have to. No one should have to refuse godhood twice."

"But you don't mind asking her to take the risk again."

Aidan did not smile then. "I'm just sent to fetch the Emerald. You will be the one to do the asking, bard."

Dail drew a sharp breath. "Me? You're wrong, Aidan. Dekar's going to do that. He knows I won't ask Nikia to take the risk again."

"Dekar's gotten you to come this far, hasn't he? I know this:

He has the feeling that while his daughter might well refuse him, she won't refuse you if you come asking with the Jewel in your hand. You and she are . . . good friends, aren't you?"

Dail carefully ignored Aidan's pause before the words "good friends." For the rest, the mage's words had the ring of truth. A truth which Dail hadn't wanted to consider when he'd agreed to ride north in search of the Emerald.

Of course crafty Dekar would not do the asking himself. His daughter was not the innocent she'd been when the Elf-King had sent her into foreign lands to marry a stranger. She'd learned a thing or two in the years past, and one of those things was how to say her father no. But Dekar was gambling now that Nikia would not refuse Dail should he come asking for magic.

You and she are . . . good friends.

Dail felt as though he was both betrayed and betrayer. And yet he knew that there was, in truth, very little difference between being the man to fetch back the Emerald and being the man to ask Nikia to use it.

Still, he did not answer Aidan. He tried to keep his face expressionless, as he thought—all the while wondering whether the Elf-King's Mage knew what he was feeling—that Nikia surely *wouldn't* refuse him. Because he wasn't going to ask her to risk soul and self again in an attempt to use the untamed magic of one of those lost Jewels. Dekar would have to do his own asking.

Yet this remained: What chance did Nikia or anyone else have if she did not use the Emerald to heal the land so badly damaged by the Sorcerer's last spell? Unless she called the Emerald's magic, Nikia, like every other woman, man, and child, would soon die of hunger.

Nikia is the strongest among us.

Calmis had said that in another context, but Dail believed that his friend's estimation held true here and now.

And the strongest, he thought, *the best, the fairest, are always chosen for sacrifice. And the ones who offer up the sacrifice? The ones who offer sacrifice, of course, are the weakest.*

Dail laughed bitterly, such a sound as to make Aidan flinch.

The Elf Brys walked for a while in the noonday sun, head low and heading east away from the River Altha, north, away from Lindens Lee. Though the air was fragrant with the aged scent of old bracken, Brys breathed only shallowly. He made no good speed, covered no great distance. It was hard walking. His knees and the joints between foot and leg ached terribly. He felt the pain even in his toes, as though the small joints had become filled with sharp-toothed ice.

But he walked on, and kept his eyes on the path, though the relentless throbbing headache made it hard to see. Weaker now than when he'd set out this morning, he was afraid that if he stumbled and fell, he might not be able to get up again. And the raspberry patches were a ways into the forest. Sick, he was; too weak to hunt, too weak to fish. But he needed food.

Brys walked, lurching a little now, and tried as hard as he could not to think about the pain in his legs and feet, the cold aching in his elbows and shoulders, wrists and fingers. The gentle air of springtime felt like fire on his skin, hurt his lungs when he breathed. He felt as though his chest had somehow shrunk, his lungs shriveled. He was afraid that soon he would no longer be able to take in air or squeeze out breath.

His throat tightened with dread, and he prayed all the Deities that he didn't have the sickness. But he didn't know how it could be otherwise: Brys was sixteen and he felt very old, as though he'd come to the end of his days.

Stone-Elves . . .

Dail thought that the village looked like little more than tumbled boulders, massive stones rolled down the hillside and left to lie where they'd stopped. Beyond, the ground was flat, billowing with plumed sedges and sweetly green reeds, a whispering, waving border between the tumbled stones and the Altha, whose water ran blue-silver as a legend's eyes. But the boulders—surely they made no village?

Aidan touched his arm, then pointed to the wide, tall stones. "Do you see the circles, bard? They're hard to make out from this angle; it's better if you're standing higher, but look hard."

Dail squinted. And then, cued by Aidan's suggestion, he saw the circles made by the boulders. Seeing that, it was as though the whole pattern of the place suddenly revealed itself. A broad, loosely laid outer circle of stone, a smaller, neater inner circle.

"Where are the buildings?" he asked. "Where are the houses?"

Aidan pointed to the boulders again.

"Beyond that wall?"

"No, the stones are no wall. They are the buildings and the houses. From here they look like boulders. But they are not. When we come closer, you will see that these 'boulders' have windows and doors." Aidan smiled tolerantly. "And you will hear the folk brag about how cool their homes are in summer, how warm in winter. The boasting is worth bearing, bard, for when it is done, you will get hospitality worthy of a song-making."

Aidan urged his pied gelding down the slope, and so Dail let his next question go unasked. Undoubtedly they'd see plenty of people once they'd gotten into the village proper.

They did; men, women and children. But none of them was alive, and the late afternoon sun sitting heavily on the village made the corpses reek. The wind, light-voiced and sweet in the forest, sounded like banshees howling in the streets of the Stone-Elves' Lindens Lee.

Brys leaned against the slender linden tree, pressed his back against the rough bark. His face ran with sweat, yet he shivered uncontrollably. His breath bubbled in his lungs and he coughed, a racking spasm that felt like knives in his lungs. He wiped the blood from his lips, and staring at the red flecks on his fingers, he remembered the strangers who had wandered into Lindens Lee at winter's end. They'd come looking for shelter from cold rains.

Mannish, they'd claimed to be hunters, and so the elders of the village had granted them hospitality. And it had been good hospitality—fine food, shelter and company. The elders knew that folk from the hungry lands had been given permission to hunt in the forests, and it was always the way with the folk of Lindens Lee to say: What Dekar in his southern forests can offer, the Stone-Elves can better.

But these two strangers were not of a mind to appreciate hospitality. One of the Men had been tall and rangy, with yellow hair, narrow eyes and disdainfully curled lip. He'd had the look of the thief about him, and had proven himself such: In the morning a valuable dagger had been missing from the home of the elder who had hosted him. The other, his companion, had been smaller in stature, and as thin. Balding and rheumy-eyed, that one; and he'd been so often taken with violent coughing that he could not speak even a full sentence. Brys had heard him coughing all through the night, for his parents had been this sick man's host. And once, in the late watches, Brys had gone to bring the man water and seen blood on his lips.

Afraid, he'd left the water where the man could reach it and backed out of the room. It was as though he could smell death in the room, and he hadn't wanted to be near when the dark-eyed Deity came to claim the man. What passed between mortals and Diwan-Deyja in the last moments of life was best left private.

But the Deity of Death had not taken the sick man in the night. The man had left with his companion at dawn, lurching as he walked, coughing terribly. And though the tall man had been a thief, the short man had left something behind: his sickness.

Not all folk fell sick at once, and the young and strong stayed well for a time longer than infants and old people. Still, the sickness had crept, unstopped, through Lindens Lee like ice inexorably stealing across the river's surface. Brys had helped with the sick folk, then tended the dying for more than a month, until the last of them was gone, leaving him to wonder how it could be that he was the only one the sickness had passed by. Now, alone and afraid, he knew that just as the plague could strike fast, so could it hide in a man; crafty and silent and lurking for weeks before it sprang.

Brys coughed again, gagging on mucus and blood, and sank to his knees. He did not try to rise again. What use to try to find food? Food was for those who hoped to live. Brys did not believe that he had more than a few hours of life left to him. And so, because he was very tired now, he stretched himself out on the ground, blessed the welcoming bed of old soft leaves there under the tree, and waited for Diwan-Deyja to come whispering his name.

Chapter Eighteen

AS THOUGH HE WERE UTTERLY ALONE—AS THOUGH SOUNDS OF horses stamping restlessly, Dail's ragged breathing, were not sounds at all—Aidan prayed to the Deity of Fire. His voice rang strongly down the stony hillside as he greeted the god Vuyer, chanted a hymn to the goddess Fyr. His eyes soft-focused, vision inner-focused, he did not see silent, dead Lindens Lee below. Nor did he see the sunlight shining on the Altha's still water beyond. He saw his prayers stretching out on the air before him.

"Warm Vuyer, hear me," the Elf whispered. "Bold Fyr, see me. I ask in the names of those whose voices are forever stilled. Lend them your wide wings, Vuyer. Give your bright shelter, Fyr, to the dead."

The prayer hummed like an echo around the hilltop. Unformed, colorless images drifted like fragile gossamer in the motionless air; an invocation waiting for Vuyer-Fyr to choose whether to fulfill it.

The air stirred. A breeze grew, and then a small warm wind. Sunlight slanted low and red across the Altha, tipping wind-called wavelets with gold the color of flame. Aidan felt the light of crimson sunset warm on his face, on the palms of his uplifted hands. Eyes yet on the frail threads, the shimmering manifestation of his prayer, he held his breath, waiting. He heard his heart beating, heard the hissing of his blood racing through his veins, heard a rumbling in the air.

Came a broken sound of breath being hard sucked in, a sound of fear from Dail behind him. Aidan did not turn, did not look. The wind became still. The ghostly, drifting half-images of his prayer, thin lines of need-fueled energy, hung in the air above silent Lindens Lee. And the sun, dropping lower in the west, lent them light. The images, the lines, the threads of need and prayer quickened with color, gleamed red-gold.

Dail let his breath go, made a hard, painful, choking sound. Aidan only remembered this later. He had no time for the bard's fear: In another instant, in the space between this heartbeat and the next, the fragile images of a prayer granted would fall to earth, the boon unaccepted.

Gently, as though offering a resting place to some timid weightless butterfly, Aidan reached out his hands, gathered the lines of power which had a moment ago been prayer, braided the red-gold strands around the silver threads of his magic, wove a spell.

Kicva smelled the Altha well before she saw it. The river's fragrance filled the air, made earth-scent richer. In the past days, tall pines had fallen away before a march of linden trees as she and her friends went ever southward. The birds of the forestlands, woodlarks and stonechats, were replaced by sedge warblers and reed buntings who loved the riverside. In the sunny gaps between the trees butterburs, golden saxifrage and sweet-flax were more to be seen than the violets and bellflowers and enchanter's nightshade of the highlands.

She watched Islief as he walked in the shadows, his wide-set eyes gleaming with delight as a flock of purple-winged butterflies whirled up from a sweep of golden primrose. Aeylin had said that he'd lived through centuries, condemned to wait. *How long has it been*, Kicva wondered, *since Islief had gone abroad in the world?*

Kicva shuddered, thinking about the burden all those many years must represent. But the chill died aborning as Islief raised his head to smile at her. His was a strange smile, because his face was all craggy and grey as rock. When he smiled, it looked like a piece of stone moving. And yet there was a warmhearted gentleness about Islief that had nothing to do with rock and stone. Kicva could well imagine that the Lady Aeylin had found him to be a good friend, then all the long years ago.

Kicva glanced over her shoulder, looked for Joze, who had been following. He was nowhere in sight.

"Where'd he go?" she muttered, scanning the path and the woods to either side.

Islief pointed to the west.

Kicva noted the length of the shadows, the color of the light. "The day's getting old," she said impatiently. "I wish he'd stay with us."

Islief shrugged. "Maybe he has something to do, Friend. And—"

But Kicva didn't hear the rest of what Islief said. A crashing came from the west, nearby, like something heavy running through the undergrowth. Islief raised his head, eyes suddenly huge with alarm. Fitting arrow to bowstring with the speed of long practice, Kicva stepped deliberately in front of Islief, bow ready.

And had no reason to use it.

Joze, face pale above his black beard, breathing hard, shouldered his way through the brush, tripped over a maple's twisted root, and stumbled into the path.

"By the Seven!" Kicva gasped. "What's wrong?"

Breathless, he pointed back over his shoulder. "Back there—hurry!"

"What?"

He grabbed her arm, pulled her off the path and into the darkness beneath the trees. "Don't argue with me, Kicva; he doesn't have time."

"*Who* doesn't—?"

But Joze didn't waste further breath, only held tight to her wrist and pulled her along in his wake. When she looked over her shoulder, Kicva saw that Islief was gone, vanished from the shade at the side of the path as though he'd never been there. Then she didn't have time to think about Islief, for Joze stopped suddenly and Kicva saw why he'd come running so hard to find her.

But she thought that they'd come too late, she thought that the young Elf was only a breath or two away from his last.

Joze went down on his knees, lifted the Elf in his arms. But the Elf did not move. His dark lank hair trailed over Joze's forearm, hair wet with sweat and to which small bits of old leaves clung. Then, with terrible suddenness, a spasm of coughing took him, like wracking, despairing sobs. Joze held him close, tightly, as though afraid that this violent coughing would break the Elf, bone from bone.

Huddling like a child in his father's arms, the Elf buried his face in Joze's shoulder, coughing, coughing. Then, between one gasp and the next cough, he stiffened, arched his back, pulled away from the man holding him. Kicva saw his pale, northern blue eyes staring at Joze's black-bearded face, saw those eyes flare, as though he recognized someone both dreaded and welcome.

Kicva knew that look. She'd seen it many times before in the year past. It was the look of one who saw the two faces of the Death Deity; Diwan-Deyja—dark and terrible warrior-king, bright and welcoming queen of final peace.

And she saw something else: A small blossom shaped and colored like the reddest of roses, a splash of blood, stained Joze's sun-browned shoulder. Blood like that on the dead boy's lips. Blood like that which had fouled the patchy, greying beard of one of the men who'd attacked her at the rock pool. Kicva fingered the rough cotton of Joze's shirt, wishing suddenly that Joze were wearing it.

The wind shifted, just a little, and soft on the air she smelled smoke. At the same moment, Islief—until then forgotten—came to stand beside her. "Fire," he said, his voice low and sounding like crooning, as it did when he was troubled or disturbed. "There is a fire by the river, Friend." He pointed south. "I saw fire in the stone-rings!"

Fire burst from between the ringed stones, roared and leaped and ran through the streets of Lindens Lee. Dail held the horses, a hand on the bridle of the skittish pie, one on the neckstrap of the wide-eyed brown mare as he watched the blaze from the hill.

He didn't want to watch, any more than he'd wanted to watch Aidan sketch those gleaming lines of magic against the sunset sky. But the leaping, dancing flames enspelled him, as had the weaving of red-gold and silver lines. Though it was not possible to feel the flames' heat from the hilltop, distance did not keep him safe from feeling the red-hearted rage of the fire.

Dail forced himself to look away from the fire, made himself look at the mage. Aidan's long eyes were wide and unnaturally bright, not silvery now, but red as though they were mirrors reflecting the flames. He had done his chanted prayers, finished

making magic's incantation to a god whose name was Vuyer or
Fyr or both. When their eyes met, bard and mage, Aidan took
Dail's arm and moved him several steps back into the safe shadows
of the lindens that crowned the hilltop.

Hoofs rattled stone as the horses backed away from the edge of
the hill, obliged to follow. Aidan held as firmly to Dail's arm as
Dail held to the wild-eyed, quivering horses. It was as though he
understood that Dail was not reacting to the fire he saw now, but
to the blazing violence he'd seen at the end of the Ruby War.

Aidan let go Dail's arm, took the pied gelding's bridle. "Be
easy, bard. Now is not then." He pointed down the hill, down to
burning Lindens Lee. "This is a cleansing fire."

A cleansing fire . . .

The fire swallowed everything that was not stone. It devoured
little gardens, carefully tended and growing neatly before the
boulder-homes of the Stone Elves; the ashwood-handled tools
used to till those gardens; split-oak water buckets, clothing and
blankets; the carved wooden furniture that Dail and Aidan had
dragged out from the cool, round stone houses. Fire consumed the
people themselves. Men and women, old and young, children and
infants, all stiffened and dead, markless as though they'd fallen
before an army whose weapons left only invisible wounds. And
the black smoke of that fire billowed high, curtained the red sun,
fouled the deepening blue of the sky: a dark banner proclaiming
that Lindens Lee had been a plague village.

A twig snapped in the forest. The pied gelding snorted, jerked its
head and thus Aidan's arm, hard enough to make the mage wince.
The brown mare tried to sidle away, then threw herself back on
her haunches, twisting, ready to rear. Dail reached high, grabbed
both sides of the mare's bridle and pulled her head down. From
the forest came a whispered sound, like wind over leaves, then a
sharply drawn breath which sounded like shock and pain.

The mage heard it, too. Head up, tense as the horse he held,
Aidan looked beyond the pie's shoulder and into the forest. His
high-boned face assumed a carefully neutral expression, worn as
though it were a seamless mask. When he spoke, even his voice
had changed, deepened.

"I am a mage," he said to the shadows beyond the lindens.
Narrow-eyed, Aidan warned: "If you are Elf-kind, you know what
that means."

The shadows took on a solid seeming; a voice spoke with
the kind of forced flatness Dail sometimes heard used to hide
surprise:

"I know what that means, Mage Aidan."

Hanging on to his own brown mare, grabbing the reins of the pie before the Elf could let them drop, Dail saw the careful mask fall away from Aidan's face. The expression beneath that mask, mingled wonder and ghosty traces of both anticipation and reluctance, was like none Dail had seen on the face of the Elf-King's Mage before then.

A slender Elven stepped out of the lindens' shadows, looking like a child in the too-big shirt she wore. She was no child, though; Dail could see that when fire-stirred wind from the village below pressed the shirt tight to her body, made the rough cotton hug her breasts. Her cropped hair—girlish golden curls—was burnished almost red by the light of the flames. The look on her face belied her voice's previous flatness, mirrored Aidan's expression almost exactly.

"What have you done?" she whispered. Long, canted eyes on the burning village, voice shaking, she said: "Oh, Aidan! What have you done?"

But Mage Aidan didn't answer. He was looking beyond the Elven, into the shadowed woods.

Dail squinted into the darkness, saw a black-bearded young man of his own people, leaning, head bowed, against a linden's grey trunk. He was grimy with road-dirt, shirtless. Maybe injured, for Dail saw that a splash of blood, red, unbrowned by time, stained his shoulder.

The very moment that Dail's eye fell upon him, the young man raised his head. In the sharply etched lines of the man's pale face, in his wide-pupiled dark eyes—which reflected Aidan's magic-made fire even at this distance—Dail read a horror, a panicky terror that was kin to his own.

But he did not think this pale, frightened Man was the cause of Aidan's staring. Dail, too, saw the creature lurking behind the Man; the short, thick-shouldered, bulky creature with wide-set glowing eyes.

"Who are you?" Aidan asked, his voice low and filled with wonder.

A prickling—like foreknowledge—skittered up Dail's spine as the creature lifted its head, turned shining eyes, gentle as a homecoming light, on the both of them.

"I am Islief of the First People," it said.

In the creature's voice, a quiet voice like the deep echo heard in vast empty stone places, a voice the sound of which seemed to make whispers of the snapping roaring fire below, Dail found a sudden, startling memory of something Nikia had told him she'd read. A thing written in thick bold script on yellowed parchment found in Seuro's Keep.

I am Islief of the First People.

The things of which I write are things most sacred, things most holy. And I write of hope, always keeping in mind the sin which was committed in the name of hope. Old I am, old and old.

The Crown is lost, and lost again . . .

The jeweled crown Aeylin had taken from distant caverns in a far time; the crown she'd broken.

A feeling that was both anticipation and fear clutched at Dail's heart, made his knees go weak. He closed his eyes, in the darkness saw the image of the Lady of the Blue-Silver eyes, dark-haired Aeylin, the long-dead queen for whom he had made songs all the winter past. When he opened his eyes, saw the creature standing in the shadows, Dail let his breath go on a long, wondering sigh.

"By all the dear gods," Dail said, who seldom swore by gods. "You've come back, too."

"Not come back," Islief said. He cocked his head, squinted as the fire of burning Lindens Lee leaped higher, sent its light even to the shadowed woods. "Harper, I have never left."

Chapter Nineteen

AIDAN MADE THE CAMPING FIRE THE HARD WAY, WITH FLINT AND striker. For this Dail was grateful. He'd seen enough of enchanted fires. And this time Aidan made the simple little fire safely, without burning his fingers or setting his clothes to smoldering; for he'd chosen a place well out of the wind, in the eastward lee of the hill. When the flames were crackling merrily, tamed and contained, the campfire drew them all—Kicva from her hunting, Islief from the lightless shadows at the forest's edge. Dail came from picketing the horses, and Joze returned from the small brook, shirtless yet, but cleaned of blood. Simply made though the fire was, it drew them as though it were a magic summoning.

By unspoken consent, Aidan and Kicva had spoken only briefly on the hill above burning Lindens Lee. (Though Dail noted with some interest that they seemed to know each other well.) Surprised was Kicva's greeting; Aidan's had been spoken awkwardly, his words stiff and uncomfortably polite, and mostly having to do with the fact that someone called Cowan and his wife, Erla, were well and awaiting her homecoming.

"Where have you been, Kicva?" the mage asked mildly.

"Wintering in the Kevarths," she said.

"Yet winter is well over and spring soon gone. Your parents have been wondering whether they should be mourning you war-killed."

Kicva had flushed, ducked her head as though she felt Aidan's mild words for sternest admonition. But she'd not tried to defend her absence. And then the two had gone about the business of making a camp and finding food, as though they knew that the place for asking questions and finding answers was not on the hilltop overlooking the burning. The young man Joze, and Dail himself, had followed their lead. Islief had gone to haunt the shadows.

Now Dail watched as all but Islief found places to sit, took up the small tasks of making a meal; tasks to occupy their hands while they watched each other, strangers and companions alike.

Aye, we're all people with things to say, he thought.

But no one was saying anything. Alone on the side of the fire opposite Aidan and Kicva and dark-bearded Joze, Dail took his *Dashlaftholeh* upon his knee with some thought of checking the harp's tuning. Joze and Kicva bent industriously over their work of skinning Kicva's catch of two rabbits and a squirrel. Aidan kept silent, sitting motionless, nearly invisible behind them, beyond the fire's light. Islief stood squinting thoughtfully at the flames. No shadow touched him now, only ruddy firelight; the small grey man was the brightest thing in the darkness.

Islief had spoken no word after their meeting. He'd kept to the shadowed forest, kept quietly to himself as though the gathering of food and fuel did not concern him; as though he'd had matters of his own to consider. Now he put his back to the fire, came to stand before Dail. And the bard, catching expressions of both eagerness and relief on the faces of Islief's companions, realized that Joze and Kicva had been waiting for Islief to speak first, by their silence deferring to him.

Only hip-high to Man or Elf, Islief stood before Dail seated on the ground so that the two were eye to eye; a creature of distant legend making ready to speak to a weaver of legends. Dail saw Mage Aidan look up from his fire tending; saw Kicva lean forward, Joze put aside his skinning knife. But he noted these things only absently. The wide-set eyes of ancient Islief held him,

kept him as though they were a candle's flame and he a moth
drawn to the light.

"Harper," Islief said, his voice deep and sounding like a long
underground echo. "Why have you left the Elf-King's daughter
all alone?"

The question caught Dail by surprise, and it hit him like a blow
or an accusation of abandonment.

"Harper, is she well?"

Dail did not answer at once. He closed his eyes, and in the
darkness found a memory of Nikia. On Midwinter Night, as had
become her habit, she'd been walking the paths of the Queen's
Garden. Moonlight had dressed her silvery hair; the thin cotton
bedshift she'd worn had rippled around her bare ankles like soft
blue shadows. She'd stopped her walking to sit upon the stone
bench, looked at the Elf-light in the east. She'd been so still that
she might well have been a statue made of marble. Then she'd
moved, rested a hand gently on the new-swelling life within her.
Such an intimate gesture! As though she'd been in deep converse
with someone dear to her and, speaking, must caress.

On that Midwinter Night, from the window of his tall tower
room Dail had been too far away to see the expression on Nikia's
face. But there'd been something in the way she had wrapped her
arms around herself which made Dail think that she was hugging
her unborn babe close, speaking to that newly made child. Of
what? Of hopes and joys? Of the secret longings mothers have
for their children?

Watching Nikia, he'd taken up his harp, seeking refuge from his
own longings in the songs he made for ghostly Aeylin. And working, he'd changed the words of a song he'd been hard at making
all the week past. That night a Topaz became a Flame-stone, and
a Sapphire a Wind-stone; a Ruby became a War-stone, a Diamond
a Sea-stone. That night an Emerald became a Heal-stone.

"Harper," Islief said again. "Is the Elf-King's daughter well?"

"Yes," Dail whispered, his hands tracing the shape of the harp
on his knee. "She's well."

"And her babe—has it come?"

"No. Not yet. Not for near a month." Then, realizing suddenly
that Islief was speaking of Nikia as though she were someone he
knew well, Dail left the memory, asked sharply, "How do you
know about Nikia's child?"

But Islief shook his head as though to say, *Later, we'll talk
about that later.* Wide-set eyes bright, he said, "Harper, you should
be with her. Why are you here?"

On the other side of the fire, Kicva returned to working on the catch. But she watched Dail carefully, for all that she seemed busy. Joze took up one of the skinned rabbits and spitted it. And Aidan sat still as stone in the shadows behind the two. It was the mage Dail looked to for his cue. But Aidan said nothing, made no gesture, gave no clue as to how Dail must respond. In the end, Dail stalled, countered Islief's question with questions of his own.

"Why are *you* here, Islief? Why have you come looking for me?"

"Because I need your help." Islief gestured behind him, indicated Joze and Kicva. "Harper, we need your help. But we have not come looking for you. We only hoped to find you. We have come looking for the Elf-King's daughter."

Dry-mouthed, feeling like the dark night had drawn suddenly closer to press all around him, Dail looked at no one but Islief. "Why?"

The sounds of the forest—leaves whispering to the breeze, an owl's distant wondering, a fox barking—all seemed like voices raised to echo his question. And then these voices fell silent. Wind, wandering from the forest, slipped past the fire, came to caress *Dashlaftholeh*'s strings like a gentle hand. That wind-made music shaped a melody Dail knew well. In the words which fit that melody, Dail heard the answer to his question.

"I found the Flame-stone," he said softly, speaking the words of his song.

Islief nodded as if to encourage. When Dail did not continue, he whispered: "And the Wind-stone."

"I held in my hand the War-stone," Dail said, the hair rising on the back of his neck. Had the Elf-King been right? Were these words not his, but Aeylin's? He turned his head, lowered his eyes, not wanting to catch even a peripheral glimpse of the fire. Even all these months later, he did not like to think of the Ruby in the presence of flame. "I took the Sea-stone and the . . ." He stopped, unable to continue, though he knew the words well, though he heard them whispering in his heart.

"And the Heal-stone, Harper," Islief said gently. "And she took the Heal-stone."

Dail sighed the inevitable name. "Aeylin."

"The Lady. Yes. I have come from her, Harper. *We* have come from her. There is a magic needing to be made."

Fire snapped, sent sparks spiraling into the darkness, and then Mage Aidan spoke, who had sat silent through question and answer, through even the wind's song. "You have the Emerald?

You have the Heal-stone with you?"

"No," Islief said, answering though he never looked away from Dail. "It is in a safe place. It is waiting."

"Waiting for what?"

Islief didn't answer Aidan, only continued to look at Dail.

"Waiting for Nikia," Dail said flatly, the words tasting like ashes in his mouth. "Islief, have you come to ask Nikia to make the magic?"

Islief shook his head. "No, Harper. We have not come to ask her to do that. We have come to ask for her child. It is the child who will make the magic."

Dail found himself unable to respond, unable to do more than look around the circle, perhaps hoping that Joze or Kicva would speak up, say something to let him know that he'd misunderstood Islief. But they didn't. They kept silent, their silence confirmation.

Again the fire snapped, spat sparks. Smoke, caught in the changing wind, swirled high. For a long moment, no one moved. Then Aidan said:

"That's madness." Long eyes narrowed, he turned to Kicva. "You've fallen in with madmen, Kicva."

Kicva's face flushed, sudden anger springing to color her cheeks. When Joze laid a hand on her wrist, she turned, looking as though she might vent her anger on him. But he whispered something, a word Dail couldn't hear, and the Elven nodded curtly.

"Aidan, it's *not* madness," she said. "I've seen the Lady. I've seen Aeylin! She's—"

The mage did not stay to listen. He rose abruptly, dusted off, and walked away from the fire, strode into the woods. Kicva scrambled to her feet, shook off Joze's restraining hand.

"Friend, wait," Islief warned.

But Kicva paid him no heed, and ran after Aidan. In the wake of their leaving came silence, broken moments later by a sudden barking cough from Joze.

Kicva found Aidan standing between the pied gelding and Dail's brown mare. He stroked the gelding's neck, whispered quieting words as the pie stood quivering beneath his hands. The horse danced skittishly when it sensed Kicva's presence. Aidan turned, his movements slow and easy as though he didn't want to further startle the pie. Or as though he'd expected that someone would follow him.

"Kicva," he said, nodding once. And that gesture too was ambiguous, either greeting or confirmation. Kicva was not often able to tell what Aidan's gestures meant.

She stayed where she was, several paces distant from him. "Aidan," she began, then stopped as she realized that the forest had become unnaturally silent around them.

The horses pricked up their ears, shuffled nervously. The gelding snorted again, head high so that Aidan was obliged to turn and speak softly, urge calm upon the anxious beast. Sharp from the direction of the camp came a hard coughing and Aidan said, over his shoulder and as though casually:

"Your friend Joze would be the better for that shirt of his."

"No doubt," Kicva agreed. "All I need to do is convince him of that."

"If the problem is that between you there's one shirt too few, I've an extra in my scrip. You'd better wear it, though. I doubt it would fit your friend."

Kicva thanked him, wrapping her arms around herself, suddenly chilled. Somewhere within herself she wondered at that, for with the stilling of the breeze the air felt warmer than a moment ago. But she only noticed this briefly, for she was suddenly acutely aware of how comfortable Joze's shirt felt against her skin. Even after many days of wear, she imagined that the rough scent of him still clung to the fabric. And she was distracted by wondering why Aidan *didn't* wonder how she came to be wearing another man's shirt.

"Aidan, about what Islief said—"

Aidan raised an eyebrow. "Ah, yes. Islief. He talks about Aeylin as though he knows her personally."

"Aidan, he *does*. He's been years and years alive because of her. He's . . ." She stopped then, trying to sort out the things she needed to tell him to make him believe that they'd come from Aeylin with a charge so important, so vital.

And in the pause, Aidan shrugged. "Well, he looks old enough to be someone who'd known her, I'll grant you that." He smiled indulgently. "But Aeylin is ages and uncounted years dead, Kicva. Don't you think your friend Islief is perhaps just a little . . . confused? Aye, I'll grant you he's a kind I've never seen before. Some old creature left over from legends, he looks like. But surely—whatever kind he is—age can make his mind as weak as it would make Elf's or Man's. What's he been doing, talking to ghosts all these ages past?"

"Yes!" Kicva snapped. Then, feeling as though her assertion had been translated to absurdity by the look of tolerant amusement in Aidan's eyes, she drew a deep breath, tried to find patience and the words to explain what she knew to be true. "Aidan, *I've* seen the Lady. And Joze has."

"Oh, yes?" The pied gelding shuffled restively, and Aidan reached up to stroke a broad flat cheek. Head cocked, the mage listened to the night. But there was nothing to hear. Not the sighing of wind, not the rustle of bold foxes stalking, not the bright songs of crickets, not the grim ponderings of owls. It was as though nothing remained alive in the night but the two of them and the restless horses. "Tell me, Kicva: Where have you all seen this marvel?"

He was baiting her, she knew it. Yet Kicva was unable just then to stop to think about why he—a mage whose smallest daily work was among wonders—should doubt her. Judging, he was; always judging, watching her from behind that unshakable mage's calm of his.

And Kicva realized that this was nothing new. He was always watching her and weighing what he saw, trying to come to some conclusion about her. Or to justify one.

"I'll tell you," she said, at once angry. "Aye, and listen well, Mage Aidan, for it's truth you're about to hear. There are caverns, in the north, in the Kevarths. They're out east, a week shy of a month's walking from here, beyond the Landbound Sea. You've never seen such caverns as these—they're a whole world beneath this one, Aidan!"

Kicva stopped for breath, and felt herself calming as she remembered the caverns, the chamber of the crystal hearth, and the Lady who'd put all her hopes for the world's safety in the hands of ancient Islief and two soldiers. And calmer, she spoke slowly, choosing her words carefully.

Wanting Aidan to believe her, to stop regarding her as though she were a tale-weaving child, she told him about Aeylin, told him about the Jewels and the Crown, told him about Islief; about sins and payments, promises and hopes. And she told him about the Emerald, the Heal-stone; and the Lady's need for Nikia's child. She even told him—though with an odd reluctance which she did not then try to understand—that Joze had questioned that need, doubted.

"But even Joze believes it now, Aidan. For Islief and the Lady have told him: No mage alive has the skill to call the magic from the Emerald. Only Aeylin and the child who was born for it can do that."

Aidan watched her for a long time, so still and silent that Kicva felt a chill touch her. It was as though his narrow-eyed intensity were something to fear. "And clearly you believe this strange little creature and his ghost, too."

"Yes."

"Kicva," he said, his voice low and so flat as to be emotionless. "There *is* no child. You heard the bard say it to Islief: The Princess has not given birth. By his account she's yet a month away from that." Came a note of what could only be called pity in his voice, and indignant as she was in the face of his doubt, Kicva recognized it as genuine.

"Kicva, do you mean to say that you've come all this distance to take a childing woman—only one month away from her laying-in—across two kingdoms to these wonderful caverns of yours? How do you think she'd fare on the journey?" He shook his head, as though disappointed. "You've changed. Was a time when I thought you were the most sensible person I knew."

Then he said nothing more, turned his back to her, and returned to the business of soothing the horses.

Kicva stood wordless. It was as though she were alone, as though Aidan had walked away from her and left her standing in the eerie silence by herself. After it became clear that he would not take up the conversation again, she walked away, back to the fire, back to Islief and Joze. She felt foolish, childishly incompetent for not having explained things more clearly.

When she returned to the campfire she saw that only Joze sat there, turning two rabbits on a spit over the flames. His face was all grey pallor and dark hollows in the changeable firelight.

"Where are Islief and the bard?" she asked.

Joze jerked his chin toward the west, toward the hilltop and burned Lindens Lee below. "They went to talk."

"Does the bard . . . does he believe?"

Joze smiled, just a small twitch of his lips. "Aye, he believes. He's a bard, hunter-scout. That kind knows about ghosts." He gave the spit a turn, carefully so as not to lose supper to the flames. "And your mage?"

My mage, she thought, feeling bleak and again cold.

"He thinks Islief is addle-minded." She sighed tiredly. "For all I know, he thinks we're addle-minded, too."

"Ah? Strange thing for a mage to think. I'd have figured that— next to bards—mages know best about magic and ghosts. You're sure he knows his business?"

Kicva would have retorted sharply, spurred to indignation by his question. Why was everyone trying to bait her tonight?

But before she could speak, Joze began to cough again.

Saying nothing, she pulled his shirt over her head and tossed it to him. She took up Aidan's scrip, rooted around in it until she found a fine white linen shirt. It was rolled into a bundle, and she withdrew it carefully, for the bundle was heavy. Parting the folds, she saw that Aidan had used the shirt as a protective wrapping for a small crystal bowl. The feel of magic hovered faintly around the edges of that hollowed garnet bowl, like echoes. Firelight called flickerings of deepest wine-red from the black crystal. This was Aidan's scrying bowl.

Joze coughed again, but only softly this time, as one coughs who is too near smoke. He moved back from the fire. "Come turn the spit for a while, Kicva."

She looked hard at him, at his face showing pale against his dark beard, at his hand shaking just a little.

Tired? Ah, likely. Well, so are we all, she thought, feeling sullen and sour.

But she didn't speak that thought aloud, for in the part of her mind where she kept the things she didn't like to think about there stirred a small, dark fear that Joze was more than tired. And so she went to tend the spit, said nothing when Joze stretched himself out on the ground before the fire and went at once to sleep.

The fire in Lindens Lee had dwindled to embers, and those embers shone like red stars now. Islief standing silently beside him, Dail sat on the hilltop, chin on drawn-up knees, watching the glow and the darkness. Islief had talked long; about his cavern home, and his Lady Aeylin; about need and promises, and the long, long time he'd stayed waiting to be healed of his sin. Around Dail the night grew strangely quiet. Nothing for him to hear now but the sound of low voices from the camp as he watched the embers in Lindens Lee. And watching, he thought that this was a fair crazy thing to do when the flames those embers used to be had looked too much like the fearful, magic-called fire he'd seen Nikia command scarce a year ago.

Ah, but maybe not so crazy. A year ago he'd seen the terrible Ruby of Guyaire work wide and deep magic; only this afternoon had he been reminded of that again. Now he was being asked to help make it so that another one of those Jewels could realize its own magic.

And this the *second* invitation, he thought. The first a disguise for the Elf-King's command.

"Harper," Islief said into the silence. "What promise have you made that is so troubling to you?"

Dail looked up, startled from his brooding by Islief's question. "Only one, Islief. And that one you'd like me to break. I promised Dekar that I'd bring the Emerald to him."

"He cannot use it," Islief said gently.

"So it seems. Though he'd never intended to. He wants his daughter to use it."

"Ah. The Hunter-Defender. Do you think that is how she understood the Lady's words to her?"

"The Lady's words? Aeylin's?"

If he knew that he was being offered a final test, Islief showed no sign of it. He answered simply. "Yes. Aeylin's. 'Heal the damage. Daughter, find the strength to mend what the Sorcerer has broken.' The Lady said that to her." Islief looked at him keenly. "But you knew that, Harper. You were there to hear when those words were spoken."

"I know it. I was just wondering if you did."

"So you were." Islief smiled, his wide-set eyes glowing warmly. "And you are wondering how it is that I know you were present when the Lady spoke to the Hunter-Defender. I will tell you: Not all fire is dreadful, Harper. A fire there is in my home which shows me many things. And so there is a lot that I know. Ah, maybe even things that you didn't know could be known, yes?"

Undoubtedly, Dail thought, sourly. *It seems that everyone I meet knows every secret I've ever had without having to bother about waiting for me to reveal it.*

"Harper, is there anything else that you wonder?"

Dail went back to watching the embers. "I wonder how you'll convince Mage Aidan to believe you. He doesn't."

That didn't seem to bother Islief. "What else do you wonder?"

"I wonder how we're going to get to Damris. I wonder if we're going to encounter more plague. I wonder if we'll even make it through the borderlands where the brigands run. I wonder if we'll make it through the hot lands. I wonder if . . ."

He fell silent, not willing to discuss this last wondering of his; not willing to give voice to the sudden-springing image of himself striding into the Citadel—past guards, past servants, past friends, past Garth himself—to take Nikia up in his arms and carry her away to some far place beneath northern mountains where magic slept waiting for her babe to be born.

He shook his head, got to his feet. "I'll tell you what I *don't* wonder, Islief. I don't wonder if I've gone crazy. I've been that way for some time now. I'm likely to stay that way for a while longer. I'll have to, if I want to break my promise to a king and make a new one to you."

"And do you want to do that?"

"Stay crazy for a while longer?" Dail shrugged. "I haven't died of it so far."

"No, no, Harper. I don't want to know if you are going to stay crazy. I want to know if you will make the promise we need you to make. Will you help me show your Nikia that the strength Aeylin needs is within her daughter? Will you help your Nikia to see that, Harper?"

"Her . . . daughter? You know that this child will be a daughter?"

Islief nodded. "I know that."

And aye, that was one question Dail had. But he didn't ask the other question, did not dare ask why Islief referred to Garth's wife as "your Nikia."

Instead, he looked down the hill to the ruined plague-village, looked out across the Altha. The water's surface lay still as glass under the starlight. Then a small breeze stirred, ruffling the wide, glittering blackness. He'd been a while in Elflands, been a while feeling the changeable spring. But the seductive kiss of damp wind, the charming embrace of green-scented forests, the delight of hearing again the world's music of rain and wind, bird and beast—none of these pleasures had caused Dail to forget what the damaged lands beyond the Altha's western banks were like. Nor had he forgotten the farm-wife's daughter, her sweet, tender youth hounded away by drought and desperation.

To bring healing to those seared places, hope to those people . . . aye, that was worth staying crazy enough to make a new promise to Islief, even knowing that it meant he'd break his promise to the Elf-King. And worth the risks of crossing back into his damaged and dangerous homeland.

But he wondered if he'd be able to figure out a way to take Nikia away from Damris, for even if she did not object, there would be others who would. And how to bring her safely to Islief's cavern home?

But likely Islief himself didn't have the answer to that question. And so he asked another, one which had been troubling him since first he'd heard Islief's tale.

"What will happen to you, Islief, when the healing is done?"

Islief was a while answering, and when he spoke at last, Dail heard a deep, ages-old longing in his voice. "Ah, Harper, when that healing is made I will rest at last."

"Rest?"

Islief nodded. "But I wonder sometimes, Harper, if when I go to rest, my kin will recognize me after all this long, long time."

"Where are your kin, Islief?" Dail asked, though he knew the answer.

"They are dead, Harper."

In that moment Dail became aware that the hilltop was quieter than it had been. A silence came creeping out of the forest, a stillness so complete that the two looked at each other, unspoken questions between them.

There was something wrong about that silence, for it was deeper than even the quiet of night's longest hour. Every dark-roaming creature was voiceless; the wind no longer stirred. It was as though something big, something dangerous, prowled the edges of a once-safe perimeter, and all the forest around held its breath, waiting fearfully.

"Harper," Islief said, his voice hushed to near a whisper. "All this quiet is a lorn thing. Come back to the fire with me. Give us your songs of aforetimes for leath and to fill up the quiet."

For leath, Dail thought, as he walked away from the hilltop with Islief. For comfort, he thought as he found a place near the fire. Well, maybe there was some comfort to be gotten from his songs, for surely the hard lines of tension eased away from Kicva's expression when bard and harp gave voice to the song folk sang in Verdant Hall, last before ending the day.

> In fallen cities, fair and golden,
> In ancient times misplaced,
> There hangs a banner
> Tattered and faded.
> In fallen cities.

Joze, stretched long and sleeping by the fire, seemed to fare better for the singing, for he stopped his restless stirring. And Islief, head low so as not to look too closely at the fire's glare, seemed like one who hears news of old friends when Dail sang for him the new songs.

> Of moonlight her robe is spun.
> No gem has she but starlight's strands
> Braided fair in her hair.

Of dawnlight her cheek is made.
No gold has she but sunlight's mantle
Soft to wrap her in.

Yet the brooding silence crowded close, gathered darkly in the breach made by each pause in the music and every breath Dail took. And Aidan, the Elf-King's Mage, never came back to the fire all night, never came to see if there was comfort to be found in the singing.

In the morning Kicva awoke from a dream of startling intimacy, a dream wherein she recalled each thought, felt again each emotion of the weeks past, lived again each day since first she came upon Joze at the edge of the sick lands. In this dream she'd shared all these things eagerly with another, offered insights, made gifts of her knowledge, submitted her fears for some cool-eyed inspection, bestowed her hopes as though they were favors.

And it was a strange dream; not because it was so complete, but because it was not made up of the startling flashes of memory from which most dreams are constructed. This dream had an eerie orderliness, progressing from moment to moment through each day and night. Kicva shivered, for it seemed now that even as she had been dreaming, she'd known that this strange orderliness had been imposed upon the dream from without. For there had been a light in her dream—red almost to black, like the wine-colored glints in Aidan's scrying bowl.

And so she was not surprised when Joze came from the brook with a pot of water and said that the Elf-King's Mage and the pied gelding were nowhere to be found. She knew, even as the others wondered, just where Aidan had gone: She herself had shown him the way to Islief's cavern home. In dreams she had told him every detail she knew about the things he'd pretended to disbelieve.

So troubled was she by this, she did not notice until Islief pointed it out that the silence which had blanketed the night still clung to the day, and that the grasses which had only the day before grown so sweetly green between the stones on the hillside now looked pale and weak, browning as though they'd not had a drink of rain in many months.

*Chapter Twenty*_____

GARTH CLOSED THE BROAD WOODEN DOOR SLOWLY BEHIND HIM, winced as the hinges groaned, and set his boots down beside the tall, painted clothespress near the doorway. The bedchamber was silent until, faint from without the Citadel, came the call of the watch on the walls of Damris.

"All well?" cried a piping young voice. That guard could not have been more than a boy, maybe keeping the watch with his father or brother. His question rang clearly through the night. Near, he was. Likely walking the wall where it curved inward and close to the Citadel in order to bypass the flat stretch of ground between Damris and the river.

The Duel, folk called that broad meadow, for legend and history told that several famous contests had been fought there. Duels over women, over honor, sword fights which had not ended until one man lay dead. When Garth was a boy, the songs Dail used to sing about those deadly matches on the field of honor had always been his favorites.

> Kinnan brave, gone to meet the challenge;
> Kinnan lost, gone to find his way.
> Kinnan in love, gone to win his lady;
> Kinnan gone . . . Kinnan gone.

Garth could not have been much older than ten when he'd first heard that song. And Dail, singing it for the first time, trying it out on his young cousin the prince, had been as old as Garth was tonight. That day, blue-eyed handsome bard, chronicler of duels and wars and ladies loved, Dail had looked like one of the bright shining heroes from his songs. Soon after first hearing Kinnan's Song, Garth had begun to realize that he'd be happiest did his life hold nothing more than the mere chance to be like one of Dail's wild, free song-heroes.

Ah, Dail . . . And where are you this night, cousin? Out in the sick lands, gone since April. Are you seeking 'prentices, as they say? Are you finding new songs? Are you playing your own part in them? I wish I were with you instead of trapped here in Damris!

"All well?" the young guard called again. His voice had a thinner edge to it now.

An older man finally answered. "All well!" Distance muffled his deeper voice, but not his tone of mingled boredom and amusement.

No, Garth thought. *All is not well, not in a kingdom stricken by sorcerous land-sickness, afflicted with drought and famine and the natural outcome of those two evils, plague.*

He turned away from that thought, away from his wondering about Dail, and surveyed the bedchamber all filled with light and shadow. Shadows pooling on the stone floor made dark gaps in sight; the light of the newly risen moon, clear and thin and flowing through the wide south window, fell across the bed and made a silver dancing in Nikia's hair.

Garth listened to his wife's soft, even breathing. She slept deeply, her face so still that it looked like white marble in the moonlight. Careful to make no sound that would wake her, he moved on silent bare feet to the small table near the window. It was as he'd thought when he'd searched through his papers in the outer room: He'd left the parchment here, the unsigned decree, the decision he wished he could defer.

Achingly tired from a day which had held two separate Council meetings, a day of seemingly endless talk, dire exhortations and angry warnings, Garth drew a long, silent breath, let it go slowly. Today he and those lords of the Council who were in the city had talked of plague; today they'd treated the rumors of fatal sickness that had wiped out whole villages in the north as though they were not rumors at all, but true reports.

Garth traced the edge of the parchment, the ink which had dried hours ago. Written here was the outcome of those two Council meetings, an edict unanimously urged by Liam and Calmis and Celed, urged despite the fact that neither Karo nor Fargut had been present to agree or disagree. Desperately frightened men had attended those meetings, drafted this decree. All this paper needed now in order to become law was Garth's signature.

He moved a chair noiselessly away from the table and sat to look at the decision he needed to make. From without he heard the clash of steel on stone. Like an eagle honing horny beak, a guard sharpened a dagger's blade or a sword's against the wall. The stones of the wall were scored with grooves from such work. Thus bored soldiers amused themselves on a quiet night-watch. Garth listened to the stone and the steel for a moment, then ruffled the edge of the parchment on the desk. *Soon*, he thought heavily, *when this decree is signed, watches will not be so quiet.*

Across the room Nikia stirred a little, sighed as though it were
an effort to move even in sleep. This mid-May night she was large
around with the child, due to bear in only a few weeks. All who
saw her remarked upon the miracle of roses in her cheeks, the
wonder of a woman heavy with child in a time of drought and
hunger who looked as fresh and glowing as a maiden in spring.
But it could not be easy to carry such unaccustomed weight with
never a chance for ease. Sometimes, as now by the thin light of
the aged moon, Garth saw lines of weariness around her eyes
that no one else seemed to see, blinded as they were by roses
and glow and the symbol of hope they'd made of her in these
hopeless hungry times.

In these weeks past he'd talked over all of his decisions with
Nikia. He'd discussed every choice with her. Except this one.
There had been no time to talk to her about this one, no time
to seek her opinion. He wondered now whether he should wake
her. He almost did, until he looked again at her still form.

Aye, like marble, her face, a deft sculpting of a woman in
dreamless sleep. Did Nikia ever dream anymore? She was always
so still in the bed, so silent. There was a time when he'd have
known whether or not she dreamed. There was a time when he
could hear the small sounds of her dreaming, feel the fact of her
dreaming in the way she moved and breathed. But they didn't
come too close to each other now, didn't sleep in each other's
arms as once they'd done.

Because, he'd told himself, a childing woman certainly needs
more room, less confinement, than she might once have required.

The scraping of stone and steel fell silent. Though he could not
truly hear it from this distance, Garth imagined that the measured
tread of the guard's pacing replaced it.

"All well?" the older guard called.

"All well," the youngster answered promptly.

No, Garth thought. *But maybe it will be soon.* He looked at the
parchment again, and he knew what the decision must be.

Garth had made a hundred decisions in the three weeks since
Alain had grudgingly appointed him Regent; and before those
decisions, a hundred choices between action and inaction. Some
had been good decisions. The decision to block the Council's
strident clamor that he send the Citadel Guard to commandeer
all available water in the city for rationing had been a good one.
He did not see any value in making the people of Damris more
helpless than they already were.

"They'll hoard," Liam had warned. "And they'll charge exorbitant fees for what all should have free access to. Or at least regulated access, for the good of everyone."

Fargut of Hivard, who'd not then left the city, had agreed. Celedon of Rigg and Calmis of Soran had disagreed. Each of the latter supported Garth's position that the folk of Damris would do as they'd always done: sort it out and survive as best they could.

To commandeer water would look too much like stealing, Celedon had said. And Calmis had gone further, said that it would not look like stealing, it would *be* stealing.

"And to take from a man the thing his life depends on makes him desperate," he warned. "Desperate men have fueled riots before now."

Because Karo of Raeth had not been present, had ridden from the city with pale excuses on the day Alain had announced the Regency, Garth's had been the voice raised to undo the deadlock. As Regent, he could have overridden even a unanimous vote, but he was glad that the Council's divided opinion had allowed him to appear to be casting the tie-breaking vote.

And so, as Fargut and Liam had predicted, the people of the city had hoarded water, stored it in barrels in their cool stone cellars long before the time when the A'Damran ceased to flow. But, as the others had known it would be, they'd acted reasonably. Now that the river was a muddy, unhealthy smear of standing water, there was water enough in the city for all if it was doled out carefully. And it was, though care was not miserliness. Garth had heard of no man or woman or child dead of thirst in Damris. He'd heard more than one tale of generosity. Damris was a city of tradesmen and shopkeepers. Shrewd they were, but they'd long ago learned how to strike a bargain. The man who had come to the end of his water struck one deal or another with his neighbor. It worked.

Garth had made other decisions equally good; and some not so good.

It had not been wise, he thought now, to forgo making a concerted effort against the outlaws who clustered at the border between Mannish lands and Dekar's kingdom; bandits in packs who hid waiting for men going to or coming from hunting forays in Dekar's forests; bandits like jackals waiting for a wounded beast to come be their defenseless prey.

The bandits were not found often in Raeth. Karo, he of the largest province, had yet a strong army. Garth had heard reports that Karo had been making good use of his time in Raeth. Though Ybro's grandfather could do nothing about land-sickness and drought and famine, his borders were not haunts for outlaws. But folk who lived along the border in Celed and Rigg suffered badly. They had taken to calling that corridor Brigand Home.

No, it hadn't been wise to leave the matter of Brigand Home solely in the hands of Liam and Celedon, in whose provinces the outlaws had gained strong footholds. Celedon's Rigg province had suffered greatly, it being a small and narrow length of land. Five hundred outlaws in Rigg were as dangerous as a thousand in greater Celed.

And it might be, Garth thought now, *that the men of the Guard I sent last week to Celed and Rigg will get the job done. But it also might be that by waiting this long to act, I've made of Liam and Celedon—if not enemies—at least men who are going to think twice about supporting me on another issue.*

Garth shuddered, cold-shivering, though the night was breathless and hot. Behind that thought lay the specter of another, darker decision, and that his worst fear: With eroded support, would he then have to choose to override the Council each time it did not agree with him? Would he soon become obliged to behave like a tyrant, a petty dictator with an emasculated Council?

What dark demons of rebellion would that unleash in a Council long accustomed to having its advice considered and often heeded?

Garth slew the wondering, and hastily buried the fear.

"All well?" the younger guard called.

"All well," the older answered around a yawn.

Garth closed his eyes, hearing the distant questions as more than the formula of the watch. It seemed that these voices, the young one and the older, urged him to make final his decision. He fingered the parchment again. Cold sweat, of which he had not been aware till just then, smeared a little of the ink.

Then, because he knew that he must not let time and doubt so smear his intent, he reached for an inkpot and a pen. He dipped the pen, tapped it on the edge of the pot, and signed his name boldly. No indecipherable scrawl for him, nor kingly and arrogant initial. He penned his name in a firm clear script:

"Garth of Damris, Uncle to the King who is Ybro, Son of the Once-King who is Alain. Regent."

All who could read and who cared to would know who had ordered the four gates of Damris shut, never to be opened again but by decree. All who could read and who cared to would know who had made the law which would bar all from entering the city.

There was not, to Garth's knowledge, one single case of plague in Damris tonight. When the gates did not open in the morning, he hoped that those folk who had fled the countryside for the city would understand that Damris was barred to them for the sake of those who lived within. He hoped that they would find shelter from the storm of sickness gathering without. He hoped that they would survive. But he would not let them past the gates. This for the sake of those who lived in the city.

The parchment signed, Garth undressed and slipped quietly into bed. On his own side, away from the window, closest to the door, he lay awake for a long time. He wasn't eager for sleep. He wasn't eager to meet in dreams even one man of the Citadel Guards he'd sent out into Rigg to help Celedon's men fight outlaws. Should they return alive, he'd not be able to welcome them back to the city. Nor would he admit Karo of Raeth, three weeks gone from the city; nor Lord Fargut who had several days ago quit Damris for his residence in Hivard.

> Kinnan brave, gone to meet the challenge;
> Kinnan lost, gone to find his way.
> Kinnan in love, gone to win his lady;
> Kinnan gone . . . Kinnan gone.

Nor Dail, the King's Bard, his cousin and his friend.

Dail and all others without the walls of Damris were doomed folk. They must take their chance with plague and do their best to survive.

Chapter Twenty-One

IN HIVARD PROVINCE, IN LORD FARGUT'S MOORLAND HOLDINGS, Karo of Raeth, grandfather of the infant king, made ready to burn another village. He held tight to the reins of his restive mount as he studied his band of men, twenty trusty soldiers standing like a ring of ravens round the leaping campfires. The eyes of some narrow slits, others nearly all whites, they waited on his word.

It would not be an easy word to give—no easier for having been given three times the two nights past, six times in his own stricken Raeth before that. Karo turned away, looked one last time at the huddle of thatch-roofed cottages and stone byres in the beech grove.

Fargut of Hivard was useful in Council, Karo thought bitterly, but a wretched ally in all other ways. Weak-bellied and whining, he'd let the sickness run rampant through his province while he kept himself locked away behind the thick wooden doors of his gloomy moorland residence, hiding like a rat in the dark pile of stone he called Loft. Fargut would not expose himself to plague. Not even to burn and cleanse the stricken villages in hope of stopping the plague's southward march. And so, over the squealing protests of Hivard's lord, Karo was doing the burning himself, cowardly Fargut be damned. This dismal huddling of cottages in the beeches would be the fourth Karo had burned in Hivard province.

In the east, unnatural Elf-light hung like a rippling many-colored veil beyond the naked beeches, cast slithering shadows over the village and the dead. Dead people, men and women and children claimed by plague; dead farm-beasts, cows and horses, chickens and ducks and pigs all starved to skin-hung bones. At least there'd be no one begging to have his life spared, swearing he was not plague-struck. It made the burning harder when a killing had to be done first. But this time they were all plague-dead.

"All dead and the rainbow washing over them," one scout had reported. That one's eyes had been narrow slits, as though he'd not wanted his lord to see the fear in him.

"Aye, making their grey faces into shape-shifting demons' faces," his companion had said. *His* eyes had rolled white. He hadn't cared who knew about his fear.

Karo spat. They were no shape-changing fiends down there in the village. Just poor farmers, dead of plague and drought, dead of Fargut's cowardice . . . and the Elf-King's unredeemed promise. He glared at the shimmering Elf-light over the beeches. That light seemed like nothing more than a fool's ill-fated hope of gain before a master trickster's sleight of hand.

And he's that, the Elf-King. A master prankster, prating of his mages' desperate attempts to cure the land-sickness, all the while safe and well fed in his green forests.

Karo shut his eyes tightly, ran his big hands up the sides of his face, smearing dust and soot and sweat into a gruesome mask. What did Dekar know about desperate attempts? Did *he* watch his lands burn with drought? Did *he* watch his folk die of hunger and thirst and plague, with not a weapon to help defend them? Not he. Dekar offered hunting rights with the cynical satisfaction of a man who knew that few could go to claim the mean-hearted gift, for fear of death at the hands of the bandits who haunted the border between the kingdoms. Relatively easy to get through to the Elflands to hunt; not so easy to come home again. Even strongly armed hunting parties fell before the lawless men, killed and stripped of weapons and gear, their hard-won food stolen.

Hot north wind, the wind of the pre-dawn hour, drove dust blown from the burned plains behind him, hung a gritty veil between Raeth's lord and the village at the foot of the hill. Outlines of buildings were indistinct, blurry as though seen in a dream. Wending that village was called, named for the beck, the sweet stream, that used to wander through the beeches in better days. No beck travelled through now, and the beeches were no more than skeletal hands scrabbling at the hot sky.

Still, if rain would fall, this earth would bear. Here, in this southern part of Hivard, the earth was not sick to dying. Only very thirsty. Not grey and ashy, not sucked hollow of all its goodness like all the land in Raeth.

Karo wiped sweat from his face, squinted to see the village more clearly through the haze. No light shone in any window, no sound drifted up the hill. They all slept the long sleep in plague-struck Wending. As they had in Khar's Crossing, Stag Run and Bounty. And this village, like all the others, lay on naked ground, earth holding no more than stone and what dirt the hot winds did not carry away. Any fire lighted here would find no purchase on bare dirt and stone, would not spread much beyond the borders of the village itself.

Karo's horse snorted, danced restlessly. The Lord of Raeth turned his back on the village, swung into the saddle. He gripped the stock of a brand and leaned down from his tall horse to plunge the oil-soaked rags wrapped round the end into the nearest campfire. He winced a little as acrid black smoke from burning oil billowed up from the kindling torch and stung his eyes.

Smarting like tears, he thought bitterly, *sticking in my throat like a need to weep. Aye, well* . . . someone *should weep for 'em dead down there of plague. Their own lord won't, so why not me?*

Karo kneed his mount, moved off to let the others feed their torches at the fire. He watched his men mount and form two ranks behind him. Last came old Gharey, who bore the banner of Raeth. The standard-bearer had to lay the Shield and Sheaf across his saddle bow before igniting his brand.

Karo watched Gharey's torch flare, and thought about the magic of fire. Fire could make enchantments of hot light and secret shadow on the stone walls of a bedchamber; weave wizardry to beguile a wistful dream from far places of the mind. Fire could, charm away the cold of winter.

And fire could cleanse, as it had the six villages in Raeth and the Hivardan villages of Khar's Crossing, Stag Run and Bounty.

Karo lifted his brand high, watched the last of the night's stars through the smoke. Horses stamped restlessly, uneasy with the scent of smoke. Dissonant clinking in the hot hour before dawn, bridle iron jangled.

"Colors," Karo said evenly, and the gritty wind caught the Shield and Sheaf as Gharey raised it. The banner's silk hissed, snapped a little, sounded just like the voice of fire.

"Why the banner?" Gharey had asked at Khar's Crossing.

Karo had answered that though he did not like what he'd been about to do, he would not go secretly like a marauder in the night. As was Wending, Khar's Crossing, Stag Run and Bounty were Fargut's villages and the banner of Hivard's lord should have flown over the burnings. Yet, though this task of scouring the villages was not rightly Karo's, only taken on because their lord was a puling coward, the Lord of Raeth would not do the sorry work skulking. And so he'd gone about the business of burning those villages with his colors high for his sake and the sake of his men. Regretful they might be, but they needn't be ashamed.

Now he told Gharey to raise the colors, knowing that the old man—yet among the finest horseman in Raeth despite his age—could ride his red mare with torch in one hand, banner in the other, breakneck down the hill to Wending with only knees gripping and guiding.

"Higher now than ever, old friend," he said.

And Gharey nodded his understanding, a look in his canny old eyes which said that he suspected another reason to raise the standard.

Khar's Crossing, Stag Run, Bounty—they'd all been villages well within Hivard's borders. But Wending was close enough to the border between Hivard and Soran provinces to have provided Fargut with fuel for boundary disputes with Darun Lord Calmis in years past. Should anyone beyond Wending see the village burning, Karo wanted to be able to say that he'd done this sorry but needful work with his colors high, done the burning on behalf of the rightful lord of the land.

Karo had quarrels enough with Soran's lord—not least of which was that Calmis had engineered Garth's regency, undermined his own bid to become the infant King's formal guardian. When time came to settle that quarrel, as Karo was certain it would, he did not want the accusation of contributing to a border dispute to cloud the true matter between him and Soran's lord.

Karo of Raeth lifted his torch, drove his heels into his mount's flanks. Trailing smoke and fire like another banner, he led his soldiers down to Wending.

Fire leaped and stretched from burning cottages, roaring like the thunder no man had heard in all the year past. Light and shadow, stinking smoke billowing into the paling night sky, the merciless heat of devouring flames—all these things receded, became unreal as Karo stared down at the infant cradled in his arms, trying hard to see it through his own hot and smoke-stung tears.

How had he heard the infant crying, weak mewling, above the roar of fire? Likely he'd not ever know the answer to that.

When he'd picked the babe up, lifted it from the withered breast of its plagued-killed mother and run with it from a small cottage just fired, the boy-child had been stirring fitfully, making faint kitten-sounds, little coughs. Now it lay motionless in Karo's arms, delicate lips blue and dry, eyes half-hidden behind lids as finely veined as a flower's petals.

"Kill it," one man had said when Karo ran from the burning village to the safety of the stony fields with the infant in his arms. "M'lord, it's plague-struck!"

Several others agreed with this hard advice, wincing to see their lord with the sick child held close against his breast.

Dawn-wind picked up, blew from the north and fanned the fires in the village, spread it to the tinder-dry beeches. Old Gharey used a less direct word than "kill." He spoke of giving the babe mercy.

"M'lord, the babe'll not live long now, and that living is only pain. See how aching its breathing is." Gharey shook his head regretfully. "Child has plague, he does. Y'can see it, m'lord."

Karo saw, and heard the thick wheezing in the infant's chest even above the noise of fire and horses and men. Had he and his soldiers not come to scour Wending, the babe, lone little life in this plague-village, would surely have died today anyway. Gharey counseled a painless death, the mercifully swift drawing of a keen-edged dagger across the little throat. Nothing for the babe to feel, not really, and better than suffocating on lungs filled with plague-drawn blood.

Karo shuddered, wracked by sudden nausea. This was a child in his arms, not a sick cat found in the byre! Nor a grown man who could plead for the kind of mercy Gharey spoke of—all the while knowing what the hard gift would mean. And Karo, both a father and grandfather, had never held a babe, never felt the warm and trusting weight against his breast, without knowing that it was a privilege; one paid for with the promise to ward and nurture, to protect from pain when that could be done.

Soldiers muttered, wind whistled hollowly. Behind, the fire in Wending weakened, having fed on all there was to eat and finding nothing but stone and dirt beyond the beech grove. In Karo's arms the babe gasped feebly, coughed once. Blood stained the delicate blue lips. Soon the choking would start, and that would hurt terribly.

"M'lord," Gharey whispered, urging a decision with only the tone of his voice.

But there was no need for Gharey to speak further. Somehow, without knowing he'd done it, Karo had shifted the infant to the crook of his left arm, taken his jewel-hilted dagger from his belt. Cold the weapon's grip against his palm, though the aged night was hot as summer's noon. With trembling fingers he closed the finely veined eyes, let his hand linger on the babe's head like a blessing.

The child stiffened, then convulsed suddenly, gasping desperately for air that was not there. Karo closed his own eyes, loosened his grip on the dagger's hilt a little so that the sweep of the blade across the infant's throat would be swift and smooth, as painless as such a thing could be.

And so it was.

The babe sighed and sagged, a limp, lifeless weight, heavier now in Karo's arms than it had been. The Lord of Raeth knelt slowly, placed the dead infant gently on the ground at his feet. His men backed away from the tiny corpse, hissing whispers and making the sign against ill-luck. All but Gharey, who took the dagger from his lord's hand and cleaned it in the dirt, wiped it on his breeches, and handed it, hilt-first, to Karo.

"Where to now, m'lord? Loft?"

Karo, scrubbing the heels of his hands against his bloody shirt, jerked his head south, toward Damris.

Though he'd originally planned to, he'd not now return to Loft to tell Fargut that his dirty work was done. And he'd left a strong enough army in Raeth, an army determined to protect from outlaws what villagers and stead-holders yet lived. Cold in the place where his heart used to be, Karo decided that he would go to Damris, go to tell the Regent about this night's work and ask Garth if he thought such work would have been needful if they'd not spent the past year waiting for the Elf-King's false promises to bear fruit.

"But m'lord," Gharey whispered, "what if we are plague-carriers? What if we bring the sickness to the city?"

Karo worked at the bloodstain with his knuckles. "What if we are; what if we do? They can't hide forever, and it's time they knew that. And what matter to us, old friend, if we die of it out here or behind the walls of Damris?"

Gharey said nothing, only followed his lord as he was used to doing. In that he was no different than the others.

By night's end they sighted the walls of the city. In the long dark moments before dawn Karo wearily answered the challenge of the guard on the north wall. The guard, a youngster who looked to be no older than twelve or thirteen, admitted the Lord of Raeth with no further query and only weary and perfunctory courtesy.

As he and his soldiers rode through the tall wooden gates and into the city, Karo heard the sharp cry of one man seeking to get another's attention. He looked up along the wall, saw a man hurrying toward the young guard. A question was asked and answered, but Karo did not hear the words for the whistle of the hot dawn wind and the ring of shod hoofs on cobbles. He did see the youngster gesture in his direction, saw the other man stop, then shrug.

Behind him Karo heard the young guard cry: "None through the gates!" to a watch-mate. That second guard caught the order and sent it on to a third, that third to a fourth.

"None through the gates! None . . . the gates! . . . The gates!"

The cries ran like echoes around Damris, carried by hot winds, and the hair rose bristling along the back of Karo's neck the way a wolf's hackles rise when it has entered the sheepfold and knows why it has come.

Chapter Twenty-Two

THE CATS THAT FREQUENTED THE HOMES OF THE ELVISH FISHERS all sat by hearths or in doorways, grooming themselves with the fastidiousness of their kind. As cats do when rain is about to fall, they licked their coats upward, against the grain. In the forest beyond Verdant Hall a doe trumpeted, another answered.

A fall of woodcocks skimmed a tree-ringed meadow, their flight sounding like faraway drumming.

An owl alighted in the large oak that stood like a sentinel beside the Elf-King's bedroom window, stayed to hoot at the cloud-hidden dawn. The scent of the forest, a rich incense of wood and earth and leaves and animals, hung heavy in the air. Dekar, who'd lain wakeful through the long night, tending to his sorrow and tendering his prayers to the seven Deities, rose now and went to the window. He listened to the owl, and watched the rain as it began gently to fall. A soft misty vapor like a secretly whispered blessing, the rain did not pock the grey surface of the Altha, only mingled with the thin veils of fog rising from the river.

A blessing, the Elf-King thought. Well, maybe. A blessing for the two mages who had died this night, wasted and sapless as last year's fallen leaves. Dead of their efforts, all their strength spent in magic not made, prayers not answered. And in the night, after the two had taken last breaths and died, the silvery, ever-present twilight which filled the southern forest and veiled Verdant Hall had darkened noticeably, grown more like true night.

"Tonight in Mannish, they'll not see the rainbow lights they once saw over the forest," he told the owl. "Our mages are too few and too weary to send their light that far now. When they see only the stars and the dark sky, will they wonder whether we have abandoned our efforts?"

Will they wonder—as I wonder—whether the Deities are deaf and all hope of help is nothing more than the subtly played, wistful chords of a bard's song of long ago?

The owl had no answer, and the river only sighed.

Dekar turned from the window, then spun quickly back as he heard the hard and urgent drumming of hoofs on wood, the grunt and pant of a horse mercilessly driven as it galloped across the bridge that connected the island to the eastern forest.

"Cry the King!" someone shouted. A young woman by the sound of the voice.

"The King!" called another, likely a guard complying promptly. Then, hastily: "Let the rider by!"

The Elf-King drew cool water from the ewer at his bedside. He washed hastily, changed clothes quickly and went to wait for the rider. He steeled himself to patience, did not for even a moment engage in the game of trying to guess what would have sent a rider galloping recklessly along muddy forest tracks as though her own neck or her horse's were worth nothing.

Such guessing was a hazard to clear-thinking, and Dekar had only to remember the high thin edge of panic he'd heard in the rider's voice to know that clear-thinking would be needed now. As he walked the cool corridors, went to the hall and the Forest Throne, he listened to the rider's approach, tracked it by the cries of the watch.

"The King! Let the rider by!"

None through the gates . . . None through the gates! The terrible order passed from man to man, rolled through the dreams of Darun Lord Calmis like the heavy, unstoppable tread of an army marching. He woke startled, heart pounding, sweat trickling down his ribs. The questions he'd asked yesterday—of Garth, of his fellow Council members, of himself all the night before—still weighed on his heart.

How many people beyond the gates of Damris would die of plague because they could not flee the countryside?

And then, as always before, hot on the heels of that question came another to torment the Lord of Soran, a question guised as an answer: How many in Damris would die if but one carrier of the dire sickness were admitted to the city, his illness to share?

(And soft-footed, whispering, came the question he'd not asked of anyone but Garth, that question filled with private pain of the kind only reluctantly shared. What of Dail? Where had he gone? Neither the Regent nor the Lord of Soran knew, and now Dail's bards and 'prentices were no longer talking about their master having set off upon the usual spring journey. Now they had the tight-eyed, pinched look of men who feared for a well-loved friend.)

Dawn's light scattered the night darkness to shadows, and those shadows, that light, fell in confusing patterns across the bedroom. Beneath their burden of light and darkness, the sweat-damp sheets of the bed seemed somehow heavier than they were. Someone groaned, a soft sound of secret pain, and Calmis knew the voice for his own. Bedsheets rustled, and Lizbet, her long Elvish eyes clear and bright as though she'd been hours awake, leaned up on her elbow, drew him close.

Calmis breathed the richly mysterious scent of the oils she used to keep her skin soft in these hot dry times. The scent of other people reminded him constantly that the luxury of bathing had become nothing more than a memory. But by miracle or magic, Lizbet's fair skin and thick dark hair smelled always of witchy wood-scents, musky oils pressed from strange trees that grew in

foreign lands beyond the southern seas. An Elvish fragrance—
and one which had always enchanted him, wrapped him in peace
the way her very arms could do.

Not so now.

"The gates are closed," he said dully.

Lizbet did not try to reason with him, did not offer him the
shallow comfort of telling him what he already knew: that no
other course of action could have been taken.

"Ah, Lizbet," he sighed. "I feel like everything's gone out of
control."

She stroked his face gently, with one finger traced the line of
his jaw beneath his closely trimmed beard. Once such a caress
would have sent shivers of delight through him. Now Calmis felt
nothing, not even the easing of the tension that made neck muscles
rigid, jaw muscles ache.

"And had you hoped to control drought, Darun? And hunger;
now plague? These are not things a man can control. These are
only things he can endure."

"No," he whispered fiercely, feeling no longer ragged and hopeless, but deeply and painfully angry. "Only victims endure."

Lizbet, not daunted, went on with the same quiet determination
that Calmis had always admired. "Wise men endure," she said,
"until they can find a way to make a change."

What change? he thought bitterly. *What change can be made
when no one has control?* He, who had managed—and often with
ease!—to keep a firm and steady hand on the reins of events,
could control nothing now. And so he could change nothing.
All he could do was react, and hope that reaction would be
sufficient.

"Darun, be easy. All that could be done, you have done. You
have worked hard to convince Garth that he must become Regent,
and he has. Dear one, I remember the time—and not so long ago—
when you despaired of doing even that."

He smiled, but only thinly.

Lizbet, as though she saw into his thoughts, sighed. "He *has*
made mistakes. But he's also done good things. It's not a god
you convinced to become Regent, simply a good man. And that—
though it seems little to you—may still be enough. You know him
better than I, Darun, but I know this: Garth has endured much, and
will endure more. Sometimes endurance is all we have. And, my
love," she said, leaning to kiss him, "it is not only victims who
endure. Another word for endurance is survival, and often it is
only heroes who survive."

And what does that make us? Calmis thought. *A kingdom of victims or a kingdom of heroes?*

Came the distant thunder of horses' hoofs on cobbles, the ring of bridles and mail; then, closer, from the courtyard below the window, a sharply barked order. Calmis, to escape his thoughts and angers, to flee his helplessness, left the bed, went to the window to see who had come into the courtyard.

He saw the Shield and Sheaf streteched out across the hot blue sky, the gold thread of the banner's design glittering in the red dawnlight. Karo of Raeth, gone since April, now led a band of men into the court. As Calmis watched, he swung down from his mount, threw the reins to a stableman, and spoke a word to one of his soldiers. Then he strode up the stairs, a set of his broad shoulders which spoke of some grim and stony determination.

Calmis shivered as though winter had touched him. He'd seen blood on the Lord of Raeth's shirt, a great long smear of it. Saying nothing of this to Lizbet, he dressed quickly, all the while wishing that if one person had managed to get to the gates of the city before the order to close had gone out, that one person would have been any other than Karo of Raeth.

A steward ushered the rider into the hall, guided her to the Elf-King where he sat upon the Forest Throne. Surrounded by beauty, by wood-paneled walls polished to gleaming, by ancient tapestries which glowed warmly in the light of braziers newly fired against dampness; surrounded by delicately blown glass ewers and thin stone goblets, by rush-woven rugs so tightly made that they could have been fabric—surrounded by all this, the rider strode long-legged into the hall and did not seem to notice that she'd come into the most beautiful of all Dekar's chambers. Head high, nostrils flared and trembling, she gave off the same restless, skittish energy a sensitive and overdriven horse might.

The young Elven had the look of a northern Stone-Elf about her; not nearly so tall, she, as her southern kindred, nor were her eyes so long, her ears so elegantly canted. Often the look of these northern folk recalled Mayne's fathering, though that fathering was long, long ago.

And, aye, she was no young woman, Dekar thought as he stood to greet her. She was no more than a near-grown child, all lean angles and coltish as adolescent girls are. She had ill news. Dekar felt it the way he could feel the charge in the air before a summer storm. He gestured toward the chair the steward set before him, said:

"Sit, child, you look weary."

She gulped, still catching breath from her long ride, but she did not sit. All that quivering energy would not let her. And though it was proper to accept whatever the Elf-King offered, Dekar did not insist. He nodded dismissal to the steward.

"King," the girl said, breathless and trying for calm. "I've been in the northern woods." She stopped, shook her head, her pale, rain-wet cheeks flushing. "Pardon," she said, realizing her lapse in manners. "Pardon, King. I am Neysa, a hunter-scout with Lundr's band. We ride the northeastern borders—"

Dekar raised a hand, stopped her explanation. He knew where his old friend Lundr rode. He himself had given Lundr charge of the stony lands between the Landbound Sea and the arrow-straight border across which the Mannish province of Celed lay. "Tell me your news, Neysa."

She did, and spoke evenly now that she'd caught back her breath. "King, the land-sickness has crept more eastward. We saw trees on the borderland— Oh, King, the leaves were dead on them as if winter had struck in summer! The bark was peeling off branches and trunks, and around them withered grassland, and earth no stronger than ashes!

"We went hungry for two days, had to ride deep into the forest before we could find even squirrels to hunt." Tears welled in the girl's eyes, and she gulped again, but not for breath. "These were not Mannish lands so stricken. This I saw a half-day's ride into our own lands."

Dekar groaned, but only inwardly. Last night his grief for the two mages dead had been for them; this morning it was for the land. *Now*, he thought, *the land-sickness will be like a terrible army marching, advancing, invading, destroying more and more as my brave mages weaken and die*. He listened to the rain—not a drumming but a whisper, for it was still a misty fall—and felt his belly go tight with fear.

How long, he wondered, *before the last mage kills himself with unanswered prayers? How long before we, too, have heard the last of the rain?*

"Neysa—" he said, but said no further. The hunter-scout, hearing impending dismissal in his tone, shook her head.

"King, there is more. Our hunt for food took us northward into foothills of the Kevarths. There we saw two things. A village—" She swallowed hard around pain. "My own home-village was burnt to the ground. The stone-houses were black, the streets filled with bones and ashes. They were all dead! Not a one—no man or woman or child—escaped the fire. King, it was mage-made fire, and I spoke with the one who did the magic. Aidan, he said he was: your own mage. He told of plague, told that the whole village was stricken, and when he'd come there none had escaped the sickness, all were dead. He made the fire to make a cleansing.

"And he charged Lundr with a message to you; one which Lundr said that I must bring. It was this: 'Your hope is alive. The stone is where we thought. I have gone to take the magic.'"

Your hope is alive!

And so it was—alive, quickening, growing. Neysa spoke of plague and the advance of the land-sickness. The rain fell heavier now, beating furiously on the river, the wooden roofs of Verdant Hall. It sounded a wonderfully strong beat, like hearts rising to hope's anthem.

"Neysa," Dekar said, surprised to hear the catch in his own voice, surprised to feel his hands trembling where they rested on the arms of the Forest Throne. "Hunter-scout, you've brought me good news indeed. Now, before you go to your well-earned rest, tell me this: How was Aidan? Are he and the bard faring well?"

Neysa cocked her head in puzzlement. "Mage Aidan was well when I saw him. But, King, there was no bard with him. He was alone."

"Alone? Had he no Mannish companion?"

Neysa shook her head. "There was only Aidan, and he in a great haste to be riding northward."

A thin shadow of uneasiness crept across Dekar's new hope. Where, then, the bard? Had he taken sick of the plague? Had he been hurt or killed along the way?

Or had he been unconvinced after all? Had he gone back to Damris and Nikia?

He was not fainthearted, the bard. Fear would not have sent him back to Damris. But love might have; the love that Dekar had heard in his voice when Dail had protested the idea of bringing the Emerald back for Nikia to use.

Nikia almost lost her soul to that cursed Ruby!

And protesting, the bard had felt that Nikia would risk the same loss were she to call the Emerald's magic.

But surely Aidan would have sent word if Dail had left him to bring warning to Nikia . . .

Dekar leaned forward, now gripping the carved arms of the Forest Throne so tightly that he saw the blood drain from whitening knuckles. "Neysa, hunter-scout, think: Did Aidan say anything about the bard?—Dail, his name. Did he mention a companion at all?"

Neysa answered at once, and with certainty. "Mage Aidan said nothing about any companion. He was in haste and barely took time to give his message. But . . . could it be that this bard Dail fell to the plague?" Her eyes darkened. "How sad to lose a bard's treasure that way."

Aye, sad, Dekar thought. If it were so. But another treasure was still within reach.

Your hope is alive. The stone is where we thought. I have gone to take the magic.

The Elf-King warmed his heart at Aidan's words as a man warms ice-bitten hands at a leaping blaze. He'd planned to use Dail for more than a way to the Emerald. He'd hoped the bard would be able to convince Nikia to use the Emerald were he himself unsuccessful. Still, a way would be found without Dail's help. Nikia had become strange since her wedding in Damris, and filled with the kind of independence of spirit Dekar had never encouraged in her. But even she—so newly independent—would not refuse to call the Emerald's magic when presented with the stone. Whatever else she was, Nikia was about to become a mother.

And what question there was about the fathering did not seem to affect Nikia's feelings toward the unborn. The foolish child cherished that babe as though she had no thought that circumstances might well dictate that the babe be taken away from her, a traitor's get not allowed to live at either court. Perhaps not allowed to live at all. This had long been a source of frustration to Dekar, but now he saw that Nikia's affection for her child would work to his good. No mother would turn away from the chance to save her babe from the terrible fate of sickness and starving.

"Neysa," he said kindly. "Girl, get yourself some food and rest."

She left him silently, and, alone in the hall, the Elf-King left the Forest Throne and went to watch the rain pouring in rippling sheets like watered silk outside his window. Likely the bard was dead, he assured himself, for surely Aidan would have warned otherwise.

And then, because he was a cautious man, a careful planner, Dekar went to find the captain of his guard. He gave her orders, and warned her to take only the best of her soldiers, the strongest. For they were to go into the damaged lands west of the Altha.

"Ride north along the border between Mannish Celed and our own lands, Maida. Look for a Mannish bard, Dail whom you saw here not long ago. Belike he's dead. If so, leave him where you find him, for he'll have died of plague and it will be worth your own lives to get too near the corpse. If you find him dead, send a fast rider with word to my daughter's husband at Damris. They'll need to know that news, but tell your rider to speak it gently. In Damris they'll know his death as a great sorrow.

"But if you find the bard alive, bring him here to me. Don't harm him, but know that he must not return to Damris."

Chapter Twenty-Three

THE LATE AFTERNOON SUN BEAT LIKE A FORGEMAN'S HAMMER on the walls of the Citadel, and Liam of Celed cursed the heat as he walked through the close, hot dimness of the windowless gallery. As he passed the chambers of the old king, a servant noiselessly opened the door, nodded greeting.

Ah, Brita, he thought. Brita, fair red-haired maid, used to be plump in all the right places before hunger and thirst came. Liam eyed her sideways and almost smiled. She was yet no rail-thin starveling, and pretty still, despite the rigors of heat and drought.

He was a sly one, old Alain, to keep such a soft and winsome girl near. Liam wondered now, as he'd wondered times before, whether Brita warmed more than the old king's wine of an evening. In his youth, and well beyond, Alain had kept a keen eye on the pretty ones.

Ah, but that was a time ago, and before he'd gone all broken-hearted to his chambers like an old dog with nothing to think about but licking his wounds.

Brita spoke a quiet greeting.

"How is he?" Liam whispered, asking the question everyone asked whenever they came upon one who might know. A question ventured a little guiltily, for it seemed that when Alain had put aside his crown and given the Regency to his son most people had forgotten him.

A forgetting, Liam thought now, that Alain himself had fostered, him keeping so tight within his dark and closed chambers. As though *he'd* forgotten *us*!

Brita shrugged. "He goes on. Neither gets worse nor well. No Sorcerer's war could kill him, nor this drought and hunger the evil one left behind." She jerked her head toward the closed door. "Him, his heart'll kill him."

Surely that, Liam thought as Brita bobbed a curtsey and took her leave. *If broken hearts can kill.*

He went past the Council Chamber, past the chambers of Darun Calmis, and went to stand at the balustrade which overlooked the Great Hall. Leaning on the stone, he looked down into the well of the Hall, then up along the smooth walls of stone which were dressed in tapestries and embroidered silk hangings. The soaring walls of this central hall made the spine of the Citadel, and from either side broad-stepped stairways swept up to galleries like this one, to residential suites and reception halls and the wide, stone-flagged corridors on which they fronted.

Liam waited where he was, not too near the Council Chamber, not too near the Regent's suite of rooms; rather, somewhere between both. From below came the sounds of harps and voices raised in song as masterless bards schooled their younger fellows in the old songs of the land, the new ones crafted in the wake of a war. There were more apprentices than bards these days, Liam thought grimly. Not many of Dail's old troupe had survived the war; a few of the older survivors had not withstood the drought and the hunger.

And the King's Bard himself? Well, who knew where he was? Vanished like the last deep chord of one of his own songs as it fades into the night and the silence.

The Lord of Celed smiled a little, despite his gloomy thoughts, as one voice, a strong, even baritone, took flight and rose above the others. A bard, impatient with his slow students, snatched the song from the mouth of a youngster and set it free to soar as it was meant to do, let it fly on the wing-strokes of his harp.

> I am the hunter bright, north-fled
> To dark places where no light shines.
> Dark's foe I am, hard-hunted
> To stone places where nothing grows.

A song of Ylin, of the queen whose face and form adorned a tapestry now hanging in the Great Hall, who long, long years ago had made the garden that lay brittle and burned, dried and dead outside the Hall today. Aeylin the bards all called her now, giving her an Elvish name. One and the same, those two women of legend; or so the King's Bard said, so the Regent's Elvish wife claimed.

One way or another, Liam thought, *and for all the good it does anyone, those bards do make fine songs about her. Songs to make your heart rise when it'd rather be sinking.*

Drawn by the music, Liam almost turned toward the wide stone steps that would bring him down to the Hall. But he didn't. He'd promised Karo that he'd wait nearby until the Lord of Raeth's interview with the Regent was done.

"For we've some talking to do, Liam," Karo had said.

And so he waited, listening to the songs of the bards. And as he waited, Liam of Celed had time to realize that when he'd agreed to listen to whatever it was Karo would talk about, he'd not thought—as once he might have—that he'd make certain to listen carefully so that he could repeat the conversation to Darun Calmis. Instead, he'd thought nothing, only found himself responding to the dark fire in Karo's eyes, to the hint and unspoken promise of fighting.

We need *to fight—something*, he thought now. *No good'll be done locking ourselves up behind walls like old men taken to hiding in their beds*!

Old soldier that he was, Liam heard his heart say: *We need to take some kind of action against—something. If Karo knows what that something is and how to fight it, I'll listen. And I'll do no talking to anyone who might want to get in his way.*

Nikia's small harp had a voice like spring, and when she caressed the strings she made music to remind one of the dreams to be had during misty twilight. Sweet music, dreams of day's end and the things to be hoped for from the night.

There was no better place to be when Nikia played like that, Calmis thought as he dropped flat on the floor, stretched his arm under the bed. In all the Citadel, likely in all of Damris, there was no better place to be than with Nikia in Ybro's nursery if it was hope you were looking for.

Then he smiled. *And no better place to look for the ball Ybro always loses than under his bed.*

The mattress rustled a little as Nikia put aside her harp and moved from the center of the small bed to peer over the side. When the music stopped, the hot chamber seemed to become even hotter, the air thicker. But no change had really come, except that now the grinding drone of cicadas could be heard again.

"Don't bump your head, Darun," Nikia warned, her voice soft with the mingling of fondness and amusement peculiar to a woman who watches a friend indulging a loved child.

He grunted a wordless reply as his fingers brushed red cotton, the rag-stuffed ball. Then he grunted something else when he realized that he couldn't quite reach the ball.

Ybro cried: "Ba!"

Calmis shrugged himself farther under the bed. With his right hand he swept the ball into his left, then rolled it along the length of himself to where the yearling King sat near his feet waiting for play to resume.

"Ba," Ybro whispered, clutching the ball to himself. He wrapped his arms around the ball. "Ba!" he crowed.

Calmis, still on the floor, put his back to the bed to watch the child at play.

"He reminds me of Gweneth," Nikia said. She brushed her fingers across the small harp's strings, called a wistful chord. "It's his eyes."

Calmis nodded. Ybro's were wide grey eyes, bright with satisfaction now, but most often mild and meditative. (Upon what would a year-old child meditate? Calmis wondered.) Most who saw him seldom looked past his thick, curling red hair, his well-made limbs, the stamp of his father. Long-jawed he'd be, like Fenyan was. But his eyes, his smile, these were gifts from his gentle mother; from Gweneth, Karo's daughter, who had spent all her own strength in child-bed so that her son would have a chance to live.

And live, he had; even prospered in this year of drought and famine. Fenyan had never been a friend to anyone, not even to himself, but Calmis was grateful now that the prince had made a strong son, one who could withstand the rigors of the hard year that was his first. His mother had given him the chance, his father the strength. And Nikia nurtured him as fondly as though he were not her nephew but her own son.

Ybro climbed to his knees, precariously balanced with his hands planted squarely on the ball, and began to rock back and forth.

"Boy," Calmis warned, moving away from the bed, reaching for the child. "You'll fall right on your face if you don't—"

The ball slipped; the child, gasping, tumbled forward. But not to the hard stone floor, only into the Lord of Soran's waiting arms. Ybro wriggled, turned himself around, reaching for the ball which had rolled away. "Ba!" He drummed his heels against Calmis' belly.

Calmis endured the pummeling, tilted his head back so that he could see Nikia. "Ba?" he asked.

"Only if you want to continue rooting for it under the bed. That's where it always seems to go."

Ybro squirmed harder in his arms, wriggling and kicking again. Calmis glanced at the depth and the angle of the hot sunlight pouring across the window ledge. Several hours past noon, the time, and like a dark thread of unease woven through the brightness of the afternoon, he realized that if he didn't leave now, he'd be late for the meeting in the Council Chamber.

One of the first things Karo of Raeth had done upon his arrival this morning was to go find his grandson, only just awake in the nursery. Calmis yet heard the deep shudder in Lizbet's voice when later she'd told him of that meeting, how Karo had stalked into the nursery, all grim and silent and filthy with blood to hoist the boy high and dandle him on his knee.

"Ah, Darun, I thought he was a wolf come stalking," Lizbet had said. "To see him all blood-covered, and the child in his arms! And the look of him! Darun, he looked . . . hungry. Strange and hungry."

The next thing Karo had done was to visit the old king, pay his respects to Alain. He'd come from there to demand an audience with the Regent. He'd gotten that, and what matters Raeth's lord and Garth had discussed in that private audience none knew. But word had been sent to the Lords of the Council that a meeting had been called. And the page who'd carried the message to Calmis had been white-eyed and nervous, had looked as though he'd seen ghosts.

Calmis lifted Ybro, swung him up and over his head, sat him on the bed beside Nikia. "Sit here, little King."

"Ba!"

"No," Nikia said. "No ball. Little one, I think it's time for a nap."

"Ba!"

Calmis, half-turned to rise, saw Ybro bang his fist down on Nikia's harp in a fit of childish temper. A string snapped loose from its fret, made a sharp wailing cry. Ybro echoed the instrument's jarring protest. Calmis reached for the boy's hand, turned the little fist over to see whether the snapping string, sharp enough to cut, had drawn blood from Ybro's hand. But he stopped mid-gesture, the King forgotten.

Aye, the King forgotten, the Council forgotten, all else forgotten but the sight of Nikia's stricken expression. Tears stood in her long silver eyes; tears come so suddenly, so incongruously, that Calmis almost didn't know what they were for not knowing *why* they were.

He checked Ybro's hand, checked his arm, saw no mark. "Nikia," he said quickly. "The boy's not hurt."

She said nothing, only turned her head. The gesture sent a tear sliding down her cheeks. One slender hand reached blindly for the wounded harp where it sat in a long shaft of reddening light. She lifted the instrument, held it close against her shoulder. In the sunlight, a quick and sharp dazzle, the simple gold ring she wore on her left hand gleamed.

Garth's ring, Calmis thought.

But it was not Garth's name Nikia whispered as she wept over her wounded harp; though a well-known name she spoke. And, as though the leaping light from that golden ring were not a thing to be seen but a thing to be heard, Calmis remembered—no, *felt*, along nerves and heartstrings—a song of Dail's.

> Of dawnlight her cheek is made.
> No gold has she but sunlight's mantle
> Soft to wrap her in.

And Calmis, his eyes on Nikia's wedding band, knew suddenly and completely why the Elf-King's daughter sat weeping over the unstrung harp.

No gold has she but sunlight's mantle soft to wrap her in . . .

Calmis set Ybro down upon the bed, took the harp from Nikia and laid it aside. She was a king's daughter, a regent's wife. Such women are not approached familiarly. But she was also a friend, and so Calmis did not ask permission, but sat on the edge of the bed, took Nikia very gently in his arms and let her weep there, the yearling King still sobbing between them.

Dail . . .

Nikia shivered, though Calmis held her tight; cold, though her friend's arms were warm. She ached in every part of her: heart and soul and body. And the weeping did not ease the pain.

When had she first understood that the man she loved was not the husband who slept beside her at night? When had she known that the affection, the gratitude, even the admiration she had for

Garth were not love, but only parts of it?

Ah, Dail—gone away quietly in the night with no word of farewell to his friends; trapped in dangerous places outside the closed gates of Damris. When had she first understood that she loved him?

Nikia shivered again, and Darun held her closer. She remembered a day in the fall, when the world still knew seasons. On that day she'd looked into Dail's eyes and known what it would be like to be loved by him. *His love is like his music*, she'd thought—*low, soft hymns, bright anthems, canticles, and cradle songs*.

But that day she'd been about to take up the burden of convincing Alain and the Council that they must trust in her father's mages to halt and heal the land-sickness. And so she'd closed her eyes to the promises Dail wanted to make her. She did not permit herself to wonder what it would be like to accept such promises— to offer like promises. Instead, she'd asked for his friendship, and with it she'd made herself strong enough to convince the old king and his Council; strong enough to find and use every way possible to make her marriage to Garth a good one.

But then she'd told Garth about the child, then had come the unspoken questions and the fear of not knowing how to answer. How lonely those fears! How lonely she, as she shared her hopes for her unborn child with no one; kept secret her joy as the babe grew within—as she and Garth grew apart.

And at night, alone in the Queen's Garden, she would walk, and watch the Elf-light in the east. Then she'd feel closest to her child. Secret and alone in the garden, she could tell her babe how welcome he'd be, how dearly she'd cherish him . . . no matter who his father. And when the moon would set, the garden become filled with Dail's music, she'd sing the songs to the accompaniment of those distant harp notes. She'd sing each one softly to her child as she'd learned them from Dail, the bard who was cousin to princes, the bard whose mother had been sister to Garth's own mother, but who did not know who his father was.

Had it happened one night that she'd recognized love in music and a moonless sky?

No.

Nikia had understood only this morning, when she'd waked to hear the cry of the watch on the wall passing orders that none would now be admitted into the city. She'd known then, as she'd lain beside her husband and felt the first rising of a love finally acknowledged even as she heard a watchman's voice crying Dail's doom.

And a moment ago, when she heard the broken harp scream in pain, she'd heard an echo of the scream that had been within her all day. As she'd hidden from her dreams all these long, weary weeks past, taken up calm as though it were a cloak to conceal her from herself, so had she tried to hide from her love all this long weary day.

And so, she wondered, *have I really damped my dreams at all?*

Nikia sat away from Calmis, took Ybro upon her lap and hushed his sobbing. And calming the child, she used all her will to stop her own weeping. After a time, Ybro grew quiet again. His fright forgotten, he yawned, then cuddled against her shoulder, his right hand fallen lightly to rest on the swell of the babe in her womb.

The unborn stirred, and Ybro opened his eyes, startled.

"That is your cousin, little Ybro," Nikia whispered, her head bent close over the yearling King. She stroked Ybro's red curls. "Do you feel him moving?"

Ybro sighed deeply, gone quickly as children do to the edge of sleep. Nikia looked up at Calmis, and she knew that her air of peace had returned.

Once she'd wielded fire and war, with the help of a Ruby's magic become a creature with no other name than Hunter-Defender, no other purpose but to defeat in deadly combat a ravening Sorcerer. And she'd come back from it, to be again a mortal woman. It was not, after all, so very hard to still weeping and restore calm.

"Nikia," Calmis whispered. "I wish . . ."

"You wish you didn't know," she said. "I wish I didn't know, too, Darun. If I didn't know, it would be easier to live the life my father chose for me. But, easy or hard, I *will* do that; for I agreed to."

"Ah, Nikia, I'm sorry."

She shook her head. "Don't be. It's not a bad thing I agreed to do." She stroked Ybro's shoulder, thinking of Gweneth, of her sad ruin of a marriage to Fenyan. "Or even a very hard thing; my husband is a good man. Many women are not as fortunate. On my wedding night, my father said that by my marriage to Garth I would found a new house, for my child will one day rule Elvish. He and Ybro will be raised as cousins, Darun, close as brothers. No jealousies, no fears, no cause for war between the kingdoms they will grow up to cherish. 'We will bind our two kingdoms through the generations,' my father said that night. 'And not simply for one lifetime.'

"He was right, Darun. These children must have nothing but peace, and a kingdom each to rule. I could wish nothing better for Gweneth's son. I could wish nothing more for my own child."

"And for yourself?"

Nikia looked out the window, at the hard blue sky as it deepened toward day's-end. She tilted her head a little, listening to the ceaseless droning of cicadas, the ever-present sigh of hot dusty wind.

"I could wish for rain," she said, pretending to lightness. "I could wish for that."

She turned, met the Lord of Soran's eyes calmly. She covered Ybro's small hand with her own, touched the child on her lap and the child she carried within her.

"And, of course, I wish what every woman wishes: That my child comes healthy and strong, that he will be brave and good. And—" She took a quick breath, remembered fear making it sound like a small sob. "And that all will love him."

"How not?" Calmis said. "If this child is only a little as good and brave as his mother, how could anyone help but love him?"

Then I hope the Deities are kind to him, Nikia thought as Calmis left her for the Council meeting. *For his mother is not brave. And I do not know who his father is: the mage I killed, or the prince I admire but do not love.*

Karo of Raeth reeked of burning, trailed the stench behind him like an evil memory as he paced the length of the oaken table; like memories of the tale he told now, of smoke and sorrow. When Raeth's lord passed in front of the window, Calmis winced to see the last sunlight stab at his breast, change the brown smears of old blood to blazing red. There had been time for Karo to change his shirt before the Council meeting, but he hadn't. He wore that blood like a badge of hopelessness, and each man he passed— Liam of Celed, Celedon of Rigg, Garth, and Darun himself— recoiled from the sight.

Karo stopped his dark tale, stopped his restless prowling, stood near the window, a little turned, so that the light shone full on him. With a bard's skill for pause, he glanced down at his shirt, touched the edges of the bloodstain.

"And this . . ." he said softly, fingering the stiff material. He raised his head, looked directly at Garth. Calmis shuddered to see the icy, brittle light in Karo's eyes. "This is babe's-blood."

On his right, Calmis heard Liam's indrawn breath hiss between clenched teeth. On his left, Celedon stirred restlessly, a man afraid that he was about to have a terrible guess confirmed.

Though it was to the others he spoke, Karo never looked away from Garth. "Aye, babe's-blood," he said relentlessly. "We found the poor mite in Wending, all but dead of hunger and sickness."

Calmis looked at Garth. Face pale, fists tight, the Regent kept his eyes on Karo. None could call him cowardly, Calmis thought. But Garth didn't ask the expected question. Likely he knew the answer to it.

Ah, but I *don't.* Nor did Celedon, and Rigg's lord asked for them all.

"And how is it you're stained with this babe's blood?"

"How do you think?" Karo asked, his voice dry and flat, barren of emotion. Absently, he touched the jeweled hilt of the dagger at his belt.

Celedon made a hard, choking sound of disgust. "You never killed a babe!"

Karo twitched his hand away from the dagger, as though the touch of the jewels stung. "Didn't I? Better, Celedon, to let him die choking? Better to ride off and leave him to make a feast for jackals and foxes? They're not always patient, those carrion-eaters. Especially now in these hungry times. Often they don't wait for their dinner to die."

And then Calmis saw something the others didn't. Too taken by their own revulsion, by their need to make sense of the terrible deed, none seemed to see that the brittle cold light in Karo's eyes had become like a mask. And ugly as that mask was, Calmis knew that it hid something uglier: barely contained rage, and something very like self-loathing.

Someday, Karo's hard eyes warned, *someday soon you will have to do what I did. You will have no choice. But that won't stop you from hating yourself.*

And each of the men at that table—Calmis himself—shuddered deeply. Not at the thought of Karo's killing. At the sure knowledge that as plague advanced, each of them could well be faced with a like decision: mercy or no mercy.

"Regent," Karo said. He glanced at each of the others in turn. "My lords, you're not going to keep the plague without the city walls. And so I've come here to discuss the matter of a solution to our problems."

"What solution?" Calmis demanded. He eyed Karo narrowly, the way he'd eye a poisonous snake come slithering. "Have you suddenly turned enchanter that you've a solution to the problems of drought and famine and plague?"

"Enchanter?" Karo shook his head. "No, Calmis, I'm no dab-bler in magic and useless enchantment." He looked at Garth again, smiled coldly. "And besides, we know that doesn't work, don't we?"

"We know nothing of the sort!" Celedon insisted.

Karo shook his head, slowly, sadly, as though over some tragic folly. He turned his back on the room, went to stand at the window. Head back, he twisted his neck, his shoulders, as though trying to ease tense muscles.

Those gestures might have been affected, Calmis thought, but surely the sudden stiffening of his back, the small sound—much like a groan—which escaped him was not.

Karo turned from the window, eyes glittering like diamond chips and about as warm. He laughed, a deep booming sound like winter surf. Calmis heard Celedon take a short, sharp breath. The Lord of Rigg had seen something in Karo's eyes to frighten him. Liam kept quiet; Garth did not even stir.

And Karo, playing to his audience again, gestured expansively, swept his arm round the chamber, extended his hand to the window and the hot sky bruised with twilight.

"Come look at the Elf-King's enchantments, Celedon. Aye, all of you: Come see what Dekar is doing for us tonight."

They went to the window, Celedon, and Liam. Garth stayed where he was, eyes tightly closed like a man marshaling strength. Calmis only followed the others slowly, his mouth drying up with fear.

"He does *nothing* for us," Karo snarled. "He's given up on us, my lords. Like a wise man, he's decided to cut his losses and fall back to consider what can be gained next."

Out beyond the walls of the city, beyond the dead river and the seared meadows, out in the east where once the shimmering rainbows of many-colored Elf-light had veiled the sky over the dark line of the forest—there only darkness hung, and one or two early stars.

"Aye, given up on us," Karo whispered, deadly soft, again working at that terrible bloodstain with the heel of his hand. "And do you think he'll welcome our hunters now that they may be carrying plague? Do you think the Elf-King will do anything but shore up his border defenses and give orders to kill any one of us who sets foot in his forest?"

No one answered, and so, cold inside himself, Calmis chal-lenged. "You don't know that," he said, and nearly groaned aloud to hear how feeble his defiance.

Karo only laughed again. "Ah, I don't. But *you* should, my lord of Soran. You know the Elf-King better than all of us. It was you who urged the treaty with him two years ago—and that treaty years in the crafting. You know he's no fool. Tell me: *Will* he let plague-carriers into his lands?"

Not if he's got any sense, Calmis thought bleakly. But he did not voice this thought, let Karo's question go unanswered.

Karo walked away from the window, went to the oaken board and sat. Celedon and Liam followed. Calmis remained behind, still looking at the empty sky.

Have all the mages died? Is there no more hope?

At the Council table they began to talk of precedents for the unmaking of treaties, of gathering armies if need be, of raiding into Elflands to take what was needed. They talked of war—declaring one or causing Dekar to declare one.

Who talked the loudest was Liam, with Celedon muttering and wondering and finally giving way. Who spoke most calmly and reasonably was Karo. The Lord of Raeth had thought this all through, offered sound suggestions, well-made plans.

Who remained silent was Garth, quiet as stone, never moving, not showing by word or gesture what feelings were hidden behind the silence and the tightly shut eyes.

And Calmis, for he did not take part in the discussion, only heard it vaguely, as though it were taking place in another room. He could not focus his thoughts on anything but the blackening sky and—sometimes—his memory of the look in Nikia's eyes when she'd spoken of her marriage and her hopes for her yet-to-be-born child.

We will bind our two kingdoms through the generations, and not simply for one lifetime.

That binding was being undone now . . . or would be if Garth didn't come out from his silence and stop this mad and dangerous talk.

But Garth said nothing, offered neither protest nor agreement, and the talking went on.

Chapter Twenty-Four

RAIN SWEPT DOWN IN THICK GREY CURTAINS FROM THE KEV-arths on the first day of Mage Aidan's solitary northward journey. And that was no surprise. Thunder had been growling even as he'd given his message to Lundr; a sheet of lightning flashing white had shown him the pale face of the near-grown girl Lundr had chosen to bring Aidan's message south to the Elf-King.

Your hope is alive. The stone is where we thought. I have gone to take the magic.

Lundr had looked like he wanted to ask questions when he heard those words, but he'd kept his peace. This was business between a mage and the Elf-King. And so, in the end, Lundr had charged his rider with the message to Dekar and only bid the Elf-King's Mage safe journey and good speed.

The rain had poured from the deep cloud bellies even as Aidan spoke a word of thanks to Lundr and turned the pie's head north and east. That rain had fallen all day, made the ground a thick and treacherous mire, the rocks slick and dangerous. Still, Aidan went on. He estimated that he was yet two weeks' hard riding from the caverns and the lost Jewels.

These hours of riding had put many miles behind the mage, and with this distance between himself and those he'd left behind on the hill above burned Lindens Lee, Aidan began to believe he'd completely misunderstood the original reasons for his decision.

He hadn't been fleeing a bard's dangerous harp music, Dail's songs of Aeylin, which carried, unsung, dreams of the Elf-King's daughter . . . unfulfilled dreams whose merest echo stirred Aidan's own dreams of hunger for power. Too close he'd come to that bard in the scrying, too alike their separate wants. But that wasn't why he'd left. Not truly.

And he hadn't left quietly in the night because he'd seen a thing in Kicva's dreaming which he'd never expected: a whirlpool of emotion centered around a dark-bearded Mannish soldier. What matter, that? What matter that she was not the calmly sensible young woman he'd always thought her to be? War changed people; times of fear and strife made them behave in extraordinary ways. Come times of calm again, and Kicva would find her way free of the whirlpool and the confusion, Aidan was certain of this.

He'd left for no other reason than that he believed there could be no sensible thing to do but find Islief's cavern home. And this, he told himself, had been a hard choice to make. Despite what he'd said to Kicva, Aidan did not in the least believe that Islief was anything other than what he claimed to be—an old, old son of a race no living being had seen before now. Islief must surely be filled with the kind of lore and learning no one alive today could do more than guess at. Hard to leave that!

But in the end, Aidan had left; taken the horse and begun his northward journey to the Kevarths and Islief's caves. For the Jewels were there, and among them the Emerald that he so desparately sought.

I want to bring that Emerald back to Dekar, he thought as he urged his pied gelding up a stony slope. *I want to bring the Heal-stone to him so that he can put it to the use he'd intended all winter.*

And no, he *didn't* want to use the Emerald himself. That would be insane, for the one with the best chance to call and control the magic was the one who'd used a Jewel like that before. Nikia.

Exactly, he thought as he bent over his horse's neck to avoid the low-hanging pine boughs. *Nikia is* exactly *the person to use this Emerald. No matter that Kicva and her strange friends rant about unborn babes.*

Then came a frightening whisper escaped from a secret dream.

Kicva had said that no mage alive had the skill to call the Emerald's magic. But she was wrong. One mage possessed the skill to find the Jewels; just as Aeylin herself had found them. And that mage—and *he*—would surely have the power and skill to . . .

Aidan drove his heels into the gelding's flanks, rode as recklessly as a man rides who is grievously afraid. For now it seemed to him that the words of his message to Dekar were changing with the drumming of his horse's hoofs. It seemed to him that there was a small and dangerous difference between what he'd said and what he'd meant.

I have gone to take the magic . . . to take the magic . . .

"I have gone to make the magic," he whispered.

And when he spoke those words—those terribly changed words! —Aidan himself changed.

He became like a torch, afire with visions and shining; shedding the concerns of others, the promises he'd made his king, as a fiery brand sheds shadows behind, for this is what it is like to acknowledge a dream.

Armed with Dekar's orders to find the bard Dail, Maida took ten good soldiers and left Verdant Hall. She kept to the forest's northward tracks for a day and a half until she found a good place to ford the Altha. Now, as she led her troop across the river, she smiled a little, coldly. She knew this ford well, had led soldiers across it often in the days when there was no agreement between the Elf-King and Mannish but the simpler one that war was a good way to settle ages-old differences. Rich Celed, with its farms and pastures, was a day's ride from here, and in those war-days it had been a fine place for raiding when armies were on the move and could take no time for hunting. Much faster to sweep down upon some Mannish farmer and relieve him of fat cattle or plump sheep, the corn from his fields or the chickens from his henhouse.

Ah, but that was two years ago, she thought as she watched the last of her troop cross the water. Sometimes it seemed a lifetime ago.

She looked eastward. Only true twilight hung over the forest, soon to fill up the woodland with night. Strange to see that, for no night had come to the forest in near a year, held back by the silver sheen of mage-work; night rendered no more than gloaming for all the hours between sun's setting and rising.

But now the mages had stopped trying to work their magic, ceased the making of prayers. Only a few men and women remained of that prayerful host Dekar had gathered in the autumn. And they were not strong enough to do more than sit alone in dark corners, wrapped in silence and despair, wondering how it was the Seven no longer heard them.

Maida snorted, waved the last soldier on and spurred her horse, cantered along the line of ten to its head again. And wasn't that typical of mages? Prayers unanswered meant that each of the Seven Deities was deaf.

The Deities weren't deaf. They just weren't of a mind to listen. *And you can shout at one who has no intent to listen until you are hoarse and your tongue falls out*, Maida thought. *That one's still not going to listen.*

When she and her troop had gone a short distance into the river meadows, Maida wished heartily that the Deities *were* of a mind to listen to the prayers and spell-chants. The lovely meadows of spring were a silent ruin, and the wind hissing through seared and lifeless grasses had an evil sound to it.

What was it the Deity of Wind wanted if not prayers? What did the others want?

Maida shivered, though this first hour of night was far hotter than even noon had been in the forest. That the Seven wanted something, she was certain. Goddesses and gods, they always wanted something. But what?

"Make camp," she told her young second, come up from the line to await her orders. His face shone pale in the light of the rising moon; his northern blue eyes showed more white than color. "Build the fires well and strong. We're not far from Mannish now, and there's like to be bandits and thieves near. But watch the campfires well, Truite. Else Waian will conspire with Vuyer and burn the world down round our heads."

Truite nodded, went back to his fellows and gave the orders. Alone again, Maida looked out over the meadows, the land flat and empty, seared as brown as though the heavy hand of drought had lain upon it for years. But no drought had touched these river meadows until just recently. She'd been here not long ago—ah, not a seven-day before!—and then the meadow had been noisy with birdsong and springing with life.

Anyone would think this place lies in Mannish Celed, she thought. *But we're yet a half-day's ride from there.*

In the east the dark line of the forest showed like a black, black wall. But for how long? The land-sickness was on the march, advancing like a pitiless army; enemies come not to conquer, but to destroy. How long before the forest died of this land-sickness?

"What do you want," she whispered to the silence and the sky. "All you Seven, *what is it that you want?*"

But there was no answer, only dry wind-whisper, and Maida turned her horse's head, went to join her troop.

Were he dead or alive, she hoped they'd find the bard Dail soon. She hated being in these blighted lands. She wanted to go home to the woodlands, wanted to return to Verdant Hall the way a woman feels the urge to return home when word has come that a beloved, a parent, a child, a friend is dying.

Ah, bard, she thought, *if I find you dead—I'm fleeing this place as fast as horse will take me. But if I find you alive, you'd do best not to argue with me about coming back to the King!*

On the second day after leaving Kicva and her companions, Mage Aidan woke wet and chilled, but hopeful. The dawn sky had shone clean-washed and brightly blue between the branches of the pines. Warm sun gilded the edges of brown puddles. The way would be muddy yet, the rising rocky ground slippery, but Aidan would not be wet and cold, and he would be able to see and better find his way. But he could not ride now, for the pied gelding had thrown a shoe early in the day, and now limped behind him, bleeding from the hoof's tender quick.

At the end of the third day Aidan came to the rock pool, the place where Kicva had been attacked, and weary of walking, he lay down to sleep.

On the fourth day, dawn came brightly. The misty air smelled of honeysuckle and a vagrant thread of pine come down from the northern heights. Mage Aidan stood beside the rock pool, watching the rising sun light the water. He prayed, and his prayers were answered. The pool became as a scrying bowl, and Aidan tasted the dreams that had been dreamed in this place a month before.

Dreams of what an old cotton shirt smelled like; dreams of green things—ribbons and emeralds, and the sunlight on ver-dure; a small grey man's sleepless dreams of hope. Aidan bent to pick up a stone, tossed it into the water and watched the ripples take the dreams away. He had a dream of his own. The dreams of others were no more important to him than if they'd never existed at all.

He left his injured horse, stripped of saddle and gear, by the side of the pool and started his journey on foot. And he comforted himself for the loss of the pied gelding by telling himself that he'd be travelling rising paths now, steep-sided trails that climbed along the giddy heights, treacherous paths not meant to be taken on horseback. He'd not come to Islief's cavern home as quickly as he'd hoped, but come there he would.

As he walked, he dreamed waking, as Islief himself did. But Aidan's dreams were of power and wild, wild magic, as Islief's had never been.

Chapter Twenty-Five

DAIL THOUGHT OF THE ALTHA AS A DIVIDING LINE. ON THAT first day, when they crossed the river at the ford near fire-blackened Lindens Lee, they'd left behind all things of springtime. Though a poor springtime it had become; faded in the night and failing in the morning. The river was as much a border in time as of

place. Three days had passed since he and Islief, Kicva and
Joze, waded across the Altha. Dail was certain that during
the passing of those days springtime had died in the eastern
forests just as it had here in the meadows on the western side
of the Altha.

On the first night of their journey they'd seen the sky in the
northeast darken, seen a haze of rain, a grey wavering curtain
hanging over the woodlands. But they'd not felt any of that rain.
Dail and his companions had come into sick lands where the sky
glared with painful blue brightness. On that first night they'd yet
at least three more days of walking before they reached Celed
province and the true border between Elflands and Mannish. Three
more days and they would enter that deadly strip of land known in
Damris as Brigand Home.

Aye, walking. They'd only Dail's brown mare, and she carried
nothing but the light burden of Islief, his sack full of cooking
pots, and the harp *Dashlaftholeh*. The heat and the sun were things
each of them tried to endure as best they could. Kicva and Joze,
soldiers each, knew how to settle into a steady gait of walking
which would cover distance but not become exhausting. Dail did
not find it difficult to match their pace. Islief should have been
able to keep the stride, but he could not.

"Not the heat, Tall," he'd said that first night when Joze asked
him about it. "Heat doesn't hurt me. Light. The light . . ."

Of course the light. Those wide, wide eyes of Islief's were
for gathering all the light there was to be found in deep cavern-
darkness. Small gleams of starlight or sunlight at shadowed
entries; faint drifts of illumination wandering down the length
of stone chimneys, spilling over the sides of cracks and fissures
into the world below the earth. Even in the forest Islief had
been a shadow-haunter; the terrible abundance of light in these
unsheltered meadows must be very painful. And so they'd all
agreed that Islief must ride the brown mare. This would save
him no pain, but it might save strength.

There was another whose strength Dail worried about. Joze had
become quieter as time went on. He did not speak unless spoken to,
and he had always a look of concentration about him, as though he
were continually checking on some troubling situation. "Watching
for these brigands and bandits you talk about," he'd said when Dail
questioned him. But after a while of watching, Dail understood
that what truly concerned Joze was his breathing. He did that
carefully, but there was always a point beyond which exertion
set him to coughing.

On the second day, following a wide-reaching arm of the Altha along the southwest curve, they saw no white herons laying siege to the shallows of the river. Dragonflies did not hover in jeweled clouds over the water. And on the third day, after they'd filled their water flasks and hung them from the brown mare's saddle, they left the river behind, walked into the broad meadows stretching ahead. They saw no yellow buttercups growing, no snowy flocks of ox-eye daisies or ruddy bells of wild hyacinth nodding in the sun.

Ah, but hadn't there been brown and shriveled leaves clinging sadly to withered stalks! Plants so badly savaged that none of them could guess what they might have been.

Except for the wind hissing and the unrelenting drone of cicadas—so unnerving to the others, so familiar to Dail—the meadows were a silent place. They heard no scurrying of mouse or vole, no sudden startling leap of woodcocks winging for the sky. Small whitethroats did not nest here; willow-warblers did not hungrily hunt insects here. The butterflies of spring—with their wings of white or gold or softest green—did not come to dance.

Dail was used to these sad absences. But Joze, with the dazed expression of a man struggling to accept news of a death, asked where the winged and feathered could have all gone.

"Tall, they have fled along the secret paths all creatures know when they must flee," Islief said. "The ones their fathers and their fathers' fathers knew."

And Kicva, looking pale and belly-sick, had pointed to a clump of withered grass, to the little nest hidden there. Four tiny speckled eggs lay cradled in the nest, untouched, their life arrested.

Islief nodded sadly. "See, Tall. Mother, she is gone; but no hungry thief stopped even to taste."

So it must have been, Dail thought as he watched Joze struggle to accept this. Predator and prey fleeing the sick lands together as they'd have if a wall of wildfire were pursing them.

That night they built no fire for the sake of the tinder-dry meadows. At Dail's urging, they granted themselves only scant sips of water. They found it hard to sleep that night, for the din of the cicadas filled the meadows. When Islief brought Dail's harp to him, asked again for music, for leath, for comfort, Dail obliged. But he heard the droning insect noise at every stop and pause, and it seemed to him that soon the terrible buzzing groan would fill the world and leave no room for the songs of birds or beasts or men.

• • •

Came a day when, sighting landmarks familiar to both of them, **Dail** and Joze agreed that they'd crossed a true border early in **the morning**. They were in the part of Brigand Home which maps named Celed. They wasted no time or attention on conversation. All agreed that they'd like to be out of Brigand Home as quickly as possible.

And what to say? Dail wondered as he walked beside Islief and the brown mare, watching the rising ground ahead where seared meadows swelled in small hills and dipped to sudden hollows round which skeletal cottonwood trees staggered. Should they point out more signs of land-sickness to each other? Ah, no. They all had eyes to see—often wished they hadn't. Should they talk again about the reasons for Mage Aidan's vanishing? Should they wonder one more time why he'd gone away north?

Aye, north he'd gone. His track showed that, and Kicva's dream had confirmed it.

Dail glanced at her now, sideways, and so she could not see him watching. But she must have seen, for she gave him a narrow-eyed look and dropped back to walk with Joze. The Elven didn't like to be watched; Dail had learned that early on. Watching, in Kicva's parlance, seemed to mean the same thing as judging. In these days past, she'd felt as though she'd done something worth judgment. She felt guilty about that dream of hers.

Ah, but we can't control what shape our dreams take, Dail thought. *Or we shouldn't be able to. Where else to go but to dreams when we need to be alone with memory or hope?*

But she *hadn't* been alone, or so she'd said. And Dail, who'd had his own uncomfortable experiences with Aidan, did not doubt Kicva when she said that Mage Aidan had been with her, picking and sorting among her memories until he'd found the way to Islief's cavern home. When Aidan had finished sorting through Kicva's dreams, it must have been as though he himself had been in the chamber of the crystal hearth, as though he'd made that long walk from the caverns to Lindens Lee. Easy to find the way back there armed with the map of Kicva's memories.

"He wants the Lady's Emerald," Islief said.

The aptness of his words, so well matched to Dail's own thought, was startling. Dail looked up, cocked his head to better see Islief on the brown mare.

"Yes, Harper, I know: You wish we could do something about that. But we must go to your Nikia; we must tell her about the magic her little daughter can make."

"But if Aidan takes the Emerald?"

Pain-weary, the small grey man; head low to protect his wide eyes from the sun's merciless light. Still, he had it in him to smile a little, to offer what consolation there was to offer. "We must let the Lady ward her treasure."

From behind them came the hard sound of Joze coughing, the softer sound of Kicva's question:

"Are you all right?"

"Fine," Joze muttered. "I'm fine. It's the dust. This place is so dusty . . ."

But Dail didn't think it was the dust that made Joze cough that way. The young man had been trying to hide his coughing long before they came into these dry places.

Please, Dail thought, *not plague*. And when he looked at Islief again, he saw the same unvoiced prayer for the friend he called Tall in his eyes. *Maybe we'd do well to pray for us all*, Dail thought. *For one of us with plague will surely doom the rest.* Then he turned from that fear, went back to another concern.

"Islief, can Aeylin keep the Jewels safe?"

"She is the Lady," Islief said simply. "She is Aeylin."

"And so we needn't worry about Mage Aidan."

Islief shrugged. "I did not say that, Harper. We must only worry about what worrying about will help."

Dail didn't know how to answer that, and so he didn't.

Then suddenly, sharp from behind, he heard Kicva shout a warning, Joze echo it. Like a baleful ghost, a tall, powerfully built man rose up from the grass only two yards from where Dail stood. As if by magic, with soldiers' swift, silent moving, Joze stood at Dail's right beside the mare's off shoulder, Kicva at his left. For a long moment the only sounds Dail heard were the brown mare breathing, the whisper of wind in the grass and the drone of insects.

The tall man lifted his left hand. Like a claw, that hand, missing thumb and two fingers, half the palm itself. But his right hand was whole, and in it he gripped a short-handled scythe. Dail and Joze drew swords, their blades hissing free of sheaths with one voice.

"Ah, no," the tall man said.

He whistled low, and at once the meadows were empty no more, but filled with weaponed men sprung suddenly from hiding places in tall seared grass and shadow-filled hollows. Two dozen men and half-grown boys, afoot and armed, formed a silent semicircle behind their leader. Some bore short-swords and dirks, several only sharp-honed farm tools. But all wore some piece of mail—helm, hauberk, or ring-shirt—that Dail recognized as gear of the Citadel Guard.

The brigand leader grinned at Dail, a cat's cold grin. "No, no, my friend. You're in Brigand Home. Not courteous to draw weapons in someone's home, is it? Toss 'em down."

Dail glanced at Joze, and when the young man let his sword drop, the bard did the same. The sound of the steel ringing on an earth-embedded stone made a hopeless peal.

"Now you, little Elfling, unstring the bow."

As Dail knew she would, Kicva bristled, but the half-handed man looked away as though she were nothing for him to worry about. One of the brigands snickered; another laughed in such a way as to send chills racing along Dail's spine.

"No, no," the leader said, "later for that. Later. First I'd like to know who these visitors are." His eyes narrowed, he studied them all. When he got a good look at Islief, the tall man spat, then said, "What have we here? I thought all you Sorcerer's spawn were dead."

Dail went cold. If this half-handed man had been a soldier in the war, he'd have seen enough of the Sorcerer's brutish creations to dislike the sight of Islief—small grey creature so different from Men and Elves. Nor did he seem like one who would be willing to consider that Islief might be other than one of that terrible horde.

But Islief said nothing, kept his head low, his eyes closed, for they were facing west and directly into the sun and all its painful light. The half-handed man took a step forward and the mare snorted, danced skittishly. Islief, caught off guard, grabbed the saddletree. Dail reached for the mare's bridle, steadied her.

The brigand laughed without the least sign of humor. Sunlight gleamed sharply on the wickedly curved blade of the scythe. He jerked his chin at Islief. "I'm still waitin' an answer. What are you?" His pale eyes cold as rime, he held up his maimed hand in a parody of a salute. "You one of those filthy sorcerous things took the fingers right off me all sharp-fanged? You one of them?"

And Kicva, who had only barely managed to keep still for her own sake, did not keep quiet then. "Leave him alone, you! He's no creature of the Sorcerer's. He's—"

Islief looked up then, wincing against the light, flinching against pain. By design or by chance, his sudden movement caused the mare to throw her weight against Kicva.

"I am Islief," he said quietly as the Elven caught her balance.

"And the Seven made me; as they made you. I am not evil-willing. Will you let me and my friends pass onward from here?"

The half-handed man shrugged, not as though he believed any word of Islief's, but as though he'd lost interest in his own question. "Probably not. We're what you might call tollmen, eh? Cost you to come into Brigand Home. Down from the mare, now, and let's see what y'got to pay the fee."

"Harper?" Islief whispered.

Dail looked at Joze and Kicva. The Elven, tight-eyed and thin-lipped, shook her head sharply. But Joze took a step away from the mare, a long step that Dail knew would give him room to use his short-sword should he get his hands on it in time.

"Stay where you are, Islief," Dail said, his voice as cool as though his heart were not pounding wildly against his ribs.

The half-handed man laughed again. Brandishing his scythe, he stepped close to the mare, inspecting the gear hanging from the saddle. With a satisfied growl, he hooked the two fingers of his left hand around the water flasks and tossed them to one of his fellows. "That'll do for a start. Now let's see what else y'got."

"Nothing else," Dail said, his eyes still on the precious water flasks.

"Ah, surely something else, Harper." The brigand took the harp case, heard the instrument's soft sigh, and met Dail's eyes with a cruel smile. "Well, well. You're right after all. This isn't worth passage. Naught but a noise-maker."

And he did not toss the harp aside. He dashed it to the ground, then kicked it hard and far.

Dail said nothing, nor did he move, for the world around had gone small and narrow, filled with pain and the sound of *Dashlaftholeh*'s breaking. If he'd had a sword in his hand, he could have done nothing to avenge that destruction. Inside him the harp's dying cry echoed, and it was as though he were feeling the tearing and rending of each song she'd sung with him, the death of all the music she would have made with him. He was helpless to move now, as he'd been helpless to prevent his harp's ruin.

Sneering, the brigand leader signaled to those behind him. "Get that Islief-thing off the horse, m'lads."

Wind moaned down the sky, hissed through the brown grass, sent small clouds of dust spinning as three men came forward, bent on doing their leader's bidding.

They'd not taken two steps before Joze began to cough. He coughed deeply, a hard, wrenching sound of gagging that stopped the three dead in their tracks, their eyes rolling to show the whites.

"P-plague . . ." one whispered, that whisper a fearful stutter as Joze sank to his knees, grabbing at the ground as though to hold himself up.

"Tall!" Islief cried in real fear.

Kicva bolted past Dail to Joze. Still on his knees, shoulders heaving now, the young man struggled in the Elven's supporting embrace. Nor was he struggling against any pain, Dail realized. He was struggling because he'd been reaching for his sword, and there was no way to do that now with Kicva's arms so firmly around him.

Before Dail could do more than understand that Joze's ploy was about to be negated, the earth beneath his feet growled with the thunder of hard-ridden horses, and the blue, bright sky filled up with high, keening battle cries as a mounted troop of Elvish soldiers came sweeping from the south and east.

Panic spread among the brigands, already unnerved by the dread that a seemingly plague-struck man was so near them. They broke and ran, fear-driven, for the cover of scanty cottonwoods. Dail snatched his sword from the ground, shouted to Islief to hold tight and slapped the brown mare hard, sent her galloping. He grabbed Joze's arm, hauled him to his feet, and Kicva with him.

"Go, Joze! Catch up with Islief!"

Joze did not question but ran, head low and staggering a little.

"What are you doing?" Kicva cried as she pulled away from Dail. She pointed to the approaching riders. "Bard, those are Elvish soldiers! That's Dekar's own guard!"

"I know it," Dail said. He grabbed her arm again, dragged her along in his wake as he ran to catch up with Joze.

"They're *friends*!"

Dail did not answer, only held tight to her arm and kept on running. He did not think the Elvish soldiers were friends, for one had pointed to him, shouted an order before she engaged the bandits.

"Truite, there's the bard! Stop him!"

But Truite, whichever of the guard he was, did not have a chance to carry out that order. The bandits, finding no cover among the cottonwoods, had rallied and were among the Elvish soldiers, fighting fiercely, striking at mount and rider alike. No one of those soldiers had thought now for anything but the battle around him.

Dail ran, and he ran hard, following the high cloud of dust raised by the brown mare, leaving behind the sounds of battle. Hard as he ran, though, he could not leave behind the memory of his ruined harp's desolate wailing cry. That music, as all she'd made since first Dail's old master had put her into his hands, would stay with him forever.

A long run through dusk and night that was, and neither Dail nor Kicva wasted breath trying to talk. They were a long time catching up with their companions, for the brown mare had run far and fast. But always they had dust to follow; dust to see, and when night came, dust to taste and breathe. And at last, when they topped a small rise and were able to look around them by the light of bright sweeping stars, they saw one shining red light in the darkness at the foot of the gently sloping hill.

"A fire," Kicva said, panting hard, wiping sweat and dirt from her face. She pointed past the light to a dim tall shape rising behind it. "That looks like a house."

It did, Dail thought, and the shape of it suggested the broad roof-beams and deep stone walls of the kind of house wealthy farmers made for themselves and their families. Houses like that had comfortable hearth-rooms, and still-rooms fragrant with drying herbs; weaving-rooms filled with the clack of shuttles; spacious lofts for sleeping under eaves of sweet-smelling thatch.

He looked back over his shoulder, saw no sign of pursuit. Hard to be glad for that, though he'd been fleeing those Elvish soldiers. The silence behind meant that there was no one—brigand or soldier—left alive to hunt them down. He looked at Kicva, her face white in the starlight, and saw that she had the same thought.

"I'm sorry, Kicva," he said. "Those were your countrymen."

"I'm wondering why they were so hotly on your trail, bard."

"I'm not. Aidan must have gotten some message to Dekar. Your king knows we've parted company and so he must know that I'm heading for Damris." He smiled wryly. "And not to do his bidding."

When he offered nothing else, she nodded wearily, took her bow from her shoulder and fitted an arrow to the string. She jerked a thumb at the house at the bottom of the hill. Shadowy and dark before the flickering firelight, two figures moved.

"Now we'd better be worrying about *your* countrymen, bard. We're only hoping that's Joze and Islief down there. If that's the campfire of more bandits, we're not out of trouble yet."

Dail laughed humorlessly. "Hunter-scout, we're not going to be out of trouble for some time to come. No matter who's down there."

He started down the hill, hand close to sword hilt, but they were not halfway down the slope before he realized that here, at least, they'd get a welcome. Joze came walking to meet them, hands raised and empty to assure them that he was no enemy. His greeting was spare, barely more than assurance that he and Islief were well. Swallowing with difficulty as though around a great lump of pain, he gestured toward the dark house behind him.

"Welcome." he said, his voice shaking. He lowered his head, coughed softly, then swallowed hard again. "Welcome to my home. I'm used to giving better hospitality than I can offer tonight. But . . . at least it's shelter."

It was barely that. The building, which seen from a distance had put Dail in mind of wealth and comfort, was a derelict. A season or so gone, fire had swept through, devouring roof thatching, blackening beams and deep, thick stone walls. The campfire he'd seen from the hill was not outside the house, though it had seemed so from a distance. One wall of the house had collapsed, and Joze had built a campfire in what might have been a comfortable front room in better days, fed it with pieces of broken furniture. Outside, there was nothing to see of garden or pasture or farm-field except dark patches on the land.

That night Joze refused all company as he wandered from room to ruined room of his house, pausing to look out each window as though searching for something he'd lost. And he did that most of the night, though both Kicva and Islief tried to convince him to rest.

"Tall dreams ill dreams at night, Harper," Islief said when Dail suggested that they leave Joze alone to come to terms with his sorrow in his own way. "He dreams of fire and rending. He saw the Sorcerer's fortress burn and fall. Now he sees that fire has taken his own home. He does not know where his kinfolk have gone. This is terrible for him. But he *must* rest, Harper."

"He will," Dail said. He stood in the doorway, watching the hot stars wheeling through the night, thinking about his own nightmares of fire and war, and thinking that Joze surely had a heartful of courage to have set out upon a journey to the Hunter-Defender whose works haunted him still. "Joze will rest when he can."

Islief glanced at Kicva, who was making ready to sleep. Then he came to stand beside Dail. "And you, Harper? Will you rest?"

"I will. When I can."

"But not until you stop hearing your poor harp crying?"

Dail shrugged. He looked down at the ground, saw a piece of broken glass nearly the size of two spread hands. He went down on his heels to peer at the glass. The dark earth made of it a mirror.

Whose face, that in the mirror? Who was that grimy, bearded man? How came his cheeks to be so sunburned, so thin? How came his beard to be so rich in silver? How did he come to be weeping here?

"He misses his harp," he whispered, answering his own questions. "And he's going to be haunted by her forever, and all the songs he sang will be drowned by her last."

Islief touched his shoulder, said gently, "You will always miss her, Harper, for you loved her voice. But if you sleep, maybe you will dream of other songs she sang before this last one."

Dail shook his head, looked away from the mirror and back to the stars again. These, by their pattern, were the stars of Midsummer's Eve. In past years Midsummer's Eve was a time of joy and wonder, a time to revel in the long sweet days between planting and harvest. How many Midsummer festivals had he and his *Dashlaftholeh* celebrated?

"Aye, you bring your harp, master," the farmers would say. "Us'll bring the ale and the food and a pretty girl or two. . . ."

But that was so long ago, when farmers planted with reasonable hope to harvest. Long ago when girls were not blighted by care and sorrow. Long ago when the King's Bard used to have a harp, and went riding the length and breadth of the provinces looking for apprentices and, along the way, for pretty girls.

Tonight Dail felt as though he'd lost everything, hope and music, even the shape of his own face. He thought that Joze was right to be wakeful and watchful against nightmare.

Chapter Twenty-Six

AN HOUR AFTER SUNSET ON MIDSUMMER'S EVE, RED-HAIRED Brita made up a supper of thin broth, dry, tasteless flatbread, and precious water from barrels stored deep in the dark cellars below the Citadel, and brought it to the chamber of the old king. There she found him coughing so hard that he could not take breath enough to do more than lift his hand in a plea for help. Trembling, she hastily set down the tray of food, took the short ewer of water and went to help Alain drink.

Must be that he's been coughing so all afternoon, she thought as she propped his head against her shoulder. *He has the look of it—all white and weak and weary!*

An ache of pity and sorrow shivered through her. She kindled the small brazier near his bed and sat beside him, held him while he coughed. The old man in her arms had no more weight to him than a child. His skin was grey, his lips tinged faintly blue. The rosy light of the brazier lent no color to his face.

Oh, poor King, she thought, tears welling. And she was truly sorry to see him this way. Brita knew what speculations were whispered about the Citadel regarding her relationship with the once-king. People wondered how much and what kind of use Alain was making of her, wondered how warm she kept his bed of a night. But Brita employed the strict policy of letting the wonderers wonder—she did not think that the truth would do either of their reputations any good.

What good braying it about the Citadel that Alain had no more use for her than to plump his pillows, fetch and carry what little food he'd take, and keep him quiet company of a long, long night while he tracked the stars in the hot sky? Servant and lord alike, they'd laugh at him, say that all the sap had dried up in the old tree. And likely they'd laugh at her too, and say that she, who could once have had any man—aye, servant and lord alike!— had grown so poor in charms that she could not even tempt an old man.

But it hadn't been about tempting, she thought now. It had never been about that, unless the tempting of a heartbroken old man to get himself through another night, another day of brutal heat and cruel despair. Some, they die like withered flowers when they lay aside the long hard tasks which kept 'em going for years and years. Even kings who had once been strong as stone.

Brita held the once-king close, whispered words of encouragement, tried to sound briskly matter-of-fact and confident. She did not feel that way at all as Alain swallowed the water she urged on him, though he had to tilt his head far back to do so. A spasm of coughing wracked him again and he lost most of the water down the front of his bed-shirt.

Not plague, Brita thought as she wiped the old king's chin, sopped the water from the bed with her apron. Not plague. It couldn't be that! All the rumor from outside the city had it that plague took its time growing in a person. Maybe weeks. They did a lot of secret coughing, the newly plague-struck, hiding the signs of sickness as though they could deny the hard bleak truth. But time—unpitying as the terrible sun itself—always showed them truth, whether they wanted to see it or no.

Alain coughed again, thin shoulders hunched, head low as though hoarding what breath he had, and that not much. Brita held him in the crook of her arm, and with her free hand she piled up pillows against the headboard.

"King," she whispered. She had never got used to calling that babe in the nursery aught but Prince. "King, rest you easy and I'll go call your son."

But Alain shook his head. "No."

"Shall I stay with you?"

"No. Go away."

"But, King—"

"Go, child. And . . . don't come again. Plague."

"No! It isn't that, King!"

But he—who well knew what enemy had come looking for him—did not answer, only fell to coughing again, and Brita saw blood on his lips.

But how? No one had come into the city from the outside in near a week. Only Karo of Raeth and his few men, and *he* was well enough, that stormy surly lord. This couldn't be plague, all come in one day. But maybe it hadn't come all in one day. The old king had been quieter than usual this week past. And if the stricken one was old and weak and weary of living, could not the plague work its evil so much faster?

Terrified, Brita ran from Alain's chambers, and in the corridor she found the Lady Lizbet just coming from her own chambers. Weeping, she told the wife of Lord Calmis that Alain was ill. "Coughing and bleeding from his mouth! Oh, Lady Lizbet, what will we do if it's plague that's caught him?"

The Elven did not hesitate, spoke quickly in that quiet capable way of hers. So calm, she, that her words did not even go to echo in the well of the Great Hall below them, as most words did.

"Brita, run find the Regent."

"But he doesn't want to see anyone." Brita flinched, for she was not calm; she was filled with the wild whirl of panic and her words flew in echoes all along the gallery. "Oh, Lady Lizbet, what if he has plague?"

In the Great Hall below a boy passing through upon some errand stopped. When he looked up to stare at the two women, Brita recognized him as Saer, the sea-fisher's boy who used to come to Damris without fail every week to barter his father's catch to the Regent's wife. Many people had been caught outside the city when the command had come to close the gates. This lad had been caught within and had stayed to serve in the kitchens. Closed those gates, and barred strongly against any who would enter, and so against any who would leave.

"Hush, now, Brita," Lizbet said as Saer looked away. She laid a hand on Brita's shoulder. "It may be that Alain doesn't want to see the Prince—"

"It's so, Lady, I asked him—"

Aye, capable, that Elf-Lady, even masterful though she never raised her voice. "Nevertheless, Brita, you must go find the Regent. And if you see my Lady on the way, say nothing, else she'll want to come."

Brita nodded, silently agreed that Nikia should not go into the sick man's chambers, carrying as she was. Then, for good measure, she made the sign against evil.

Oh, poor old king . . . !

Brita ran down the stairs, flew past young Saer, the sea-fisher's lad, and went seeking the Regent.

The newly risen moon dressed the Queen's Garden in a motley of light and shadow. In the east, beyond the garden wall, stars hung pale and small.

"Light, and no light at all," Garth said, his eyes on those stars. "Just like my choice, aye, Darun? Choice, and no choice at all."

Calmis winced as Garth kicked the garden wall, kicked it hard as though it were one of the walls hemming him so closely. But it wasn't. It was only flaking mortar and dense grey stone. And the patterns it wore were only the faintest blue shadows of long-dead lichen, the driest rusty outlines of once-soft green moss.

"Prince," Calmis said gently, "kicking the wall isn't going to help get the choice made."

"Darun, there is no choice to make."

"Maybe it seems that way, but a choice is still before you."

Garth closed his eyes, shut out the sight of the garden walls as though he hoped to shut out the unarguable fact that the choice was upon him whether to make the decision or to let others make it for him.

He must, as all the Council but Darun demanded, set aside the treaty with Dekar and go warring into Elflands—or he must refuse to do that and face the real risk of civil war. Karo and his fellow Council members had made that very clear. Either way, violence and bloodshed lay beyond the walls of this sad Queen's Garden, beyond the walls of choice and decision which trapped Garth now.

Cicadas droned, scraping their incessant dirge. Crickets shrilled, a terribly empty sound. Often it seemed to Calmis that these two creatures, noisy insects, were the only things to thrive in this enduring drought. Day and night, they allowed no silence in which to find peace.

"Garth," Darun said, again gently. "There's one thing you need to consider."

Garth snorted. "Only one?"

"Not only one, but this one's important. The treaty your father made with Dekar was not only for the present. They made it to ensure the future."

Garth twisted an ugly, bitter smile, frightening to see in heartless moonlight. "What future might that be, Darun? Plague is within the city now—you know it. That's no broken heart my father is dying of. Though he tried hard to kill himself with grief and sorrow, didn't he? Well, too bad for him. Plague's going to get him first."

"And yet," he said, his voice suddenly soft. "And yet, Darun, I can understand why he'd want to leave all this care and trouble of ruling. It's hard and painful work. But I could have made use of his help."

Garth turned his back on the garden wall as though, stone and mortar, it were the old king himself and all the decisions Alain had not helped him make.

"Ah, Darun," Garth said, "I used to think the two words—decision and choice—were of a kind. That was before I argued with my father for the Regency and won."

"And now?" Calmis asked.

Cicadas groaned, crickets screamed thinly.

"Now I know the words don't have exactly the same meaning. You choose to decide, to follow a certain path of action. Or you choose not to decide and leave the pattern of your life to the whims of events."

Calmis nodded. "The whims of events have been graceful until lately, eh?"

"They haven't been hard."

No, they hadn't, Calmis thought. In all his short life until now, all his twenty-two years until this one, Garth had found the whims of events to be generally kind. A prince and a second son, privileged and not too much bothered with responsibility, events or fate had taken little interest in him. Even his marriage to the Elf-King's daughter—a marriage he had not chosen, but had accepted gracefully—had looked to be a fair bargain: peace between two old enemies, and a pretty wife.

Ah, but a pretty wife who'd come to love another man! And yet, there was even a slim grace to be found in that: Nikia knew what she was going to do about this new love of hers—nothing. But what will happen to them, Calmis wondered, if Garth gives in to the pressures of the Council and sets aside the treaty, lets Karo go raiding into Elflands? Surely their union, like the treaty, will fall into ruin.

Garth ran a finger along the rough stem of dead rosemary. No ghost of the herb's pungent fragrance remained to haunt the bush.

"Darun," he said, voice low, eyes averted. "It's a matter of choosing which war I'd like to fight—when I don't want to fight any war at all. I'm trapped, and I don't know how to get out of this trap."

Calmis held still, waiting for a question. When none came, he dropped to a seat on the ground, put his back against the stone wall. Above them the Citadel loomed, tall dark pile of rock; beyond the garden walls the world stretched dry and hurt and filled with the deadly promise of wars to fight.

"Garth," he said, offering the only advice he could, the advice he'd once offered two warring kings. "Choose for the future."

"Choose for civil war, Darun? I couldn't win, even if I wanted to fight one. The King's army is all the combined armies of the provinces. You know that. What army does that poor babe in the nursery have for me to command if I'm to fight the provinces?"

"None but my men of Soran." Calmis hesitated, then summoned all his faith and went on. "But if you have to fight them, Dekar is still your ally, Garth."

"Is he? Maybe."

"You don't believe what Karo says; you don't believe the Elf-King's abandoned us?"

"No, I don't. He's worn out his mages, he's run out of prayers. But do you think I'd lead his soldiers against my own people?" Garth shook his head. "Darun, do you think he'd even send them?"

"I know he'll defend his kingdom. And if you choose for the future, choose to uphold and defend the treaty between you—you'll take what army you can personally command and help your ally defend his lands while he helps you defend yours."

"Against my own people. Civil war."

"*For* your own people. For their future." Calmis sat forward now, spoke eagerly, and the words he used were not his own.

"Dekar said this to his daughter on your wedding eve: 'We will bind our two kingdoms through the generations, and not simply for one lifetime.' Garth, that is the only hope you have. The child Nikia carries now is the future of both kingdoms. Abandon that treaty now and you will have to fight Dekar. Abandon that treaty now and Ybro will not only inherit a kingdom torn apart by a war that will gain nothing but delayed fate—he will inherit a bitter enemy, the next ruler of Elvish. *Your son.*"

Garth was quiet for a very long time. The ceaseless noise of cicadas and low-moaning wind spun a dry and eerie song. When he spoke at last, his voice was an echo of the wind's, dry and empty and without life.

"Darun, I'm not sure Nikia's child is mine."

He knows about Dail!

Calmis moved suddenly, backed up as though he'd spoken his fear aloud and wanted to distance himself from the speaking. But there was no distance between him and the garden wall, and feeling the solid stone behind him, he knew he had no place to go, and knew he had no question to ask but one.

"Garth, why do you think that?"

He expected anger, or dismissal. His wasn't a question a man would like to answer. But a strange look of something very like relief softened the hard lines of Garth's face. He ran a hand along the side of his jaw, dragged his fingers through his beard. Even in the pale light of the moon that beard was more red than brown, as a deer's coat is.

"I'm not the only one who wonders, Darun. Nikia wonders." Garth drew a long breath, let it out slowly. "My father wondered. Dekar wonders. I'll—I'll tell you the tale if you've heart to hear it. But I warn you, it's a painful one."

His back yet to the garden wall, Calmis nodded, vowed silently that if Garth had the heart to tell it, surely he would have the heart to hear it. But as the telling unfolded, he wished that he had no heart in him at all. For it would have been far easier to hear a man tell the tale of his wife's rape and helplessness were he heartless and sorrowful.

Reynarth—mad mage and traitor! Like his master the Sorcerer, the consequences of Reynarth's malevolence had outlived him. As the land-killing spells cast by the Sorcerer yet poisoned the world, so did Reynarth's rage and violence threaten to poison hope. And they did threaten that, for behind the words of Garth's tale Calmis heard grim possibilities for choice and decision:

With Alain's death would come at least a thin and shabby political excuse to break the treaty with the Elf-King should Garth choose to employ it. The man who made the treaty would be no more. Compacts had been broken that way before. And should Nikia's child prove to be Reynarth's, the next ruler of Elvish would be the son of the man who had betrayed both kingdoms. Calmis shuddered. Dekar would never permit this child to rule if it did not bear strong, incontrovertible evidence of Garth's fathering.

From the far end of the garden came the sound of the solar door opening and closing again. Calmis looked up to see his wife come along the shadowy path. She had news; this Calmis knew because he knew her so well, her every gesture and the meaning of her very posture.

A full burden of news, and it given in a voice which was caught in trembling at every word.

The old king was dead.

"Long life to the King," Lizbet whispered, the words of the old formula dry on her lips. "And, Regent," she said, "my Lady has gone to her chambers and asked for the midwife. Her pains came upon her in the very moment she heard that your father was dead."

Garth got to his feet, his only offer of thanks a nod as he went back to the Citadel with Lizbet.

The Lady A-bearing, Calmis thought as he followed behind. Nikia, for so long the only symbol of hope people had, might this night give birth to a traitor's child. Like the words of a ghost passing unseen and unseeing, came the memory of a conversation he'd had with Nikia only week ago:

And, of course, I wish what every woman wishes: That my child comes healthy and strong, that he will be brave and good. And that all will love him.

No one will love him, Darun thought now. No one will want him. And his birth may well signal the end of hope. For if this child is Reynarth's, what choice will Garth have now but to make war on his father-in-law in order to avoid making war on his own people? What sense risking civil war by upholding a treaty with the Elf-King when that accord might soon collapse under the weight of a dead mage's atrocity?

Chapter Twenty-Seven

NOT UNTIL HE WOKE DID DAIL REALIZE THAT HE'D BEEN SLEEP-ing on his feet, still leaning against the smoke-blacked doorjamb of Joze's ruined farmhouse. What noise had wakened him? For surely a sound had pulled him out of sleep. Joze walking? No, not that, though Joze still wandered his house in lonely search of what used to be. Another sound had wakened him. Dail heard it yet, a tantalizing echo in memory. A wail, a full lusty cry, a shout, a protest. The sound had been all these things.

Hand on the hilt of his short-sword, Dail stepped silently into the night. There beneath the stars he held his breath, listening. Wind whined; insects droned. The brown mare snorted. None of these sounds matched his memory of that which had wakened him. He squinted at the stars and the dark places between.

"Ah, *Dashlaftholeh*," he whispered, his heart all filled up with pain again. "My poor girl, it was you I heard."

Soft behind him came the sound of a footfall, a drawn breath. Dail turned sharply, sword leveled. Beyond the gleam of starlight running on steel he saw Islief standing in the doorway.

"It was not your harp's voice," Islief said.

Dail sheathed the sword. "What do you mean?"

"Your harp did not sing in your dream."

"How do you know what I dreamed?"

"Came to me the same dream, Harper."

Dail frowned, tugged at his beard. "I've never known you to sleep, Islief. Were you sleeping tonight?"

"No. I have not slept in a long, long time. But still, I dream. All creatures must." Islief's eyes glowed warmly, long and wide and bright. "Came a cry in the night to wake you, yes?"

"Yes."

All the world grew silent around them. Dail no longer heard the measure of Joze's sad progress. The wind dropped. The brown mare lifted her head, ears pricked. In the high vaulted sky, in the deep blackness, even the stars did not breathe, and their countless lights became still.

So it had been when, in Elflands, the land-sickness had come stalking. The hair rose prickling on the back of Dail's neck. What

magic prowled near them now? What worse sorcery could come
into these sick lands? Hoarsely, afraid to ask and afraid not to
know, Dail whispered:

"Who cried in the night, Islief?"

A child, Islief told him. A child of Man and Elf, shouting to
greet her bright life at the same time she cries farewell to safe
sweet darkness. "Nikia has given birth."

Dail felt his heart shake and begin to tremble. "Is she well?"
he asked before he could stop to realize that there should be no
way for Islief to know.

"I think she is. The babe did not sound mother-lorn."

Dail felt the sharp sting of tears behind closed eyes.

The Elf-King's daughter at last held the fulfillment of a treaty
in her arms; Garth's wife had the child denied her by miscarriage
two years before. The Lady of the Bards had at last made the
song women long to make. The Hunter-Defender who had fed
upon fire and magic to find the strength to defeat the Sorcerer
held a hungry babe at breast and used a gentler magic than she
once had.

The Lady A-bearing had borne her child, and so who was
she now?

"Harper," Islief said gently. "Your Nikia kindled the heart of
hope. With our faith we will kindle the babe's soul and all its
shining magic. Her mother dreamed of me once. Now the babe
dreams. She knows that we are coming to find her.

"And do not fear the silence. The world has quieted that we
may hear hope beckon." Islief pointed past Dail's shoulder to
the hill beyond. "And so that we could hear the horses coming."

Dail turned sharply, thinking of the Elf-King's guard, thinking
that, after all, some of Dekar's soldiers had survived the afternoon's battle to take up their pursuit of him. He saw, instead,
two riderless horses standing on the hilltop. More weaving of
enchantment?

"Islief, are these magic-sent?"

"No, Harper. They are only horses who have run away from
the fighting. Now maybe it is best to take Tall and go bring those
horses here before they decide to run another way, for we will
come to the Elf-King's daughter and her little one faster with them
than without."

As Dail ran past him, calling for Joze, he saw Islief smile, saw
the light of weary satisfaction in his wide, wide eyes. One might
have thought that he'd assisted at the birth.

• • •

Fire kindled in the many-colored hearth as Vuyer touched sleeping embers, as Fyr breathed light and life. Driven from dreams—by dreads, by voices of fire and magic, by old longings for redemption—Aeylin rose high above the rainbowed hearth, became smoke and the wispy image of a woman who had once lived.

Now, said Vuyer, *look at the fire!*

Quickly, said Fyr, *see what only moments ago happened!*

Aeylin watched the fire, saw a maze of images—the achingly dry bed of the drought-killed A'Damran; Damris city with its cobblestone streets; the dark stone Citadel rising tall over the small brown oval of the Queen's Garden.

My garden! Oh, garden! How carefully I planted and watered and shaped you in the years after Mayne died! Planting for sorrow, they'd said of me. But I was planting for memory, and for all the things that Mayne and I had not made together. . . .

The images in the fire stilled, became focused, and Aeylin saw sunlight, harsh and hot, fall upon a tiny hand. That hand, delicate fingers curled so that it looked most like a bud not fully unfolded, reached through the flat, heavy light, reached into a slender spill of shade to touch a woman's white breast. The ghost heard wind mourning, cicadas droning, dust whispering with the small secret rasp of grit on stone.

The Elf-King's daughter bent her head over her babe, leaned over the child as though to shelter her from the hot sun, and Aeylin heard the infant's soft breathing mingle with Nikia's sigh. Aeylin knew that sigh; she'd sighed so herself each time a midwife had laid a child in her arms. She'd sighed that way to feel the lusty kicking of her sons, to feel the tender softness of her daughters. Warrior she'd been, soldier and hunter-scout; she'd also been a mother and so had known what weights of satisfaction and hope freighted such a sigh.

Those hopes and satisfactions she saw now in Nikia's long silvery eyes. And she saw something else. Nikia, king's daughter, treaty-warrant, Hunter-Defender, knew about magic. How not? She was Ylfish. She'd used many small magics when she was a child, spoken with the birds in the forest, the deer in the glade. And she'd used other magics when she was a near-grown girl, called light from prayers, called healing from brews and simples. Nikia had used a wild magic when she was only just woman-grown, stood with the War-stone in her hand and made the world fall silent and still, breath-held and waiting for her will.

But the Elf-King's daughter had never encountered a magic like this one she held in her arms. No one had ever encountered such a magic. For there are magics and there are magics; there are children and there are children. But the infant Nikia held in her arms—this daughter of Elf and Man—was not simply one who would be skilled in the use of magic. This child *was* magic.

Yes, magic, Ylf said.

Magic, Chant whispered. *Now see what else is abroad this Midsummer's Eve, Aeylin.*

Then Vuyer and his Fyr, working in union, caused the flames to reach high, and when the fire had fallen again, Aeylin saw the image in the embers shift and change.

The ghost saw an Elf walking. He walked in a gentler clime than that of afflicted Damris, in the northern marches of the Elflands, where land-sickness, though close on his heels, had not yet come. Aeylin had known mages, and she knew that this Elf was one of that kind. Trees rose tall around him, and his way wound upward, twisted round stony falls of rock. Westering sunlight slanted low across the earth, made shadow-pools between the rocks and rich gilding for the tips of small tufts of vibrant summer-green grass. Dog-rose twisted, briars and blushing petals, across his path; venturesome honeysuckle wrapped the trees. Aeylin could smell the sweetness.

As she watched, the Elf looked around himself and nodded once, satisfied that he was making good progress on his journey. Then he went on, though he was weary and footsore. This was a man with a purpose, a mage with a narrow focus. He cared not for weariness, Aeylin realized. She knew, as she'd known how to recognize the weight and the wonder in Nikia's sigh, that this mage was following a need. And she knew that he would follow that need until he found fulfillment in the only place such a treasure could be found: these very caverns below the Kevarths, where she watched and waited.

Mage Aidan went on with the singlemindedness of a force of nature, came toward the caverns as though the Emerald were a magnet and he longing steel.

Aeylin knew how that was, too.

He hopes to find a path to a dream, Chant said. *And if he does, that dream will become nightmare.*

"I will stop him," Aeylin said, and the ghost became more solid than smoke, looked more like the queen made of flesh and blood, bone and heart, than she'd seemed in many long years.

No, Ylf whispered. *Your part is to watch the fire. You will see a wolf stalking hope. You will see another hope stalking like a wolf. But never leave these caverns, no matter what you see! What you do, you will do here.*

Then all the Deities spoke; seven gods and seven goddesses in unison said gently, as though they offered not admonition but comfort:

Patience, Aeylin! Your part is not ended. But all these events—and those which they engender—are weights in the balance to come. No matter what you see, add nothing to the weights by your actions now, else what must be, however good or ill, will be changed.

And so Aeylin tried to be patient, the ghost, the long-dead queen. Her every instinct demanded that she do else, but she kept to the hearth, watching and waiting. It chafed her to do so. For she'd not yet learned all the ways of forbearance, and she thought she heard Deities whispering about that, gods and goddesses murmuring doubts and fears that she would never learn in time.

Chapter Twenty-Eight

KARO OF RAETH PACED THE LENGTH OF THE GREAT HALL. TODAY this public place was best for meeting secretly. Two nights before, the Hall had held Alain's mourning feast, and last night a quiet gathering to celebrate the birth of Garth's daughter, the child they called Gai. Poor hungry meals those had been, feasts in name only, with no fresh food and little enough of dried. There'd not been much to clean afterwards. The servants had done that in the night and would have no reason to come here today. Nor did bards gather here this morning. Caught between Alain's death and the birth of Nikia's daughter—end and beginning—those bards attended mourners and rejoicers alike, made songs for each.

"We're all caught," Karo whispered to the emptiness. "And I between things no one else sees." He laughed coldly, and the echoes of his laughter pursued him like dark-winged ravens. As he walked, Karo rubbed the heel of his hand down the front of his bleached linen shirt, scrubbed at a stain he could not see, the weight of which he felt nonetheless. He scrubbed hard enough to feel the bruising pressure along his breastbone, but he did not wince. He'd become used to the pain.

Karo stopped his pacing, gauged the time by sun's height and shadow's length. They were late, damn them. And why late? Were they mourning or rejoicing? Karo snorted. Not those four! They had no hope to ever feel sorrow or joy again. Each had kin trapped without the city walls when the order came to bar the gates; kin left to die of hunger and thirst and plague. Karo had chosen his henchmen well, and none of them a man of Raeth. Not even a birthplace would point the blaming finger in Karo's direction. These were citymen; men of Soran. In later days folk would say they'd risen up against the two men—the Regent and their own Lord Calmis—who would not act to help them.

Karo began his restless pacing again, and with each step he took, resolve and fear warred in him.

Did he dare do what he planned?

Did he dare not?

And, caught between the questions, he comforted himself with the knowledge that he would not do the deed; he would only set it in motion. "And those are only the same thing if you let them be," he told the echoes. "Who is to say that *I* killed them, when another's blade strikes?"

Who is to say that you brought plague to the Citadel? the dark-winged echoes whispered. *Who is to say it was you caused the old king's death? And the boy in his cradle—who is to say that it was* you *brought sickness to him?*

Karo pressed his hands to the sides of his head, moaned softly as he remembered how it had felt to hold Ybro only hours after he'd held the doomed infant in Wending. One holding had been mercy. The other was not something he could think about, not anything he could admit.

Lay the blame at Garth's feet, the echoes said. *He's earned it. The plague is his fault, for he did nothing about getting the food and water that would have kept it at bay. Such terrible sickness seldom finds footing where people are fed and clean.*

And as the raven-winged echoes laughed at how quickly he leaped to embrace that conclusion, Karo thought: Yes! Yes!

In Elflands there was food and water, but Garth had not moved to do anything about that. He'd only taken the meager crumbs his father-in-law let fall from his table. And the crumbs had never been enough; were not now. Yet, claiming that he was mourning for a father already entombed, Garth refused to answer any question on the subject of dissolving the Elvish treaty. Now the time for questions had come and gone. Answer would be found in steel, and murder would be remembered as execution once this weak and puling Regent was dead. Once Karo ruled.

And he would rule. Ybro's closest kin, and all the Council but Soran's lord in agreement with him on the wisdom of treaty-breaking, he would rule. Come night, there would be no Regent; no Lord of Soran to disagree with his plans for war. Come darkfall no man would be able to stand against him, and the first blow— maybe the surest—would have been struck in a new war against the Elf-King. Come the night, Garth would be ready to take his place beside his father in an old tomb; Darun Calmis would be no more. And Dekar would have no heir at all, not daughter, not grandchild, when tomorrow dawned.

Soft behind him, as though a route of wolves had come padding into the hall, Karo heard the echoes of footsteps other than his own. He turned, saw the four. Each had hidden in his belt a dagger, plain-handled citymen's weapons. They were ready.

"Today?" the oldest asked. He was a squint-eyed fellow, his thoughts well hidden.

"Before day's done," Karo said.

When the echo died, the narrow-eyed man said, "We'll come tell you?"

"No." Karo scrubbed at the front of his shirt again, hard with the heel of his hand. "I'll know. And if vengeance is still not satisfaction enough for you, you will be paid as we agreed."

The four left the Great Hall silently, and Karo, yet worrying the front of his shirt, followed a short time later. On the broad stairs to the gallery he met a half-grown boy, shabbily dressed and pale-faced. But though the boy tugged at his forelock, stammered a courteous greeting, Karo did not answer. He had no time for tongue-tangled servants; he was thinking about Ybro. Karo wanted to sit with him now, his grandson whose death the Regent had caused. He'd hold him, rock him in his arms, and talk to him for as long as the child could hear.

Saer, the sea-fisher's son, flattened himself against the wall of the staircase as Karo passed by. He pressed so hard against the wall that stone bit into his shoulder blades.

Too late for that! The lord's already seen ye, witling!

Ah, but maybe Karo didn't know that, passing near the Great Hall, Saer had heard whispers and echoes. Surely the lord had seemed preoccupied as he'd brushed by, and not with worrying what dark whispers a fisher-lad might or might not have heard.

Today? one of the four had asked.

Before day's done, the lord had growled.

Whispers and echoes, but telling of what? There was nothing to truly speak of ill-doing in those overheard words, not if you weighed word against word.

Saer's heart took a sick turn in his chest. But if you put shifty eyes and secretiveness into the balance, and four daggers, the plain dudgeon of one showing above a broad leather belt, the shapes of others outlined beneath shirts and so not hidden as well as their owners thought . . . then would you have an inkling of evildoing? Saer didn't know, and the not-knowing was nearly as frightening as any knowing.

He wanted to tell someone what he'd heard, wanted to rid himself of this sudden, terrible foreboding. But who to tell? Mother Ina, she who tended the little King now that the Regent's wife had a wee one of her own to watch over? Ah, not Ina. She'd scold and fuss and tell him his head was all full of fancy, his wits weak from long days spent with the sea and the sun-dazzle. She'd done that before. Ina was a citywoman and such seldom had use for sea-folk.

Brita, the dead king's fine and handsome servant? Ach, but no one could speak to red-haired Brita these days. She mourned old Alain hard, like a woman who'd lost both a lover and a child all in one bleak night.

Who to tell, then? Who to tell that he smelled trouble in the air as surely as he'd be able to scent a storm abrew at sea though the sky shone blue and the water lay calm? Maybe there was no one to tell.

Shaken, Saer took the stairs slowly, went walking along the gallery toward the chambers of the Regent's wife. For this had been his original destination before he'd been stopped by overheard words. He'd gotten himself as clean as possible this morning—hair combed, shirt tucked and tidy, breeches brushed—so that he would look presentable. He was going to visit the Elf-King's daughter to tender his good wishes upon the birth of her child. It was only polite, for the Princess had been a keen and skillfull barterer each time he'd come to sell his father's fishes to her. She could strike a cunning bargain, that Elf-Lady! Saer respected her for this. But, more, she'd been kind to him when he'd found himself trapped within the city. Homeless, he, until she'd given him a home within the Citadel and work to do with the kitchen-folk. And she always had a pleasant greeting when she saw him, ever a smile, sometimes even a small jest to hark him to the better times when they'd both bargained over fishes.

"Be good to them as is good to you," his mother always said. And so Saer believed it would be poorly done if he didn't pay his respects in person to the Princess and her little daughter.

Well, well, he thought. *Maybe I'll find someone to tell after they let me speak a good wish to the Princess. If they let me do that.*

For they weren't so free with permission to see her. Her waiting-woman, Lord Calmis' Elf-wife, was like a lioness watching her cubs, keeping day and night to the Princess's anteroom, not letting too many folk come near. Everyone was worrying about sickness these days, and the Lady Lizbet seemed to make it her bounden duty to keep all plaguey folk away from the Princess's door.

And after all, Saer thought as he walked along the gallery, *maybe that's what I'm scenting: plague-fear, like storm-fear. Maybe I'm worrying for nothing.*

The voice of Lizbet's lady-harp in the outer room came to fill the bedchamber as Nikia lifted her daughter from the cradle and held her to breast. Singing soft songs to quiet Gai's hungry crying—Dail's songs, the very songs she'd sung in dark nights as she'd walked the lonely paths of the Queen's Garden—Nikia made herself comfortable against pillows and nursed her daughter. The babe sighed, for the milk and the music. In the same moment that she felt Gai's hungry nuzzling Nikia felt herself fill up with wonder again. She marveled at the perfect beauty of her daughter, fell silent in amazement when she realized that she'd carried this dear child through terrible seasons of want and hunger, yet still had milk to nourish. She joyed in the bond, forged in an instant, which had sprung up between them. It was as though they were two who had known each other many long years gone and, separated by time and events, had found each other again at last.

"All the things I used to be," she whispered to the child, "were like masks and costumes that I wore, tried on and found ill-fitting. I see who I am, Gai, when I see my image reflected in your eyes. . . ."

But even these amazements and mother-magics paled when Nikia understood again—and again as though it were the first time—that she at last had the answer to the question that had tormented her countless times since she'd first known she was childing. She no longer wondered whose child Gai was. She knew, and the understanding brought a sweeter kind of joy than she'd ever felt.

Gai was *her* child. A daughter borne safely through dire months of drought when the bearing was seen by others as a symbol of hope, but was in reality a lonely joy not able to be shared. And with this knowledge, all things of care—wounded world, tangled loves, all the hard strivings and mazy politics of her life—fell away when Nikia held her baby. Even the harsh sunlight of this day's end seemed soft. The winding drone of insects—ever present, often felt these days like scraping along nerve-ends—seemed gentler, mere weightless sound again.

In the outer chamber the music stopped. Came the sound of a door opening, then Lizbet's voice. Though her words were whispered, Nikia heard Garth's name spoken in quiet greeting. They talked for a while, Lizbet's voice low and questioning, Garth's deep and troubled.

Garth had been like a man haunted these last few days, a man dogged by danger. Isolated though she'd been since Gai's birth, kept to her bedchamber as much by choice as by the weariness of having so recently given birth, Nikia still knew that something threatening, dark and fearsome, stalked the hot, breathless corridors of the Citadel. She knew it by the conduct of those around her, by their foolish and fierce determination to play at happiness and contentment when they were with her. Yet Nikia, daughter of a king, wife of a ruling prince, was well used to sensing the secrets behind a gesture, a glance, a word not spoken. Some storm prowled near; and not a storm of nature, unless of men's natures.

Came a pause in the conversation; then Nikia heard Lizbet speak clearly.

"My Lady is within, Prince, and your daughter is awake. Won't you go and see them?"

Nikia bent close over her child again. Lizbet would not persuade Garth to visit the child. He was yet ambivalent, caught between wanting to believe that Gai was his daugher and fearing to know that she was a mad mage's get. He'd chosen the babe's name, and that was a father's duty; among both Mannish and Elvish an unspoken acknowledgment. But between them, husband and wife knew that he'd chosen the name for Nikia's sake, not the child's.

"Call your daughter Gai," he'd said to Nikia on that first night. "Name her for happiness, Nikia, for you deserve some. Wife, you've more than earned it."

And so the child was Gai, named for gaiety and joy. Nikia had hoped, by his choice of name, that Garth himself would find joy in the child, that he would believe she was his daughter. But she was always *Gai*, or *the child*. Never but once had Garth spoken the words, *my daughter*, and that when he formally acknowledged her in the company of all the Citadel folk in the Great Hall.

But as the days passed, Nikia saw that Garth had not made up his mind about Gai. By night's darkness, firelight and shadow wrapping the peacefully sleeping babe, Garth was solicitous, even kind. But his kindness had a wistfulness woven through, and he never came to see Gai in daylight. He dreaded to see the shape of an old enemy's face in Gai's.

"Ah, Garth," she whispered, "you'd not see that if you came to look."

Neither would he see his own face echoed. It seemed that the shape of Gai's face would speak to all of her mother's kin, her cheekbones handsomely high, her chin made in just that way a chin is made when people speak of heart-shaped faces. Her eyes were long, as an Elven's eyes are, and startlingly blue as a Mannish child's are in the early weeks before the true color comes to tint. She had fine hair, more to be felt than seen, for it was pale almost to white, soft as catkin's down. But Gai had not even the merest trace of an Elven's graceful cant of ear.

Beyond these mere details of appearance, within Gai, within her very heart, shone something that spoke of a Deity's touch. And beyond a mother's fond hope, Nikia knew that a potential for grace filled this little one; a promise of strength. Among the Elvish it is said that magic speaks to magic, and each time Nikia looked at her daughter she saw the potential and the promise of magic surrounding. It was as though she were seeing the very lines of a mage's bright prayers weaving round and round to make spells and enchantment. Gai was history's child, harking to a time when there was only one race, reaching for a time when the broken bonds might be knotted again. It might be that her like had never been seen in the world before now.

"You are neither your mother nor your father," Nikia whispered, her contentment for the moment regained. "Gai, you simply are, and that will always be enough."

From the outer room came the sound of a door closing. Moments later, Lizbet took up her harp and her music again. Gai cuddled against her mother's breasts and sighed, sated and sleepy. She seemed sure—with an infant's trusting certainty—that there was no safer place than where she lay. But Nikia, remembering the deep and troubled sound of Garth's voice, feeling in her heart the approach of storms, shivered suddenly. For no reason that she could name, she hoped her Gai's trust was well-placed.

Peace now, peace, whispered a voice from memory.

And Nikia fell peaceful, for this voice was one she'd heard at the birthing, soft and deep, and full of comfort when the pain was worst. A physician's perhaps . . . or only imagined. Still, she never failed to find comfort in the memory.

Peace, now. Peace . . .

"Have we come a far distance today, Tall?" Islief twisted a little in the saddle to look at Joze astride the brown mare behind him, and twisting, his shoulder rubbed against Joze's shirt, caused rough cotton to scrape across sunburned skin. Joze winced, and Islief hissed a sigh for his friend's pain and for his own.

Islief's skin was no longer grey, but a strange blue-white. It made Joze think of iron stock thrust into fire and gone beyond red to white-hot. These past four days of riding through the agony of land-sick places had taken a toll of Islief's strength.

At night, soothed by darkness, Islief seemed to regain what the day had stolen from him. But during the day, when the sun was burning brightest, Islief would often lean back against Joze, head low and turned into the poor shadow of Joze's shoulder. At these times Joze would wrap his arms around his friend and hold him gently.

Islief tried his question again, but this time he only twisted his head to look up. "Tall, have we come a good distance?"

Joze shrugged. "Good enough."

Beside them, Kicva spoke a calming word to her nettlesome horse. Hot as the afternoon was, the sun low in the west and burning there like nightmares, that dun-colored beast still wanted to find a faster pace than this steady canter which the others, the brown mare and Dail's bay gelding, found so wearying. When the dun settled, Kicva said:

"Have you ever been to Damris city, Joze? Will we get there before dark, do you think?"

Joze shrugged again, hoped she'd take the gesture to mean that he wasn't in the mood for talking. Kicva glanced at Dail, riding beside her, and at some gesture of the bard's fell silent. Joze was glad that she did. He had no heart for conversation. He did not know how to talk about small things anymore, and he dared not talk about his sorrow for lost kin, lost home. That pain could be translated in no other language but that of endless tears.

And how to answer her question, how to answer Islief's? Ever since the morning they left his farm, he'd been haunted by the feeling that there was no longer anything solid in the world, no longer anything upon which he could depend. Certainly not memory! Joze failed to recognize a single feature of the land about, as he'd not recognized a single board or stone of that sad, fire-blacked farmhouse which used to be his home.

He didn't recognize a foot of ground in the anguished place that used to be his homeland. Over the past four days Joze had come to believe that the haunting feeling of uncertainty sprang from the eerie sense that, though he rode through lands he'd known from childhood, nothing was familiar. This grotesque unfamiliarity left him feeling unmoored, helpless as though he were being blown down nightmare's landscape by mindless winds.

Joze glanced at Kicva, watched her secretly, as though the sight of her might offer comfort. Her cropped hair had grown longer in these weeks past, curling over the collar of Mage Aidan's shirt. A fine shirt that had been once; linen, and white as the memory of snow. Now it was grey with ashes and dirt and sweat. Her hair had become lighter, bleached by sun. The gold had fled to her skin, a kind of red-gold from tan and sunburn, like an apple near ripe. Thin, she was, thinner than she'd been, and her long Elvish eyes held lurking sorrow.

Does she miss the mage? Joze wondered. *Does she worry about him?* Ah, Mage Aidan! And what was he up to now? Had he come to the caverns? Was he even now laying hands on the Emerald?

We must trust the Lady, Islief had said, and we must trust the newly born babe.

Joze tried to trust, he tried to match Islief's faith. And he tried to believe that Dail was right when he counseled that they could only go on. But it was hard, for Joze hadn't forgotten something else Islief had said, all those many long weeks ago in the caverns:

No good—and much harm—would be done if someone other than the one who was made for this tried to call the Emerald's magic. This the gods have said, Tall. The Lady and I, we know it.

Mage Aidan, thief of dreams! What would he do if he managed to take the Emerald back to Verdant Hall? Would he, upon learning that Dekar's daughter had gone off to the mountains with strangers, try to call the Jewel's magic himself? Or would he even wait? Would he try to use the Emerald there in the caverns?

Kicva had said that she didn't know. Thereafter, she hadn't talked about the mage but once more, and that only to say that they two were betrothed. That intelligence she offered grudgingly. And if she felt that the mage had somehow betrayed her by stealing

her dreams like some padding thief—well, she said nothing about
that either.

Joze wanted to ask her about it. Cool as ice, that mage, and
Joze wanted to know how Kicva, fiery Elven, had come to be
betrothed to him. But mostly, when he saw her sitting alone at
night and staring at stars, he wanted to know whether the theft
of her dreams had hurt her. But he never asked. Though she
was quieter these days, less abrasive, Kicva still did not invite
confidences, the giving or the receiving. This change to brooding
quiet made Joze shy of her. In former times, at least, he'd known
what to expect if he'd inquired about her feelings or dared to offer
comfort. She'd have snapped and snarled, long eyes blazing as she
bade him tend to his own business. Now he had no idea what to
expect, and so now he, too, kept quiet.

And the quiet between them made room for an unexpected
hope to rise. For, late at night when he watched Kicva watching
the sky, Joze didn't think about Mage Aidan. He thought about
how, when brigands had threatened, he'd faked plague's deep and
terrible coughing for time and a gamble to reach his short-sword.
Kicva, not recognizing the ploy for what it was, had run to him
and held him tightly, clung to him as though he were someone
she cared about. She'd ruined his chance for regaining his sword,
but Joze had not minded that, not even then when he'd been
certain they were about to die of ruined chances. Even now,
days later, Joze well remembered what her arms felt like as she
held and supported him. Often he comforted himself with that
memory when nightmare raged or the sadness of days threatened
to overwhelm him.

Kicva had run to what she thought was a plague-struck man,
held him as though holding were healing. And, oh, who would
have thought that the holding would feel so good! But therein lay
a snare to tangle hopes: One hope—that Kicva had held him so
because she truly cared about him—became tangled with the other
hope that he had indeed been faking plague's dire coughing.

Ah, but surely it's not plague. Surely it was only the wretched,
ever-present dust that made him cough.

And then he thought no more about either hope, for suddenly
Dail put his heels to his horse's flanks and the dust of the road
flew high behind the bay, setting them all to coughing—Joze,
Kicva and Islief.

When the air cleared again, Joze saw the bard atop a small
rise and waving them forward. Kicva gave her restless horse its
head, Joze followed, and as he rode he realized that if he'd only

recognized the twisted and changed landmarks around him today he could have given Islief a better answer to his question about good distance. Looking around, he began to suspect that they'd come a good distance indeed. The suspicion was borne out when he topped the rise. He pointed down the slope to a broad brown sweep of flat land and the long twisty line of brown beyond it.

"That's the A'Damran, Islief. Damris city is beyond."

Islief leaned forward, shading his eyes against the red light of sunset, then squinted hard, trying to see, this once ignoring light's pain. "A river, Tall?"

Joze nodded. "It used to be."

"Ah. And what is that big, big pile of stone beyond?"

Dail answered, clearly amused by Islief's description of the great stone-built palace. "That's the Citadel."

"You are home-come, Harper?"

Cicadas droned, filled the air around them with sorrowing. But the bard smiled. "I am home-come."

"Will they be happy to see you?"

Dail hesitated, then said: "Some will."

Joze, newly acquainted with not-to-be-spoken yearnings, heard one now in the bard's voice. He glanced at Kicva, saw her head-cocked and frowning. She'd heard it, too. Uneasy, Joze brought his mare closer to Dail. Remembering that two of the horses they rode had once belonged to the Elf-King, a king who didn't seem to harbor friendly feelings toward the bard, he asked:

"Are they going to welcome you, Dail? Or is there another king in there who'd like to send soldiers out to chase you?"

Dail laughed, seemed genuinely amused. "Joze, I'm thinking I've not been much of a bard these days, not much of a news-bringer. Likely I should have told you before now, and would have if events hadn't been daily conspiring to scatter my wits."

Joze frowned, his sense of uneasiness growing. "What news haven't you given, bard?"

"This: Last I heard about it, the king in there is a babe in his cradle. Alain has abdicated in favor of Fenyan's son. As far as I know, I've done nothing to offend either king, old or new. As for the Regent, he's my cousin. Aye, that warrants nothing, I'll grant you. But last I heard, Garth yet considered me a friend. No one will be chasing us away."

Not at first, Joze thought, as he and Kicva sent their horses down the slope after the bard. *Not at once. But Prince Garth will probably want to do some chasing when we come to tell him that we'd like to take his wife and his newly born daughter out into the sick lands. Or maybe,* he thought darkly, *if he's a kind man, the Prince will just throw us into a dungeon, lock us up for crazy people so we can't harm ourselves or anyone else after we try to explain that an ages-dead queen has sent us upon this errand.*

He was very careful not to think of the nightmares of burning Souless, the great stone fortress blasted to sand by the might of the Hunter-Defender's magic. Best not to remember that! Best not to even think about what the Princess herself might be moved to do when she learned that they had come to take her babe to a ghost in far-off lands.

But, after they'd crossed the blistered mud bed of the poor A'Damran, after they'd crossed the wide expanse of the Duel and ridden in the welcome shade of the winding wall for a while until they came to the north gate, Joze realized that neither of his gloomy predictions—likely not even his unspoken fear—stood much of a chance for coming true.

The north gate, and every other gate to the city, was barred, defended by guards on the wall who bristled with weapons and were armed with orders to use those weapons to repel any comers. And those guards didn't care who'd come seeking entry.

Be he beggar or King's Bard, they would open the gates to no one.

Chapter Twenty-Nine

SAER, THE SEA-FISHER'S SON, SAT OUTSIDE THE REGENT'S CHAMbers. He sat with his back to the gallery wall, his head against the stone balustrade in the place where the low wall curved and wound gracefully down to become a stair-guard, the balustrade a handrail. He sat all wrapped in shadow because no one had come to light the torches yet. So dark was that corner that the Regent and Calmis of Soran had not seen him when—moments ago—they went past. Deep in talk, those two, their heads low as though they were speaking secrets. Likely they'd not have seen him were he sitting with a torch in each hand.

The Lady Lizbet had not let Saer in to see the Princess this morning. He hadn't been surprised, though he'd been sorry and disappointed. "Can I wait?" he'd asked her. She'd said he could, and he had for a while, until he'd had to go back to the kitchens and his work. But he made time during the day to return, found reasons to come back up here to let the Lord of Soran's wife see him and be reminded that he was waiting.

"Boy, you're too stubborn by half," his mother used to say.

Maybe so, Saer thought now. *But I'll wait here till nightfall and till dawn-rise if I have to. That fierce watchdog of an Elf-Lady will have to let me in to see the Princess one of these days! What's right is right, and it's right to be good to them as is good to you.*

And sitting, he began to think again about the whispered words he'd overheard between Lord Karo and the four dark-looking men. Some business of the lord's, he thought now, and nothing more. And the fear? What more than plague-fear? The whole Citadel was a-quiver with it. One rumor—quickly denied, but maybe too quickly—had it that the little King himself was plague-touched. Terrible that fear! No need to add any groundless fancying to that.

Came the sound of a booted man running up the stairs. Saer peered around the corner, saw a stocky man, sweat-grimed, dressed like a guardsman and taking the stairs two at a time. He had a strange look on him, that guard, like an in-and-out day, sun struggling with clouds, as though he was hoping for something he wasn't sure he'd get. Curious, Saer tucked himself deeper into the shadows, watched as the guardsman went into the Regent's chambers. He listened hard, but they shut the door tight, and he didn't hear what it was the guardsman might have been hoping for, or whether he would receive it or be denied.

While sunset became twilight and twilight moved toward the brink of night, Kicva made herself hold tight to her patience, paced a short path before the walls of Damris, always taking care to keep her hands away from her weapons and trying to appear unthreatening. She was the only one pacing; it seemed like she and the ever restless wind were the only ones moving. Dail sat on his heels before the tall wooden gate. Twilight's eerie gloom bleached all color from him so that he looked like a stone carving of a man at prayer. Or a man sitting siege. Joze stood exhausted and disheartened in the shade of the wall. Sometimes he would cough quietly, and Islief beside him would look up. "Ah, Tall," he whispered, once. "Tall . . ." But Joze only shook his head and cursed the wind-driven dust.

That didn't sound like a dust-cough, Kicva thought. And then she turned away from that, not wanting to think about the things she always thought about when Joze coughed: the young Stone-Elf dead of plague in the forest, Joze's naked shoulder smeared with his blood. Nor did she like to think about how she'd held him so tightly that day the brigands threatened and he had played at desperate sickness. She flushed to remember that, and berated herself again for her foolishness. He'd not been sick! He'd been trying for his sword, and she could have cost them all their lives if fate and doomed Elvish soldiers hadn't intervened.

She glanced up at the guards on the wall, men who had kept uneasy watch over them since first they'd refused the four entrance into the city. They'd been quiet, those guards, offering no hope, though at Dail's insistence they'd sent one of their fellows with a message to the Prince. Now, as the thin moon rose above the Elvish forests, riding the deepening blue sky, the elder of the two remaining guards came to the parapet and again studied Dail and his companions.

At another time, Kicva thought, the guard might have considered it strange to see the bard in company with an Elven and a ragged-looking Mannish soldier. But now, as it had initially, his attention lingered longest on Islief. He had not asked—as the half-handed brigand leader had—whether Islief was one of the Sorcerer's beasts left unkilled at war's end. He'd taken it for granted that Dail knew all about the strange creature he travelled with.

Nevertheless, Islief fascinated him.

"King's Bard," he said, "ye've a strange lot w'ye. Me, I'd like to let y'in just to hear the tale of 'em."

"The tale is for the Regent, guard," Dail said grimly. "He's not going to thank you for keeping it from him."

"Nor would he thank me for opening the gate. I've done as y'asked, sent word to the Prince. Y'can see that no message from him has come back. Seems our prince is not going to let me open the gate to you."

And that admitted of no argument. They would not gain entry, they would not see the Princess. They would fail Aeylin.

Kicva drew a long, steadying breath, tried not to think that she'd failed the Lady long before, when she let Aidan know where the Jewels were hidden; when she'd let him plunder her dreams. She'd been more helpless to prevent that than she'd been to prevent that ragged scarecrow of a man, the intruder at the rock pool, from trying rape. Her dreams, her memories, her hopes and secrets—he just took them, and she hadn't been strong enough to stop him. Or was it that she hadn't possessed the courage to try?

Kicva lost her pacing path, wandered aimlessly for a time until she found herself near the wall, staring at the winding expanse of stone. Then, suddenly, and for no reason, she put her back to the wall and laughed. Just a bitter chuckle, that sound; just that at first. But soon the chuckle became a snicker, and that snicker changed quickly, rose to such heights of laughter that the giddiness made her legs unsteady. She slid down the wall, sat hard on the dusty ground, wiping tears from her cheeks on the sleeve of Aidan's linen shirt.

The guards on the wall peered over, one shaking his head, the other—much younger than his comrade—looking pale and unnerved, as though he feared that these ragged strangers who accompanied the King's Bard were in fact a scouting party for a contingent of madmen with plans to storm the city. Kicva laughed the harder to see him trying to master his nervousness, and then tried to regain some control as she realized her friends were passing looks among themselves as if to ask whether her mind had become unbalanced. Islief came to stand beside her, stroked her arm gently as though trying to soothe a skittish horse.

The older guard leaned on his spear, spat over the wall and called: "Elven! What's so funny?"

Kicva patted Islief's hand absently and craned her neck to see the guard. "Well," she said, "it's this: When I took it into my head to become a soldier, our two peoples were still warring with each other."

The guard nodded. "Maybe just. Y'look a bit young, lassie."

"I am young. But the war I trained for was the one against the Mannish." She climbed to her feet, stepped back to see him better. "And you know, guard, when I was little girl—knowing as I did that I wanted to be a soldier—I used to play at storming this very wall."

"Girl-children play strange games in Elflands," the guard observed drily.

Kicva nodded, and then, suddenly clear of mind, as though her cataract of laughter had been nothing more than a sluice for frustration and fear, a torrent to wash a clear space to think, she realized that a small idea had been born of that laughter.

She smiled up at the guard. "They might seem like strange games to you."

"Tell me, then, Elven: What are your plans for storming the wall now that it's not games yer playing?"

Kicva shrugged, hoping that not the least hint of her new-come idea echoed in her voice. "The plans are in need of repair, guard. All my games played out with me at the head of a thundering army." She spread her hands, looked around, tried not to notice that her friends were regarding her as though they were not yet certain that she was returned to sense. "As you can see, I've no army with me. Otherwise, we'd be having a very different conversation tonight."

"Ah." The guard spat again. "Too bad for you."

"Yes, it is. Do you mind if we sit for a while in the shade of the wall?"

"No matter to me, lassie, as long y'know that the conversation we *are* having means ye'll be sittin' on *that* side."

"You've made that clear." With studied nonchalance, she started to turn away, then looked up at him again. "You call me 'lassie.' You come from the north, yes?"

The guard allowed that he did. "From up top of Celed near where the mountains are."

"Ah. So does Joze here. Come from Celed, I mean. So I suppose you're compatriots. He used to have a farm in the south part of Celed." Kicva drew a soft breath, remembering the ruin of Joze's home, sorry to have to remind him of it. Still, she went on, trying to grow her germ of an idea into a seedling. "I guess you know he doesn't have that farm now, though. And I guess you know why."

The guard nodded sympathetically, then said with gruff humor: "Elven, yon Joze could probably tell y' that flatland Celedmen and northern Celedmen don't often think of themsel's as compatriots."

Joze snorted, and Kicva heard in the sound a thin appreciation for what surely must be the guard's understatement. She winced inwardly, wishing she knew a little more about where these Mannish found their sense of fellow-feeling if not in their own provinces. She tried another tack, revising her idea as she talked.

And, she thought, this might just be the better way after all.

"Our friend Islief comes from North Celed, don't you, Islief?"

Islief watched her carefully, trying to understand how he should answer. In the end he said: "I am from where the mountains are, yes, Friend."

"So tell me, Celedman," Kicva said to the guard. "For the sake of a compatriot, would you have any food or water to spare? It's been a long hungry ride only to be turned away."

The guard laughed skeptically, as though he'd have to go a long way before he'd consider such a creature as Islief a compatriot, and far past the point of considering a flatlander one. But he said that, though he had no food with him, he did have water. He tossed a half-filled leather flask over the side of the wall.

"Thank you, guard. Good night to you."

"Good luck to you, Elven."

No, Kicva thought, good luck to *you,* guard.

She shared the water with her friends, then went to sit in the shade of the wall again. Each of her companions looked like he wanted to ask questions, but she halted the questions with a gesture and suggested that Joze and Dail unsaddle the horses and get some rest. But of Islief she asked another thing.

"The sun's well down now, Islief. Can you go sit in front of the gate? The moon's light isn't so bad as the sun's, is it?"

Islief said that moonlight was always gentler than the sun's. "But why should I sit before the gate, Friend? The wall-ward will not open it."

"Maybe not," she said. "Then again, maybe we don't care about that anymore. Just sit where that Celedman can see you."

"And then what?"

"If he talks to you, talk to him. If he asks questions, answer as you think best. Tell him stories, sing him songs. I don't care. Just keep his attention."

Joze coughed, cleared his throat and said, "What if the guard's not interested in talking to Islief?"

Kicva drew breath to reply. But Dail, who'd been very quiet all this time, cocked his head, glanced keenly at Kicva. The Elven saw by the light in his quick blue eyes that he understood her thinking. Clearly, he too, had just then heard the third pause in the guard's measured tread. That man up there was stopping to think again.

"He'll talk to him," the bard said.

Joze looked skeptical, but Islief accepted it. "And then what, Harper?"

"And then," the bard said, "we'll see what can be done about getting inside the wall."

Islief asked no more questions. He went to sit in the thin moonlight, keeping himself well in sight of the guard from Celed.

The child coughed, then coughed again. The light of day's end, thin and diluted by twilight, spilled across the window ledge, poured into the nursery. Karo got up from his chair, his grandson cradled against his shoulder, and went to sit on the broad stone ledge. Ybro's red curls were all matted with sweat, but his lips were faintly blue, and so surely he must be cold. Karo sat in the window, back propped against one wall, feet against the other. He placed his grandson on his lap.

Ybro coughed again and Karo lifted him, held him tighter. But he was always careful to hold the boy against his shoulder, careful not to let the child rest against the place where blood stained—No! Had once stained!—the front of his shirt.

Babe's blood, blood spilled in a killing he'd never wanted to do. He rubbed at the front of his shirt, scrubbed with the heel of his hand at the blood which foretold this killing he'd never thought he could do.

Karo lifted his head, heard soft footsteps, a stealthy whisper from the corridor. Not servants passing. In sadness or in gladness, servants chattered among themselves like crows in the fields.

Had he heard executioners walking? Wolves taking the route of murder, down the stone gallery to the Regent's chambers? Wolves stealthy on the scent of the Prince and the Lord of Soran? He thought he heard—between the padding footsteps—the small hiss of steel coming free of leather, a dagger drawn from a sheath. Then he thought no more about it, for Ybro was coughing again, and there was a raspy sound to his breathing. Karo looked out the window. A moment until dark fall.

The Lord of Raeth left the window, placed Ybro gently in his cradle. The boy did not move, did not cough, and no longer breathed. He looked as though he were sleeping. But he wasn't. Ybro, the son of Fenyan and Gweneth, his grandson, was dead.

Karo covered his grandson to the shoulders with a light blanket. He left the nursery, went down into the Great Hall. It was not empty now, but host to the men he'd brought into Damris on the day the gates had closed. One or two had found food in the kitchens, several others contented themselves drinking old soured wine found in some far storeroom.

And seeing them, Karo knew that he dared not leave the workings of fate in the hands of four paid murderers. His voice calm, low and steady, he bade his men arm themselves and make ready to fight.

"Fight, lord?" old Gharey asked. He wiped wine from his lips with the back of his hand. That wine looked like a thin bloodstain. "Fight who?"

Karo eyed him coldly. "The King is dead."

Gharey stared, perhaps thinking that his lord was talking about Alain, perhaps wondering why Karo would tell them something they'd known for days. Then understanding dawned, a frightened, cold kind of understanding.

"Lord, your grandson? How—?"

"The Regent killed him."

Killed him with the plague he'd let grow in Ybro's own kingdom. But Karo didn't say that, and he had to say nothing else. Gharey put his wine goblet aside, drew sword from scabbard. The others did the same, and they were hard put to listen while Karo laid out his plan, hard put to wait until their lord would give the word to fight.

Kicva kept to the shadow of the wall, silent while her friends loosened their mounts' saddle-cinches, silent when they returned. Moments later she heard another pause in the Celedman's pacing and the hawk and spit that meant he was preparing to talk.

"From up top of Celed, are ye?"

Islief raised his head, tilted it far back to see the guard. "From where the mountains are," he said, his tone curiously gentle.

The Celedman grunted. "Can't say I ever seen the like of ye up there."

"From where the mountains are," Islief said again, his voice so low that the guard had to lean over the parapet to hear; his tone so tender that one would think he spoke to soothe a restless, night-frightened child.

The second guard, the younger, came to listen.

"From where gardens take root in stone. From where forests are shaped in rock."

Came a third guard, and a fourth asking questions. His fellows hushed him.

"From where floors are roofs and there is no direction save high or low. I come from the place where all songs are kindled."

Darkness fell, snuffed all light but the moon's and the small gleams of stars. Kicva got to her feet, motioned Dail and Joze to do likewise. Islief's voice, though low, carried clear on the hot night wind.

"I come from the place where history was driven out. From the place where history will live."

Silently the three put their backs to the stone and edged their way down the wall, Joze and Kicva following the bard to the place where the shadows were deepest. Dail stopped in a corner where south and west walls met. Kicva checked the full quiver of arrows at her hip, slipped her bow over her shoulder. Then Dail made a stirrup of his hands and boosted her high. Heart pounding, she grasped the parapet, pulled herself up to peer over.

The way was clear!

Oh, Aeylin, she thought, *maybe I* haven't *failed you—maybe not yet!*

She listened for Islief, satisfied when she heard his voice in the darkness below, a voice as deep as cavern echoes. At this distance, she could no longer make out the words of his chant, could only hear the rhythm, the persuading cadence. Yet, despite distance, she knew what words he spoke, and so maybe she heard them in her heart or her soul.

I come from the place where hope did die. From the place where hope will thrive . . .

Kicva pulled herself over the parapet. Not only was the way clear, but a length of rope—dark and twisted as some great snake frozen in slithering—lay on the wooden walkway. Kicva grinned broadly, feeling generous enough to pity the guardsman who was going to have to answer to his captain for leaving that rope lying around.

Quickly, she looked around her. The bard had chosen this place well. The tall dark Citadel rose directly ahead of her, embraced by this corner of the wall. She saw a series of windows, darker holes in the stone's darkness, and orange light moving, gleaming faintly, as though someone passed through an inner room with a torch. She was so close to those windows that she could have leaped to the ledge of one with ease. She looked below, saw a narrow alley between the wall and the Citadel, smiled again. It was empty of all but night and shadows. Not even moon's light penetrated.

Kicva cocked her head, listening. She heard men talking, the low voices of bored watch-keepers. But they were not near enough to cause her worry. This was going better than she'd dared hope.

She tied the rope round her waist, braced against the base of the wall where it met the walk, and tossed the line over the side to Joze and Dail. Joze came first, hand over hand, and landed silent as a cat on the walk. Hand on her shoulder, he pulled her so close that his whisper was more a thing to be felt than heard.

"Dail's gone to fetch Islief. Says he'll make it look like he's apologizing to the guards for Islief keeping 'em from their work." He jerked his head in the direction of the guards, who were yet standing fascinated by Islief. "He figures it'll only be a moment before those guards start walking watch again after Islief's gone. Likely they'll think we're all sleeping down there. But their turn'll bring them to this part of the wall soon. We've got to get off this walk fast."

Kicva felt a tug on the rope, saw Dail below with Islief, and in the same moment saw a guard walking, head low and thoughtful, in their direction.

"Joze, that's the one they sent to the Prince."

"Get down!"

But she couldn't duck into the shadows, for the rope around her waist grew taut. Dail had already started climbing. Heart pounding so hard that she was sure half the people in the Citadel would be able to hear the drumming, Kicva braced herself against the double weight of the bard and Islief, prayed hard that the guardsman would not stop his deep thinking for a moment or two.

Joze stepped between her and the wall, grasped the rope and took most of the weight of the climbers.

"Where's the guard?" she hissed against his neck.

"Turned back; looks like he heard something."

And then there was no more time for talking. Dail clambered over the parapet, Islief clinging to his neck. Kicva loosed the rope from around her waist while Joze gave Islief a hand down. In that moment, with the suddenness of wildfire igniting, light blazed from the windows behind them.

Dail dropped flat to the wooden walkway, Islief vanished into the shadows. Before Kicva could but breathe, Joze hauled her to the ground, shoved her into the concealing shadows of the wall, held tightly to her as echoes of *Murder!* rang between the wall and the Citadel.

Beyond Joze's shoulder Kicva saw that the very window she'd only moments ago thought she could leap to with ease was now filled with the glare of torches. Framed in the opening, face smeared with light and shadow, distorted by terror, a half-grown boy leaned far out over the window ledge.

"Guards to the Prince!" he shouted, his voice cracking under the weight of desperate fear. "Guards to the Prince!" And then he was gone, vanished as though he'd never been.

As though the boy had called storm down from the sky, the wooden walk thundered with the running of booted feet, shook beneath Kicva. From the shadows she counted four, five, then six guardsmen running by. The last came so close that he'd have trampled Kicva's hand had not Joze caught it away in time. When they were gone, all fled down some stairway beyond her sight, Kicva twisted around in Joze's arms, looking for Dail, a suggestion that they gain the Citadel by the window already on her lips.

But she saw only Islief, wide, wide eyes bright in the darkness, and when she turned back to the window Kicva saw Dail backlit by the orange torchlight. He'd already made the leap.

"Follow?" Islief said in her ear.

Kicva and Joze answered with one voice. "Follow."

Then Kicva turned quickly, laid her hand on Islief's shoulder. "But not you. Get back to the horses and have them ready."

"No, Friend—"

"*Yes.* Please, Islief. Fetch the horses. Watch and be ready."

And she did not wait to argue further, for Joze had already made the leap to the window ledge.

Chapter Thirty

NIKIA CLOSED THE DOOR BETWEEN THE BEDCHAMBER AND THE outer room, but she could not shut out the memory of the guard's plea that the King's Bard be admitted into the city. She could not forget Garth's denial of that plea. How high her heart had leaped when the guard came bringing news that Dail was safe, that he was near! And how fast and far it had fallen when Garth told the guard to refuse him entry. Lizbet placed an arm around her shoulder, led her to the bed, bade her sit.

"It hurt him to say no," she said. "It hurt the Prince to do that."

Nikia nodded. It had; she'd seen the pain in Garth's eyes as he looked to Darun for help, to Nikia herself. But even as he turned to them, he knew that there was no escape from the order he himself had written, the one the guards on the walls had carried out time and again. And so he forbade his friend, the cousin whom he loved, entry to the city. And though she was aware of Garth's pain, Nikia could do little but feel her own.

There would never be a time again when she would see Dail. Never again a time when she would hear his voice, hear his harp's songs. Nor would there ever be a time when she could see him and wonder, so privately, how it might be between them if she were not who she was.

Lizbet held her and tried to soothe her. No word had Nikia spoken—even to Lizbet—of her love. Darun would have said nothing; not even to his wife. He knew how to keep secrets.

Yet Lizbet knew. Princess and waiting-woman, they were old friends, they were as mother and daughter, they were as sisters. It had always been that way, from the time Nikia was a little girl.

In the outer room Nikia heard Darun speaking quietly; no words, just the familiar sound of friend speaking to friend. Then the voices stopped, not suddenly, but trailing away as though someone else had come into the room. A moment's peace there was, an empty time when only the hot night wind whispered, only the ever-droning cicadas whined. In her cradle, Gai sighed, uttered the small sounds of an infant on the edge of waking.

Then came a cry to scatter all the smaller sounds, a boy's voice raised in a bellow of outrage to freeze Nikia's heart. She heard Garth shout warning, then a man's scream, high and terrible sound of dying.

Nikia leaped from the bed, hardly aware that she'd run to Gai's cradle, hardly aware that she'd snatched her daughter to her breast until she felt the infant jerk awake, heard her startled wail. Trembling, shaking so hard that she feared her knees would give way, Nikia held Gai close, watched as Lizbet ran to the door.

"Lizbet, what is it? Lizbet—!"

Steel whined against steel, that thin sound at once drowned in a crash like a table overturned.

Lizbet slammed the door, and beyond it someone—surely that was Darun!—roared, in pain or rage or both. Lizbet's face drained of all color to hear her beloved husband cry like that, but she flew to Nikia, wrapped her arms tight around mother and child. The cries in the outer room rose and fell, one voice tangled with another.

Nikia felt Lizbet's breath catch, felt her friend's heart pounding in the same frantic rhythm as her own, and the door flew open before a hard kick. Nikia clutched Gai tighter as a boy ran in, torch in hand, shadow and light flowing behind him like a banner. With a strange sense of unreality, she recognized Saer, the sea-fisher's son.

As though he were a captain ordering a troop, Saer stabbed a finger at the two women. "Get me a weapon! Murderers—four of 'em! They've hurt the lord! They want to kill the Prince!"

"Darun—" Lizbet gasped.

Saer ran to the window, leaned far out over the ledge. "Guards to the Prince! Guards to the Prince!"

From without came the sound of booted men running, cries of alarm, the whisk of steel unsheathed. But fast as they ran, Nikia knew that they'd be a while getting here to help. Quiet now, surrounded by a calm as eerie as that at the eye of a storm, she returned Gai to her cradle, went to the tall, painted clothespress near the door. From beyond she heard the fighting, the sound washing over her like waves, sometimes loud, sometimes muffled. She smelled smoke, oily from Saer's torch.

"Lady, please—Lady, a weapon!"

Her mouth dry with fear, Nikia found a short-sword among Garth's clothes. It was only for ceremony, but its edge was keen, as all Garth's steel was. She gave this to Saer and the boy nodded curt thanks. As he left them, the sound of fighting, the cries, the outrage, the belling of steel on steel, increased. There were no longer four outside the door. Before Nikia slammed it behind Saer, she saw a room filled with weaponed men, a room which seemed to rock wildly with shadow and light; orange, streaming fire from torches and men fighting.

Came a shuddering blow to the door just as she closed it, came a cry to make her heart shiver. "The Elf-King's daughter! She's hiding in there!" A roar followed upon that cry, men's voices raised in the kind of rage that would only be damped by killing. Lizbet screamed, a choking cry which died suddenly, and Nikia whirled round to see what new danger threatened.

None did; not from this quarter. For it was Dail who leaped down the window ledge, her bard who gestured to someone behind him. A dark-bearded young man dropped through the window; a waif-thin Elven, arrow nocked to bow, replaced him on the ledge. But Nikia barely noticed them; all her attention was for Dail. Changed he was, thinner, whiter of beard, sunburnt and with a lean and dangerous air about him.

She went to him, stepped into his arms as though there were storm-haven to be found there. But there was not, not even for a second. Beyond the door another man screamed in dying.

Garth! Was it Garth?

Nikia turned away, started to run to the door, but Dail caught her back, held her hard. And she, tightly held in the arms of the man she loved, struggled desperately, pushed and beat her fists against his shoulders, trying to free herself so that she could run to her husband.

Dail was leaner—but he was no less strong. He gripped her hard in one arm, quickly slipped a dagger from his belt.

"Nikia, listen. Listen!" He freed her, pressed the dagger into her hands. At a gesture from him, the dark-bearded young man gave his own dagger to Lizbet.

"Defend yourselves," Dail said. In the outer room steel screamed against steel and Nikia winced as Dail gripped her shoulders. "And always defend your child, Nikia."

And then he was gone, the Elven and the young man close behind him; gone beyond the door and into the storm of fighting which had descended so swiftly upon them all.

Garth kicked a shattered chair out of his way, sidestepped a downed man who was gagging on his own blood, and tried to find room to use the sword he'd snatched from the body of a dead Raethman. But there was no room, only the stone wall behind and bloody steel before. And there was no aid to be had from Darun, bleeding from wounds and harried steadily toward the gallery by a swordsman with flashing steel; none from Saer, who faced his own opponent with little skill and only the fierce and terrified determination of a boy who is closer to his life's end than he'd ever thought to be. There was no hope or help to be had from any quarter now as Karo, flanked by two of his soldiers, pressed advance.

Trapped, Garth felt the wall against his back and saw Karo's feral grin all at the same time. No way out, he thought coldly. None now, and there had never been a way out of any trap he'd found himself in this whole year past.

In the gallery without, carnage and battle reigned, screams and cries of rage as the guard of watch engaged Karo's treacherous Raethmen. And those Raethmen were shouting *King-killer!* out there, shouting *False Regent!* and *Murder!* so fiercely that the echoes themselves screamed.

And so, with no way to go back, no way to go forward, Garth went sideways, feinted left, ducked under Karo's thrust and kept going down. He left the three with nothing but air to slice at as he rolled into one—took his feet out from under him!—and kicked out at the back of Karo's knee. This did not bring him down, only ruined his balance. But that was enough, for when another swordsman came at Karo, steel flashing over Garth's head, Karo had to fight awkwardly and limping.

Heart pounding, blood warming him again, Garth scrambled to his feet with decent space now to fight the other two who must surely have gotten behind him.

But there were no others now, or none standing. Only one dead of a green and white fletched arrow in his back, the other dead with Dail standing over him—and no time to question, no room to wonder how that could be, for the fighting in the gallery poured into the room, steel clashing, men bellowing in rage and pain.

Time enough for his heart to rise leaping in hope, though. Time enough for that. With his cousin at his back, Garth fought fiercely, as savagely as a chained beast at last freed. And they did not fight alone, for there was a dark-bearded young man always near, and he fought just as hard, his back protected by a tall thin Elven whose long eyes blazed with the kind of war-fire Garth had learned to respect when their two peoples were enemies.

Then came silence, deep and dark as night fallen on a battle-ground, stillness like the pause between thunder's crashing. Garth looked around him to see that the only men standing were those of the guard, and these friends who had come to fight beside him.

Like a man wandering, he went to search among the fallen, looking for Darun, seeking Saer, who had been the first to come to their aid. Saer he found, bloody but not bleeding, gripping the silver-chased hilt of Garth's own ceremonial sword as though it were a lifeline in a raging sea. Virgin's luck, Garth thought, grimly amused. He steadied the boy, waited for the battle-terror to calm in him, then said:

"Saer, go take what guards are left and get the Council lords. Boy, I'd like to think they haven't heard any of the murder's been done here today. But I fear you'll find them hiding, each in his own chambers and trying to preserve his ignorance. If that's the case, use the guards—round them up like sheep if you have to. I will expect to see them in the Council Chamber within the hour."

"Aye, P-prince," Sear stammered.

The boy gone, Garth looked again for Calmis, for the one lord of the Council who'd stood by him in talk and in battle. But Darun was nowhere to be seen, not among the dead nor among the injured.

Neither was Karo of Raeth.

In the moment Garth realized this, in the very moment he turned to see the stout wooden door to his bedchamber shattered and hanging by one hinge—in that moment did he hear Lizbet scream, hear Nikia cry out as though her very heart were being broken.

"Don't move," Karo whispered, his voice terrible and empty. "Lady, do not move."

Helpless, Nikia watched as Karo held her daughter high by the heels and out before him as though the infant were a shield. Every part of her demanded that she run at Karo, clawing and fighting for her child, but she used all her strength to make herself as motionless as stone. Gai wailed and sobbed, and from behind Nikia heard Lizbet moan.

For whom did Lizbet sorrow? For Darun, who had failed to stop Raeth's lord from snatching Gai from her mother's arms and now lay still and bleeding on the floor before the overturned cradle? Nikia did not know, and she dared not look to see. With great effort, trying to make no motion that could be interpreted as threatening advance, Nikia said:

"Lord Karo, please. Give me my daughter."

Karo laughed, a hard, heartbroken sound. "No, Lady. No." He brought up his sword, steel all covered with blood.

Nikia screamed. And her cry was drowned by a commanding shout:

"Karo! Put up your steel!"

Karo turned, the wailing child still in his grip, the heartbroken laughter still on his lips. He did not back away when he saw Garth standing in the doorway. He did not change his stance at all, though the Prince was backed by Dail and his two friends.

"No, Regent," Raeth's lord said, "there's a death to be paid for. A king's death. My grandson's death."

Nikia shuddered, wondered what Karo was talking about, wondered if he were insane. Ybro dead? How could that be? But she had no time to think. Garth stepped into the room, walked surely and steadily toward Karo.

"Give me my daughter, Karo," he said. "You've no reason to harm her. Nothing to avenge. I didn't kill my nephew."

Trembling, Nikia saw Dail and his friends enter behind Garth, saw them widen the distance between themselves so that they encircled the Lord of Raeth, until Dail, sword leveled, stood on his left, the dark-bearded young man on his right. The Elven stood behind and laid a hand on Nikia's arm, moved her gently aside.

Karo himself did not seem to notice any of this maneuvering. All his attention was on Garth.

"Aye, you did kill him, Regent." He spoke the title as though speaking a curse. "You killed Ybro the same way you killed his kingdom. You *let* him die of plague, as you let his kingdom die of land-sickness. And so there is vengeance needed."

Garth swallowed hard. His brown eyes darkened. Like pain twisting, Nikia realized that he did not much disagree with Karo's insane charge.

"Then your quarrel is with me," Garth said. "Not my daughter. Give her to her mother."

He gestured to Nikia, and now she saw a warning to courage in his eyes. "Come take our Gai, Nikia."

Karo went taut and tight, seemed to see for the first time that he was surrounded. He turned sharply, holding the screaming babe at arm's length. "Don't move, Lady." He raised his sword, and Gai wailed louder. "*Don't move!*"

But—hearing her child shrieking, seeing the steel above her—Nikia was simply not capable of staying. She ran to her child.

"Dail!" Garth cried. "Hold her!"

And as though his mere words made it so, Nikia found herself held tight in Dail's strong arms, all the breath nearly crushed out of her.

Nearly, but not fully. She had breath to scream when she saw Karo's sword flashing down, breath to wail as she saw her child fall, heard her husband cry out. She had breath to sob when, swift and hissing, an arrow flew past, caught Karo full in the throat in the exact moment the dark-bearded young man drove his short-sword into Karo's back, full to the hilt. Neither struck in time. Arrow and sword, they killed the Lord of Raeth. But only a scant second after Karo drove his own steel deep into Garth's side. The Lord of Raeth crumpled to the stone floor, and in the same moment, Garth fell.

A terrible quiet, an awful stillness, filled the bedchamber. A torch guttered somewhere and went out. The night became darker. Dail's arms tight around her, Nikia watched—as though from a great distance—while the dark-bearded young man cleaned his short-sword on his breeches. She watched—as though from far, far away—as he bent to touch Garth's wrist, his neck.

Then, shoulders hunched, he knelt to pick up Gai. He cradled the child in his arms for a moment, hushed her crying and soothed her terror. He bent his head over her to whisper something. When he looked up again, his eyes met Nikia's and she saw tears make bright trails on his face, watched one trickle all the way down his cheek and vanish into his black, dusty beard as he rose and came to stand before her.

"My—my Lady," he whispered. He coughed, then cleared his throat, tried again. "The Prince is dead. And I think . . . I think he was a king, Lady, if what Lord Karo said about his grandson is true." He looked down at Gai, still sobbing fitfully in his arms. "But—but the King's daughter isn't hurt."

The young man held Gai carefully, offered her to Nikia. The King's daughter . . .

Dail let her go and Nikia looked up at him. He was so pale beneath his sunburn!

"Lady?" the young man said.

Dail shook his head. "A moment, Joze. Give her a moment."

Nikia barely heard them. She looked around the ruined bed-chamber, at Lizbet standing near the window. Lizbet did not stand alone. She and Dail's Elven companion supported Darun, weak but on his feet, between them. Nikia looked everywhere but at Garth, at everyone but her husband.

Softly, the young man—Joze—said, "Lady, here is your daughter."

And like an echo, she heard in memory Garth saying, *Come take our Gai, Nikia.*

Our Gai . . .

She held out her arms, received the child. But the weight of her was too much, and Nikia sank to her knees, huddled on the floor, alone and cold and empty. She neither sobbed nor moaned; she shed no tear. No feeling had she, in heart or limb. Vaguely she saw thin black smoke from the guttered torch, but she did not smell it. She was somehow so far away, so distant. She did not truly believe that she was in this bedchamber at all. Surely she stood in some high and remote place, looking down upon herself, looking down upon people she did not know.

She heard these people talking, heard questions—one sobbed in sorrow—and she heard answers. But nothing they said made any sense to her. It was as though the speakers used a language she was not capable of understanding.

"We've got to get out of here," someone said.

"Soon," another agreed. "But how?"

"I've a way. I've a way," said a third person. Saer? Wasn't that Saer?

And there was more talk, low and urgent voices. It seemed to go on forever; but though Nikia heard the words, meaning slipped by her, sense evaded her. They talked all night, all day—or they only talked for moments, words spoken swiftly, urgently. Nikia could not tell. To try to concentrate on the words would mean going back to the place where terror was, going back to the place where Garth lay dead.

Then someone raised her gently, kissed her cheek. She felt that, and the return of feeling made pain out of even this tenderness.

"Lizbet?" she whispered, and wondered how her own voice could sound so terribly weak and tattered.

"Yes," Lizbet said. "I'm here."

Lizbet touched her face, let her fingers linger on Nikia's temples as she used to do when Nikia was a child and in need of sleep. "Trust me, Lady. All will be well."

Then there was no pain, only a prayer, a gentle whisper, and the overwhelming urge to leave this place where she was for the places of sleep.

Nikia felt someone else embrace her, but weakly, and this person smelled of blood. Darun? She tried to see, but she could not. Perhaps another torch had guttered and died. It was very dark now, and Nikia felt as though heavy weights dragged upon her. She could not turn her head to see who smelled so bitterly of sweat and blood, hurt and sorrow.

Came a moment, a terrifying moment, when no one held her, when she stood alone in darkness at the edge of a sleep that could not be denied. She heard Gai whimper, felt the child taken from her arms.

"No," Lizbet said. "Hush, Nikia. Gai is well."

Then Nikia knew nothing more than that she was held close again. But even so warmly held, so carefully sheltered, she could not escape emptiness. She did not dare try to fill herself with anything, for fear that there was nothing beyond this cold hollowness but terrible sorrow for her husband who was dead.

A voice came into the darkness. Deep as echoes heard in hollow cavern depths, it followed Nikia all through her sleeping, hunting her and haunting her until she at last understood the words.

Now you must take courage, Hunter-Defender. Elf-King's daughter, now you must find power and heal your memories of blood. Now you must find the strength to weep. You must find peace now. Peace . . .

And so she wept. Because she knew that this deep, deep voice was one she'd heard before. She knew it from the weary hours of childbirth, and she understood now—where she had not before— that she'd heard this voice in a long-ago dream. In that dream it had spoken to her of courage and power, of blood and strength. She'd obeyed that voice a long time ago, had become a fiery Hunter-Defender with this one's words on her lips. Asleep, a-dream, she knew that this person spoke with magic in his voice, but a softer magic than the one she'd first learned from him.

And so it proved.

Watered by weeping, Nikia's dreams of aching sorrow grew to become visions of a season she'd not known how to dream about for nearly a year. She dreamed of spring, of misty rain, of richly scented meadows filled with green and growing things.

Chapter Thirty-One

MAGE AIDAN KNEW WHERE TO FIND THE LONG CRACK IN THE EARTH which led to Islief's underground home. He had Kicva's clear memory of that place. And so he was not deceived into thinking he'd gone astray simply because brush and stone concealed the entrance to the caverns. He had a deal of hard work to move the stones, and sometimes he was obliged to use stout branches for leverage. But he worked steadily, did not stop to rest, for he was bound upon an unrelenting path which did not admit of obstacle. After a time he cleared the entrance.

It was the hour of sunset, and in the west fading light tinted the sky rose and gold; the tops of the trees were all gilded. Jays and stonechats, woodlarks and hooded crows—the forest birds grew boisterous, as though noise could hold back the night. An early owl woke questioning. Above the Kevarths' broad eastern shoulders the moon sat, flushed with sunset's glow. The direction of the wind shifted, came now from the east, smelled of the sea gleaming and tossing beyond the mountains.

Aidan noticed none of these things, for he was listening to magic as it spoke to magic, listening to his own dream speaking to the vast powers he felt hovering beyond the dark entrance to the cavern world. These might have been the voices of Deities speaking; the Seven whispering. Or they might have been the echoes of the dream he'd dared not acknowledge, all the need he'd kept in dark places within, as though need were a bastard child whose existence would serve to point the accusing finger at a mage who'd dared to dally with dreams he should not have.

Aidan dreamed of a masterwork. He ached to feel the full stretch and reach of power, his own and that of the Emerald. Mage in a time when only small magics got made, only little prayers were answered, Aidan longed to feel the mere trappings of skill fall away before the wild rush of need and dream. He hungered to know whether his was the potency of true genius.

He was a hawk, trapped by the hood, hungry to fly.

He'd been hungry that way since first he learned that the Ruby had been used in the war against the Sorcerer. His hunger had turned to starvation this year past as he damped his dream and, for the sake of his king, ventured along the planes of magic in search of the Emerald for someone else to use. But now the hawk had no hood. Now Aidan could walk into the caverns and take the one Jewel he needed. His magic free to fly, he would soar with the Emerald's great powers.

He would heal his hunger and heal the world's sickness.

Turning his back on the sunset, on the moonrise, on the songs of birds and the fragrant wind, forsaking the earth above, Aidan went into the dark. He breathed a prayer to the Deities of Magic and Fire. Hands cupped, he waited for cool blue light to fill them.

Light came, and it was cool, it was blue. But it was not weightless, as light should be. The familiar gossamer glow weighed as heavy as the stones he'd pried away from the cave's entry. The burden of it made Aidan's arms ache, made his shoulders hunch inward. Sweat trickled down the sides of his face, his heart thundered, warned loudly that he taxed his strength too greatly.

But this was only hand-fire! A child's exercise—the smallest of magics!

Small when a god helps, distant voices whispered.

Too great a burden to bear when a goddess turns away, other voices hissed.

Breezes, cool and damp, smelling sharply of stone, thinly of age, drifted around the cave entry, brushed past Aidan's face like teasing fingers.

Turn away, Mage!

Aidan, go back!

Mage Aidan, flee!

The hand-fire faded, guttered and died. Aidan groaned, for the release and relief from godless magic. The darkness held him prisoner again, like a hood on a hawk. He screamed.

"NO!"

And the echoes ran around him, his own voice tangling with the mysterious voices. He would not stumble on through the blackness. He would have light, whether the Deities helped or hindered. He did not offer prayers, for he knew that they would not be answered. He took everything of strength that he had and pulled it into the very center of himself. He did not offer it to the earth, did not offer it to Deities. He held tight to what strength and power he had in mind and heart and soul. By his own will, not the will of the Seven, Aidan made a magic, made a light as red as blood.

Deep inside himself he knew that his was not the earthy magic he'd been taught to use and honor. He knew that the magic he worked now was the same kind which had fueled all the Sorcerer's evil. Godless magic, brute sorcery created with no balance between a Deity's will and a mage's need. But he did not turn back from it. Now he was willing to take power wherever he could find it. He was a man dreaming. And after a time that sorcerous light became easy to support, for it seemed to both feed on his strength and regenerate that strength. This kind of power existed for its own sake. It was not mastered, it was a master.

Aidan didn't care about that either. He was so near the Jewels now; he'd gladly give the sorcery what it needed as long as it kept him walking in light. He told himself that he could let the sorcery go, turn away from it, once he found the Emerald. He told himself that he had the will to do that.

And so he found that the caverns beneath the Kevarths were not, as the old song said, low and cold. Nor were they dark and drear. His sorcerous light showed him wonders—the least part of wonder a stone forest so wide, so tall, so endless-seeming, that he had trouble understanding how it was that such a vast place could be filled near to bursting with voices, each calling his name, each followed by another, so that MAGE AIDAN . . . MAGE . . . MAGE . . . AIDAN . . . AIDAN . . . MAGE AIDAN . . . echoed round and round in the endless underground. Yet he would not be bewildered, the Elf-King's Mage would not be daunted, for a hawk cannot be held from flight once he feels the wind of his dreams under his wings.

Above her rainbowed hearth, the ghost prayed hard, prayed to all the Seven at once, for she was afraid. She'd felt the dark workings of sorcery, and she knew that the Elf-King's Mage had crossed some border, had left behind his dream for the lands of nightmare.

"Let me stop him!" Aeylin begged.

But gods did not answer, goddesses kept silent.

"Please! Let me leave this hearth and stop him!"

No, gods said. *You will not move against sorcery, Aeylin. Remember what happened when once you did.*

Stay, goddesses whispered. *Aeylin, stay where you are. You cannot kill to heal—and you would have to kill him to stop him. You will have a part to play, but not yet.*

"But if he should find the Jewels—!"

If balance is to be restored, the Seven said, *you must have patience, daughter.*

And they said no more.

Islief! the long-dead queen cried to one who could not hear her. Alone in silence, she begged: "My old friend, please hurry!"

Salt spray hung a misty curtain above the little fishing boat, dazzled with dawnlight. Gulls hovered near, crying high around *Skimmer*'s red sails, sweeping low to feed in the little craft's frothy wake. Because Yan, Saer's father, guided his *Skimmer* close to the coast for the warm swift winds, Nikia could see the white waves, the sea's foamy mane, leaping against the shores. But no gulls fed there, for there were no fish in the rocky inlets, no clams or mussels to dig from the shores off the damaged lands. Still, the waves were lovely in their grace and power, and it had become Nikia's habit, day and night, to stand at the ship rail to watch the wealth of water leaping and playing for the joy of expending its strength.

By night Nikia often stood alone, but she was not lonely. For company she had the deep boom of the sea and the soft creak of Yan's boat. She had time to grieve for Ybro, her nephew, the little King, the child of her friend Gweneth. And she had time to be with her memories of Garth.

She thought about Garth often, and often she wept for the husband who had been kind to his foreign bride. She'd hoped to love him, for a time believed that she had. Yet even in the absence of love, there were many things about him she admired, things that she cherished. She sorrowed for the prince who had become a regent; for the regent who was—so briefly—a king.

Come take our Gai . . .

And she mourned for the man who had, at last, known Gai for his own, and who had died for his daughter's sake.

By day Nikia watched the brown lands slip by. Brown in Soran, brown in Hivard province. Yan's boat sailed past the drought-lands for two days. But the lands were not brown in Raeth, and this morning she'd come to the rail to study them again, to know the difference between these lands and the southern provinces. Raeth, as seen from beyond the coast, was a grey land, as though a terrible fire had burned and left nothing but ash.

Islief had said that land-sickness ravined up Raeth. Devoured it, made it sad to see.

Sad, yes. But Nikia studied these grey lands carefully. Here people had forgotten about hope. She wished they could know, those starved and sick folk, that hope had not died. She wished they could know that a sea-fisher's small craft bore hope swiftly northward to the place where magic lay waiting.

High above, a gull screamed, and when the screaming stopped, Nikia heard a footfall on the deck behind her.

Dail came to lean his forearms on the rail. He watched the gulls hanging in the blue sky, and he was quiet, gave only a nodded greeting. Feet wide, braced against the roll of the deck, he did not stand close to her. He never did, always kept an arm's length between them. And if he spoke, he always called her Lady, never used her name.

"Lady," he'd said on the day she'd waked from the sleep Lizbet had imposed. "Lady, we are bound for the sea, and we will be there tonight. But we will stop now, for a moment. Gai needs you."

He'd slid down from his horse's back, still holding her, and came foot to ground so lightly that she never felt the jolt. Later, when they resumed their ride to the sea, he'd held her so carefully that she fell at once to sleep again, but this time naturally, and she'd dreamed no dream, good or ill. Safe in his arms, no nightmare of violence or death could find her. Safely held, she had no need to fill her sleeping with fancies of better places.

"Lady," he'd said that night, *Skimmer* rocking beneath them, the sky all filled with stars and the sound of the sea. "Lady, Yan wants you to have his cabin, but you must share it with Islief, for light is pain to him."

When he saw her settled, Dail had spoken in whispers with Islief, then gone away to study sea charts with Yan, later to make his own bed on the deck with his friends. And that night, in the dark cabin, by the warm light of Islief's wide eyes, Nikia had heard again the voice she'd heard in dreams. They talked for a long time.

Elf-King's Daughter, Islief called her. And Hunter-Defender. This last name she did not like, and when she asked him to call her Nikia, he nodded solemnly and thanked her. Then he'd told her, with grave courtesy, that he would be pleased if she would make free use of his own name. And he told her the reason he'd come out into the upper lands, said that he would answer any questions she had. But Nikia asked no question. She'd known from the first moment she'd looked into Gai's blue eyes that this girl-child was made for magic. The course had been chosen nine months before. Islief's tale only confirmed that.

One question she had no answer for, but she did not pose it to Islief. Why did Dail keep himself so distant, so far from her that he would not even use her name?

Lady . . . Lady . . .

"Lady," Dail had said a day later, when the sky was filled with golden sunlight and the creaking of gulls. "These friends of mine are Joze and Kicva, and they are your friends, too. They have come to find Gai. They will help us bring her to Aeylin."

Kicva had bowed before the Elf-King's daughter; Joze had stood silent and shy, dark eyes lowered. Then they'd gone back to their work—for Yan needed crewmen and Kicva was good help, Joze a quick learner. But Joze did not seem to have much stamina, and he had to rest often.

When Nikia commented on this, Dail nodded slowly. "I know, Lady. I know."

She'd asked her question carefully, afraid because she thought she knew the answer. "Dail, do you think it's plague?"

Dail hadn't answered for a long time. When he spoke at last, his voice was low and troubled. "I don't know, Lady. He's been exposed to it. You and Gai at the Citadel, Joze and Kicva and me in the outside—we all have. Any one of us could fall sick now. But, Lady, I don't know whether Joze is plague-struck, and he's not talking about it."

Lady . . .

"Lady, Darun will see to the Council and the Kingdom. No, I don't know how he'll manage this tale of your vanishment or Gai's. I don't know how he'll manage your father when Dekar learns about it. But he will. You know Darun."

She *did* know Darun; dear friend who had put himself between Karo's sword and Gai, helpless and sobbing in her cradle. She knew him and she trusted him.

Lady . . .

"Yes, Lady," Dail had said one night when she'd come to the ship rail to watch the dark headlands slip by, the reaching arms of land which enfolded Carnach Bay. She'd surprised him with tears on his face. "Yes, Lady, I'm sorrowing."

But he hadn't told her why. And he was so changed, so close and quiet, this bard who carried a sword but no harp. She could not, as once she might have, guess what sorrow cut so close as to wring tears from him. And she hadn't asked for fear she would learn that time and events had changed him so much that he now sorrowed for a love dead for lack of nurturing.

Again a gull cried, hovering close about the tall mast and the yardarm where Kicva stood high above the sea, keeping watch. Kicva looked down the distance to the deck and waved a morning greeting. The river-fisher's daughter looked fresh and bright in the heights of a sea-craft, like someone who was in a place which reminded her of home.

Nikia called her good morning, but Dail did not even turn. His eyes still on the grey Raeth shore, Dail drew breath to speak. He let that breath go, wordless, and looked at her sideways. Nikia saw an expression in his eyes like a question long pondered.

But he had no chance to ask the question, for from the small aft cabin came the sound of Gai's waking cry. Nikia excused herself and went to see to her daughter.

Nikia stood still, tried to get her bearings in the cabin's darkness. Though a whale-oil lantern hung within, it hung cold and dark, for light was pain to Islief and this cabin was his only refuge from the sun's glare. When Nikia's vision adjusted, she saw a short, stocky figure bend over a small blanket-lined box—Gai's makeshift cradle—and lift the child.

"Hush, alderliefest," Islief whispered, stroking Gai's cheek. "Mother, she will come."

Alderliefest. Best beloved. Dearest of all. When Nikia heard this creature of legend and dream address her child so, she knew he was speaking to hope.

It was, ever, delightful for Nikia to see her little child cradled in Islief's arms. He'd not held a younger—his word for child—in many, many years and he shared the tenderness he felt with all who were near to see. And she was fascinated by Gai's reaction to this strange small creature. When Islief was near, Gai saw no one but him, her eyes opening wide as a babe's eyes will when she sees light playing—the bright glint of sun on water, the moon's silvery path across the sea, light leaping from a gull's white wings. Or the warm soft glow of Islief's eyes in the shadowed darkness of the cabin.

Magic speaks to magic. Nikia saw it each time Gai looked into Islief's wide, wide eyes.

"Younger," he said now, rising to put the child in Nikia's arms. "She is hungry."

And then he went deeper into the darkness of the cabin, went to sit against the far wall while Nikia nursed the babe, and footsteps, hollow and heavy, traced a pacing path beyond the cabin's walls. When Gai was satisfied, sleepy again, Nikia rose to return her to her makeshift cradle, but Islief nodded toward the door and the light.

"Maybe you should take her into the sun, Nikia. Take Younger into the warm." He cocked his head, listening to Dail's pacing, then nodded as though the sound confirmed something. "Let her harper walk in company, for he is lonesome."

Yes, he was lonesome. And lost-looking. Nikia held her daughter close, and the closeness felt so good. "Why is Dail lonesome, Islief?"

Islief shrugged. "That is for Harper to say. It may be that he will tell you if you ask him."

And it may be, Nikia thought, *that he will not.*

There was so much Dail hadn't told her. Why, she did not even know what had become of his *Dashlaftholeh.*

"Islief, where is Dail's harp?"

"Raveners took her and broke her. Do you think this may be why he is lonesome and lass-lorn?"

Caught by a sudden and startlingly painful memory of her own grief at a harp's breaking, Nikia could not answer. But when Gai began to squirm and kick, she whispered a gentling word to her and went back onto the deck and the sunlight, looking for Harper, for Dail.

Joze sat with his back to the cabin wall, warm in the sun, tired though he'd slept through the night. Sleep, good food, rest—these things did not help the bone-deep weariness which haunted him always now. They had entered the Straits of Carnach, and Yan's best guess had it that they'd come near the Kevarths and the sea entrance to Islief's caverns before noon. Joze was glad the journey was nearly over. He nodded to Nikia as she passed, watched her return to the ship rail and the bard. When Nikia was out of hearing, he peered around the corner and into the cabin's darkness.

"Lonesome and lass-lorn, Islief? For a harp?"

Islief came closer to the doorway, large eyes bright, the rest of him no more than a dimly seen shadow in the blackness. "He loved her, his harp. And she loved him, for she made the leal-songs for him. The true music, Tall."

Joze said that he supposed this was so. Privately, he thought that if the bard was "lass-lorn" it was not only for his harp. Anyone with eyes to see knew for whom Dail yearned. But this princess had only days before seen her husband murdered, and from the sad sound of weeping he'd heard of a night, Joze didn't think there was much room in that tale for the bard to offer his heart to his cousin's wife.

Clearly, Islief had other thoughts on the matter, but he didn't offer them, only said: "Sun warms, yes, Tall?"

"Sun warms fine."

"And so you do not hurt much today?"

Joze's smile withered before cold dread. He looked away from the doorway, as though he could look away from the certain knowledge that he was ill.

But he found no refuge from fear. *Skimmer* now ran the narrow channel between the blunt cape where the city of Seuro lay and the coast of the northern land where once the Sorcerer's fortress had stood. He closed his eyes, tried not to remember what that fortress had looked like when wild magic had torn it stone from stone. Magic made by the hand of the young woman who now walked *Skimmer*'s deck with Dail.

This was the god-woman, this was the Hunter-Defender. This slender young Elven with the babe in her arms was the terrible being who had stolen away his will and left him helpless to do anything but crouch upon the very shore they were passing; helpless to do anything but watch the awful destruction of Souless.

And she hadn't known. In her magic and might, she'd never known that a Mannish soldier had cowered on the crumbling shore, prayed that the world would not collapse around him, that the fragile shore would not break apart and spill him, helpless, into the sea.

"Tall?"

"I don't hurt," Joze said roughly. "I'm fine."

Islief sighed, a sound like sand drifting. "No, Tall. You are not fine. You cough, and you think people don't hear. You breathe hard from pain, and you think people don't see. You are sick. And you try to think that you are not."

"Don't worry about me, Islief. You should worry about yourself, aye?"

"Why?"

"All this light you're hiding from. Maybe there will be more after we leave the ship, and it will hurt. *I* worry about you."

"Ah." Islief was silent for a while. Then he came still closer to the doorway. "No need, Tall. I will not die of light. I will not even die of pain."

"You're sure about that, are you?"

"I am sure. I know when I will die, Tall, and why. It will not be of light."

The brisk morning wind played around the edges of the cabin like a whisper. Despite the sun's warmth, a chill crept along the back of Joze's neck, like a memory waiting to be recalled. "Islief, how can you know when you will die?"

"Gods told me. Goddesses made the time. I have been waiting, Tall, to mend what was broken, to heal what was damaged. And now the waiting is nearly done. I know that when this is—"

"You *can't* know."

And yet he did know. Of Islief, the ghost Aeylin had said: *He felt the Ruby's power like a wild wind in his ancient soul when Nikia lifted it against the Sorcerer. He rejoiced when that evil creature finally died, for he knew that a new age was being born. He understood that the end of his long punishment was near.*

Islief knew that the end of his long punishment meant the end of an immeasurably long life of waiting. And Joze knew it, too. But he did not accept that knowledge. He buried it deep and far, hid it in the place where he entombed the understanding of his own illness. He did not know how to do anything else.

Yan called a sharp order from forward and Joze watched as Saer and Kicva shinnied up the mast to untangle a sail-line. They were swift-handed, those two. Sailors' children, Man and Elf, and they enjoyed a companionable rivalry, contending river-fisher's skill against sea-fisher's. This time Saer was slower, and Kicva's laughter showered down like silvery sunshine as she leaned far out from her perch and deftly untangled the lines. *Skimmer*'s red sail filled with wind again, billowed proudly.

"Islief," Joze said, trying to mask his fear of Islief's death, of his own illness. "Tell me something."

"What should I tell you, Tall?"

"That. Names. I'm Tall; Kicva is Friend; Dail is Harper. Even little Gai is Younger." Joze hitched around, looked into the cabin. "Why is Nikia the only one of us you call by her name?"

Came a cry from overhead and Joze looked up to see Kicva leaning far away from the mast, clinging with one hand, risking limb if not life to wave in the direction of the cabin.

"Islief!" she cried. "Islief! You're nearly home!"

Islief's eyes shone brightly. "Nearly home," he whispered. "Tall, nearly home. Go look. Please. And come to tell me what you see."

His question unanswered and likely to remain so for now, Joze got to his feet, bit back a groan for the pain in his knees and feet. He limped to the ship rail, stood near Nikia and Dail. "Are we near the Kevarths?"

"More than near," Dail said. He pointed south and east, toward a stony shore and a rocky cliff rising dark against the sky. "That's the back door."

"The back door? You don't mean we'll have to scale that cliff?"

Joze squinted out over the sun-gleaming water, shaded his eyes for a better view. The cliff, all sheer stone with surely not the least handgrip or foothold, towered over the shore, seemed to rise higher over the strait than the Citadel did over the small buildings in Damris.

Yan shouted an order, and another, bellowed instructions to Saer and Kicva as *Skimmer* turned into the changing wind. As *Skimmer* came close to the shore, navigating treacherous rocks, Dail pointed again. Now Joze saw dark gaps in the cliff. Cave openings.

"According to Islief, one of those is the back door."

"Bard!" Yan called. "Bard, come forward!"

Dail did as he was bid, left Joze and Nikia. Eyes on the cliff face and the cave mouths, Joze tried to breathe easy, tried to quiet the pounding of his heart. Hard to do, though. Breathing was never easy these days, and harder still because he stood nearly elbow to elbow with the Hunter-Defender.

Those rocks warding the coast did not always use to be there. Was a time when this was a clear shoreline. The rocks were chunks of Souless; dark, worked stone, the edges of some still smooth from an ancient stoneman's chisel. As *Skimmer* came tentatively closer, threading the toothy maze of stone, Joze could see decorative work, carvings and the fluting of a nearly submerged pillar which once stood sentinel at some entrance to the Sorcerer's fortress. Joze glanced at Nikia standing still and quiet beside him. The strong morning sunlight made her hair shine like silver, and it gilded a tear, a thin trace of gold as it slid down her cheek.

"Princess," Joze whispered. "Princess?"

She shuddered, and one tear followed another. In her arms Gai began to whimper. Nikia held her daughter close, bent over her as though protecting her from something. Joze touched her shoulder, and when she did not move away from him, he patted that shoulder, feeling awkward and clumsy.

And he thought: *My nightmares of that time are horrible. What must* hers *be like?*

Thinking that, he realized that she was, after all, not terrible. She was, after all, a young woman who had used all her strength to master a wild magic, a woman who would soon give her infant daughter the same kind of task to do.

And you can talk about babes who are made for magic, you can go on about destiny and Deities all you like, Joze thought. *This lady is only a mother caught between fear and hope for her child.*

Chapter Thirty-Two

KICVA DID NOT WANT TO LEAVE THE SEA. SHE FELT IT AS AN ache in blood and bone that she must give up the gentle rocking, the sturdy sway, the pitch and roll of *Skimmer*'s decks for the motionless floor of the caves. To leave the spangled light of sun on water for the dark of the caverns, to trade the strong boom of the sea for weary drip and echo of the underground— this was pain to her. She stood for a long time at the cave's mouth; for a long time she looked outward at the bright, heart-breakingly clear blue of sky and sea, at *Skimmer*'s retreating red sail. The craft ran well clear of the dark rocks now, and Yan navigated alone. High in the mast, Saer worked among the ropes.

Likely trying to free that ever-twisting rigging again, Kicva thought.

Behind her, at a distance, she heard the retreating footfalls of her companions, the soft cooing of the babe. Closer, she heard a muffled coughing and turned to see Joze lagging behind the others, waiting for her.

He looked terrible, unsteady on his legs, his dark eyes glittering in the last of the light. Here in the cave, with no sunlight to lend even false color, his lips looked blue, his face all grey and so thin; like a hunted man, a haunted man, like the Stone-Elf, the poor sick boy they'd found in the forest. Kicva had to swallow hard against a painful lump in her throat when he held out his hand. She had to blink back tears when he said:

"Come on, hunter-scout. We don't know the way, and it would be a sorry thing to get ourselves lost now when we're so close to the journey's end."

No challenge in his voice, not now. No wariness in his eyes like he was bracing for some heated exchange. He just held out his hand. Kicva turned her back on the sky, on the sea, on the light, and went into the darkness. She did not take Joze's hand. Rather, she flung her arm around his shoulders, as though they two were old friends, old travelling companions who were glad to walk the last miles of the journey together.

"Well, Joze," she said, taking more of his weight against her than maybe even he realized. "Turns out that you didn't have to commit child-theft after all."

He nodded, his eyes on the stony floor, for it was very dark here, and the others were only dim forms ahead of them and not worth watching for guides.

"I suppose you're glad about that," Kicva said.

"I am." He coughed again, and muffled though it was, it felt as though it came from deep in him. "That Lady loves her daughter. Now the Prince is dead, it would have been cruel beyond nightmare to steal little Gai away from her."

It would have been that. And yet, though they had the babe to bring to Aeylin, though Islief had assured them that they would not walk many hours before they came to the crystal hearth, Kicva could not find the joy of a task well done. She was afraid, and fear had a name to freeze her blood like winter winds freezing water to ice.

Aidan.

This was not an unspoken dread. She'd discussed it often with Islief on the sea journey. He'd not tried to allay the fear. He was too honest to offer false comfort. But he believed that, should Aidan find his way to the caverns, Aeylin would find a way to protect the Jewels.

Such faultless faith! Such steadfast trust!

Kicva wished for that kind of conviction as she'd never wished for anything before. But wishing proved nothing. She did not know whether Aidan had found his way to this underground world. She did not know whether the Elf-King's Mage had stolen the Emerald as he'd stolen her memories. She was frightened, and Joze's weight against her was not the only burden she walked with as she followed along behind Islief and the others.

She walked with a burden of guilt, for she was the one who had showed Aidan the way to the caverns. She was the one who had not been strong enough to resist the theft of her dreams. All she had done before that, after that, could not make up for this one weakness, this crucial failure of strength.

Beside her, Joze stopped, glanced back over his shoulder. Kicva, looking where he did, saw the light at the entrance to the caverns as no more than a pale white glow. Ahead lay darkness.

"He's here," Joze said. He coughed again, stood away from Kicva. "The mage is here in the caverns."

The skin along the back of her neck prickling with fear, Kicva said, "How do you know?"

Joze gestured ahead, pointed not into the darkness, but at it. "No light. Remember the light, hunter-scout? Aeylin made it for us. There is none now, though surely she must know that we're here. But to light the way for us would be to light the way for him."

"She's making him find his own way," Kicva murmured. "Making him use his own magic if the Seven will hear his prayers."

"And if they won't?"

Kicva tried to put something of hope into her voice. "Maybe he will realize that he must not take the Emerald away from here— or ever use it himself."

"Do you think he will understand that?"

Kicva didn't answer, because she didn't know. There was so much she didn't know about Aidan; so much she had never known about the man she'd meant to marry. Aidan kept himself distant from all, cool and safe to judge everything and everyone from behind a wall of calm. Now she thought that she'd be better able to tell someone what Joze might do than to make a guess at what Aidan might do.

The dark pressed closely around her, seemed to weigh heavily. Kicva lifted a hand, breathed a small prayer, and a cool blue light sprang up.

"The Deities still answer my prayers," she said, smiling to see the startled look on Joze's face. Ahead, a similar light leaped to life. By her light and Nikia's, Kicva saw that her friends were stopped, waiting. "They have an ear for the Princess, too."

Joze eyed the handful of light, head cocked and wary. "I've never seen you do that before," he whispered.

There would have been a time—and that time not long ago!— when Kicva would have sneered, and, seeing his uneasiness, might even have flung down a challenge to his courage. Now she did neither of those things. She did not doubt his courage, would never doubt it.

"I never had a need to before," she said. She gestured for him to hold out his hand.

He did, bracing not to flinch when the cool glow spilled over into his own cupped hand. When the light remained steady, he looked up, frowning. "Why doesn't it go out?"

Kicva smiled gently. "The light doesn't come from me. It's prayer-made. Keep it. I can make another. Come now, we have to catch up. If we're lucky, Aidan's been wandering in these caverns for some time, no way to know where the Jewels are. It could be

that we'll have done what needs doing before ever Aidan finds
his way out of the stone forest."

So saying, she put her arm again around his shoulders, again
as though she were offering no more than comradeship. Together,
they went to join their friends.

Aidan passed through the stone forest with the map of Kicva's
dreams for his guide until he came to the stony path leading away
from the underground river toward the small chamber that held a
rainbowed hearth and a ghost. Here he stopped, eyes on the red
light of sorcery, on the dark patterns of shadow that it cast.

He did not let himself listen to the echoing voices that seemed
to fill the caverns. Ah, but only seemed. These were the voices of
Deities. It was no more than an aural fancy that their voices filled
the caverns. Their voices were heard nowhere but inside himself.
And so Aidan did not let himself listen, refused to hear, for he
knew that the sorcery he embraced now had nothing to do with
the Seven.

It might be, he thought, that even Deities could not stop him.
For surely they would have before now if it were possible.

Upon that thought, the voices fell silent.

But Aidan did not pause, did not stop to tremble that the
Seven had turned away from him. And he did not think, he
who had revered these Deities for all his life, that this was a
thing for fear.

Hadn't he come this far without them? Hadn't he worked magic
without them? He would have his dream, and not have to beg for
it. He would take the Emerald and soar with the power, ride the
winds of enchantment. Let the Deities call that sorcery if they liked
the word. Aidan no longer saw the difference. He was not much
thinking about healing now. He was not much thinking about the
world without. He was thinking about the power growing within
him, a power he did not have to pray for, or even work for. This
power came to him with no effort, no humbling plea.

Kicva's dreams had shown him no more than the way to the
caverns and the way through the stony forest to a ghost. Aidan
abandoned those dreams now as useless. They would not lead
him to the Jewels, for Kicva had never been to see them, had
only been to Aeylin.

But, though this underground world be vast and its paths winding, Aidan knew that he would find those Jewels. For, beneath
the silence of the Seven, he sensed other whisperings. He did not
hear them as one would hear a voice, or wind, or a sigh. But he,

who had ranged along the planes of enchantment through all the
winter past in search of these Jewels, knew that these were the
voices of the wild magics within the Sapphire and the Diamond,
the Topaz, the terrible Ruby and the long-sought Emerald. Magic
speaks to magic, and the Jewels spoke a language that sorcery
could understand.

Aidan turned his back on the chamber of the crystal hearth,
walked away from the path to Aeylin without another thought, as
though he'd made up his mind about that long ago. He followed
the stony banks of the underground river until he came at last to a
long and narrow corridor, a winding, high-ceilinged hallway. The
Elf-King's Mage did not hesitate. He entered that corridor boldly,
sending red light and black shadows questing before him.

I have been here before, Nikia thought. By blue hand-lights, small
globes of radiance in Dail's hand, in Kicva's, in Joze's, she saw the
spires of stalagmites rising tall from the stony floor, saw the ceiling
above hung with thin, fragile-seeming stalactites, and knew that
she walked through the landscape of an old dream.

And in that dream, while in the waking world the Sorcerer had
advanced upon the Keep of Seuro, she'd come to these caverns,
filled up with need, and found a voice to teach her how to turn
need into the spell that would set the Ruby's magic free.

I am Islief . . . of the First People!

Nikia shivered, held Gai tighter, pressed the sleeping child
close to her heart for warmth and for courage. That voice, deep
and terrible, had rocked the cavern, the world itself, to its very
foundations. It had taught her spell-words, magic incantations. It
had taught her how to use the War-stone to become the Hunter-
Defender, a being with the undeniable might of a Deity, with
the strength to fight the Sorcerer and his godless magic. And
that voice, sounding like earthquake and avalanche, belonged to
this small, gentle creature who walked beside her and even now
looked up at her with sure understanding.

"You remember," Islief said, his words spoken as softly as
though they were not words at all but wind sighing across sand.
"You remember our dream."

"I remember."

"And you know that what must be done next is not yours to do."

Nikia was longer at responding than she'd thought to be. It was
not a matter of believing that Gai had the power to enkindle the
Emerald's healing magic. She knew that, who saw the grace of
power each time she looked into her daughter's eyes. The world

had not known Gai's like for long ages past, perhaps never.

She held Gai close, took courage from feeling the sleeping child's breath warm on her neck. They walked through wonderful places, people afraid that the chance to make the magic which must be done could yet be snatched away. Yet Gai slept peacefully in her mother's arms, calmly, as though she were waiting for something and, waiting, knew nothing better to do than sleep.

Nikia glanced at Dail. The bard met her eyes, and Nikia knew— for he watched her so gravely—that he understood the fear she dared not express. Gai sighed, made a small, sleepy sound.

"It will be all right, Lady," Dail said. "It won't happen for Gai the way it happened for you."

"How do you know that? Oh, Dail, how can you be certain?"

It was not Dail who answered, but Islief. He touched her hand, said gently, "You were alone, Nikia, when you called the Ruby's magic. Hard it was for Harper and my Lady to call you back from that power's terrible promises. But Younger will not be alone when she uses the Emerald."

He said nothing more, only continued walking, tracking over trackless stone with not so much as a pause to look around himself for a landmark. And Nikia followed him as she had once before followed his voice.

Soon the rough stone floor became smoother, the walls wider and higher. Now Nikia could not see the cavern's roof even when she tilted her head far back. Once Kicva sent a handful of blue light drifting upward, hoping to find some sense of height. The blue light faded from sight, swallowed into the darkness, though Kicva said it had not been quenched. It had simply been lost in the height.

"But I hear the river," the hunter-scout said, glancing at Joze, who nodded confirmation. "We're not far from Aeylin now, Islief, are we?"

"Not far, Friend. But on the wrong side of the water. We must cross to come into the forest."

Forest? Nikia glanced at Kicva, but the Elven did not see the look, for she was speaking to Joze, head low and murmuring encouragement. Not long after, Nikia understood what Islief meant by his use of the word "forest," and she had no words for question, none to express her delight in the beauty of this underground woodland which had nothing to do with wood at all. And Dail, like her a stranger to this place, drew a long breath and let it out in a long slow sigh. It was that familiar sigh, the one of which he was never aware, breathed in the moment before his fingers touched a harp's strings. He had no harp to touch, but he touched her shoulder—perhaps the first time he'd come so near in days—and pointed ahead.

"A . . . tree has fallen across the river," he said, though he did not apply the word "tree" with any confidence in its aptness to that great stone column. "We can cross there."

Islief, hearing, agreed. "Just there, you are right, Harper." He glanced over his shoulder, spoke to Joze, who was yet some distance behind. "You know where we are, Tall?"

Joze, leaning heavily on Kicva's shoulder, limping now, said that he knew. He coughed, hard and painfully. "And I know the way to Aeylin. But I've got to rest, Islief. You go on, I'll catch up."

"Ah, Tall, you cannot stay alone."

Joze was slow to answer, coughing hard again. When he looked up, Nikia saw that the blue hand-lights lent his face a horrible grey pallor. He sat down on the stony floor, though it looked more like his legs simply went out from under him.

"Islief is right," she said. "Joze, you can't stay here alone."

"Well, maybe Kicva can stay with me. Just for a few moments."

Nikia glanced at the hunter-scout and did not have to ask the question. Kicva went down on her knees beside Joze, held him tightly while he coughed.

"It's all right, Princess," the Elven said. "I'll stay. You go on with Islief and Dail. We'll catch up."

Islief looked from one to the other, eying Joze closely. Then he spoke, briskly for him:

"Yes, yes. We must go on, Nikia." He glanced keenly at Dail. "Harper, you had best hold your Nikia close when we cross the water, for the stone is slippery and wet."

Dail did that, and not reluctantly. But Nikia wasn't thinking about reluctance or eagerness. She was thinking about Joze, coughing weakly now, and she was thinking about the mingling of tenderness and terror in Kicva's eyes.

So far those two had come to bring hope to a world bereft of hope! Could it be that one would not see the results of their struggle?

Joze leaned against Kicva's shoulder, let her hold him for many long moments after he was certain that Islief had brought the others safely across the water and into the stony forest on the other side. It felt good, here in her arms; a warm place to rest. He'd happily have rested there for all the time left to him. But he could not do that. He tried to push away from her and had to give up the effort, for he was taken by a fit of coughing. This time he did not cough for effect, and the coughing hurt.

"Oh, Joze," Kicva whispered, her breath warm against his cheek. "Oh, it's plague, isn't it?"

He felt a thick and alien wetness in his lungs, prayed that it was not blood. The coughing done, he wiped his lips with the back of his hand, heart rising a little to see that he was not bringing up blood yet.

"No," he said. He moved away from her, pushed himself to his feet, and did not groan for the sharp, cold pain in knees and ankles. "No, it's not plague. Just more of the same kind of trickery you've seen before, hunter-scout." He cocked a grin and almost felt better for it. "I was just stalling."

"What—?"

Joze took her hand, pulled her to her feet, though the effort hurt. "Come with me."

Her struggle between disbelief and suspicion played out in her eyes. "Joze, what are you up to?"

"I'm up to trouble, hunter-scout. Though it's sanctioned trouble, never fear. Islief knows what I'm about. I'm going to see if I can bring some trouble to Mage Aidan."

"Aidan? But—you don't know where he is!"

Joze squinted across the stone column bridging the underground river. "No, I don't. But I know where he wants to be, and I know the way. Maybe we can get there before him." Joze put an arm around her shoulders, led her toward the water and the stone bridge. "Want to come with me?"

She let silence be her answer, and Joze didn't complain when she held him nearly as closely as Dail had held Nikia as they crossed the fallen stone tree to the other side.

As from a great distance, Nikia heard Dail say that Joze and Kicva had not followed behind; she heard him tell Islief that he'd go to find them. And she heard Islief say that Harper must wait, that he must let things fall out as they would. She heard these things, but she paid them no attention, for she had come to the chamber of the crystal hearth. She had come to Aeylin, the queen of ancient memory, the Lady of the Blue-Silver Eyes.

The layers of crystal hearthstones shimmered like bright memories of exquisite gems. Green, blue, white, orange and red—the color-shadows all mingled and moved in the irregular, unpatterned dance of firelight. But, elegant as that delicate weaving of light and shadow was, it seemed like nothing more than the fine gown worn by a woman who needed no rich silks or patterned damasks to make her splendid. Nikia had no eye for anything or anyone but the tall, ghostly Elven rising high, smoke-thin, above the heat-rippling, brilliant coals in the hearth. And she could listen to nothing but Aeylin's voice, the familiar ghosty whisper not heard since the day she'd known she was childing.

"Set your Gai down, Nikia," the ages-dead queen said.

Nikia went close to the hearth, and, eyes still on the ghost and the smoke, knelt and laid her daughter in a smooth depression on the stone floor. Gai did not move but to open her eyes, so wide and blue, and to look up at the ghostly queen.

Blue-silver eyes shining, Aeylin asked, "Who named your daughter for joy, Nikia?"

Nikia drew a long breath, let it go shaking. Close around her a shadow of sorrow breathed. She tried to speak, but no words made a way past the pain closing tight around her throat. For now, though it had never seemed so before, she saw Garth when she looked at Gai. She saw his smile mirrored in Gai's, saw his face—the very shape of it!—echoed in the shape of his daughter's. As Gai regarded the ghostly woman above the crystal hearth, so had Garth looked when he bent his thoughts upon some serious and grave matter.

Dead, her husband, her Gai's father. And though, in the end, she hadn't loved him, still she would miss him.

Nikia looked away from the ghost, looked to Islief, looked up to Dail standing close beside her, as though they—one or both together—might provide her with a voice for answering. Islief said nothing, only stood watching her, his wide, wide eyes alight. But Dail put his hand on her shoulder, squeezed gently, as though pressing courage upon her.

"Lady," she said, "Gai's father named her."

Aeylin smiled. "And he said, 'Name her for happiness, Nikia, for you deserve some. Wife, you've more than earned it.'"

Nikia nodded, wordless before sorrow.

"Did you think, Nikia, that *he* took no happiness in his Gai?"

Nikia felt Dail's hand tremble, for he did not understand the question. But again he pressed her shoulder; again she found that she could speak. "Lady, I don't know. But he died for her, and so I must believe that he loved her."

"Daughter, before the end, he had as much joy in her as he had love. And she, your little Gai, has as much courage as he did. Never fear for her, Nikia. For when the last work is done, she will prove herself worthy of the name her father gave her."

"The last work . . . Lady, will we do that soon?"

Aeylin made no reply, but her image thinned, wavered as though a breeze had come wafting. But no breeze stirred the air, not the least breath. It was then Nikia remembered that Joze and Kicva were not present. She looked from Islief to Dail, and their worried exchange of glances alarmed her.

"Islief, have they gone for the Emerald?"

Islief said gravely that he hoped so. Dail said nothing, only went to his knees beside her and held her when she began to tremble with fear.

"Aidan," she whispered. "My father's mage . . ."

The words had not left her lips before Gai, till then so still and placid, began to cry. Not the lusty wail of hunger, nor the weak, uncomprehending sob of fevered illness. Gai screamed, shrieked with the wide-eyed, blind staring of a terrified child, and no one, not her mother, not her bard, not Islief, could comfort or still her.

Chapter Thirty-Three

JOZE RAN DOWN THE HIGH-CEILINGED CORRIDOR, STAGGERED coughing down the winding hall which led to Crown Hold. His heart pounded hard in his chest, hammered wildly, painfully, and with a sound to fill his ears like thunder. So Islief had run on a night so far distant that time no longer measured it. So Islief had run down these very hallways when he'd determined to give the Crown and the Jewels to Aeylin. And now a mage had come to steal one of those Jewels; now all Islief's waiting for redemption might be in vain.

Joze ran harder, sucking in breath when coughing would permit. He didn't want to think about what redemption would mean to Islief, or what the end of Islief's long waiting might mean to him. And he dared not think what terrible thing would happen should Aidan try to use the Emerald.

He wished desperately for the cool white sheets of illumination like lightning's glow which had filled the stone hallway the last time he'd come this way, following Islief in sedate step, wondering where they were bound, wondering whether he himself had made up his mind to go seeking the daughter of the Hunter-Defender. He prayed for that light, pleaded with Deities whose names he'd known in childhood, but none answered. He had only Kicva's blue hand-light to guide him now, and that made more shadow than illumination.

He stopped at a joining of hallways, at a crossroad, leaned his back against cool damp stone, trying to catch his breath, trying to choose the right turning. Kicva stood waiting, impatient for him to make up his mind. Her long eyes were dark with dread.

"Joze," she whispered, that whisper echoing like bats' wings rustling. "Do you know the way? *Do you?*"

He coughed again, bent over and trying to breathe through the thickness in his lungs. "This turning . . . I don't remember this turning . . . or where it leads. . . ."

What was it Islief had said to the Celedman, the guard on Damris' wall? *I come from where there is no direction save high or low . . .* It was true! No north or south; no right or left!

Joze looked around wildly, and in that moment a fierce and spinning light filled the corridor, splashed a wild rainbow of colors up the stone walls to spill back from the ceiling. Joze grabbed Kicva's wrist, pulled her hard, and they ran again, taking neither the left turning nor the right. They ran straight toward the light's source, straight toward Crown Hold.

When they entered the small chamber behind the Hold, they saw a horror.

Making no prayer, surrendering his will to the coldly whispering sorcery within himself, Aidan laid his right hand upon the Crown. He had no intent to use the Jewels; intent would be shaped by the limits of the Jewels' power and his own strength. He spread his fingers so that he touched each Jewel: Sapphire, Diamond, Topaz, the dreaded Ruby. Just for exploration, just to test and try, he lifted the Emerald from the stone worktable and placed it in the empty setting.

A connection was made, the kind crafted when lightning leaps up from the earth, flares high in the sky, and falls back to ground again, fiery spears of deadly, unbridled power. Aidan's vision filled with madly spinning color. His heart became charged with fear, his soul with elation. He could not tell dream from nightmare, though dreams and nightmares surrounded him, sighing sweetly, howling madly, offering promise and snarling threat. The small stone chamber filled with raining light—green and red, blue and orange, and purest white.

He knew no difference between balance and instability. Confused by the lights, by the great and many powers, he did not know tame from feral; docile from savage; surrender from resistance. And the whirlpool of feelings—he himself!—was all at the same time fierce and wonderful, terrible and magnificent.

Someone screamed: "AIDAN!"

He could not answer. He did not know who he was—where he was. He knew only that he held the spirit of the world in his hands and that spirit was heavy enough to tear muscle from bone, heart from soul. Enlivened and exhausted, both, Aidan leaned against the low stone table, sweating and shivering, trying to block out the echoes of that one screamed word, trying to find and hold on to the dream that had led him here.

But that dream did not let itself be seen. Aidan knew only nightmare, felt only reckless flight, heedless speed, unmeasurable height. Homage and horror, both, he knew; the unhooded hawk caught in a gale of terror, snatched up by stormwinds of power and might so strong they could blow him wherever they willed.

But these winds of might and magic had no will. Will must be imposed upon them, will forged by reason and strength. Aidan had neither and, mindless, those winds raged for rage's sake, screamed and howled and tore at him for no other reason but that they could. For power unbalanced by reason is merciless.

Filled with terror, sightless in a chaos of color and whirling light, Aidan searched desperately for answers to questions which tore past him like fragile leaves in a tempest. What reason had brought him here? What purpose, what will? He could not recall a time when he'd known. As though reason and memory were foreign concepts spoken in alien tongues, Aidan could not understand even the need to know or remember. He was without memory, without experience, without the least reference point in the pitiless maelstrom of power he inhabited. The experiences he had now— the terror, the groping, the attempt to tame the raw and raging power surrounding him, filling him—did not accumulate or grow into knowledge.

"Aidan! Control it! You must control it!"

CONTROL . . . AIDAN . . . AIDAN . . . CONTROL . . .

Staggering, falling against the table, a gem-smith's stone workbench, he clutched the Crown, the Jewels, and tried to follow echoes as though they were paths to a dream. But these fey echoes ran taunting all around a place with no direction, disembodied wraiths fleeing.

And the wind howled, the wind screamed, the wind roared curses and laughter. Power mocked him, shrieked for all to hear that the Elf-King's Mage was helpless to comprehend even the idea of control. Wrenching strength from himself, Aidan turned away from the stone workbench. He saw them, then, Joze and Kicva. Desperate, they looked, all wide eyes and mouths distorted with terror.

"Aidan," Joze cried. "Aidan, look at me!"

Aidan lifted his head, tried to meet Joze's eyes. But he couldn't. There was all the light, the many colors of power, between them.

"Look at me!"

How to see him through the storm of light? How to see him through the fear? How to even hear his words, so faint and far beyond the vortex?

"You can," Joze said, and said it gently. A spasm of coughing took him, shook him hard, as though he too were caught in some deadly, pitiless storm. When he looked up again, he had to gulp for air before he could speak, and when he spoke, his voice was thin and tattered. "You can see me, Aidan. Look. Look at me."

And he did see. Beyond the wild colors, on the other side of the whirling light, he saw a thin, grey-faced young man, filled up with fears; terror of the great powers that flew howling all around the small stone chamber; dread of the mage with no control. And something else.

"Joze, you are dying," Aidan thought. "Plague is killing you."

And perhaps he'd spoken that thought aloud, for Kicva, yet holding to the young man's arm, drew a ragged, sobbing breath. But Joze, though he flinched like a man who'd just been delivered a death sentence, only nodded slowly.

"I know it, Aidan. And this power you're holding is killing you. Put the Crown aside."

He couldn't, though now he wanted to, more than he'd ever wanted anything.

"Aidan, put it down. Those powers will tear you up. Mage, let the Crown go before it kills you. This isn't how it was supposed to be. Aidan, don't you remember? This is not what your king wanted."

No, it wasn't what Dekar had wanted. Not for the theft of power had his king sent him ranging along the planes of enchantment. Not for that.

And Aidan knew, this the first knowledge he'd been able to find since he'd touched the Crown, that this wasn't what he'd wanted either. He'd wanted flight, he'd wanted the sure knowledge that all his hard-won skill, all his carefully nurtured talent, all his yearning and hope, could become something more: the realization of a dream. But he'd been lured away from that dream, seduced into the arms of nightmare by the lies sorcery had falsely disguised as promises. He'd been beguiled by his own certainty that he could control the wildest things known to Deity or man: the spirits of the earth.

Aidan searched for words, searched for a way to tell Joze that he could not lay aside the Crown. This was more power than anyone had known, and it was at once horrifying and beautiful; at once a thing for despair and a thing for joy. Easier to cut heart from breast now—simpler to make the blood dry up in his veins!

But he could find neither word nor way to explain this to Joze, and helpless in the whirlwind, he clung to the only thing he could feel: the Crown. He clutched it to his heart, so close that the faceted Jewels tore his shirt, bruised his flesh, their sharp edges raked blood from his breast.

"Aidan!" Joze cried. Stop! Put it down!"

AIDAN ... AIDAN ... STOP ... STOP ...

But he could not stop. He pressed the Crown closer, embraced it now as though it were a lover and he starving for love; as though it were sleep and he a dream needing to be born. The Emerald, the green, shining Heal-stone, fell to the floor, rolled a short distance. But Aidan had no thought for it now.

He hunched over the Crown, the bound stones, pulling all their power into himself. It would break him apart, he knew that. But maybe, when he was all broken and scattered and the pieces of himself taken by the storm, the nightmare would end, the dream be found again. Feeling as though he were drowning, burning up, torn apart, blown down the landscapes of nightmare, Aidan took all of power into himself that flesh and bone, heart and soul, could bear.

That was not, in the end, much at all. He was not a long time dying. And dead, there was nothing but the memory of him left behind; remembrance echoed in Kicva's sobbing and the hollow sound of the gold and silver Crown hitting the floor. The Jewels were only stones again, dark and quiet, their fierce and spinning brilliance extinguished all at once, as though there had never been even the least glimmer of light in the world but that in a mage's hungry dream.

Islief's small workroom was filled with darkness so heavy, so thick, that Joze did not know how he would ever find the Emerald

now. It had fallen, at the last, from Aidan's grasp, fallen and rolled
a little, until the rough stone floor and its own facets stopped it.
Staggering on legs that had gone cold and weak with pain, Joze
took a step, and then another. He bent, for no reason but that he
could not stand erect for coughing, and reached—for no reason
than that his legs could no longer hold him. He was only hoping
to break his fall. When his fingers closed round the Emerald, he
drew a hard breath, just like a sob, and lifted his hand, called
softly for Kicva.

"I'm here, I'm here," she said.

But she needn't have spoken. He felt her arms close around
him, felt her breath catching, her heart pounding. He pressed the
Jewel into her hand, said hoarsely:

"Bring it back to Aeylin. Hurry, now. I'm sorry for your Aidan,
but there's no time to mourn him. Hurry! We've been too long
waiting for this."

"I won't leave you—" She shook her head and Joze felt her tears
on his neck. "And I'm not crying for Aidan, or not just for—"

She held him gently, and when he understood the other reason
for her tears, Joze groaned, then laughed, then coughed again.
"Ah, Kicva, what a time for us to finally admit it, eh? But you
must bring Aeylin the Emerald, as we promised. I'll follow. Just
as soon as I can."

Kicva held him for a moment longer, kissed him again, and then
left. He listened to her retreating footsteps for a long time before he
found himself able to marshal his little strength and grope through
the darkness again. He did not retrieve the Crown. Though he
knew that no touch of his would set those powers raging again,
he shrank from the thought of touching it. Someone else would
have to do that.

He didn't get very far before he at last acknowledged what
he'd been too afraid to consider before now. Aidan, who had
been wrong about so many things, had been right in one: Joze
was dying of plague. He took what strength he had and used it
to get out of Islief's little workshop.

Alone in Crown Hold, wiping the first warm flecks of blood
from his lips, Joze knew he couldn't go farther. And so, he went to
the black diamond pedestal, the tall dark column he'd once thought
looked like a lonesome cry of yearning, and sat himself down to
wait for whatever would come for him out of the darkness.

Dail stood away from the others, prepared to assume the role he'd
always played, made ready to take the observer's part. He kept

a distance between himself and Nikia, though he'd have liked to stand close beside her to offer what he had of strength and courage. If he dared not offer her his love—she who had wept each night of the sea voyage for her husband dead—these, at least, he could offer. But he did not; he kept his back to the wall as Kicva placed the Emerald in Nikia's hand.

He kept a distance between himself and Kicva, though he would liked to have tendered her some comfort. She had come back from Crown Hold alone, and Dail thought he knew what that must mean. Of magic or sickness, Joze was dead. But he did nothing as Kicva went to stand beside the crystal hearth, empty-handed now.

And he kept a distance between himself and Islief, though he would liked to have stood near and be warmed by the light of hope in Islief's wide, wide eyes when Gai, cradled in her mother's arms, at last fell still as though the Heal-stone had worked its first magic by comforting her infant terror. But he stayed where he was; Dail believed that he had no role to play here but a bard's part to mark and remember.

The Lady of the Blue-Silver Eyes knew otherwise. "Come close to the fire, bard," she said, her lovely eyes shining bright in smoke. Dail could do nothing but obey this ghost who'd kept him good company through the weary winter.

"Nikia, give Gai to her bard."

But Nikia questioned, asked why it was that she could not hold her child through the making of magic. "Lady, I know what it is to use a Jewel. Gai must not be alone."

The smoke rose higher above the many-colored hearth, the ghost became more solid-seeming. Blue-silver eyes shone brightly and raven-black hair gleamed in the firelight.

"How could she be alone in the arms of her bard? We have spoken of balance, Nikia. We know the need for it, and have gathered all the weights. How is it that the Deities find balance?"

"God and goddess move together," Nikia answered. "Male and female, each with their own qualities, make a whole."

And so the Deities each have two names, Dail thought, his understanding like a pulse of joy.

"Just so," the ghost said. "Let this man hold your daughter. Let him, who has sung many songs, guide your daughter, who has never voiced one. Let him, who has seen one of the Jewels wreak despair and destruction, watch as another sows hope and renewal. Let Gai's bard stand with her. You her mother, these her friends, will watch and witness."

Nikia looked around the chamber, from Kicva to Islief, and finally to Dail. Silvery eyes luminous, she placed the infant in Dail's arms. Gai moved, stretched a little, and Dail held her close, feeling at once awkward and full of the very simple fear of a man who'd not often held infants: What if he dropped her? But Gai was not concerned. She smiled sleepily. She was warm in his arms, warm against his breast, and her eyes, canted as an Elf's are, blue as any Mannish child's before they have found their true color, held him for a measureless time. Dail saw both Garth and Nikia in this child. He saw, too, the shape of the future; the child who would rule both Elflands and Mannish.

And I am your bard, he thought, wondering and joyful. *Gai, Aeylin has said it: I am your bard.*

Gai reached up, brushed tiny, perfect fingers against his sun-burned, bearded face. Perhaps the beard tickled her, for she laughed, as infants do—a sudden burst of delight.

"Nikia," Aeylin said, her voice thin, somehow more distant though her image never moved or faded. "Give the Heal-stone to the child."

The Emerald was no small stone, nearly as large as Dail's fist, and many-faceted. Nikia rested it gently upon her daughter's breast. Gai did not move, though she must have felt the weight.

"Bard," Aeylin said. "Are you ready to see the magic done?"

He didn't know; he wasn't sure. He'd stood near such magic before, and he'd nearly died of it. And, aye, this magic-working would not be like the Ruby's pitiless rending and war-making. Nothing could be more unlike. And yet . . .

Dail looked from Aeylin to Nikia—the ghost and the living woman—each in her way part of the voice of every song he'd made since winter; one the heart, the other the soul.

"Lady," he said, because they were both 'Lady' to him now. "Tell me what must be done."

"Gai will tell you," the ghost murmured.

He would have questioned that, asked how a weeks-old infant could instruct him, but the answer came before he could draw breath to speak. When Gai touched the Emerald, laid both hands upon it, Dail knew that he must go closer still to the hearth. When the flames fell, the fire quieting all at once to leave nothing but bright embers and a ghost hovering above, he knew that he must hold the child near, so that she could see the embers reflected in the Emerald's facets.

And when his eyes were drawn to those reflections, he did not look away, did not think—even once—that here were things not meant for him to see. He *knew* he must look, knew he must go as far into reflection as Gai would go, stay close beside.

He must be there to bring her back home again.

They went to brown, broken lands, the man and the babe in his arms. They went down from the mountains, down from the place named for caves. In Elflands they saw no bird or beast, only dying trees, withered grass. They went through stony glens which had not long ago been filled with tumbling water. Now the ground was cracked and dried, and no moisture relieved the land's pain. Honeysuckle did not cling to the bare black trunks of trees and the air was foul as a dying man's breath. No white wood sorrel, no golden primrose, no red rosebay grew to abate the forest's loneliness. The empty sky longed for the company of hawks; the blackened graveyard of the forest's floor groaned, aching to feel the soothing touch of a woodcock nestling. Windborne dust stung tears from the babe's eyes. Memories, echoes from another time, wrung tears from the man. Not a month before he'd seen this place, and it had been alive then.

The babe cried, sobbed for better places. But there were not better places, only worse.

They went into Mannish lands, the man and the babe in his arms. They went into hungry places, into villages where children never felt the sweet kiss of rain; they passed farmers' cots where children never smelled the earth quicken to welcome spring, nor heard a gentler breeze sigh as it rippled across a green and gleaming sea of young wheat. Along the coastlands, no tall grey heron stalked, no turtle warded sandy nest, and only hungry gulls sailed the hard blue sky.

The babe sobbed, she cried out for better places. But there were no better places, not outside the borders of memory and dream. The man told her that she could have them only if she made them. But she did not know how, that little child, to make what she wanted. She could see nothing but stark emptiness, and she had no memory of anything but a dying land.

He sat down, the man with the babe in his arms, sat on the sandy shore; the place where the land ends and the sea begins; the in-between place. He took the Emerald from her breast, placed the Heal-stone in her hands, held it steady for her. He watched as she touched every facet of the Jewel, listened as she sighed and murmured over the hard, cool, green brightness.

She looked up at him, her eyes so blue; as a babe's are before the turning, glossy and deep as the color of juniper berries. Eye

to eye, she spoke to him, but the man did not understand, for she
used the wordless language of infants.

She spoke again, and again he failed to comprehend. He looked
around himself, at the white, white sand, at the sun-glinting ocean,
as though there he could discover a way to understand what the
babe said. For deep in himself he knew that she was asking for
something, and he knew that he must grant it, else the Emerald's
magic would not spring to life.

Then he bent close over her, the babe in his arms, felt her
breath warm on his cheek. He closed his eyes, trying to take
the wordless sounds she uttered and make of them the kind of
language he could understand. But he understood nothing more
than that these sounds embraced a language of the heart; all
prompted by feeling and sensation; all uttered without the confines
of thought.

This language of infants was like music, a tune without words,
a fall of notes born of a breeze come caressing. Songs of the heart.
And that language, that speech, he knew well enough.

He opened his eyes, looked at the babe again, and saw her
smiling secretly and to herself, as though over the change which
had come upon her while he was not watching. Her eyes were
no longer blue-before-turning. They were lighter, now; the color
of shadows on whitest snow, blue-silver and lovely. They were
Aeylin's eyes. When the babe smiled up at him, murmuring and
sighing, her tiny hands clutching the Heal-stone tightly, the man
understood what she asked for, knew what she needed. For he'd
always understood the Lady of the Blue-Silver Eyes.

Harper without a harp, he whistled the wren's three sweet
notes to turn her smile to laughter. He sang wordless songs about
thunder and about rain. His voice a sigh, he let her know about
grass growing and what secrets the rain whispers as it passes
over. With no words, he told her what the woodlands smell like in
the moment before a storm, all charged and sharp and dangerous.
He told her how snow feels, light swift kisses.

Wordless, he told her what the world is like when it is alive;
while she, blue-silver eyes bright, made a chorus of delighted
laughter for his song. And she let him know that she loved these
wordless songs; that she—now in these moments both Aeylin and
Gai—had heard all his worded songs in her hearth in the caverns,
and in her mother's womb.

When the time was right, they left the shore, went back inland,
through the farmlands, into the forest, up to the mountains again.
Misty softness followed them, wrapped the land in a silvery cloak

*of rain so gentle that even the most sorely wounded places felt it
as a blessing.*

*And the mist, it seemed, followed them even when they went
back below ground, for when they came back to the place from
which they had set out, the man smelled the heavy, damp odor
of a quenched fire. He did not understand what this meant, but
the scent of an extinguished fire is sad and final, and he wept.*

By the blue glow of Kicva's hand-light, Nikia saw Dail turn away
from the dwindling glow of the hearth, then sink to a seat on the
stone floor, Gai in his arms, his back against the hearthstones.
She needed no light to show her that he was weeping; she heard
that. And hearing, she could do nothing but kneel beside him,
wrap her arms around him, and hold him close.

"She's gone," Dail whispered against her shoulder, his voice
hollow with loss. "Aeylin is gone, and she will not come back."

It was so. Nikia knew it, had known it since first her daughter
touched the Emerald. In that moment the smoke had thinned, the
image of the long-dead queen had lost shape and substance. In
that moment, Aeylin's voice had sounded like nothing more than
wind sighing through tall grass, a breeze soughing through a
thickness of forest pines. But she had not gone away until her
hearth's embers revealed a vision of rain, soft and misty, to those
waiting for the magic to be done. Kicva had breathed a prayer of
thanks for that vision. Nikia, who stood watching the embers as
though she were attending the birth of a miracle, had echoed that
prayer.

But Islief, standing between the two, had been perfectly silent,
as though only silence were called for; silence to confirm, silence
to welcome, silence to make ready for something more. Yet
nothing more had happened but that the embers had darkened,
the smoke dissipated, the ghost vanished on a sigh that sounded
like a voice whispering.

At last . . .

And Dail, bending close over Gai, had placed the Emerald on
the crystal hearth, turned away from the dying embers, turned
away from the image of what he'd helped the infant accomplish,
and sat down upon the floor to weep.

Nikia held him for a long time, soothed him while he tried to
find a place of balance between gain and loss, while he worked to
understand that he no longer walked on the planes of magic and
would not again speak with the ghost who had kept him company
throughout long seasons of sorrow.

Kicva came to take Gai, and Dail—arms empty—turned and took Nikia in his arms. He held her tightly, and this was not about weeping and sorrow for loss. Nikia knew, heard it in the measure of her own heartbeat, felt it in the rhythm of his, that this was about happiness, and the understanding that something a long time yearned for was about to be found. For, holding her, he'd whispered her name as though it were a question, and she had spoken his as though it were an answer.

Chapter Thirty-Four

ISLIEF TOOK THE HEAL-STONE FROM THE HEARTH, DID NOT EVEN look at the last smoky ghost of a ghost hanging empty and cooling above the fading embers. This was not his Lady; Aeylin had gone elsewhere, and she was waiting. With the Emerald cupped in his two hands, held with as tender a care as though it were a creature only moments ago kindled, he walked past Nikia and Harper, close in each other's arms. He left them to ask and answer their questions of each other. He walked past Friend and Younger, and he only stopped for a moment when Friend looked at him, her pretty eyes still wet.

"Where are you going, Islief?"

"To finish," he said.

She understood, and she bent to kiss him, a soft brush of lips against his cheek. Younger, all sleepy from her work, sighed, and Islief could feel her warm breath. She smiled, as over a dream, and Islief felt that smile as a blessing.

"Alderliefest," he said. Best beloved; dearest of all.

Then Friend gave him farewell as a soldier does, clear-eyed and silent, the silence filled with trust that parting companions understand what need not be said: *I will see you again. Someday . . .* Her hand, so warm and young, lingered on his shoulder, then fell away.

Islief left them all behind and walked out into the darkness and his caverns. No need to tell Nikia and Harper where he was going. They would know he'd gone when they had time to know, and the knowing would change nothing for them, or for him. The paths—his and theirs—which had run side by side for such a brief time, were separating again. They must go out into their bright world to remake all the bonds which had been so long ago shattered. He must go—at last—to remake the Crown which had been broken; to keep his promise to Aeylin and the Seven.

Old he was, old and old, and as he walked into the forest of stone, Islief felt the weight of each day, each month, each year spent here. Time did not know how to count the years he had spent watching a forest grow from stone. Water dripping, just like tears, made the stone trees; carved them from rock, or shaped them one tiny grain of sand at a time. There were no words to describe the length of that making. Counting did not know how to measure how many years he'd spent again hearing the water kiss the rocky shore of a secret river, the caresses seeking to find the shape of the stony banks as a lover seeks to know his beloved, delighting always in a new reason to kiss.

Nor could measure tell about the years spent in vast darkness, loneliness relieved only lately by a ghost's company; they two hearing the echo of each other's prayer for forgiveness of theft, each other's plea for a way to find redemption. And now Aeylin was no more, the desperate ghost, the sad and sorry queen gone to be among Deities.

At last! My dearest and most cherished friend, at last!

Islief was alone again, and now more truly so than he'd ever been. For even in the time before Aeylin's return he'd had hope to keep him company. He wondered, as he walked to Crown Hold, how it could be that the path to the final deed of hope's fulfillment could leave a soul feeling so lonely.

Well, he would bear it, the loneliness. He'd borne it this long, surely he could carry it for this little time longer. And a little time it would be, easily measured by the rule of the single task left to do.

But when he entered the Hold, Islief saw what he'd not expected to see: Tall, brave Tall, sitting with his back to the pedestal. Not dead, not killed by magic, not ravined up by sickness, as all had feared. No, not dead, for there was light in his eyes, and that light—so faint—spoke of life.

And so maybe it is that I can dry up some of Friend's tears, Islief thought.

For, seeing Tall, Islief was minded of a promise he'd made, a promise offered months ago. And he wondered, as he went to stand beside the young man, whether the Deities, who were so fond of promises kept, would grant him some time to keep this one he'd made to his friend Tall.

Am I to die, he asked, *the very moment I set the Emerald in the Crown?*

He listened hard, who had been long used to listening for the voices of Deities. But he heard no answer, no yea or nay.

Shall I die with a promise unkept?

Yet there was no answer, and Islief decided at last that what he had always known still remained true: Silence was an emptiness that must be filled up with trust, or remain forever hollow.

There is rain, Tall. There is rain . . .

Joze sighed, a thin exhalation, as though it were his last breath fleeing, no hope for another to be found in this heavy and hurtful darkness. Then light flared, a torch streamed, and he saw a small and bulky shape standing not an arm's reach away. Light, familiar and warm, showed him Islief.

Joze coughed, but only weakly. He had no more interest in clearing lungs that would no longer take or hold enough air. Islief laid a hand, broad and cool and moist, against Joze's cheek. His voice soft as wind sifting through sand, Islief said:

"There is rain, Tall. Out and above, there is rain."

"Have all the promises been kept?"

"Not every promise, Tall," Islief said, rattling a little in his throat, familiar soft laughter. "There is yet one more."

"The Crown . . ."

"No. Not that. See."

Islief put the torch into a bracket on the stone wall, came back and helped Joze to rise, took all his weight on strong shoulders and lent him balance by letting him lean. The black diamond pedestal no longer looked lorn and empty. Now it held the Crown, the silver and gold band. Emerald, Diamond, Topaz and Sapphire embraced their most dangerous sister, the fifth Jewel, the War-stone at the Crown's center. Each Jewel pulsed with light, as though the lone torch's illumination were fuel for a heartbeat. What had seemed terrible in Aidan's hands now was lovely, a masterwork whose beauty lay in the perfect balance of light and color and form.

"You've remade the Crown, Islief."

"I have done that. I have kept my promises to Deities, and they will keep theirs to me."

"And now?" Joze asked, though he was afraid that he knew the answer, afraid that he knew what redemption meant for Islief.

I know when I will die, Tall, and why. It will not be of light.

It would be here in the darkness of his ancient underground home. Islief would die here, within sight of the Crown he had stolen, the Crown he'd restored.

"Yes. Here, Tall. But not alone, not alone."

Not alone. Joze coughed, deeply and painfully. "No, you'll have company on that journey."

Islief did not agree. "Not company, Tall. A friend to see me on my way. Now come, sit down again, for you are weary."

Weary to death, Joze thought. And he did not believe that Islief would go his dark way alone, he did not believe that there was anything of life left to either of them now, for he would die of plague and Islief would die of a promise kept to Deities.

But he sat, as Islief bade him do. When he saw the small grey man close his eyes, shivering a little in the wake of some vagrant breeze wandering far from the river, Joze took him in his arms, held him close. And there was something about the holding, something about the feel of his arms round his small friend, which called back two memories from among many—one recent, one older. Moments ago Islief had said that not all promises had been kept. And months ago, in the workshop behind the Hold, he'd offered to Joze a promise: *Should you come to a time when you have no more strength to use, you will have mine.*

Joze realized then that it had been some time since last he'd coughed, or felt the need to; some time since he'd had to strain for breath. There was yet a thickness in his lungs, still the cold ache in his joints, but the warmth of holding Islief seemed to promise that soon breathing would not be difficult, one day the pain would ease. Yet, though the warmth was like a cloak around him, like an embrace, like a blessing, Joze felt Islief himself grow colder, his small body shaking as though winter breathed on him.

"I wish I could make you all well, Tall," Islief said. "I wish I could do that. But I am not very strong now, and I can only give you what strength I have."

"No," Joze whispered. "Islief, don't."

Islief turned a little in Joze's arms, wide eyes bright and earnest. "Please, Tall. Let me keep this promise, too."

Joze gathered him close again, held him tightly. After a time, when the torch was low, when Islief had been quiet for a long while, Joze whispered:

"Do you remember, Islief, that I asked you a question when we were on shipboard?"

"I remember a lot of questions, Tall."

Joze smiled, surprised that he could. "And you answered most of them. Do you remember the one you didn't answer: Why is it that the Princess is the only one you ever called by her name?"

The torch hissed a little over its dying, the light grew dimmer, the shadows longer. Islief said:

"Nikia is the only one who said that I could use the name given to her. You, Tall, did never say that I may call you by the name given to you. And it is yours, not mine. Not for me to use until you say that I may."

Joze blinked, drew breath to speak, then blinked again. "Islief—" He stopped, wondering if he was being rude now to use a name without permission, absurdly wondering whether he'd been rude for months. "Why didn't you ask?"

"That would not have been polite, Tall."

When Joze said nothing, for not knowing what to say, Islief looked up, his wide, wide eyes gleaming; but not so brightly as they once had. "Tall," he said gently. "You did not know that you must give me your name, and I have never known it for a polite thing to ask for such a gift."

Joze cleared his throat, started to speak, and had to try again. "My friend, will you call me Joze?"

"Yes, thank you."

"Ah, Islief," Joze whispered. "Islief, you go at this dying so calmly."

And what will I tell Kicva—how will I tell her that you are dead?

"First you will tell her that you love her, Tall, for she will want to hear that. And then you will say that the Seven still hear prayers, for it is mine to die now. Tell her both things gently. But if you are wise, you will step back. You know how the friend is when her feelings get all tangled up inside her."

Joze drew a shaking breath, and when he let it go he heard it as both a kind of laughter and a sob. "How is it you always know what everyone's thinking?"

"I have been a long time living in caverns. I know how to hear the echoes."

"What echoes?"

Islief did not answer. Joze held him close again, and when the torch went out at last, he did not find the darkness heavy or frightening, for there was, yet, some warmth in Islief, still some light in his wide, wide eyes.

The weight of years, the burden of promises waiting to be kept— his own, Aeylin's, the promises of Deities—fell away from Islief as gently as snow falls away from clouds. And it was a cold thing, this dying, a thing to make him remember a night long, long past, when his punishment was new and he still liked to go up to the edge of the darkness to see what could be seen.

That night he'd gone out from the caverns to listen to the winter, to hear ice ringing like bells on the trees, and wind like a pack of hounds at chase, baying down the mountainside. Then, that very night, he'd understood how alone he truly was; he'd known how alone he'd truly be as the wind rushed by and the ice-bells rang. That was the night that Aeylin had died, a lonely queen in a land of strangers, and that night her wedding-fee, the five Jewels, went one to each of her children, took five lonely paths away through the ages.

That night, too, a long and sweet sleep fell upon his own kindred; the First People went back to the Deities, dreamed themselves away. All but him, all but Islief who must never sleep, but must spend his long life waiting and watching for the time when his promises could be kept.

And now the time had come, stealing upon him like winter, but not so silent that he could not hear the ringing of the ice-bells, as he had that night . . .

How if his kindred did not know him after all these ages past? How if they had forgotten him? How if they remembered and, remembering, would not welcome him?

"Joze," he said, warmed a little by the sound of his friend's name. "Joze."

Maybe it was that his dear friend Tall had at last learned to understand the things not said, hear the echoes of the feelings behind the words.

"They'll know you, Islief. They won't have forgotten. They'll welcome you."

"What shall I tell them? After all this time, what shall I say to them?"

"Say that you come from where the mountains are."

Islief smiled to hear his own words.

Joze drew a long breath, a cleaner breath than he'd drawn in a long time. He was not all well, but now he had the kind of chance for health that a young body would accept; the kind of hope that a willing heart could hold.

"Islief, say that you come from where gardens take root in stone, from where forests are shaped in rock."

It *was* like snow falling free of clouds, the shedding of these last sad burdens of time and fear.

"Say that you come from where floors are roofs." Joze rocked him gently, as though cradling him to sleep. "Where there is no direction save high or low. Tell them you come from the place where all songs are kindled; from the place where history was driven out."

Like approaching footsteps, the measured pace of Joze's heart, heard and felt.

"Tell them you come from the place where history will live. Tell them you come from the place where hope did die, and from the place where hope will thrive."

Like the embrace of all Islief's kindred, the warmth of Joze's arms around him. As in a dream, or from a great distance of time and place, Islief heard his own voice.

"Joze, you have been my good friend. You have walked with me and let me see all the wide world I had not seen in so long a time. With you I felt the wind again, and the softness of flowers; I heard birds again, knew light again. I have had no better gift."

"Islief—oh, Islief! I will miss you so much."

Islief closed his eyes. "Tall, you must let me go, for I am weary and now I remember how to sleep."

"Then sleep," Joze whispered.

For a time without measure—an age or a moment—Joze's tears were the only thing of warmth Islief felt. Then, like the welcoming of a Deity, came the touch of Joze's lips upon Islief's forehead.

And very much like sleep, the gentle hands that received him when Joze at last let him go.

Later, knowing that something must be done for dead friends, Dail went alone to Crown Hold, Nikia's hand-fire spilling blue light through his fingers, tangling dark shadows on the floor around his feet. But he found only one friend—and he was alive. Dail saw no sign of Islief; only Joze sitting alone by the pedestal, his arms wrapped tight around himself for warmth.

"He's gone," Joze said softly, when he saw the bard. "Islief has gone away."

Dail lifted his eyes to the empty column. "And the Crown?"

Joze did not answer for a long time, but when he did, he smiled wearily. He told Dail that the Crown was gone too, that this was how it should be. Islief had returned what he'd stolen to the Seven—and to the First People, who on a winter night in long ages gone had dreamed themselves all away.

Epilogue

KICVA WENT AWKWARDLY TO HER KNEES, HAMPERED BY THE skirts of her gown—an old faded red one, borrowed from Nikia for garden-work. She missed her hunting leathers! She longed for their comfortable familiarity, the ease of the walking, sitting, kneeling, riding in breeches. But the women of the Citadel did not wear hunting leathers for daily use, and so she would not either. Somehow she'd learn to endure skirts, though breeches would have been better for the garden-work she'd been busy at these months past.

Kicva took a wooden flat, inspected the leggy green seedlings of thyme and marjoram, sage and horehound, rosemary and basil. These, and the tender young rootings of golden yarrow, pink cranesbill, and crimson pheasant's-eye, were gifts from the Elf-King to his daughter from Verdant Hall's own gardens, taken late in autumn and kept safe through the winter.

Nikia had spent time each day since their return to Damris working in this garden. In autumn when the rains came she turned the earth, letting even the deepest parts rejoice in the rain—always soft and misty, for the god Wazer and the goddess Vetr knew that did they let the rain fall harder it would wash away the drought-ravaged soil. In winter the Princess had embedded all the varieties of bulb-rooted plants her father could send her. Nikia saw to it that the snow was always brushed over those beds to keep the bulbs warm and insulated from the cold.

Now in spring, Nikia dug and turned the earth again, checked the tender green shoots from her winter-planting, and made ready for a new season of growing. These spring days had gilded her fair skin so that she now seemed as brown and rosy as any wandering hunter-scout. That gilding made her silvery hair seem almost white. Nikia loved her garden, and took great joy in it. Yet this walled and tame place seemed almost a little dull to Kicva, who longed for the forest and all its wildness and surprises; some delightful, as many dangerous.

After a visit to her parents she'd returned to Damris, kept herself here at the Citadel because she had a decision to make. She thought it best to make it behind tall walls and in a foreign place, for she felt that this decision had to do with walls and foreign places.

"Will you marry me, Kicva?" Joze had asked at autumn's end. He'd looked at her with all his love ablaze in his dark, dark eyes and said: "Will you be my wife?"

Oh, why hadn't he simply asked: *Will you love me?* How much easier that would have been to answer!

But he hadn't. He'd asked for marriage, and Kicva could not hear the word without thinking of Aidan. It was not that she'd loved the mage. She hadn't. But she'd been ready to marry him, for the sake of what had seemed to be good sense and sound judgment. In these months past she'd come to realize how sad a mistake that would have been.

A hawk flew over, his shadow skimming the ground, his harsh cry only briefly filling the sky. Wild as wind and as free, that hawk. And lonely. Kicva sighed and looked out over the wall, and she could see nothing but deepest blue sky, a few white clouds riding.

And if she married Joze? Would that be a mistake?

Not a mistake to love him—never that!

But would it be a mistake to allow herself be bound to him by expectations as she'd let herself be bound to Aidan? The Elf-King's Mage, who had controlled his life, his dreams so sternly, could find little to prize in her but good sense. She'd tried so hard to be sensible. But she hadn't been sensible about very much this year past. She'd tried hard to be someone who could become a worthy wife. But Mage Aidan had not needed a wife. He'd needed a dream, and that dream had killed him.

What would Joze expect? How well would she meet those expectations? Expectations and fear of them: is that what marriage was? Kicva didn't know, and she was afraid to ask.

But she'd asked Joze for time. He'd granted that and gone away to search for his family, to winter at his farm, the poor ruined placed that he'd mourned for in summer and now longed to tend and heal.

And if I married him, would that be my lot? Would I be farm-bound, never to range the forests again? She didn't know that either, and she was afraid to ask.

Coward! Always the coward, Kicva!

She ran a finger along the underside of the rosemary, released the fresh tangy scent. Then she glanced sideways at the Princess kneeling beside her, skirts of her blue gown kilted high and showing a long, tanned leg as she leaned to trowel another row of earth.

"Lady," said the hunter-scout, "do you remember what we of Verdant Hall say of rosemary?"

Nikia sat back on her heels, wiped rich brown earth from her hands. "I remember: Where rosemary grows, a woman will rule."

"They don't have a long history of queens here in Mannish, do they?"

"No, we don't, Kicva. This will be something new for my husband's folk."

Kicva watched to see the soft rosy blush grace her cheek. Nikia never spoke those words without smiling. And the bard never heard them without sighing for pleasure, just as he always did when he took harp to hand.

No ghost of murdered Garth came between the woman who was once his wife and the man who was his cousin. They'd not have come near each other were Garth still alive. Now that he was dead, they saw no betrayal in their marriage. For these two, princess and bard, there could be no guilt where love was free to grow.

Was this what marriage was made of? Elvish princess and Mannish bard—these two loved, and love always seemed to be enough.

Kicva looked around her, at the sunny walls and the pools of shade they cast; at the brick walkways and the freshly turned earth those walks bordered. The Citadel folk used to call this place the Queen's Garden. They did not anymore. The place was called Aeylin's Garden now, named for the queen who had planted it long, long ago. The change in name was more than a nod to historical accuracy. It meant, as it was declared throughout two realms, that Mannish and Elvish understood whose children they were: Aeylin's children.

Children of the Smoke, as Gai's bard had it.

There had been a deal of talking and thinking on the part of the Mannish before they accepted that. But in the end it prevailed that what is, must be. Gai would grow up to rule both realms as one.

For a brief time in winter a faction of Raethmen, who had never been friends of the Elvish, had risen to put forth a claim for another; for Dail, who was sister's son to Alain's queen. That queen, herself, had been the daughter of a Raethman. But few made much of it, and Dail made the least of all. He said he wanted no truck with kingship. He said that he knew who the rightful ruler should be. Thereafter, though he did not like to mix in politics or matters of state, none spoke more strongly than Dail for Gai's rights, none more fervently supported his stepdaughter's claim.

But he would not stand as regent for her. "I am her mother's husband," he said. "That gives me no rights. And I am her bard. That carries other duties."

He had in mind another man, one of whom Nikia herself approved and counted as a friend. But that man was reluctant. As Kicva heard it, Calmis of Soran wanted nothing more than to be quit of the matters of state; desired only to spend his time administering his province and spending his days with his Elvish wife. But even Kicva, who did not know this man well, knew that his was a thin kind of wish. She could hear the thinness every time he spoke of it. Yet, he remained reluctant.

Who then? After an autumn and winter of talking, they'd all agreed, Mannish and Elvish alike, that Gai, this daughter of Elf and Man, must be raised up to rule both kingdoms as one. Dekar, yet strong and vigorous, could teach her how to rule her mother's folk. After him, should it be needful, Nikia herself could do that. But there must be found among the Mannish one who would show Gai the way to rule these fractious folk who were yet so stubborn of mind as to say, one Celedman to another: We are not compatriots, for I am from the flat southern lands and you are from the northern mountains.

Kicva raised another seedling from its wooden flat and placed it in the bed. And where was her own Celedman these days? When would he come back to the city, asking for his answer? Spring was well advanced. She'd looked for Joze to return before now. She wondered if this bittersweet ache of disappointment was, in fact, an answer to a question.

Dail sat cross-legged in the window of the tall tower room, his old hiding place. Tugging absently at his beard, he wondered again, as he'd wondered all the winter past, when he'd get around to shaving. It was again the fashion for men to be cleanshaven. Here in the Citadel, in Damris city, there was not a beard to be seen but the one worn by Gai's bard. Odd about that beard. He'd forgotten about it over the months since he'd been back, no longer saw his face in the mirror to think that here was a stranger's face. One day, when he wasn't thinking about it, he must have come to like the damn beard.

"Things change, my girl," he said to his harp.

Ah, things changed. Places changed, as had his tower room, for he no longer hid here, and people did not fear to come here. Ghosts had been sent to honorable rest, and Dail was no longer haunted or haunter. And he was not only a bard in this room; here he was also a luthier. Not a fine luthier, not even a journeyman. But he was a dogged craftsman who could look forward to his harp-making skills improving.

Comfortable and content, Dail enjoyed April's new warmth as he worked to polish and tend his Song-Bringer, the new harp modeled on the old, named for memory and *Dashlaftholeh*. All morning he'd reveled in the songs of birds, delighted in the sweet scents of earth and planting carried even this high by spring's soft breezes. And here he watched his wife working, all gold and silver as she planted in Aeylin's Garden.

Your Nikia, Islief used to say. Ancient Islief had been right about that, as he had been about so many things.

"Who are you, Lady?" he'd asked on their wedding night.

"How can I know?" she'd said. "Only a short time ago I thought I would never again be more than Gai's mother. Not a month later I was the King's widow. Ah, Dail, I have been so many people in my short life. But I know one thing I am and will aways be: your Nikia."

Dail had asked no more questions.

Came a footstep in the corridor, a familiar tread.

Darun, he thought. *I hope you're coming to say that you've made up your mind. The kingdom is waiting, old friend.*

But Calmis hadn't come to a decision yet.

"What?" Dail said as the Lord of Soran came to stand beside him. "Are you still thinking?"

Calmis looked out the window for a while, watching the clouds scudding across the blue, watching the glint of sunlight on the A'Damran. The river was not wide yet, but it was growing, and the clear sweet scent of water reached them even here.

"Still thinking," he said.

"Darun, Gai could have no better regent."

Calmis said nothing.

"Are you feeling trapped?" Dail asked gently.

Calmis shook his head. "No. Not trapped, except by inadequacy."

"Darun, Nikia thinks there is no one better suited to be her daughter's regent. Dekar doesn't argue, and even most of the Raethmen agree. No man could do this work better than you. I know you've no yen for kingship. And you put your own life between steel and a murderer—I know you love the child. So tell me, Darun: What is it that's keeping you from accepting the Regency?"

Calmis drew a long breath and let it out slowly. "I don't think I've the courage for it. It takes a hard hand to keep all the reins of power straight; a steady hand to keep the separate needs of five provinces balanced and met. I know this, and I know that— more—it takes courage. Garth had that courage."

"And in harder times than these," Dail said softly. "How is it that you think you lack the courage he had?"

Calmis smiled, not without a certain hint of dark humor. "Because every day that Garth ruled as Ybro's regent I saw how much courage was needed. In the last days he spent that courage like the well, for it was bottomless. I know how shallow my own well is."

"Ah, you know that, do you?" Dail looked out the window again, watched his wife move from a newly planted bed to a fresh patch of dark earth waiting. From out beyond the garden wall came the faint clatter of hoofs on cobbles as some rider pushed a horse to a canter up the long hill to the Citadel. Nikia looked up from her work, and Kicva got quickly to her feet, ran to the garden gate.

Another one wondering about courage, Dail thought. For he well knew what kept Kicva here in the Citadel.

"Darun," he said. "Tell me this: How can a man know how much courage he has until he's called upon to use it?"

Calmis drew breath to answer, but Dail did not let him.

"He can't. *You* can't. You, my friend, are not in the least worried that you haven't the courage. You're afraid that you aren't going to be able to control every tiny detail of the kingdom. You're afraid that you won't be able to hand over the rule to Gai—twenty or so years from now!—with each snag and problem all tucked and tidy and perfect, the sun shining regularly, the rain falling when it should. Darun, you are an ass. And one who's going to die all crushed and broken under the load of all the countless expectations you place upon yourself.

"All you have to do, you dear fool, is teach her what you know about dealing with Raethmen and Riggians and Celedmen and Hivardmen and your own stubborn men of Soran. And if you've time, you might want to teach her how to deal with her clever grandfather of Elflands. Old he is, but not nearly at the end of his days. If Dekar goes on like this, could be our Gai will be ruling here before she'll be ruling there."

Darun smiled wryly. "Not much, as you put it."

"A lot, I know it. Don't do it if you can't."

Calmis stared out the window for a long moment, then said:

"A favor, if you will, bard: Go down to the garden and your wife. Leave me alone to think for a while longer."

"Here?"

"Here's where *you* spent a year thinking."

"And will you take a year?"

The soft warm breeze wandering from without breathed a song upon the new harp's strings. A wordless song sung in the language of the heart. A language with no rules, no grammar, no impetus but emotion. And maybe that wordless song was something that Calmis could understand, for when he answered at last, his voice held the kind of quiet acceptance which speaks of the understanding of a challenge's hardships and joys.

"No. It shouldn't take that long for me to draft a message to Dekar. We will have things to say to each other, the Elf-King and I, if we are going to train up a queen between us."

The gentle spring sun was not warmer, nor more tender, than the feeling filling up Kicva's heart as she stood in the cobbled lane outside the garden, close in Joze's arms. He kissed her and kissed her again, his dark beard tickling her cheek and throat. He smelled of sunshine and freshly turned earth, of sweat from a long morning's ride and faintly of smoke from a night's campfire. He smelled so good! Kicva hesitated, then asked a question which might have a hard answer. "Did you find your family?"

"I've found them, my father and my mother. They are glad to be home again. And folk are saying that there hasn't been a man, woman or child to fall sick of plague in nigh a month. I think it's over, Kicva. I think we will be well again."

She held him closer, listened to the strong beat of his heart, heard him breathing clean and easy and silent. He'd been finally well when he rode away from Damris in the winter, but she'd feared for him, dreaded that sickness would find him again as he searched through the ruined lands for his kin. Beyond the gate, from within the garden she heard Dail and Nikia talking. They spoke in low voices, the quiet confiding tones of two people who know that should words ever fail, there is a language of trust, a speech of the heart, which must be wordless to be understood.

I will do it, Kicva thought, but thought a little desperately. *I will marry Joze, and let what happens happen. I've been two seasons in foreign lands, behind walls, and I haven't died of it. I don't have to be a soldier. I needn't* always *be in the woodlands.*

She smiled ruefully. *And I'll learn to manage these tangling skirts somehow if only I can be with him. . . .*

Oh, but it hurt the heart to think that she'd not roam her forests of Elflands again, not take up a bow and go wandering. The pain of that hurt found her even here in Joze's arms. Pain enough to make her catch her breath, to make that catching sound like sobbing. And Joze heard the sobbing, held her away from him, brushed her hair away from her face. Hair that she'd let grow and wore long now to her shoulders.

"Now tell me," he said gently. "Tell me what's troubling you."

His question was honestly asked, and bravely for all that he might well suspect that she sobbed for sorrow over the word she might give him about marriage. She wanted to tell him all about the hurt and the loss she knew would haunt her should she go to be his wife. Who better to tell about this than the man she believed loved her so well as to know what this pain meant; whom she loved well enough to know that a word from him, a hug, a kiss, would go far to soothe any of her hurts or sorrows? She tried to answer, but she couldn't.

Joze smiled, put an arm around her waist, and walked with her down the cobbled lane, his horse following tiredly after.

"I'll tell you something, hunter-scout," he said as they passed beneath an arching bough of dogwood. He reached up, plucked a delicate blossom and tucked it in the bodice of her gown, set it gently to rest in the place where a long war-scar began its faint trail lower between her breasts. His fingers, warm and roughened by a winter of working, lingered for a moment, then fell away. "I've been thinking about something Islief said to me. He said that there are certain things I must tell you gently. And then step back. 'For you know,' he said, 'how the friend is when her feelings get all tangled up inside her. Then, Tall, it is always wisest to step back.' "

Kicva smiled. "That sounds like him." She glanced up at Joze. "And so you have something to tell me that will tangle up my feelings. But you're not stepping back."

"Well, I don't want to. I want to walk with you always, have you right here beside me." He drew a long breath, let it out in one quick gusty sigh. "But I've had some time to think over the winter."

Kicva's heart fell, sank further than she could imagine a heart could sink. Aye, time to think; time to regret the offer of marriage. And so all this fret and worry was for naught. All the winter trapped inside this stone city behind these walls, in these miserable, foolish, foot-tangling skirts—! All to hear that he'd come back to tell her he'd had time to think and regret a hasty speech?

She pulled away from him, angry and hurt, and hoping that the tears she felt rising now would not betray her. "You've had time to think? Aye, well, so have I, Joze. And I'll tell *you* something. I'll tell you—"

But she stopped, for he was shaking his head gently, smiling as over sure and certain knowledge. But he didn't reach for her, took no step closer. Maybe he was heeding Islief's advice.

"Wait, now," he said. "Wait. Whatever it is you're going to do, hunter-scout, just wait and hear me out."

Hunter-scout . . . Not she, not if she went to marry him, went to live on his farm and never saw the forest again. Not she. And then her tears spilled over, tears for the thought that she might lose her old life, tears for the fear that she might lose her new love.

"I'm no hunter-scout," she said. "I can't be, if I'm to be your wife."

"Ah, you think so?"

"Well, of course I think so! What kind of a farm-wife goes running off to her soldier band in spring and summer? What kind of farm-wife can't plough a field, bake a loaf of bread, tend a fold of sheep, weave a rug, keep a kitchen garden? What—" She gulped and went on. "What kind of a farm-wife would your parents consider me then?"

Joze shrugged. "They'd say you were a poor farm-wife."

"And not one you'd want."

Now he frowned, but just to hide the smile that was beginning. "Damn right I wouldn't want a farm-wife like that. But what I've been thinking, hunter-scout, is that I don't want a farm-wife at all. Kicva, I don't want you to give up what you know, the life you chose and the one you love. But I want you for my wife, hunter-scout."

"But how? What about your farm? You love it and—"

"And I won't give that up. Maybe there won't be a great need for soldiers in these new times. But I suppose there will always be some need. When there is, you must go, if that is what you want. But tell me this: Will you know the way home to our farm after the soldiering seasons are done?"

Kicva stared at him, wondering if he knew that what he asked required more courage to accept than to refuse. And yet, if her courage failed her now, there would be no more need of it ever, for no risk would be as great. Swallowing hard, bracing her shoulders and standing straight and tall, she nodded.

"And will you trust me to wait in faith, as I'll trust you to come home in faith?"

She nodded.

"And will you take time to see how our children grow when children we have? Will you take time to love them with me and raise them well?"

"As farmers?"

He shrugged. "Or as soldiers, if that's what they wish. Or tinkers, or tailors, or fishermen."

Aeylin had said: *Your sons are yours to keep until they go out to meet their own fates.* Had she known, the ghost, the long-dead queen, who would help make those sons? Maybe she had.

"Ours will be a strange marriage, Joze."

"Not to us, it won't be. Do you agree?"

Kicva smiled, and nodded yet again.

"Then I don't see what the problem is, hunter-scout." Joze matched her smile across the small distance between them. "And, though he was a good friend and very wise, I've no idea why we're taking Islief's advice so seriously just now."

Nor did Kicva, and when Joze opened his arms to her, she went willingly into his embrace.